PRAISE FOR *GIVEN*

"Kristyn J. Miller's *Given Our History* is such a lived-in, heartwarming romance about two childhood friends who find their way back to each other as adults. I felt as nostalgic for their camp-pen-pals-with-book-clubs-and-mix-CDs relationship as though I put the stamps on the letters myself. There are so many threads in their relationship, and then when you see the way they knit them all together! I love dreaming of a future Clara and Teddy reading history books aloud together and choosing each other as best friends, always."
—Alicia Thompson, *USA Today* bestselling author of *Love in the Time of Serial Killers*

"This book was designed in a lab for me—or, more accurately, a musty history department in an ivy-covered building: competent grown-up protagonists, second-chance-friends-to-lovers story, tweed-and-elbow-patches atmosphere. Miller has created a world I've never read before populated with fully realized, completely original characters to root for. A beyond satisfying read. My heart is happy. A+. With honors. Summa cum laude."
—Julia Whelan, international bestselling author of *My Oxford Year* and *Thank You for Listening*

"Readers are going to fall in love with Clara and Teddy's years-spanning love story, filled with delicious nostalgia, laugh-out-loud nerdiness, and sizzling romance. A must-read!"
—N.S. Perkins, bestselling author of *The Infinity Between Us*

"*Given Our History* is second-chance romance, ivy-covered academia, and complicated family history at its sweetest and most heartwarming."   —Trish Doller, bestselling author of *Float Plan*

"Sweet and sweeping, Miller's *Given Our History* is the perfect study in how our longest-held feelings can lead us into life's loveliest surprises. A master class in nostalgia and second chances crafted into an emotional and charming romance."   —Emily Wibberley and Austin Siegemund-Broka, authors of *The Roughest Draft*

Also by Kristyn J. Miller

Seven Rules for Breaking Hearts

Given Our History

KRISTYN J. MILLER

ST. MARTIN'S
GRIFFIN
NEW YORK

First published in the United States by St. Martin's Griffin, an imprint of St. Martin's Publishing Group

GIVEN OUR HISTORY. Copyright © 2024 by Kristyn J. Miller. All rights reserved. Printed in the United States of America. For information, address St. Martin's Publishing Group, 120 Broadway, New York, NY 10271.

www.stmartins.com

Designed by Meryl Sussman Levavi

Library of Congress Cataloging-in-Publication Data

Names: Miller, Kristyn J., author.
Title: Given our history / Kristyn J. Miller.
Description: First edition. | New York : St. Martin's Griffin, 2024.
Identifiers: LCCN 2023058080 | ISBN 9781250861900
    (trade paperback) | ISBN 9781250861917 (ebook)
Subjects: LCGFT: Romance fiction. | Novels.
Classification: LCC PS3613.I53986 G58 2024 | DDC 813/.6—dc23/
    eng/20240102
LC record available at https://lccn.loc.gov/2023058080

Our books may be purchased in bulk for promotional, educational, or business use. Please contact your local bookseller or the Macmillan Corporate and Premium Sales Department at 1-800-221-7945, extension 5442, or by email at MacmillanSpecialMarkets@macmillan.com.

First Edition: 2024

10 9 8 7 6 5 4 3 2

To Mutti, for being my very first reader, in-house history teacher, bus driver, spelling bee judge, and a very reluctant math tutor

PROLOGUE

I might've been on time, were it not for the parking meters. They were old, coin-fed, dotted along a narrow one-way street shaded by brick buildings. My GPS had announced that I'd arrived at my destination, and I had driven right past. Some might call it stubborn, parking at a Harris Teeter three blocks away because I didn't want to pay. I mean, this was Baltimore. You *expect* to pay an egregious amount of money for parking in a major city.

Anyone who says that has obviously never been a third-year graduate student surviving on Lean Cuisines and dreams.

I hopped out of my old Volvo and legged it to the sandwich shop, guided by my phone. It led me to one of the old brick storefronts, the entrance marked by a scalloped awning. I pushed through the door and a bell chimed overhead. The dining room was long and narrow with a checkered floor, and the smell of warm, fresh-baked bread wafted on the air.

Professor Blanchett was seated at one of the laminate tables, her sandwich untouched in a red plastic basket. "You're three minutes late," she greeted me primly. Her pixie cut was a shade grayer than I remembered, but her mouth was still pressed into the same thin line, bracketed by smile lines that seemed to indicate that she *must* have laughed at some point in her life.

"Parking," I said, a little winded as I collapsed into the plastic chair opposite her and shrugged off my messenger bag. "Didn't have change for the meters." Not true. I kept a whole heap of change in my cupholder, but that was reserved for counting out quarters whenever I needed an iced coffee to power through another ten pages of my dissertation.

"Perhaps we'll leave my thoughts on your punctuality out of the letter, then, shall we?"

Well. Off to a great start. I had no clue how to reply to that, so I gave her a polite smile. Dorothea Blanchett had been my capstone advisor during undergrad at University of Maryland, some years ago now. We didn't really know each other; a lot of her advising was done through email, and we'd had only a handful of meetings in person to discuss the direction of my paper. She had retired a couple years ago. But academia loves its letters of recommendation, so when I applied for an online teaching position that called for three references— preferably, they specified, from different institutions—I had no choice but to shoot her one last email. I wasn't even sure she remembered me. She'd asked to meet in person for a *light refresher* before she felt comfortable writing any sort of recommendation, so this felt more like a job interview than a happy reunion.

"Did you already order?" she asked now, like she didn't just see me walk in.

My gaze flicked to the cheesesteak in front of her, then over to the counter. "Ah, no," I said. "I guess I should maybe—"

"Clara?" a woman's voice asked. "Clara Fernsby?"

My old college roommate approached our table, wiping damp hands on her jeans like she'd just come back from the bathroom and was in too much of a hurry to use the hand dryer. "Mindy," I said. I was so taken aback that my brain short-circuited, and for a minute, I thought Professor Blanchett must have invited her as some sort of prank—but Mindy had barely set foot in the History Department. And Professor Blanchett wasn't the pranking type.

Mindy didn't wait for me to stand; she bent over and hugged me right where I sat, but the angle was awkward, encircling my shoulders. Immobilized, unable to really hug her back, I patted the back of her arm with a hand.

"It's been so long," she said with a sigh, drawing back. Now that I got a good look at her, I noticed that she'd stopped bleaching her hair, her mushroom-brown locks chopped in a wolfish shag that framed her round face.

"What are you doing here?" I asked.

"At the sandwich shop?" she said, a little bemused. "I'm meeting Ted for lunch."

She said this with so much familiarity, like she expected me to recognize the name, but it still took me a couple seconds to register who she was talking about.

I should have been forgiven for not immediately realizing that she was talking about my former best friend on account of two things: first, because he and Mindy had only met a handful of times in passing. He didn't even attend UMD with us.

Second, because she called him *Ted*.

"You're meeting Teddy?" I clarified. "Teddy Harrison?"

Mindy nodded. "I've been telling him that I wanted to bring him here for weeks, but he hadn't found the time to make the drive down—oh, sorry, Miranda Schooner," she said, offering a hand to my advisor. Professor Blanchett eyed it like Mindy was offering her a dead fish.

"Wait," I said. "You and Teddy, you guys are"—my brows pinched—"together?"

"I thought . . . I mean, I figured he told you."

Professor Blanchett sighed theatrically, leaning back in her chair.

"He did not," I said stiffly. Interesting that he hadn't told her about our falling-out. Maybe they were still in the early stages of—well, whatever they were.

"Weird story." She dragged a chair over to our table, metal legs screeching against the tiled floor. I would really rather she didn't, actually, because if Teddy was on his way here—

"So," Mindy said, "I was obviously attracted to him from the get-go. I mean, you remember how I asked you all those questions after he helped you move into your dorm, trying to make sure he wasn't your boyfriend or anything."

The bell above the door chimed, and I stiffened. I didn't think I was capable of saying anything at the moment, so I gave a tiny nod of confirmation. Yes, I remembered.

"And then last year, I was having this conversation with my friend where we were talking, you know, like, 'You miss a hundred percent of the shots you don't take.'"

Teddy was making his way over to the table. He didn't seem to have registered who his girlfriend was talking to. There was a rising feeling in my chest, something burning its way up my throat like it was looking for a way out—panic, or maybe bile.

"And I was like damn, that's real, because there was this guy that I met a couple times back in college who I was super attracted to, but I never had the balls to just go for it. But then I remembered that I added you"—she pointed at me, and it felt very accusatory, like I was a suspect in a lineup—"on Facebook, and I was like, 'She has to have him on her friends list, they were best friends, right?' So I looked, and there he was." She glanced up at him warmly and he snaked an arm around her back, bending to plant a kiss on her cheek.

Bile. It was definitely bile in my throat. I gave them a close-lipped smile. "How sweet."

At the sound of my voice, Teddy did an almost imperceptible double take, his eyes widening when he finally registered who was sitting at the table. His lips parted in surprise, but neither of us said anything. It had been three years since we last spoke, and longer still since the last time I saw him. He'd grown his hair back out, loose brown curls that looked like he'd just finished running a hand through them, and I found a small measure of satisfaction in knowing he'd taken my advice.

Not that it should matter. He wasn't dating me. I'd made sure of that. But when I saw him now, something feral clawed at the inside of my chest. He looked . . . good. He was wearing a black T-shirt, just snug enough to show off his broad chest, and his olive skin had a healthy summer tan. Memories floated to the surface, unbidden.

I tore my eyes away, fixating on Professor Blanchett. This was testing her patience, no doubt. Her slender arms were folded over a herringbone blazer, the shoulder pads hunching. Beneath the table, I was pretty certain she was jiggling a loafer-clad foot.

Mindy was still talking. "—sent him a message, and the rest was history."

Teddy cleared his throat and glanced at his girlfriend. "She's leaving out the part where she sort of harassed me for a date," he said. His tone was obviously meant to be light—teasing—but it came out sounding a little forced.

She rolled her eyes at him. "You loved it."

I hazarded another glance at Teddy. Dark eyes met mine from behind black-framed glasses.

"Hi," I said, because the longer I went without saying something to him directly, the more it felt like there was an elephant in the sandwich shop. But I didn't know what else to say, what I could possibly tack onto that sentence without it sounding completely hollow.

"Hey," he said quietly.

I couldn't bear to look at him for longer than a couple seconds, so I stared at the table, the laminate curling up along the edges.

"Anyway, enough about that," Mindy said, oblivious. "I'm gonna grab some food. You want anything?" She flung this question at me without any real warning, and my brain was still processing everything else, so for a few seconds, I gaped like a fish. "The food here is really good," she added. "Their turkey melt panini has me in a chokehold."

I looked up at Professor Blanchett, whose nostrils flared. Her cheesesteak was still untouched. "Actually, I'm kind of in the middle of—"

"Are you kidding? We can all eat together. Lunch is totally on us."

Us. The word was a knife slipping between my ribs. Mindy left the table to order at the counter, but a presence hung in her wake, the third chair at our table still very much occupied. I felt a little guilty that my knee-jerk reaction was to hope someone spat in her turkey melt. Mindy hadn't done anything wrong.

"Clara," Teddy began, and I sprang out of my chair on autopilot. Whatever he was about to say, I didn't think I had the heart to hear it. "I've been meaning to—"

"You know what," I said, ignoring him, collecting my messenger bag off the floor. It was heavy, laden with hard copies of old essays and unofficial transcripts. Evidence that I'd meant to present to Professor Blanchett. But I couldn't do it. I couldn't sit around and wait for this storm to blow over. "I actually need to get going. I'm sorry," I told her, a little frantic, "and I *completely* understand if this ruins my chances of getting that letter. I just—I can't stay for lunch. I'm sorry."

"Clara, wait—" Teddy tried to stop me, fingers closing around my arm, and I jerked back. Our eyes locked and he searched my face—quick, cursory, but enough that he came to some sort of conclusion. He released my arm with a mumbled apology, and then I was out the door, power walking down past parking meters along a shady one-way street. I glanced over my shoulder once or twice, half expecting him to come after me, to insist that I hear him out, but he didn't.

We'd gone three whole years without speaking. But that day, the day I walked away and he chose not to follow—that was the day I finally realized that I'd lost him for good.

CHAPTER

1

A shadow shifts behind the fogged glass and the door opens with a click. Julien's bald head materializes in the gap. "Come in, come in," he says, stepping aside to let me through. "You'll have to excuse the mess."

He shuts the door behind me. The mess in question isn't much of a mess at all—just a couple of half-empty boxes and a desk strewn with papers. Balanced on top of a stack of manila folders is a placard that reads JULIEN ZABINI—CHAIR, HISTORY DEPARTMENT. The stench of hot tar drifts through the open window. They started the remodel on the social sciences building today and the roof tiling comes first, because it's the only thing everyone could agree upon. Every step of the approval process has come down to a game of bureaucratic tug-of-war between university donors, the dean of the College of Arts and Sciences, and the Board of Directors. Anyone and everyone with a long enough track record and deep enough pockets.

"Have a seat," Julien says, waving at the straight-backed wooden chair parked in front of his desk. He wanders over to the bar cart by the window, where a set of etched crystal tumblers glisten in the bronzy afternoon sun. It's the last week of summer; the fall semester starts Monday. "Scotch?"

"No, thank you."

"Suit yourself," he says with an incline of his head. "So long as you don't mind—"

"Not at all." I'm used to this little exchange. Julien did his undergrad at University of Edinburgh, where he picked up a handful of habits—habits that, on occasion, tease the boundaries of American professionalism. I suspect he enjoys it, watching our more stuffed-shirt colleagues squirm beneath his polite offers of Ardbeg and Dalmore.

He stoops beneath the bar cart, produces a bottle of amber-colored liquor, and pours himself a glass, sans ice. A few years ago, I gifted him a set of whisky stones when I pulled his name out of the hat during the department's Secret Santa exchange. He accepted them graciously, but he's never once used them.

"Down to business." Glass in hand, he settles into the tufted armchair on the other side of the desk, the worn leather creaking with the newfound weight. "I would like to put your name forward for consideration for tenure this year."

The rush of excitement at the mention of *tenure* is just as quickly replaced by uncertainty. I give a tiny shake of my head. "I don't think I understand."

"You are familiar with tenure," he says dryly, peering at me over wire-framed reading glasses perched low on his nose. He's always reminded me of a slightly older and balder Idris Elba, and his overall presence is kind of intimidating, like he's ten times more interesting and refined than the rest of us could ever hope to be. My first year working here, I kept calling him *Professor Zabini* like a frightened freshman, no matter how many times he asked me to call him Julien. "Last I checked, we hired you on the tenure track."

"Yes, of course," I sputter, my cheeks warm. "I just didn't think—" Julien blinks at me, the very picture of patience. I pause to collect my thoughts. "My understanding was that the review typically happens at the seven-year mark."

He consults one of the papers lying across his keyboard. "There are circumstances under which an earlier review is appropriate. Circumstances in which we currently find ourselves. With Leonard and Michael both retiring in the spring, our faculty is stretched somewhat thin. I would very much like to ensure that we get some of our more competent assistant professors on the advisory committee's radar." He pauses, seeming to choose his next words with care. "You might've noticed you're the only woman in our department who's on the tenure track, at present."

It would be hard not to notice. I spent my first couple years here wearing nothing but tweed jackets and pleated slacks in hopes that it would make my colleagues take me seriously. When you're a relatively young woman in an old and stuffy department, pencil skirts and ruffled blouses don't cut it. In fact, they're counterproductive. And T-shirts and jeans will just get you pigeonholed as lazy. You need the hard materials, the rough and the rigid, the kind that are starched and ironed and dry-cleaned.

I settled in, after a while. I'm no longer scared to wear swishy floral-print skirts or gaudy, dagger-shaped earrings. And anyway, my students appreciate me, if the Rate My Professors reviews calling me "fun, for a history teacher" are any indication. But tenure is the coveted seal of approval. It's an assurance that I'm a valued member of my department, and—perhaps more importantly—it means job security.

"I feel very strongly about ensuring that an array of voices and experiences are represented among our tenured faculty." Julien runs a hand over his jaw, where white stubble has sprouted. "It might be beneficial to bulk up your services to the school before sending you before the advisory committee in December. Demonstrate your investment in the future of Irving as an institution. I have a contact from Edinburgh who'll be in D.C. in November—I'll put you in touch to see about arranging a guest lecture. You'll take full credit for organizing it, of course."

"Thank you," I say, a little taken aback. There's no rule that says he has to help me with this, and he's being more than generous.

"Not to imply we don't appreciate what you've done already with the scholarship committee. To be frank, it's more about putting in the legwork than anything. A sort of show of good faith. However," he continues, "it wouldn't hurt if we had a little more to show for it, as far as the numbers go. Larger donations, more visible fundraising efforts, that sort of thing." He pauses, giving me room to voice my protests, but I don't. "By all means, take a little while to think it over. And feel free to come to me with any questions at all."

There's really only one answer, and that's a resounding yes. I made a promise to myself, years ago, that one day I'd have the sort of stability and job security that my parents never did. This is it. And I'm that much luckier to work in a field I'm passionate about. Putting in a few extra hours with the scholarship committee isn't going to hold me back. But . . . "I do have a question, actually. About course credits."

Julien whirls his scotch around the bottom of the glass. "What about them?"

"It's my understanding that tenured professors get a certain number of credits they can use each semester, in lieu of paying tuition?"

"Fifteen credits per academic year. Which translates to roughly one semester's tuition." His mouth twists in a wry smile. "Are we considering a career change?"

"I was wondering whether I'm allowed to give those credits to someone else."

"That depends. You can't just pass them off to a random student, but generally—"

GIVEN OUR HISTORY 13

"For family?" I press. "My sister, specifically."

Julien lifts a shoulder in a shrug. "I don't see why not."

"All right." I blow out a long breath, buying myself a few more seconds. Even if I agree to try, nothing is set in stone. I'll still have to put in the work, and then accept the offer of tenure, and then sign the contract. "I'll give it a shot."

"Wonderful." He raises his glass in a toast. "Then I'll look forward to receiving your dossier."

"Thank you." I rise from my seat, the chair grinding against the hardwood floor. I'm eager to get back to my office down the hall, where I'm still unpacking everything I moved from my old office in Martin Hall. In preparation for the renovations on the social sciences building, administration has relocated the history faculty to the Hall of Letters, crammed in with the literature and foreign language faculty. "Did you need me for anything else, or—"

Julien interrupts me. "Actually, while we're on the subject of this—" He twirls a hand and takes a sip of his scotch, like he's hoping I'll be able to fill in the blank.

"Tenure thing," I offer.

"Mmm." He sets his glass back on the desk with a *thunk.* "More along the lines of services to the school. I was wondering, in your endless generosity, whether you might deign to share your office space with a visiting scholar." Another pause, another opening for me to protest, but I only raise my eyebrows. "Just for the fall semester. I'm sure you've noticed, what with us all being crowded into one building, that office space is a little hard to come by at the moment."

"Of course," I say. "I'd be happy to share."

I've always had this problem with speaking before thinking, a decades-long war between my mind and mouth.

"Excellent," Julien chirps. He shuffles papers around to clear his keyboard, tapping the space bar to wake his computer. "He's a professor of history at Carnegie Mellon, up in Pittsburgh. Relatively young, but he's already got an impressive list of publications under his belt. Not unlike yourself, actually. I have a feeling the two of you will get along swimmingly."

I feel a bit disoriented, like I've wandered into a very strange dream—the sort where random people you knew ten or twenty years ago make a surprise appearance, and you find yourself wondering why your subconscious was thinking about them, anyway. "Wait, sorry." I grip the back of the chair and shake my head, trying to reason with myself. It's the same school, I'm sure of it, but that doesn't mean it's the same person. A school that size probably has twenty full-time faculty members in their History Department. Thirty, even. "What did you say his name was?"

"I didn't. It's Morrison, I think, something or another."

I exhale, relieved. See? Nothing to worry about.

Julien clicks around on the computer for a few seconds, squinting at the screen. "No, sorry. Harrison, that's it. Theodore Harrison. Specializes in maritime history of the Mid-Atlantic colonies, so perhaps not quite your cup of tea, as conversation partners go, but—" He breaks off, staring at my hands on the back of the chair. "Is something the matter?"

I follow his gaze. I'm gripping the chair so hard that my knuckles are bone-white. I release it and the blood rushes back to my fingers, itching, tingling. "Nothing's wrong." I plaster on a tight-lipped smile and shake my head, hoping I don't look as robotic as I feel. "Everything's peachy."

CHAPTER

2

PRESENT

I push through the swinging wooden door to the women's restroom with such force that it ricochets off the door stopper. The restrooms in the Hall of Letters are vaguely Edwardian, reflective of the hundred or so years that the building's been standing: lacquered wooden stalls and glazed subway tile, the grout blackened with age. The handle on the sink squeaks as I turn it and splash cold water on my face, but even after I finish patting dry with a paper towel, my reflection still looks like I've seen a ghost. I grip the sides of the porcelain, sniffing hard. "Get yourself together, Clara," I mutter to the tarnished mirror.

Behind me, there's the *woosh* of a toilet flushing and the stall door creaks open. A lanky girl in a skater skirt and ripped fishnets emerges. Likely a freshman—classes don't start until next week, but new students arrive early to move into their dorms and attend orientation. She stands at the sink next to mine and lathers her hands with three pumps of citrus-scented soap, casting a concerned smile at my reflection. Her hair's that bluish-black color of box dye, pale roots peeking out. She reminds me a little of how I wanted to dress when I was a teenager.

I return her smile, albeit weakly. I should probably feel embarrassed, but chances are she doesn't even know I'm an instructor. I'm only thirty-one, easy enough to mistake for a stressed-out grad student having a pre-semester bathroom breakdown. And my clothes don't exactly scream professor, in part because I'm not doing any professing today: tennis shoes with black jeans and a sleeveless graphic tee. Just have to cross my fingers that she doesn't turn up in any of my classes this semester.

She digs a violently red lip tint out of her bag and pumps the wand a few times before leaning close to the mirror to apply it. "I saw their Reunion Tour," she says offhandedly. I shoot her a questioning look and she nods at my shirt. "A couple years ago."

I glance at the shirt in my reflection, the backward letters spelling out MY CHEMICAL ROMANCE. I've had it since high school. "I saw them once, during the World Contamination Tour," I say, smoothing the age-crackled graphic of the lovers from the *Three Cheers for Sweet Revenge* album cover.

Her crimson-tinted mouth drops open. "Dude. I'm so jealous. I was like, five. I wasn't even born when *The Black Parade* came out."

Great. On top of everything else, I've now been made aware that the infamous opening G note—the calling card of all former emo kids—is officially old enough to buy itself a pack of cigarettes.

She peppers me with a few excited questions before losing interest, parting ways with a rather ominous, "See you around campus!"

As soon as the door swings shut behind her, I blow out a breath. My eyes are rimmed with pink, and errant blondish hairs have escaped my braid. I wet my hand in the sink and smooth them flat against my head, hoping to salvage some semblance of professionalism.

Get it together.

Nine years. It's been almost a decade since that phone call

outside Manchester Cathedral. A lifetime, really. Empires have risen and fallen in less time. But it still stings like it was yesterday, a self-inflicted wound that never quite had the chance to heal. It's not that I think I should have said *yes*. I'm firm in my belief that the timing just wasn't right. But I wish I hadn't handled it all so recklessly. I wish he would've answered my calls or texts in the weeks that followed, and I wish I hadn't given up on calling altogether.

I wish, more than anything, that I hadn't lost my best friend.

I dry my hands on a paper towel and toss it in the wastebasket before digging my phone out of the front pocket of my messenger bag. I search my contacts for Izzy Santos and press call. While the phone rings, I push through the bathroom door and out into the hall.

The call goes to voice mail. Unsurprising. We've been playing phone tag all summer. She'll call me back later, probably when I'm in the middle of something and can't answer. By the time I'm off work it'll be 10 P.M. in Portugal and she'll be at some club where they play electro house music so loud it's impossible to think, let alone hold an actual conversation. And so it continues. I stuff my phone back in my purse and start down the stairs.

I run my hands along the handrail as I descend, tracing the places where the quarter-sawn oak has been worn smooth by a century of hands. Irving isn't that old or prestigious a school, comparatively speaking—it's a private liberal arts college, built in the early nineteenth century—but I've always appreciated what history it has, even if it's a bit recent for my tastes.

My phone buzzes in my purse. And then buzzes again. And again. I pause on the landing to check it, the etched-glass window refracting a kaleidoscope of colors across yellowed hardwood planks. I'm not so naïve as to think it might be Izzy. Our texting habits are even worse than our long chain of missed calls—GIFs and shared Instagram reels that have gone largely unanswered, nothing of substance.

> The President: Helllooooo

> The President: ?!?

> The President: Where are you

> The President: Don't tell me you forgot AGAIN

Technically, I did not forget. I remember full well that I'm supposed to meet my little sister in the parking lot so that we can go to an early lunch, but I maybe lost track of time. I zip my phone back into my purse and take the remainder of the stairs at a gallop before exiting the Hall of Letters, emerging onto the patio beside the rose garden.

The skies are clear and the air is thick with humidity—the death throes of a muggy Maryland summer. I wave at Westley the security guard across the parking lot, sitting in his Polaris, his Hi Vis vest gleaming in the sun. Freshmen stop in the middle of the sidewalk to squint up at brick buildings and consult the campus map on their phones, familiarizing themselves with campus before the start of term. Parking placards dangle from rearview mirrors. A couple of the Spanish Department faculty chat by the curb. It is, for all intents and purposes, a perfectly average prelude to the semester.

Except for the parts that aren't. But I force myself not to dwell on that, shoving it into one of the dark filing cabinets in the far corner of my brain. I'll deal with that when I come to it. Adjusting the strap on my cross-body bag, I power walk toward a bumblebee-yellow Jeep Wrangler idling in a faculty parking space. Exhaust rises from the tailpipe in billowing clouds. Our campus green initiatives are a lost cause as long as that thing is still on the road.

"William Shakespeare," Reagan announces as I approach. Her golden-blond hair is pulled back in a ponytail. She's leaning against the hood of her Jeep, arms folded over the University of Irving crest emblazoned across the front of her hoodie.

I arch a brow. "What about him?"

"He once said 'Better three hours too soon than a minute late,'" she says, pushing herself off the Jeep and walking around to the driver side door.

I climb into the passenger seat. It smells like artificial cherries, dried-up jars of gel air freshener cluttering the drink holders. "When did he say that?"

"*The Merry Wives of Windsor.*"

I pause in the middle of buckling my seat belt. "And you memorized it?" I don't recall *The Merry Wives of Windsor* being standard reading, but then again, I didn't major in literature.

"Of course not. I Googled 'quotes about punctuality' a few minutes before you got here."

I resist the urge to roll my eyes. "That would explain it."

We swerve out of the parking lot and onto a narrow one-way street, shaded beneath Federal-style brick buildings and gnarled trees. I rest my fingers in the overhead grab handle as a precaution. Reagan's driving is terrifying. She's not a bad driver, per se—she's got a clean driving record as far as I know. It's more that the Jeep instills a tad too much confidence in her. If another car gets in her way, she could probably just run them over. That's what Reagan's used to doing: just barging her way through life and hoping it works out.

She stops at a stop sign, but she only seems to remember to do so at the last second: the tires squeal in protest, and I brace myself against the dashboard.

"Stop doing that," she says, continuing through the inter-section like it's nothing. Thankfully, there are no other cars around, but there are students waiting at the crosswalk, and they're staring at us.

I hide my face by resting an elbow against the door, shooting a covert glare at Reagan. "Doing what?"

"Putting your hand on the dash like that. It reminds me of Mom."

"Seems to be a trend among your passengers. Maybe you should take it as a sign."

She huffs, but doesn't acknowledge the dig. We swing into the parking lot of Bucky's Burgers and Dogs—less of a burger joint and more of a sports bar using sloppy hamburgers as a cover story, but the good news is that it's completely dead at noon on a Monday, so I can drop the whole professor act with-out worrying about bumping into any students. We order at the counter and then grab a table beneath a lazy ceiling fan that's fighting a losing battle against smoke from the grill.

I watch in horror as Reagan pops the lid off of her iced tea and proceeds to add not sugar, but several pink packets of Sweet'N Low. "What are you doing?" I ask warily. Mom was born and raised in Tennessee and sweet tea was sacred in our household, growing up. This is blasphemy. It's like I'm sinning just by looking at it.

She mixes the abomination with her straw, ice clattering. "I'm on a diet."

"Yes, but—" I resist the urge to remind her that she just or-dered a chili cheeseburger and fries. "Wouldn't you rather let yourself enjoy things?"

Her forehead crinkles. "You're one to talk. Look at you."

"What about me?"

"Old. Single. The antithesis of fun."

Ah. There it is. The payback for my driving comment. I take

a long sip of my Pepsi through the straw, trying not to focus on any one accusation in particular, but try as I might, there's one that eats at me. "I'm single by choice."

"No one's single by choice. If they say they are, they're lying. Or maybe working through some shit. You don't even have shit to work through."

"I'm too busy for a relationship." That's always been my reasoning, but it tastes especially bitter today. Ever since finishing grad school, I haven't had the time to meet people. Always working on the next paper (right now, an article analyzing the language used in a letter from Elizabeth of York to Isabella, Queen of Castile regarding the betrothal of their children) and juggling three classes with student advising and committee meetings. University of Irving isn't exactly a hotbed of attractive singles—not ones in my age range, that's for sure—and between hours spent figuring out the nightmarish departmental transition from Blackboard to Instructure and recently learning that Facebook is for old people, it's become woefully apparent that I'm no longer tech-savvy enough for dating apps.

"Anyway, how'd it go this morning?" I ask, hoping to change the subject.

"Fine," she says on a sigh. Reagan language for *incredibly fucking boring.* "We're not really allowed to talk. This lady kept shushing us while we were shelving books."

"That is generally the nature of a library," I point out. This morning marked her first day of training for a student position in the Reynolds Library at the heart of campus. It's part of a work-study program that the financial aid office set her up with after she failed to qualify for any of the merit-based scholarships on admission.

Reagan's relationship with school couldn't be more different from my own. Not that it's her fault. She's younger than me by ten whole years; Dad's vasectomy wasn't as foolproof as they'd assumed. I was homeschooled for most of my life, but circumstances had changed by the time our parents enrolled her at a local public elementary school. When her high school GPA landed squarely at 2.4 and her SAT scores were underwhelming, our parents shrugged and told her to enroll in community college.

That's where she got it together, at least academically—visiting the tutoring center when she needed help and staying up late editing her papers until they earned her a passing grade. But while it got her admitted to Irving, it wasn't enough to earn her a free ride. Our parents are still knee-deep in medical bills, part of an ongoing battle with worker's comp. I co-signed some of her loans for this semester, but I'm still paying off the loans I took out for my Ph.D. This isn't sustainable long-term.

Just another reason tenure would work in my favor.

Which reminds me of the conversation in Julien's office this morning, no matter how hard I'm trying to push it aside.

Absently, I use the straw to push the ice around in my drink, plastic squeaking against the lid. "Maybe you were too young," I say, "but do you remember I had this friend a long time ago, Teddy Harrison?"

Reagan shakes her head.

"You met him. He was"—so many things that would be difficult to summarize, so I settle for—"the tall one, with the glasses. He came to my graduation at UMD, when I got my bachelor's. You would've been, what, ten? Eleven?"

This seems to jar her memory. "We went to get dinner afterward."

"Right." I hesitate. I promised myself I wasn't going to dwell on it. But I also feel the need to tell *someone*. To acknowledge it out loud, so that the truth of it can calcify, become tangible, and maybe then I can figure out what I'm supposed to do. "We had a sort of falling-out. I haven't talked to him in probably a decade.

And then this morning, I found out that he's coming here. To teach at Irving."

"What, were you stalking his LinkedIn or something?"

"No." I'm slightly offended she thinks I'm enough of a work-aholic to *have* a LinkedIn account. "The chair of the History Department asked me to share an office with him. Share an office with Teddy, I mean, not with the chair. There are chairs in my office. Just not, you know, *the* chair." I should really get into the habit of thinking through a whole sentence before speak-ing, but word vomit is sort of a Fernsby family trait. I've just accepted that it's genetic at this point and given up on trying to change it.

We're interrupted by an employee in a baseball cap and a bright red Bucky's polo delivering two plates to the table. "Why are you telling me this?" Reagan asks warily.

"Because," I say, self-conscious. Little sisters have a way of doing that to you. "I guess I just needed someone to vent to."

"You could try a life coach. See if they can help you get your priorities straight."

I flick a french fry across the table at her. "You're one to talk."

She deconstructs her burger, peeling slices of mayo-slathered tomato from the bun and setting them on a napkin. "So, is this supposed to be a good thing or a bad thing? Like, are you hoping to reconnect with him, or are we talking more of an 'avoid him at all costs' situation?"

"It's complicated," I say, picking at the sesame seeds on my own bun. I'm not sure that I'm all that hungry, but I should probably eat. "It's just—" I shrug. "There's a lot of history there."

That doesn't even begin to cover it.

CHAPTER

3

Rain hammered against the tin roof of our cabin, dashing any lingering hopes of playing volleyball or capture the flag today—or the rest of our first week, if our new cabin leader was to be believed. Miss Andrews had parked herself in front of an old television the size of a shoe box in the girls' common room, watching *The Office*. There was little to entertain the rest of us, at least not cooped up like this, which left us with one option: braving the storm.

I stood beside the door with Isabel Santos, my cabinmate from the previous summer. She'd grown a couple inches since the last time I saw her, bony ankles poking out from a pair of brown gauchos. "Ready?" she asked, shrugging her lanky arms out of her faded Hollister hoodie so that she could canopy it over both of us.

"Let's do it." I ducked beneath the hoodie and we charged out into the gray downpour, squealing in unison when it pattered against our heads.

We sprinted for the cafeteria. The ground was wet and sloshy, rivulets cutting between the cabins, splattering the white off-brand Converse I'd begged Mom to buy me the month before, but what choice did I have? It wasn't like this last year. Last year it was muggy most of September, hot enough that the camp counselors gave up on wrangling us for educational activities like bird-watching and gardening and instead let us spend most of our time swimming in the lake and pummeling each other with dodgeballs. *Socialization is key to childhood development,* Mom had told me when she first enrolled me in Appalachian Adventure Camp the previous autumn. That was the real reason we were all here—everyone assumed homeschooled kids couldn't possibly get enough socialization at home, so the solution was to throw us in a bunch of cabins together and hope we all turned out all right.

But there wasn't much socialization going on in that stuffy cabin, and I planned to tell Mom exactly that when she asked why my shoes were muddy.

We slipped into the cafeteria in a flurry of laughter, the rain chasing us inside. The scent of warm, dry pine clung to the air, and knotty exposed beams crisscrossed over our heads. Izzy went to hang her now-soaked hoodie on the coatrack near the old gas radiator, her wet hair sticking to her cheeks in slick black tentacles. I stomped my shoes clean on the mat so that the lunch lady wouldn't yell at us, but the lunch lady was nowhere to be seen. Lunch ended hours ago, and dinner wasn't until seven o'clock, so the cafeteria was empty except for a group from the boys' cabins, huddled around a table where they were playing one of those card games like Yu-Gi-Oh! or Magic: The Gathering. Heads turned and necks craned at our arrival, but they quickly determined that we weren't anyone of interest.

"Where are the games?" Izzy asked.

I gestured toward the pine cabinet on the far wall, one of its doors permanently ajar because the hinges were bent. "I saw one of the older girls get them out after dinner the other night."

Inside was a treasure trove of board games: Yahtzee and Life and an edition of Mall Madness that had probably been wedged back in there since the nineties—all games I wasn't allowed to play at home because my parents didn't think they were educational enough.

We were in the middle of a heated debate about Mall Madness versus Guess Who? when shouts and pitchy laughter erupted from the boys behind us. Both of us whipped around. Their heads were all bowed around the table, oblivious to our presence.

Izzy exhaled, peeling a tendril of damp hair from her face and tucking it behind her ear as we turned back to the cabinet. We settled on playing Guess Who? first, but with the condition that I owed Izzy a game of Mall Madness. We were barely at our table for five minutes before a boy with a mess of ink-black hair broke off from the rest of the group and swaggered over to us. He was the size of a fourth grader and dressed in cargo pants and a severely oversized Alaska sweatshirt that might've been hand-me-down, but he slid into the chair beside Izzy like he was a celebrity gracing us with his presence.

Mohammad Darvish, Izzy's sworn rival in all things camp-related. Last year she had beaned him so hard with a dodgeball it gave him a black eye, but he kept on taunting her anyway.

"Guess Who? is lame," he announced to no one in particular.

Izzy didn't spare him a second glance. "You're lame, Darvish."

"Seriously, it's a silly kids' game. Just look at the cartoony way they drew all the faces."

She rolled her eyes so hard they threatened to get stuck. "You'd know all about kids' games, since that's probably all you play."

"No way. Back at home, my family plays trivia every game night. I'm pretty good at it. We watch *Jeopardy!* all the time and

I always know the answers. Because I'm an intellectual," he emphasized when neither of us showed any signs of interest.

"Trivia doesn't prove you're smart," Izzy shot back. "It's just random facts."

"You're only saying that because you prefer stupid games like Guess Who?"

I dragged a hand over my face. This kid was annoying the heck out of me. "Izzy could beat you at trivia any day," I said. "Right now, in fact." A quick glance at Izzy—at the slight widening of her eyes, the almost imperceptible shake of her head—told me that she didn't actually believe she could beat him, so I hurried to add, "Let's play teams. Our team against yours. Then we'll see who the real *intellectuals* are."

Darvish frowned and glanced at his raucous friends. "There's only two of you. That's not even a fair match."

"Two on two, then," I suggested. "Pick whichever of your friends is best at trivia."

Izzy's eyes looked like they might pop out of her head. She was going to kill me later, but that didn't matter right now. Darvish was wrong and I was going to prove it.

He seemed to mull things over for a minute, then his mouth quirked in a cocky smile. "You're on." But rather than call one of his friends to join us, he popped out of his chair, remembering to toss an explanation over his shoulder only when he was already halfway out the door: "I'll be back in five minutes. I expect the game to be set up by the time I get back."

I looked to Izzy for an explanation, but she was too busy plotting my murder. "Why'd you tell him we can beat him?"

"Because we can." I went to fetch Trivial Pursuit from the cupboard. "My parents don't even let me play games like Guess Who? at home," I explained as I settled back at the table and began setting up the board. "I'm really good at trivia. Trust me, we can beat him, no problem."

By the way she was frowning, it was safe to say Izzy wasn't convinced, but she'd see soon enough. Darvish obviously had an overinflated ego and I was way too happy to knock him down a few pegs. We had this one in the bag.

By the time he returned, his thick hair sopping from the rain, I'd finished setting up. Trailing after him was a boy I hadn't seen before—a boy who was unlike him in every possible way. Where Darvish was short, his friend was tall and spindly, like he grew too quickly and the rest of his body hadn't had the chance to catch up. Where Darvish was dressed like somebody's middle-aged dad, the newcomer was wearing a knit sweater over a collared shirt, like he'd recently escaped boarding school.

And where Darvish was exceptionally obnoxious, I soon discovered that this boy was exceptionally quiet.

I extended a hand across the table once they'd taken their seats. "Clara Fernsby."

The boy took my hand and gave it one terse, firm shake, but he didn't bother with a name.

"This is Theodore Harrison the Third," Darvish supplied, looking even smugger for it.

Oh my god. Maybe he really did escape from boarding school. "Is that your real name?"

Theodore Harrison the Third furrowed his thick eyebrows at me, like he'd never heard such a ridiculous question in his life. His damp brown hair curled up at the ends and his dark eyes were framed by gold-rimmed glasses, a style I'd only ever seen my grandfather wear. "Why do you ask?"

"It just sounds sort of old-fashioned. Like Theodore Roosevelt. King George the Third. You know." I ended with a lame shrug, because I was getting the distinct impression that he did not know. He was looking at me like I was an insect, wings splayed and pinned to a corkboard for study. "Don't people call you by a nickname or something?"

"My dad calls me Teddy, sometimes," he mumbled.

"Teddy it is, then." I slapped a game piece down in front of him. "You guys are going to be orange. We're green."

"But I like red," Darvish protested.

"It doesn't matter what you like," Izzy snapped.

I ignored them, focusing on the far more interesting opponent across from me. I could beat Darvish—I didn't doubt that for a second. But I didn't know anything about Teddy. Maybe he was good at trivia. "Now we have to come up with team names."

Darvish was already rattling off a bunch of team names centered around words I wasn't allowed to say at home—words we probably weren't allowed to say at camp, for that matter—but Teddy crossed his arms on the table, a light frown curling his lips. "That's not part of the rules." He was soft-spoken, his voice a little deeper than Darvish's, which gave me the impression he was maybe a little older than the rest of us.

"No," I agreed. "But my mom says team names are conducive to team cooperation. So Izzy and I will be 'Queen Equizabeth the First.'" I gave him a self-satisfied smile. He might be the Third, but I was going to be first in this game.

Darvish scoffed. "That's the most ridiculous name I've ever heard."

Teddy ignored him, squinting at me instead. "All right. Darvish and I will be 'I Am Smartacus.'"

"Do you like history, then?" I asked.

"I like most subjects."

I couldn't help myself. I just kept talking, even when he plainly didn't care. "But you named your team after a historical figure, like I did. Spartacus, Smartacus."

"I figured I'd stick with the theme."

"History is my favorite subject. I'm going to be a teacher." There was something about being taught at the kitchen table, my math homework indistinguishable from the chicken-scratch monthly budget Mom scrawled on the back of the electricity bill, that gave me a special appreciation for teaching. It wasn't that my education was lacking, or that my parents weren't good teachers; my mom had a bachelor's in early childhood education and my dad was a blue-collar man of few words— but a whole heaping of proverbs—and eager to share the full breadth of his practical knowledge. Which often involved me standing stock-still over the open hood of his white Silverado, my arms sore with the effort of pointing the heavy Maglite at the spark plugs. But I had all this stuff in my head and no one to really share it with.

Teddy gave me a quick, assessing look that somehow managed to make me feel completely and utterly insignificant. Like I was a little girl chasing him around the playground, begging for a kiss. "Are we going to play trivia, or what?"

Warmth crept into my face. "I was just making conversation. You don't have to be rude."

His lips parted like he was about to say something, but he didn't get a chance to say it, because Izzy—probably in an effort to slice through the tension—read off a question about the Beatles, and then proceeded to bicker with Darvish over the answer. Something about Ringo Starr's eyebrow.

"Sorry," Teddy mumbled after a long moment. "I didn't mean to sound rude. I just . . ." He trailed off, his eyes cast to the game board. "I guess I don't have a lot of experience talking to—"

"Girls?" I offered.

"People." The tips of his ears went a bit red, like he was embarrassed to admit it. "I mostly just talk to my parents. And Darvish, but he's not allowed to have a cell phone, so we really only talk at camp."

"It sounds like you could use some friends." When he shot me a reproachful look, I quickly added, "I don't mean that in a bad way! I just meant—"

"She means you could use some friends that *aren't* Darvish," Izzy translated. "You know, someone with a shred of—"

Darvish cupped his hands around his mouth and made an annoying *wah, wah, wah* sound, effectively drowning out whatever Izzy was trying to say. She tried to protest, raising her voice and saying something about *maturity,* but he *wah, wahed* right over that, too.

"What I was trying to say," I said to Teddy, doing my best to tune out their squabbling, "is that I could be your friend. If you want."

I wasn't entirely sure what made me throw the offer out there. Maybe because it seemed like the nice thing to do. A small frown creased Teddy's brow. Apparently, he didn't understand it either. "You barely know me."

"I'm pretty sure getting to know each other is part of being friends."

He seemed to mull this over, narrowing his eyes. They crinkled at the corners in a way that made him look contemplative beyond his years, a deeply distrustful old man in a teenaged boy's body. I pinched my lower lip between my teeth while I waited for his answer.

"All right," he said finally. Even as he offered me his hand, he seemed wary somehow, like he was already fantasizing about dousing it in hand sanitizer later. "Friends."

"Friends," I agreed, and we shook on it.

CHAPTER

4

The first day of the fall semester, I arrive early and sit in the parking lot for half an hour, trying to work up the courage to head inside. The interior of my Volvo is a mess: crumpled-up receipts and straw wrappers are strewn around the passenger seat and stuffed in the center console. I stare up at the Hall of Letters and drum my fingers against my old Ed Hardy steering wheel cover. There was a time, years and years ago, when I thought that maybe I was impulsive enough to get a couple tattoos. I had a mood board on Polyvore and everything. But as much as teenaged me wanted to believe she was going to take risks and live life on the edge, it turns out I'm a lot more comfortable playing it safe.

Taking a deep breath, I grab my thermos of iced coffee from the cupholder and climb out of the car.

It's not like I don't have a say in the matter. I could have told Julien that I wasn't comfortable sharing my office. But I'd already agreed to share it with a stranger, so to turn around and change my mind would've required me to disclose the exact nature of my discomfort, and something about that prospect felt juvenile—like when our cabin leader used to make us swap bunks because one of the girls complained. I'm by no means a social butterfly, but I'm at least amicable with my colleagues. As nerve-racking as it is to head into work this morning, I have to weigh that against my desire to be taken seriously. And professionalism always wins out. It's not like I spend all that much time in my office, anyway. If it's awkward—and I'm anticipating that it will be awkward—I'll just schedule my office hours around his.

I pass by Andrew Greene while climbing the stairs to the third floor. He's one of three distinguished professors in Irving's Department of History, and the other two are retiring in the spring. His papercut-thin mouth flattens into something that's probably meant to be a smile, but the end result is more of a lukewarm acknowledgment. Under normal circumstances, I'd spend the rest of the morning fretting about whether or not he hates me, but I'm too far in my own head at the moment to pay him much mind.

By the time I arrive on the third floor and turn down the hall toward my new office, I'm winded. My heart squeezes like a stress ball in my chest as I draw closer to the walnut door, marked by a 326 in hammered brass numbers. My hand settles on the cool metal handle and I take a deep breath, in through my nose and out through my mouth.

Get it together.

I push down on the handle and let the door swing open.

It's empty.

Well, not empty, but there's no one else in here. No dramatic confrontation with my erstwhile friend standing behind a desk, his face cast an ominous green by a banker's lamp. There *is* an extra desk, which I suspect Julien asked someone to move in here, but it doesn't look like it's been touched. Rumpled cardboard boxes of bric-a-brac from my old office are stacked in the corner. I haven't bothered unpacking yet. The whole room is small, claustrophobic. Maybe I should've insisted that Julien find someone else to share their office, someone who has more space to work with—but I doubt any of the tenured professors would've given up their solitude, and most of the adjunct faculty are already sharing with two or three other people.

I set my thermos on the desk and duck out from beneath the strap of my cross-body bag before settling into my creaky office chair. I don't have any lectures until 1:30 P.M. on Mondays. I spend half an hour or so decluttering my inbox in preparation for the wave of confused student emails that will no doubt flood it by sometime next week. I pick up my half-melted iced coffee and take a sip, the thermos leaving a ring of condensation behind on the desk. I wipe it with the baggy sleeve of my sweater before setting the drink back down. The summer weather hasn't ceded to autumn just yet, but they always crank the A/C until it's freezing in the lecture halls, so I choose to dress accordingly.

After I finish with the emails, I lean back in my creaky desk chair, contemplating what else I can do to keep my mind occupied. I thumb my necklace, the silver coin tarnished with years of fidgeting—a reproduction of an Elizabeth I sixpence, but I always wear it flipped to the side with the quartered shield of arms. With a sigh, I push myself out of the chair.

With nothing else on my plate this morning, I resolve to finish organizing. I kneel on the floor, my floral-print skirt billowing around me, and sort through the boxes one by one. Try as I might to stay busy, there's a prickling at the back of my neck, feather-light. I know, on a conscious level, that there's no one sitting at the other desk watching me. But I keep checking over my shoulder anyway, like I'm expecting him to materialize, quick and quiet as a cat. He's somewhere on campus, even if he's not here in the room with me.

About halfway through the boxes, I reach onto the desk to take another sip of my coffee while I work, but I'm met with only ice. What time is it? I'm trying to pace my caffeine intake because too much coffee gives me the jitters, but it's already almost eleven, and there's a Keurig machine in the faculty break room calling my name. I clamber to my feet and smooth my long skirt over my knees before grabbing the thermos and heading out.

The uneasy feeling creeps back over me as I wander the halls, certain I'm going to bump into him around any corner. This feels like a game of hide-and-seek back at sleepaway camp—peering between the dense branches of a Virginia pine, fingertips tacky with sap, heart pumping because you know there might be a face peering back at you. Maybe I'm worrying for nothing. Maybe he called in sick today, on his very first day, and maybe he's already fallen out of Julien's good graces, and they'll be sending him back to Carnegie Mellon posthaste.

Not that I wish any ill on Teddy. I really don't. I hope he's healthy and I hope he has a long, successful career. It would just be a lot simpler if said career was somewhere far away from me. It's a lot easier to accept the reality that our friendship is dead and buried when I don't have to worry about bumping into him at the water cooler.

Speaking of.

I tense in the doorway of the break room, sucking in a surprised breath. Surprised, but not *that* surprised, because I knew this was going to happen at some point today—I just wasn't prepared for it to happen now.

Standing in front of the Keurig is a tall man in well-pressed slacks and a rumpled button-up shirt—meticulous enough to own starch and an ironing board but just distracted enough to toss on the wrong shirt on the way out the door. There's no pod in the Keurig, just hot water trickling out. He tears open the paper wrapping on a tea bag, dunking it in the plain white coffee mug.

Before I manage to say anything, to react at all, he turns

to leave, mug in hand, and his dark brown gaze locks with mine. There's a flicker of surprise, but not outright shock, so he must've already known that I worked here. "Clara," he says, setting the mug on the counter.

Why is he setting his mug down? It's not like we're going in for a hug—we're not on hugging terms, and he seems to realize it a second late, his hand doubling back for the tea.

"I was just coming for a refill on my coffee," I say in a small voice, hoping to give us both an out from this uncomfortable encounter. He shakes his head, faintly, like he can't believe he's seeing me again after all these years—like he's seeing a ghost.

The feeling's mutual. Well, sort of. So much about him is exactly the same as I remember, but there are things that are different, too, like the way his biceps strain against the seams of his rumpled shirt. And he's changed his glasses. They're tortoise-shell now, and rounder than they used to be, which comple-ments his strong jaw and angular Greek nose. I wonder whether Mindy helped him pick these new ones, whether this was what she thought looked best on him. If so, I hate that she's right.

"How have you—" he starts to ask, right at the same time as I blurt, "We were supposed to be sharing an office."

His brows pinch together—half confused, half wary. "What?"

"I didn't know if you knew and asked them to move you somewhere else," I say. "Julien asked me if I was okay with shar-ing my office with a visiting professor. I had no idea—" I break off, shaking my head. "I agreed before he told me your name. So if you want to ask them to switch, it's really—" If I could string a full sentence together without my thoughts getting all jumbled, that would be great. Teddy leans a hip against the counter and takes a sip of his tea, waiting for me to finish. Even after all these years, he seems to remember that I need silence to organize my thoughts—no filling in the blanks or trying to finish the sen-tence for me. "I won't be offended," I say finally.

He lowers his mug. "I don't have a problem with sharing. I don't see myself spending that much time in the office, anyway."

I relax my shoulders a little. I hadn't been entirely conscious of hunching them, but I guess I was. It's so strange, seeing him again like this, but at least I know he's not blindsided by my being here. After that painful run-in in Baltimore, I expected this would be more awkward. But that was quite a while ago. Maybe, for him, it's all ancient history.

I move toward the Keurig and he steps out of my way. He watches as I stick my thermos under the ice dispenser on the fridge.

"Did you just get here?" I ask, for the sake of filling the silence.

"I drove down from Pittsburgh yesterday."

Not what I meant, though now I'm sort of curious what his living situation is. Whether he left Mindy behind or brought her along. "I meant 'here' as in campus," I clarify, popping a cartridge of breakfast blend into the coffee maker and pressing a button to start it brewing.

"No, I, um—" He clears his throat. "I'm teaching a class in the mornings, Monday and Wednesday. American Colonial History to 1763."

Right. He's here as a visiting scholar, which means he has to teach. I remember the day he told me he was majoring in history—he said he wanted to research, not teach, because he didn't think he had the people skills for it. But we all end up teaching in the end. I wanted to, but for so many of my colleagues and classmates over the years, it's been more out of necessity. The research is their real passion.

Back then, I never gave much thought to what Teddy would actually be like as a professor. He's younger than any of the male professors I've had. And—I can't lie to myself—more attractive, too. The kind of hot that used to get the chili pepper rating on

Rate My Professors, before they realized that allowing students to score professors on their attractiveness was wildly inappropriate.

Teddy raises his eyebrows and nods at the Keurig. "Your cup—"

I glance over my shoulder about half a second before my thermos overfills—I must've pressed the button for a tall cup, too distracted to account for the ice. Frantic, I snatch the thermos out from under the dispenser. A stream of coffee splatters the drip tray, spackling the laminate counter. "Son of a biscuit," I mutter, ripping a handful of paper towels from the roll and wadding them into a ball to soak up the coffee.

Teddy watches me with an unreadable expression, brow slightly furrowed. Probably thinking about what a disaster I am. I've always been a little all over the place. Driven, yes, but disorganized in my personal life.

"Since when are you afraid to cuss?" he asks.

I suck a bit of hot coffee that splattered the side of my thumb, the skin beneath seared an angry red. "Since I started teaching."

"College, though, not kindergarten. Plenty of professors say whatever they like."

"Tenured professors," I correct him. My hand still stinging, I collect the sopping paper towels and press the pedal on the trash can to throw them away. "Which I'm not yet." I wet a paper towel in the sink to wipe down the sides of my thermos—I'm dawdling because I don't know how to wrap up this encounter without it seeming like I'm brushing him off. I screw the cap back on my thermos. "I should be heading back to the office."

He exhales. "Right," he agrees, tossing a thumb over his shoulder. "I've got a meeting I should really be—"

But for the briefest of moments, neither of us moves. We've kept our distance this whole conversation, so we're certainly not going in for a hug and a diplomatic *it's so good to see you.* "This is weird," I say instead. "Right? Seeing each other again."

He nods, Adam's apple bobbing in his throat. "Weird," he agrees, and we leave it at that.

* * *

Between class and meeting with a couple advisees, the remainder of the day keeps me on my toes and out of Teddy's way. I'm a little relieved that our first encounter is over and done with, but there's a lingering anxiety that we won't be able to dodge the awkwardness all semester. And seeing him again was like a crash course in all the little details it was easier to forget: his hair curling at the nape of his neck whenever he's gone longer than usual without a haircut, and the way he always smells like pencil shavings and Earl Grey tea. On the drive home, I try to call Izzy again over Bluetooth, but it goes straight to voice mail. It's ten at night in Lisbon, so she's probably already in bed.

My sister's Jeep is parked in the driveway when I pull up to the house. I've been renting for the past four years, waiting for tenure before I commit to buying anything, so it's not quite mine—the clapboards are painted an uncomfortable shade of pistachio green and the hedges beneath the living room window could use a trim. But it's home for now, at least. And it's given Reagan a place to stay off campus, so she doesn't have to worry about the cost of housing.

I unlock the door and hang my bag on the hall tree before heading for the kitchen, where I grab some strawberries and canned whipped cream from the fridge—it's been a dessert before dinner kind of day. Like the rest of the house, the kitchen isn't quite to my liking, all white cabinets with disinterested steel hardware and a peel-and-stick backsplash. But I do like the window behind the sink, which overlooks the old maple on the side of the house, its leaves the first herald of the changing seasons every year. They're still mostly green right now. I stare out the window as I rinse the strawberries in a colander beneath the tap. The sun sinks behind the neighboring houses, wispy clouds tinged salmon pink.

I'm alerted to Reagan's presence by the sound of bare feet slapping against the vinyl flooring. I glance over my shoulder to see her dressed in a satin pajama set, toweling off wet hair. She flips her head upside down and twists it up in the terry cloth.

"Hey," I say before turning back to the sink. "How was class?"

She settles on one of the barstools on the opposite side of the counter and reaches across to pluck a strawberry out of the colander, popping it into her mouth. "Good. I think the instructor for women's lit is going to be a real stickler about MLA, though. She made us all go to the Purdue website and popcorn read the guidelines."

I raise my eyebrows. I don't know all of the English literature faculty by name, but I can think of a few who would do that, and I can't say I blame them. "She's probably tired of juniors and seniors not properly citing their sources."

"But the medieval lit professor seems cool. He started class by reciting the opening lines from *Beowulf*. We were all like, whoa, what language is this? And then he explained that it's Old English, but that Old English isn't like Shakespearean English. Old English is a whole different language."

I toss the last of the strawberries onto the cutting board and dry my hands on a dish towel before chopping them and adding them to a mixing bowl. "I could've told you that."

"Yeah, but you didn't."

Shaking the can of whipped cream, I shoot her an exasperated look. I uncap it and squirt a mound on top of the strawberries. She pokes out her tongue before continuing. "And then I had political science with this guy who seemed like he was having a super bad day. Like I thought maybe his dog died or something."

"That's probably Gary Reid." The Poli-Sci Department shares the old social sciences building with us, so we've had our fair share of run-ins—plus he's on the scholarship committee with me. "His dog didn't die, he's just like that." I grab a wooden spoon out of the dishwasher and mix the strawberries up before scooping a generous helping into a bowl. I stick a fork in it and push it across the counter to Reagan, and keep the mixing bowl and wooden spoon for myself. "Is that everybody?"

"Mmm." Mouth full, she shakes her head and swallows. "I've got history with Professor Harrison."

I freeze with my spoon halfway to my mouth. "Why didn't you mention that first?"

"I didn't know if you wanted to talk about him," she says. "I didn't remember him being so good-looking. A couple of the girls in class already nicknamed him 'Professor Hottison.'"

I press my lips together. "That's an awful nickname."

"What's wrong with it?"

"Well, first off, it's objectifying." I point the wooden spoon at her, end coated in whipped cream. "Don't objectify your professors."

"I didn't say *I* nicknamed him that," she protests.

"And second, it doesn't really roll off the tongue." I shovel a whole heap of strawberries and whipped cream into my mouth.

Reagan arches a brow. "But you don't disagree."

"With what?"

"You think he's hot."

I'm not sure it really matters what I think. That train left the station years ago, and there's nothing I can do to change that. He's with Mindy now. Wishing things were different will only end with me getting my feelings hurt. "Teddy's always been good-looking," I say in what I hope is an offhanded way. "The only reason you don't remember is because you were, what, six years old?"

A devious smile spreads across her face. "Oh my god. You *do* think he's hot."

"I'm not going to dignify that with—"

"Come on," she groans. "Just own it."

I exhale through my nose. I'm still holding the wooden spoon and I'm considering conking her over the head with it. But instead, I grit out, "Fine. I'll admit that I'm . . . attracted to him—"

She slaps the counter. "I *knew* it!"

"—but it doesn't mean anything. That ship has sailed."

Reagan watches me with a fascinated expression, like she's seeing me for the first time, but doesn't push the issue further. We finish our strawberries and I stick the bowls in the sink, dousing them in dish soap and running the hot water.

"What actually happened with you guys, anyway?" Reagan asks.

I shut off the tap. "Why the sudden interest?"

"No reason." She rises to her feet and pushes the stool into the counter. "Just curious, I guess, if I'm going to have class with him all semester. Hoping he doesn't dock my grade when he finds out we're related."

"Teddy wouldn't do that," I assure her with a heck of a lot more confidence than is due, because the truth is, I'm not sure I know him all that well anymore. We've been apart longer than we were ever friends. For all intents and purposes, he's a stranger, and that's how it needs to stay.

CHAPTER

5

"Have you drawn your numbers yet?"

Ms. Fischer, the camp director, jiggled a plastic Planters Peanuts container full of folded slips of paper. She was wearing one of those dorky hats that covered her neck and khaki shorts that revealed legs mauled by mosquitos. I shoved my hand into the half-empty container and withdrew a number. Izzy followed suit.

I unfolded my slip of paper as Ms. Fischer shuffled away. Number six. "What number did you get?" I asked Izzy, still holding out hope that we'd be paired up.

"Thirty-one. You?"

"Not thirty-one." I chewed the inside of my cheek and scanned the crowd. Campers milled around us in the grass, awaiting further instruction. It was a sweltering day for late September, sticky enough that the sky-blue Appalachian Adventure Camp polos clung to everyone's skin like Saran wrap. The winners of the three-legged race got a two-liter of Pepsi and a whole pepperoni pizza to split. Not much motivation for utterly humiliating ourselves, but after an entire month of choking down tuna salad and deli sandwiches that were drier than the Sahara, it might as well have been a crab dinner sprinkled in Old Bay.

Unfortunately, my dermatologist had made me swear off dairy for a few months in hopes that it might help clear up my skin, so that meant I couldn't have any pizza. I had little reason to try to win this race, and I already would have preferred to be inside beneath the air-conditioning, so it was only half-heartedly that I flashed my slip of paper at faces I knew and faces I didn't. "Six? Anybody have six?" The nice thing about assigned partners like this was that it got around the embarrassment of having to *ask* people to pair up with me, but the process of trying to find whoever drew the same number was still awkward. I spied Brandi, the girl who'd been assigned to the bunk above me that summer, and I shouldered my way past a group of older kids to get to her. "Do you have six?"

With a mournful shake of her head, she flashed me a two.

"Darn," I said, standing on tiptoe to look for anyone else I might recognize. "Maybe—"

"Did I hear you say you've got six?" someone asked behind me.

I turned. There was a slight delay before I recognized him—he looked different without his glasses. Indoors, his eyes were dark brown, but in the sun they were a bright, warm amber, like holding a bottle of maple syrup up to the light. "It's you," I said, perking up slightly.

"Me," Teddy agreed, holding up a scrap of paper with a six scrawled on it.

We hadn't interacted since the rain let up two weeks ago. In part because—weather permitting—the camp program was chock-full of activities to keep us busy, but it also seemed like that day in the cafeteria had been a matter of convenience. After all, we'd both spent last September at camp as well, but we didn't interact then, so why would we interact now? Our promise of friendship might have fallen by the wayside, had we not drawn the same numbers for the three-legged race.

"My stride will be quite a bit longer than yours," Teddy was saying, arms folded as he eyed my legs, "so I'll have to slow down a bit, and it might help if you lengthen yours."

I didn't have the heart to tell him that I had little interest in winning a pizza I couldn't enjoy. "Physical activity isn't really my strong suit," I said instead. In the distance, a whistle chirruped and someone called for us to line up.

"I'll count our paces out loud, if that helps," he offered as we crested the grassy knoll, where the cabin leaders had already set to work binding participants' legs together. "That should make it easier to stay on the same page."

"Sounds good," I muttered. I wasn't sure counting would be all that helpful. I was plenty competitive when it came to board games and trivia. Less so when there was athleticism involved. We stood side by side, our feet positioned close to one another as we waited for one of the cabin leaders to come tie us together. "Do you like pizza?" I asked.

He shot me a quizzical sidelong look. "Pizza's all right, I guess."

Ms. Fischer materialized again and gave us a long, scrutinizing look as she measured out the ribbon in her hands. "Stand closer," she barked.

I was already too aware of the space—or lack thereof—between us. Being tied together would have been embarrassing even if we *were* friends, but despite our promise, we barely knew each other. Without looking at Teddy, I pressed in close, hoping I didn't smell as sweaty as I felt. Ms. Fischer crouched to bind our legs together, then ordered us to wait for the signal and moved on to the next pairing.

Teddy shifted on the spot—whether because he was uncomfortable or impatient, I couldn't tell. "Stop bumping me," I said.

"I'm sorry." He tried to adjust and nudged me with his elbow in the process. "I don't know what to do with my arm."

"Just put it around my shoulder," I suggested without really thinking. "Isn't that how this is supposed to work?"

He raised his eyebrows. He plainly took more time to think things through than I did, but he seemed to come to the same conclusion, because he tucked me beneath his arm. I'd never had a boy put his arm around me before—it was surprisingly heavy, and now I wasn't sure what to do with *my* arm, so I slipped it around his back like some of the other campers were doing, heart thumping in anticipation of the race.

Did this guy even sweat? He wasn't half as sticky as me.

"Campers ready?" someone shouted, and all of the teams hurried to make last-minute adjustments to their respective strategies—shifting arms and frantic, tangled limbs. Teddy's arm tensed around my shoulder, as though to say *don't you dare try to switch things up last minute.*

"This leg will be number one." He patted our bound legs—our thighs, actually, and for some reason, the touch caught me so off guard that my heart leapt into my throat, but he didn't seem to notice. "These are number two." He indicated his free leg.

"On your mark."

"Ready?" Teddy asked.

"Get set."

I fixed my gaze on the finish line at the bottom of the hill. "As ready as I'm going to be."

"Go!"

The whistle trilled and everyone took off at once. Half the campers stumbled and ate dirt right out the gate. It took a couple paces, but Teddy and I managed to find a sort of rhythm, all to the tune of his muttered *one, two.* The finish line was marked by a chalk line sprayed across the grass at the bottom of the hill, not that far away. We picked up speed with ease thanks to the slope of the hill.

Maybe too much speed.

"One, two. One, two—no, that's not two, this leg is two," Teddy protested, trying to indicate our legs while also trying to keep walking.

"What do you mean?" I was breathless, flustered. "That's your left leg, this is my left leg, they're both two."

"That makes no sense. If they're both two then we wouldn't—"

He went to take a step with every intention of dragging me along with him, and he sort of *did* drag me. But I had already lost my footing, my free leg buckling beneath me—followed by a sickening pop. We went down in a blur of arms and legs bent at awkward angles and sky-blue polo shirts, landing face-first in the grass with a dull thud.

I let out a muffled groan. There was a bitter tang in my mouth and I tried to spit it out, grass sticking to my lip. Teddy's arm was heavy across my back, but he shifted to push himself off the ground. I sucked in a breath as a sharp, biting pain shot through my ankle.

He froze beside me. "Are you all right?"

"No," I gritted out. "I think I broke my ankle."

My face was scrunched in pain, my eyes shut tight, too scared to assess the damage. Teddy shifted himself gingerly in the grass, and then deft hands worked to untie our legs. As soon as I was free, I rolled onto my back and lifted my injured leg to reposition it, hissing at another twinge of pain. The sunlight was a dull red against the inside of my eyelids.

All around us, people were shouting and cheering at the race and whistles were chirruping. No one seemed to have noticed that we were down—or rather, if they did notice, they hadn't noticed that I was injured. "Hey!" Teddy was shouting, too, far closer than the rest of the din. Footsteps thudded in the grass. "We need to get her to the first aid station."

Someone was squatting next to me. "Can you walk?" A gruff voice that I recognized as belonging to Ms. Fischer. I pinched my eyes tighter and shook my head. "Here. Help me get her up."

They scooped me up by the arms, setting me upright, but I couldn't put any weight on my left leg. "I'll take her," Teddy offered, and he tucked me in close, much the same as he did during the race, only this time I wasn't very good at supporting my own weight. I remembered my sweaty armpits and wanted to protest, but even if my ankle was okay, I was too light-headed to stand on my own right now. He guided me as I hopped through a gap in the crowd, down the hill toward the first aid station.

* * *

Half an hour later, I sat on the examination table beneath the stark fluorescent light of the first aid cabin with an ice pack balanced on my sprained ankle. Teddy waited in one of the hard plastic chairs, his chin balanced on a fist. I wasn't totally sure what he was still doing here, but I didn't hate the company.

"You'll need to stay off it until it's fully healed," Nurse Mendoza instructed me. "And try to keep it elevated and iced for the next forty-eight hours." She glided across the room on her rolling stool and opened a series of drawers. "It looks like we're out of ACE bandages. Let me just pop over to the supply cupboard. Wait here," she added sternly, as if patients with sprained ankles regularly popped up to go walk a 10K just for the fun of it.

She bustled out of the room, leaving me alone with Teddy. I was uncomfortably aware of the way the paper on the examination table crunched every time I shifted my weight, but I shifted anyway, because I was embarrassed and didn't know what else to do with myself. "Thank you for helping me. I'm sorry I cost you the race. And the pizza."

"Actually, I'm not a huge fan of pizza. Too greasy." The corner of his mouth quirked in something resembling a smile—the closest thing to a smile I'd seen out of him, at any rate. "The Pepsi, however—"

"I'm sorry!" I groaned and flopped back on the table, paper crinkling beneath me. "At least you'll know I'm suffering. I'll be missing the hike tomorrow and everything."

"Poor you. You get to lie in bed, reading all day."

I propped myself up to narrow my eyes at him. "How do you know I'll be reading?"

He shrugged, the shadow of a smile still playing around his lips. "Just a guess."

"Are you going to be at the bonfire?" I asked. "What am I saying, of course you are." The end-of-camp bonfire was kind of compulsory, a last chance to hang out before meeting our parents in the parking lot early the next morning. Even on crutches, Izzy would probably expect me to be there. "What I mean is, do you want to hang out that night? If you're not busy."

"Sure. We are friends, after all."

"At least now you'll remember me next year," I joked, because I apparently didn't know when to shut up. "You know, now that I've tripped you and sprained my ankle and all that."

This time, he smiled for real. It wasn't a wide, unabashed, toothy sort of smile. It was subtle and close-lipped and maybe a bit shy, but it was a smile nevertheless. "You'd be pretty hard to forget."

* * *

Balancing my weight between one of my crutches and my good leg, I fed a dollar bill into the vending machine on the backside of the recreation building and selected E-3. There was a clang and I bent awkwardly to retrieve a can of Pepsi from the receptacle. I stuffed it into the kangaroo pocket of my hoodie before adjusting my crutches and hobbling toward the lake.

The smoky smell of burning mesquite carried across the field on an early autumn breeze, warm and inviting. Campers and staff alike milled about, saying their goodbyes for the summer, exchanging phone numbers. I craned my neck for some sign of Teddy, but it was hard to pick out any one person, bodies silhouetted by the flames and the orange glow dancing off the water. I spotted Darvish, a head shorter than the campers around him, and scanned his immediate vicinity. My crutches sank into the soft grass. I wore a tennis shoe on my good foot, but I couldn't fit the other shoe over my bandage, so I just covered it with an old Bobby Jack sock because it was the only sock that was stretched out enough.

From somewhere in the dark, Izzy bounded up to me. "There you are." She had her normally long, sleek hair crimped so that it fell in small, tight waves, and she was wearing shimmery lip gloss. "I was wondering whether you planned to turn up."

"Sorry. Took me a while to get down here. Crutches, you know."

"Come on." She tugged me by the arm of my sweatshirt. "The girls are just about to start a game of telephone and I've got the best idea for an opening line."

I was barely listening. Teddy was down by the shore, skipping stones across the glassy surface of the water. "I'll catch up with you in a minute," I told Izzy. She shrugged and wandered off, and I shuffled down the hill. My crutches were more cumbersome than helpful, sticking in the soft mud by the lake. Without noticing me, Teddy stooped to pick up a pebble and tossed it at the water. It grazed the surface twice before disappearing with a *plunk*. "You want to use a flat one," I said, and he wheeled around. The gold-framed glasses were back, lenses slightly too large for his face, and he was wearing a zip-up sweatshirt over one of the camp polos. "They skip better. Here, hold this." I passed him one of my crutches so that I could bend to pick up a rock shaped like a pancake and cast it across the water. It skipped five times before sinking beneath the surface, bull's-eyes rippling in its wake.

"Where'd you learn to do that?" Teddy asked.

"My dad. He's a lot better at it than I am. Thanks," I added, accepting the crutch and tucking it back under my arm. I withdrew the Pepsi from the pocket of my hoodie, the can cool and slick beneath my fingers. "I think I owe you this. For losing you the race." I wiped some of the condensation on my sleeve like I was polishing an apple before handing it over. He took it and reached for the tab to pop it, and it occurred to me that it probably got all shaken up in my pocket. "You might want to wait a while before—"

There was a crack followed by a hiss; he let some of the air out before opening it all the way. "I'm not sure we were ever going to win," he pointed out.

"Maybe not." I tried to shrug, but the motion was stunted by the crutches. "Guess we'll never know."

He took a sip from the can. We stood like that, away from the chatter and crackling of the fire—me with my crutches embedded in the mud, him politely sipping a Pepsi that I was almost certain was shaken flat. A breeze rustled the nearby reeds. On the far shore, the golden windows of lake houses glowed in the dark. "Thank you," he said after a minute.

For some reason, my cheeks warmed. Maybe because it felt silly for him to thank me for something as inconsequential as a can of Pepsi. "It was only a dollar."

"Not just for this," he clarified, holding up the can. "Thank you for being—you know." I didn't know, so I raised my eyebrows, waiting for him to continue. "Nice, I guess," he finished lamely. It was hard to tell in the dark, with only the distant light of the bonfire, but I thought maybe his cheeks had gone a bit red, too. "I'm not good at talking to people, normally, but you've made it easier. I like talking to you."

Ignoring the funny swooping feeling in my stomach, I used my crutch to bump the side of his tennis shoe. "Friends are supposed to be nice."

He stared at his feet. "And are friends supposed to exchange phone numbers so that they can keep in touch now that summer's over?"

"They are," I confirmed, a grin stretching over my face. "But I didn't bring anything to write with."

Teddy smiled shyly and produced a Sharpie from the pocket of his jeans. I held out my arm and he uncapped the marker before steadying my wrist with a hand, the felt tip whispering across the sensitive skin and leaving tingles in its wake. I was a bit ticklish, but resisted the urge to jerk away. His handwriting was neat and blockish, and his area code was different than mine, but that was no surprise, because homeschooled kids were sent to sleepaway camp from all over the Mid-Atlantic. There was even one girl whose parents drove her down from Connecticut every September.

"There," he said when he'd finished, popping the cap back on the marker and letting go of my arm. "Now we can keep in touch."

CHAPTER

6

Thursday afternoon, I let the students in HIST-102 out of class ten minutes early to allow myself time to stop by the office. It's empty, again. Almost a week into the semester and Teddy has held true to his word—he really doesn't spend much time in the office. If it weren't for a desk organizer filled with cheap pens and a jacket slung over the back of the chair, I'd almost think I wasn't sharing the office after all.

I toss a few leftover syllabi onto my desk and begin rummaging through the drawers. Where did I put the meeting agendas? I printed them just this morning, but they seem to have gotten away from me. There's a tray next to the keyboard stacked with paperwork, but a quick flip through the top few sheets informs me that I didn't put the agendas in there. I stand on my tippy-toes to peer over the desk. It's butted up against a wall—not ideal for meeting with students, but it's an issue of space when you're sharing an office this small. And there, in the space between the back of the desk and the scuffed oak wainscoting, are my agendas. They must have fallen back there when I shut the door behind me before heading to class.

I stick my hand down the gap, but my arm's too short to reach. Huffing and swiping a lock of hair from my face, I straighten up and reassess my options with my hands on my hips. I could move the desk, but that seems drastic. Plus, the last time I tried moving furniture without asking for help, I pulled a muscle in my back and my doctor had me on Flexeril for a month. The most logical next step is to see if I can reach from underneath. I drop to my knees and crawl into the leg space, my fingers patting around unseeing behind the solid part of the desk until they make contact with a piece of paper. The pages scattered when they fell, so I pull them out one by one, creasing some of them in the process. The committee members will have to make do.

Someone clears their throat.

I straighten up so fast that I smack my head on the underside of the desk. Sucking air through my teeth, I emerge with the papers in hand, only to find Teddy standing in the doorway. "Holy guacamole, you scared me," I mutter, massaging the top of my head. He offers me a hand.

"You did that thing again," he says, pulling me to my feet. "Censoring yourself."

"Like I said, I'm trying to form better habits."

We're standing far closer than we stood on Monday in the break room. He still smells like pencil shavings and Earl Grey tea, but up close like this, I notice that he's started wearing some sort of cologne as well—it's subtle and warm and earthy. He releases my hand. My pulse thrums in my fingers, an aftershock.

"Well," I say, trying to sound light, airy, even though I'm pretty sure my throat is closing up, "I've got a meeting on the other side of campus, so I've got to—" I wave the stack of crumpled agendas at him, like that's explanation enough.

He nods. "Right."

But neither of us moves. I clench and unclench my fingers, willing them to feel normal. Finally, he sidesteps me, clearing the path to the door. I brush past him, but hesitate in the threshold, words bubbling to the surface. "Do you want to walk with me?" *Ohmygod what am I doing?* "I wouldn't mind the company."

His eyes lock with mine. For the briefest of moments, I think he's going to say no. The same old song and dance: extending an olive branch only for the other person to set it on fire, *ad nauseam.* But to my surprise, he says, "All right," and joins me in stepping out into the hall.

Half of me is wondering what I'm doing and the other half is pleased. We can have *this,* at least. Something polite, friendship vacuum-sealed in professionalism. If I'm being honest with myself, there's maybe a teensy, tiny part of me that's been disappointed not to run into him around the office more. Talking to him makes me feel a little less awful about everything that happened between us, all those years ago. Look at us: we're adults now. We can be cordial without it needing to remind us of how we used to be, and all the ways we went wrong.

We descend the stairs and exit through the north door. There's a light breeze today, the first hint of autumn beating back the sticky Maryland summer, and it stirs his hair as we make our way across the grassy quad. I try not to watch him out of the corner of my eye, but it's also impossible to pretend that he's not there. His hand rests on the strap of his leather laptop bag, his father's gold signet ring on his finger, so they must be on speaking terms again. Despite the ring and the stuffy roman numeral at the end of his name, his family doesn't actually come from old money. His dad's an auto body technician from Philadelphia, and his mom emigrated from Thessaly.

I'm about to ask him how his parents have been, but he speaks first. "You remember that hike up to the overlook, when we were maybe, what, sixteen?" he asks. "You guys all ganged up on me, trying to convince me to say a 'bad word.'"

I'm surprised he's bringing up something from our past, but it's an innocent enough memory. "I told you that there was no such thing as bad words. Just bad intentions." My mouth twists in a self-deprecating smile. "Which I now realize is debatable, for the record."

He laughs under his breath. "Every time you say things like 'holy guacamole,' all I can think about is that day."

It's a good memory. Sweaty, eaten alive by mosquitos, standing victorious on a slab of rock and shouting across the mountaintops until our voices were hoarse. A warm ache spreads behind my breastbone, not caused by anyone or anything in the here and now—it's more nostalgic, a yearning for another place, another time. Afternoons spent laid out on warm, sunbaked stone, watching the clouds drift overhead and talking about our plans for the future.

I rub my chest with the heel of my palm. "How'd you end up back in Pennsylvania?" I ask. It's a personal question, but not too personal. "You always said you were going to leave and never look back."

He blows out a breath. "Just life, I guess." I raise my eyebrows at him, waiting to see whether he'll elaborate, but he doesn't, and I don't press for more information.

The buildings in the Franklin Complex are squat, one story and brutalist. They were added to the campus in the late seventies to accommodate a flood of enrollment after the end of the war in Vietnam. Somehow, the architecture is reflective of the zeitgeist. Nowadays, though, the complex is strangely juxtaposed with the more classic brick buildings that make up the rest of campus. There is no ivy creeping up the concrete walls here, no romanticism in the dry, fluffy plumes of bottlebrush that line the planters. We enter the first building and he walks me to the conference room. I expect we'll say our awkward goodbyes and then I'll head inside, but when I stop beside the weighty metal door numbered *106*, he tugs it open and says, "After you."

Five boxes of cold hot-and-ready pizza are laid out on the

conference room table, spoils of an earlier meeting. Gary's already seated at the table. His salt-and-pepper head is bent over his phone and he doesn't bother to glance up at our arrival.

"You're free to take off, by the way," I say to Teddy as I flip the lids on the boxes in search of pineapple and Canadian bacon. No such luck. "These meetings aren't all that exciting." I take a slice of cheese pizza, cradling it in a napkin, and seat myself at the end of the table.

"I've got an hour to kill before my next lecture." He takes a seat, leaving an empty chair between us, and scoots into the table. "I hope you don't mind. You're the only person I know around here besides Julien."

It's easy to forget that Teddy isn't super comfortable putting himself out there and introducing himself to new people. He's soft-spoken, but it reads more like *quiet confidence* than *social awkwardness.* "Mmm." I finish chewing my pizza and swallow. "I can remedy that." I gesture back and forth across the table. "Gary, Teddy. Teddy's a visiting professor of history from Carnegie Mellon."

Teddy rises out of his seat to offer a handshake across the table. "Most people call me 'Ted' these days."

He probably only means to gently correct me, but it's a pointed reminder that I don't know him anymore. Gary sets down his phone just long enough to reach across the table and give Teddy's hand a firm shake. "Tartans, huh? Still haven't forgiven you guys for that touchdown in the final quarter last season."

I assume he's talking about football—I'm peripherally aware that Irving is a Division III school, but sports aren't really my thing. Last I checked, they weren't Teddy's thing either, and it seems that much hasn't changed, because he chuckles awkwardly and changes the subject. "How was your summer?"

"Great," Gary says. "It's the coming back part that's not so great. Not even a week into the semester, and Jane's already called me into her office to talk grading policies."

Gary Reid has been teaching at Irving for over a decade now. In that time, he's racked up an impressive twenty-seven official complaints, most of them centered around his insistence on guarding any grade higher than a C+ like a greedy dragon brooding over a gold hoard. Supposedly he gave an A- to a girl in '07, but that's something of an urban legend—I haven't seen any tangible proof. He's one pissed-off student away from an opinion piece about professors on power trips.

The door to the conference room swings wide, and two others enter: a long-legged man with a halo of sparse, sandy hair, and a woman with a blunt bob, her pashmina shawl whirling behind her like a cape. They're absorbed in a conversation about Zoom lectures and they don't stop on our account, though the woman does toss Teddy a quick—if quizzical—smile.

"—whether they reached some consensus about the camera policy," the woman is saying as she draws out a chair beside Gary.

"Well, not in the organizational sense." The man withdraws a yellow legal pad from his briefcase and slaps it on the table in front of him. "I'd say if there was a consensus—forgive me, that might be too strong a word—then it was an agreement that these matters need to be addressed on a case-by-case basis, with varying circumstances taken into consideration."

Now that everyone's here, I shovel down the rest of my pizza and wipe my greasy fingers on the napkin before passing out the agendas. They're short, to the point: *meeting times, application deadline, award ceremony.* I know better than to expect that we're going to cover all of this today, but I'm determined to start strong.

Before we get down to business, I introduce Teddy to the other committee members. I can't quite bring myself to call him

"Ted," so I opt for his full name instead. I point my mechanical pencil at the woman wrapped in the shawl. "This is Trina Madhani from the Art Department. She's our treasurer. And this is Dean Goodman, our secretary." The lanky man looks up from scribbling on his legal pad and gives Teddy a curt nod. The notes he's made so far are shorthand and indecipherable, like the Voynich manuscript, or a prescription from a doctor.

"Pleasure to meet you both," Teddy says. His gaze lingers on Goodman for a moment before he clears his throat and adds, "Sorry, you're the dean of . . . ?"

Goodman sighs without looking up from his notepad. "Alas, I'm a Dean by birth, not by title."

Teddy shoots me a quizzical look.

"What he means by that," I clarify, "is that Dean is his legal name. He's an instructor in the English Literature Department."

"We mostly call him Goodman to avoid the confusion," Trina says with a wink.

"And I'm just a committee member," Gary adds. Despite the lack of any real responsibilities that come with his title, he manages to make it sound very burdensome.

"All right. So, first on the agenda," I continue, "we have the matter of setting a deadline for the scholarship applications this year. Last year we set it at November thirtieth for spring applicants, but I feel like an earlier deadline might leave us more time for review."

For the next forty-five minutes or so, we knock out items on the agenda. Teddy stays quiet throughout most of it, listening more than he speaks, but his presence is distracting anyway—my eye is repeatedly drawn to him. It's true that I was always something of a social safety net for him when we were younger. But he's a lot older now. He's held down the same job for seven or eight years, brushed shoulders with scholars from Oxford and Stanford and Tsinghua. He shouldn't *need* a safety net.

Not that I don't like having him around. The problem is that I do, and I'm wary of liking it too much. Of a false sense of security, lulled by the thought that maybe, just maybe, we can be friends again.

"We've got about ten minutes to wrap things up," Gary announces, jolting me from my reverie.

"Right." I look back at the agenda. "Before we go, I wanted to touch on our fundraising efforts really quick. I've already mentioned to a couple of you that I'm putting myself forward for tenure in December." This earns a half-interested nod from Trina and a few scribbles from Goodman. I'm the only member of the scholarship committee who's not already tenured—it's part of the reason I was elected committee chair, spring semester before last. With no dossiers to flesh out, none of the others were all that interested in taking on the responsibility. "Julien called to my attention that it might be helpful if we ramp up our fundraising efforts this year."

Gary scoffs. "With what? Bake sales? Should we erect a lemonade stand on the corner of Pike Street and McCulloh?" He shakes his head. "It's a drop in the bucket."

"The majority of our scholarships are dependent on endowments," Trina points out, scratching her eyebrow with the eraser of her mechanical pencil. "And the ones that aren't typically come from the same pool of donors. Outside of finding someone with heaps of money on their deathbed, I'm not sure we can do all that much to move the needle."

"I think we're already doing all we can to raise funding," Goodman adds. "It's kind of the whole point."

I'm a little crestfallen that their opposition to the idea is so immediate, but they're not *wrong*—I've been grasping at straws ever since Julien brought it up. It's not easy convincing people to fork over their hard-earned cash, and it's complicated by the pervasive belief that upper education is a luxury.

A lot of people advocate for students paying for it out of their own pockets, no matter how many integral jobs require a bachelor's degree or beyond.

"What about a gala?"

Every head in the room swivels toward Teddy. He's got his arms folded on the oak table in front of him, and at the sudden attention, his shoulders stiffen. "I know it's not my place—"

"No," Trina says slowly, watching him with her head quirked to one side. "Go on."

Some of the tension seeps out of him, and he clears his throat. "A gala gives people something interesting to do, in a town this size." While he talks, Trina clicks her mechanical pencil against her notepad, eyes narrow. "And it would appeal to both town and gown. You lure people in with food and entertainment. Charge some sort of cover fee. And Clara's always been great at organizing things," he finishes, almost as an afterthought. He glances over at me but looks away again just as soon. I didn't think much of it when we first met, but as the years went by, I used to love studying his face in profile—the curve of his nose, and the hard angle where his jaw met with his ear. I force myself to look at the agenda, pretending to jot something down.

For a moment, only the clicking of Trina's mechanical pencil fills the silence—not frantic or anxious, but steady, rhythmic. *Click.* Pause. *Click.* Then Goodman makes an odd sound, somewhere between a huff and a cough. "We're not exactly the Met."

That's my cue to jump in. "We have countless applicants every year who would love to attend Irving if they had the proper financial assistance. But there's an obvious shortage of scholarships to go around. If we could raise—"

"But just hosting the gala would cost out of pocket," Trina interrupts, hesitantly. I know that tone—she wants to help me out here, but she's pragmatic to a fault. "This isn't some established tradition we're talking about. There's no guarantee we wouldn't *lose* money on it."

"So plan on a volunteer basis," Teddy suggests. "Reach out to local businesses, see whether any alums are interested in helping out."

"We could contact the local party supply store and see whether they'd be willing to donate old stock in exchange for putting their name on the flyers as a sponsor," I suggest. "And we could see if there are any local restaurants that would be willing to cater."

Trina leans back in her chair, arms folded, but she's not rejecting the idea outright, and I take that as a positive sign. Goodman's hunched over his legal pad, scribbling.

"Might I point out that this conversation is nowhere on the agenda," Gary says. "I move to shelve it and discuss it next meeting."

"We're already discussing it," Trina counters, a touch of impatience in her voice. She locks eyes with me. "It's a good idea, but planning a gala doesn't fall under our jurisdiction, so to speak. It's the sort of thing that would normally be delegated to a subcommittee."

I withhold a sigh. Trina is like a walking, talking copy of *Robert's Rules of Order,* which is very helpful when we need to make sure we're covering all our bases, but at times like this, it gets tedious. "In that case," I say, "who'd like to be on the subcommittee?"

Gary doesn't bother looking up from his phone. "Not interested."

"I'm busy," Goodman says.

"We haven't even settled on a meeting time," I remind him, but he just shrugs.

Trina gives me an apologetic look. "I'm already spread a bit thin between this and assistant coaching my daughter's soccer team."

This time, I don't bother withholding the sigh. "Okay, so nix the gala idea, then."

"Put me on the subcommittee," Teddy says.

I look up from the agenda, frowning. "But you're only visiting."

"And you only need the subcommittee for one semester. Right? You plan the gala for this fall and then you apply for tenure. After that, you won't need me, anyway."

Need—that's a funny word. There was a time when I thought that I needed him like I needed oxygen, that everything would come crumbling down if I wasn't able to call him every night before bed, every time I had a fight with my mom or bombed an exam. It was a naïve, childlike understanding of what it meant to love someone, because the truth, as it turns out, is that you don't *need* anyone. You can love them with all your heart, but you don't need them. When they walk away, you don't stop breathing. The world keeps spinning, and life goes on.

"As chair of the scholarship committee, I would need to be present for all subcommittee meetings," I point out, as diplomatically as I can. I want to make sure he knows what he's signing on for.

He nods. "Makes sense to me."

I hold his gaze for a couple of seconds before turning to Trina for approval.

"There aren't any rules against a visiting professor serving on a committee as far as I'm aware," she says slowly.

I mull over my options. It's a solid idea. And we've managed to be civil so far. Plus, I was already anticipating seeing Teddy around campus—a few subcommittee meetings shouldn't make much of a difference.

"Someone needs to make the motion," I say. As chair of the committee, I'm not allowed to initiate the approval process.

Trina raises her hand. "I move to form a gala subcommittee."

There's a pregnant pause, and for a split second, I wonder if the other two committee members are going to outright refuse to participate. But then Goodman heaves a sigh and tosses up a hand. "I second the motion."

"All in favor, by show of hands?" I ask. Everyone but Gary holds their hand up, including Teddy, though he's not officially on this committee yet, so his vote doesn't count. "All opposed?"

Everyone looks at Gary. Picking up on the sudden silence, he tears his eyes from his phone, forehead wrinkled, and glances around the table. "I'm sorry, were we voting on something?"

"Doesn't matter," Goodman says, adding something to his notes—or maybe doodling a stick-figure of Gary. Hard to say for sure. "It passes anyway."

* * *

It's a little after six and I'm locking up my office for the evening when my phone buzzes from somewhere inside my messenger bag. I fish it out of the side pouch. Two missed calls—one spam and one from Izzy. It must have gone straight to voice mail. Service is always a little spotty in these old buildings.

> Izzy: Omg missed you again!! I feel like we need to schedule something at this point

I smile and shake my head, pocketing my keys and tapping out a message as I make my way down the hall to the stairwell. Izzy's always been better at communicating face-to-face. For a while, after her move to Lisbon, we managed to organize monthly Skype calls—*coffee and catch-up,* we called them—where we'd each head to a local café, connect to the Wi-Fi, and pretend we were out to brunch together. But after a while, even that fell by the wayside, lost in the hustle and bustle of our two very different schedules.

> Clara: Just leaving work. Let's talk this weekend?

> Izzy: Can't. Headed to Porto Santo with the new girl I'm seeing :/

> Clara: Poor you!

> Izzy: lol shush!!

> Izzy: We'll talk soon. Promise!! xoxo

I pause at the top of the stairs, my thumbs hovering over the screen. Izzy would drop everything to hop on the phone if I gave any indication that it was important, but then again, it's not really all that important, is it? There's nothing urgent about the situation with Teddy, or tenure, or this gala I'm supposed to be planning. I can't justify creating something out of nothing.

> Clara: Sounds good. Have fun in Porto Santo. Love you lots!

"You really shouldn't text on the stairs."

A deep, steady voice echoes in the stairwell—unmistakable—and I rip my eyes from my phone. Teddy's staring up at me from the landing between floors, laptop bag slung over his broad shoulder and his hands stuffed into the pockets of crisp brown slacks that flatter his long legs. "More than half of workplace injuries happen due to negligent use of staircases, you know."

"And eighty-three percent of statistics are made up on the spot," I fire back. The corner of his mouth quirks—not quite a smile, but the ghost of something familiar. It's that feeling of passing a stranger on the sidewalk, certain you recognize them from somewhere, but when you do a double take to try to place them, you've lost them in the crowd. "What are you still doing here?" I ask.

"Just finished up for the night," he says. "I was coming to check whether you'd locked up the office."

I nod. "Walk with me to my car?" I ask, tentatively. Wes keeps a close eye on the parking lot, so I'm safe walking alone, but I want a chance to talk. After the meeting earlier, Teddy had left in a rush, almost late for his 4 P.M. lecture.

"Sure," he says. His dark eyes are glued to me as I stow my phone in my messenger bag and march down the stairs, joining him on the landing. "I'm heading that direction anyway." He sweeps a hand in front of him, as though to say *ladies first,* and follows me down the stairs.

We exit the Hall of Letters into the clear September evening, the sky a muted, dusty blue in the fading daylight. "I wanted to thank you," I say, "for the gala idea, but more so for offering to be on the subcommittee. I know it doesn't really . . . benefit you, I guess, to volunteer for a campus you're only visiting, so I just wanted to make it clear how much I appreciate that."

He's quiet for a beat, staring at the pavement as we make our way to my car. "If people only volunteered when it benefitted them, I think the world would be a little worse off."

I don't know what to say to that, so I nod. I should know better than to think he'd offer to help just for my sake, but maybe a part of me had selfishly hoped.

"I was thinking maybe we could meet Friday afternoons, maybe around four?" he suggests.

"That works for me." We reach my old Volvo—easily the ugliest of the faculty vehicles with its peeling blue paint. A pine tree air freshener dangles from the rearview mirror. It lost its freshening abilities months ago. I've been too busy to remember to throw the air freshener out, just like I've spent the last six years being too busy to go shopping for a new car. "Just for the record, you don't mean Friday as in tomorrow, do you?"

He arches a brow. "Is there another type of Friday?"

I shake my head. "Scratch that, what I meant to ask is whether it can wait until next week. I'd like to take some time to sort of get my thoughts organized, before we dive in."

"Completely understandable." He adjusts the strap of his laptop bag. "I'll see whether I can figure out a meeting space."

That should probably be my job, but I don't argue, because I have more than enough on my plate as it is. I fiddle with the keys in my hand, running my fingers over the tattered *Vampire Diaries* lanyard I've had since I was maybe seventeen, long enough that the print has all but worn off. We're once again at a strange sort of impasse, neither of us sure how we're supposed to say goodbye, and it's making me fidget.

"I'm parked over in Lot G," he says.

I twist the lanyard between my fingers, nodding. "Right. Well, I'll see you tomorrow. Or maybe next week, I guess," I throw out there, because it's not like I've been running into him every day, and I kind of want to test the waters. Figure out what days he's actually on campus, so I know what to expect.

He holds my gaze for a moment before looking back at his feet, his brow knit. When he looks back up, all he says is, "Good night, Clara," and he turns to leave.

"Night," I say to his back. Then I unlock my car and climb into

the driver side, wrestling out of my cross-body bag and shoving
it onto the passenger seat. I wait for him to disappear around
the corner of the Hall of Letters, and then I slump forward with
a loud groan, smacking my forehead against the steering wheel.
At this rate, I'll be digging my old iPod Nano out of the closet at
Mom and Dad's house before midterms, skipping around to all
the angstiest tracks I can find: Hawthorne Heights or the self-
titled album by The Used, probably.

Get yourself together.

When I straighten up, my hair is falling out of my claw clip
and into my eyes. I swipe a lock of it out of my mouth and turn
the key in the ignition.

CHAPTER

7

We kept in touch.

Mom was wary when I flashed her my forearm on the drive home from camp, the first week of October. She wrinkled her nose at the phone number like it was a new tattoo. "No boyfriends until you're eighteen," she reminded me. Her voice had a special sort of twang to it, impossible to pinpoint, which always prompted strangers to ask where she was from: half Tennessee, half Eastern Shore.

"He's not a boyfriend," I said, tugging the sleeve of my sweatshirt back over my wrist.

"Why?" Reagan asked from the car seat behind me.

I pivoted to look at her. Her blond hair was chopped into a lopsided bowl cut—the handiwork of our mother and a pair of dull sewing scissors—and a packet of Annie's Organic Bunny Snacks were crushed in her tiny fist. The bunnies in question were strewn around the back seat of the car, burrowing between the seats. She'd celebrated her fifth birthday while I was away at camp, and though I didn't mind missing out on the mermaid-themed bounce house, I was sort of bummed that I didn't get any of Mom's famous red velvet cupcakes. "Because he's not," I said.

"Why?"

"Because I said so."

"Have some patience with your sister, please," Mom interrupted. "This 'why' thing, it's very normal at this age, part of natural childhood development. It's their way of showing that they're curious about the world around them."

I faced forward and folded my arms, sinking into my seat. "Well, she doesn't need to be curious about my personal life."

In the end, I had to promise not to hog the phone line all day, and to only make one phone call a week, and a whole heap of other rules Mom had never bothered enforcing when I wanted to call Izzy—maybe because Izzy and I rarely talked on the phone. But worst of all, she insisted I use the green wall-mounted phone in the dining room, where the coiled cord prevented me from wandering any farther than the kitchen.

It took me a couple weeks to work up the courage to call. Mom was washing dishes by hand in the kitchen, the faucet running and silverware clattering around the stainless-steel sink. Reagan was playing with a See 'N Say (she kept winding the arrow back to the same place, to the same refrain of *the cat says meow* every few seconds). I plugged my free ear with a finger so I could hear better.

A deep voice answered on the second ring. "Harrison residence."

"Hi, um, my name is Clara Fernsby. I went to camp with your son and I was wondering if—"

"Clara," the voice said flatly, "this is Teddy."

"Oh." Warmth colored my cheeks; I was relieved he wasn't here to see it. "You sound older on the phone."

"I know," he said with a sigh. "Telemarketers are always trying to sell me things."

It was a far cry from the *Are your parents home, sweetie?* that I got every time the pollsters called to ask who we planned to vote for. I knew it wasn't his intention, but it made me feel a little silly and childish by comparison.

"How old are you, anyway?" I asked.

"Fourteen."

"When's your birthday?" I demanded, because I was certain he was older than me, if only by a few months.

"December twenty-ninth."

My mouth dropped open. "Shut up."

From the kitchen sink, my mom shot me a disapproving look.

"What?" Teddy asked.

"My birthday is the thirtieth." This seemed like a very significant discovery, more than mere happenstance. He *was* older than me . . . by one whole day.

"It sucks, doesn't it?" he lamented. "December birthdays. Everyone always forgets. Especially when it's right after Christmas."

"I'll remember your birthday if you'll remember mine," I promised, and I marked it on my *Pirates of the Caribbean* calendar—like I'd ever forget.

We didn't see each other all year, but we tried to talk on the phone every couple of weeks. Teddy lived three hours away in Allentown, Pennsylvania, home to a life-sized replica of the Liberty Bell and Dorney Park & Wildwater Kingdom, a massive theme park that I thought sounded awesome, but he wasn't allowed to visit because his mom thought roller coasters were too dangerous.

I'd always thought my parents were overprotective. My mom didn't let me wear spaghetti-strap tank tops because they showed too much skin and she screened R-rated movies before deciding whether or not I was allowed to watch them, but I soon determined that Teddy's parents must have been worse. My parents had encouraged me to go to camp in order to meet some kids my own age. Teddy had to beg his parents to let him enroll, and only under the condition that he would do twice the chores his first month back home. Sometimes he called me later than we had planned because he got stuck pulling weeds out of the flower bed or washing the dishes after dinner.

The more we talked, the more my mom loosened up on the phone rules. By late October, she let me use the cordless so that I could lie outside in the hammock, watching the leaves float down from the oak in our backyard.

I asked Teddy what he was going to dress up as for Halloween and he told me his family didn't celebrate.

"My dad says it was made up by corporations like Walmart to sell more decorations and stuff," he explained.

We both had far too much time on our hands; where public-school students might've come home from a six-hour school day only to slog through hours of algebra homework or assigned readings, we lived by our own schedules. We still had curriculums to follow and independent study teachers that made sure our educations were up to speed, but there were days when I'd gotten all my work done early in the month, and so—with no friends nearby—I'd wake up and spend a random Tuesday binge-watching those ridiculous documentaries on the History Channel about aliens building the pyramids, or trying to teach myself how to crochet.

It was a special sort of freedom, one that gave me plenty of room to stretch my legs and grow into whatever I felt like growing into. I enjoyed being homeschooled. Teddy hated it. "Freedom doesn't matter when you can't even see your friends," he argued during one of our many conversations about it. "And I suck at talking to people. If I went to regular school, I'd probably talk to people all the time. I'd *have* to be better at it."

It was a stormy November evening and the weather had forced me inside. Rain beat against my dark bedroom window and I had the phone on speaker on the pillow next to my head, my arms burrowed beneath the blankets. "You talk to me just fine," I pointed out.

"That's different," he mumbled, but he didn't explain *why* it was different.

"What about your parents?" I asked. "You have to talk to them, sometimes."

"My dad's not really the talkative type," he said, a little awkwardly.

"Oh." I wasn't sure what else to say. My own father was a man of few words, but I never felt like I couldn't talk to him. And my mom was a great listener. So I tried to cheer him up the only way I knew how. "I guess that means you're stuck talking to me."

* * *

The week after Christmas, I remembered to call him on his birthday and he remembered to call me on mine. My mom even let me stay on the phone for an hour instead of the usual forty-five minutes because the holidays always put her in an agreeable mood. After the New Year, the days began to blur together. Dad worked as a lineman, which often took him out of state for weeks at a time, so when I wasn't working on schoolwork, I'd keep Mom company—cold, gray afternoons huddled around the glass coffee table in front of the fireplace, drinking hot chocolate with marshmallows and working on jigsaw puzzles while Reagan played with Tinker Toys on the braided rug. Mom never asked me much about Teddy after that day in the car, but I had a feeling she listened in on my side of the conversation sometimes. "If you ever decide you'd rather enroll in public school, all you have to do is ask," she told me unprompted one evening while we worked on the outline of a thousand-piece puzzle of *La Grande Jatte* by Georges Seurat.

It wasn't the first time she'd given me a choice. I went to public school until third grade, but in a classroom with thirty other kids, I never really thrived. I was impatient and easily distracted, struggling with the pacing of the curriculum—I'd work ahead, get in trouble because I didn't wait for instructions, and then turn around and fall behind. I came home one day to find my mom seated at the dining room table, my lackluster report card and a whole mess of paperwork spread in front of her. She had asked me if I'd rather do my schoolwork at home, at my own pace. I said yes and never looked back.

"I know it would be easier to make friends," she said now.

I shook my head as I sorted out all the edge pieces on top of a coffee table book. *56 Landmarks to See before You Die.* There was a photograph of Stonehenge on the cover. "I like the friends I have."

* * *

In May, Izzy had a sleepover for her fifteenth birthday and invited a couple girls from her neighborhood; they listened to music I wasn't allowed to listen to at home and teased me for not knowing the lyrics. "You should get bangs," one of them told me. "You have a long face. Bangs would suit you better." And then she exchanged a look with one of the other girls before bursting into a fit of laughter.

When I got home the next day, I called Teddy to complain about them. But that didn't stop me from asking my mom to schedule an appointment with her hairdresser, or from sneaking onto Dad's computer to use LimeWire to secretly download songs by Nelly Furtado and The Black Eyed Peas and burn them to CDs. I wasn't even sure I liked the music, really; I just didn't want to be put in the position of not knowing and embarrassing myself again.

June brought with it three straight weeks of rain, and the

remainder of summer was too hot and humid to spend much time outside, except for the days my parents would drive us up to Oxford Beach.

And then, before I knew it, it was September again.

* * *

It had only been a few months since I last saw Izzy, but it felt like we had a million things to talk about. Her family had gone on a Princess Cruise in June to Cozumel, Mexico, and she'd met a girl onboard from Norway named Ingrid, whom she claimed to be soulmates with and messaged every day on MSN. (When she later moved to Portugal chasing after a college girlfriend, I reflected that it was part of a long pattern that perhaps started here.) Her parents had finally allowed her to get a cell phone, which made me a little jealous until I realized it was a pay-as-you-go phone and they had only loaded ten dollars onto it in case of emergencies, so she wasn't allowed to make calls to friends.

I didn't know why, but I hadn't told her anything about my friendship with Teddy. She must have guessed, at least on some level, that I had kept my promise to be his friend after that day in the cafeteria, but she never asked about it. Maybe it was a simple oversight—it wasn't like Izzy and I talked on the phone all that often, so when we saw each other in person for her birthday, we had so much to catch up on that mentioning my phone calls with Teddy didn't feel all that important. But there was also a part of me that wanted to keep him to myself. I was convinced that Izzy wouldn't understand him the same way I did, and there was the risk that if I welcomed her into our friendship, that illusion would be shattered.

But now that we were back at camp, it was impossible to keep my two friendships separate.

I interrupted Izzy's story about swimming at the community

pool to shout Teddy's name when I spotted him over by the rec building. He was feeding dollar bills into the vending machine, a weighty-looking duffel bag hanging from a shoulder, but he turned and waved wide-armed when he saw me. I raced across the field and flung my arms around his waist. His duffel bag landed in the grass with a soft thump as he enveloped me in his arms, soft breaths rustling the top of my hair. We never hugged goodbye the previous autumn, but it seemed like the appropriate thing to do, given we'd been friends for over a year now. But even having never hugged him before, he was broader in my arms than I would've expected. He was already tall last year, but now he was less gangly, a little more filled out. He'd told me on the phone that he'd put on nine pounds since his birthday, but I didn't realize the difference nine pounds could make.

"You were supposed to find me first thing," I said, breathless, as we drew back.

"I wanted to surprise you." He stooped to grab a Pepsi out of the vending machine, which he handed to me. I stared at it, nonplussed. "To pay you back for last year."

I didn't have the heart to tell him that he wasn't *supposed* to pay me back, or that my family drank Coca-Cola like it was their religion. From this moment on, I was a Pepsi girl.

His brown eyes flitted over me, everywhere all at once. "You changed your hair."

I combed my bangs out of my eyes with my fingers—they were long and side-swept, and they kept getting in the way. "What do you think?" I asked. "They're kind of annoying, but—"

"I think they look great."

We grinned at each other like idiots—or rather, *I* grinned like an idiot and he just grinned, because even at his happiest, Teddy's smile was a little reserved. Like he was scared to let himself be fully happy.

"You're Darvish's friend," a less-than-certain voice said at my shoulder. "From the cafeteria last summer."

I hadn't realized that Izzy had followed me over, but of course she had, because I'd left her standing alone in the grass mid-sentence. With a twinge of guilt at my poor manners, I reintroduced the two of them, adding, "He's not just Darvish's friend. He's my friend, too."

There was something a bit guarded in the way they greeted each other—for Izzy's part, she was maybe understandably suspicious that I hadn't mentioned Teddy all year, and even more suspicious that he was friends with Darvish, of all people. After a minute, Teddy offered up a quick excuse about needing to stow his things in the cabin and claim his bunk, and Izzy pinned me under a curious look, her amber eyes wide.

"What?" I asked, self-conscious.

"Nothing. He looks different," she said, and I got the impression that her piercing amber eyes were seeing right through me.

* * *

"Vikings relied on the North Star to navigate, you know," I announced. It was a warm September night the second week of camp, and I'd planted my butt in the dewy grass beside the telescope, checking items off a list titled "Celestial Bodies." We'd already successfully located Saturn and Mars, and now I absently added Polaris to the list. It was the easiest to find and we probably should have started with it anyway. Ms. Fischer had given us a worksheet with planets and major stars we were supposed to locate; it would've been easy to cheat, I thought, except for the fear that if Ms. Fischer caught us in a lie—like claiming to have seen a planet that wasn't actually visible—we'd never hear the end of it.

Teddy drew back from the telescope to consult the book

splayed in his lap, borrowed from the rec room. "I'm pretty sure most people relied on the stars before they had modern technology."

"They had already invented compasses in China, like, hundreds of years ago. By the eleventh century, I think it was." I knit my brow and stared unseeing at the lights on the other side of the dark lake, trying to recall a particular chapter in *A History of Maritime Technology*—a hefty tome that I'd checked out of the library during a burst of interest in The Golden Age of Piracy. "Or maybe it was the tenth."

Teddy laughed under his breath as he twisted the knob to adjust the focus. "Where do you learn all this stuff?"

I twiddled the cable to my headphones between my fingers. I'd brought my portable CD player out here with me, but we'd been talking so much that I'd left my headphones dangling around my neck, the music paused. "I read a lot. And I watch documentaries. One of the perks of being home all the time."

"Why history, though?" he asked. "No offense, you just seem too . . ." He drew back from the eyepiece, frowning. "Interesting, I guess, to care about a bunch of boring names and dates."

"But history's so much more than names and dates," I said. "It's about people."

"The one thing I don't understand," he muttered before returning to the eyepiece.

"You might understand them better if you read about them more. Humans haven't changed all that much." I meant to pause, to wait and see whether I'd piqued his interest, but excited words were already bubbling to the surface. "There's graffiti in Pompeii that just says 'Aufidius was here.' And there's this kid's homework from Russia like eight hundred years ago that's full of doodles of his teacher and stuff, the same way people doodle in their notebooks today." I hesitated, then added, "I can lend you some books, if you want."

His expression was doubtful. "You brought them with you to camp?"

"No. I mean, not all of them. Right now I'm reading this super old book by this Roman guy called Tacitus, all about emperors and politics and stuff." Not that he had asked about any of that. My cheeks warmed; I was thankful he couldn't see me blushing in the dark. "But I could maybe mail you some of them." I had no idea how much it cost to mail books. The only thing I'd ever mailed was a letter to the president when I was nine, asking for his signature on a petition I'd written to get more books for my local library. "You could read them and then we could talk about them over the phone. It would be sort of like our own book club. Except I'd have to read them first before sending them to you. Or you'd have to convince your mom to let you buy your own copy."

"That sounds sort of fun, I guess." He grinned. "The Long-Distance History Club: transcending time *and* space."

I beamed right back at him. "I've got a copy of *Lectures on the Philosophy of History* in my backpack. I'll loan it to you later."

"I'm looking forward to it already." Teddy's soft gaze lingered on me for a few seconds before he returned to the telescope. He scrunched up his face as he peered through the viewfinder and inched the telescope to the left. His glasses were hooked in the collar of his T-shirt.

I picked at a blade of grass. "My mom offered to let me switch to public school," I confessed. "A couple months ago. I think she overheard us talking."

"You're lucky."

"Yeah, but I don't want to go to public school, so it doesn't really make a difference."

He pulled back from the telescope again, this time looking at me with an unreadable expression. "Why not?"

"Well, the girls are probably kinda mean, for one," I said,

thinking of the girls at Izzy's birthday party. "Plus, if I went to public school, then I wouldn't get to come here and see you. Or any of my other friends." He didn't say anything, but his thick eyebrows pinched together. "What?" I asked.

"Nothing," he said, too quickly. He pretended to busy himself with the telescope, though I had a feeling he'd lost track of what he was looking for. "It's just—" He straightened up. "It feels weird that you have other friends and I don't."

"Just Izzy," I said. "And anyway, you have Darvish."

"Yeah," he mumbled, "I guess that's true."

But he didn't seem entirely reassured, so I racked my brain for something else to say, and for some reason, one of my dad's proverbs popped into my head. It felt apt, in a way. "My dad always says 'A bird in the hand is worth two in the bush.'" As soon as the words slipped out, I realized how odd they were. Was I the bird? I hadn't meant to imply that he *shouldn't* have other friends, no matter how much the thought inspired an odd sort of jealousy in me.

Teddy nodded sagely. "Abraham Lincoln."

I choked on a laugh. "What?"

"It's just this joke I found on the internet," he said sheepishly. Even by the milky light of the moon, I could swear the tips of his ears were turning red, and he hunched his shoulders as he resumed his search of the night sky. "People always attribute quotes to the wrong people. So every time someone quotes something, I pretend Abraham Lincoln said it."

I grinned, but the urge to correct him was strong. "It's not a quote, it's a proverb."

"Proverbs can be attributed to the wrong people, too."

"Proverbs can't be attributed to anyone. That's why they're proverbs. They've been around so long that no one remembers who said them."

"Found it," he announced. I shot him a quizzical look. "Mercury. Do you want to see?"

I marked Mercury on the worksheet and pulled my headphones from my neck, setting my CD player aside. I pushed myself off the grass and brushed the butt of my jeans with my hands. Teddy's eyes tracked the movement for a split second before he tore them away, Adam's apple bobbing in his throat. He stepped aside so that I could peer into the eyepiece. It was all black, but then I blinked and shifted and it wasn't: just slightly off-center in the vast nothingness was a pale white sliver, like a pinkie nail.

"It's so blurry," I said.

"You can adjust it—"

I knew full well that you could adjust the settings on a telescope, and I was about to tell him as much, but then he was standing right behind me, and my brain screeched to a halt. He guided my hand toward the knob. His face wasn't far from my ear, and he was breathing through his nose—unsteady, wavering breaths, like he was trying to force himself to breathe normal, and suddenly I was aware that I wasn't breathing at all. This wasn't the first time we'd stood this close—we'd been tied together during the three-legged race, and that was only our second time meeting. We knew each other much better now, so this should have been less weird, but somehow, it wasn't. "I see it," I said, heart pounding in my throat, but he was already drawing back. I pulled my face from the telescope to find him sinking into the grass where I had been sitting.

"What are you doing?" I asked warily.

"I'm curious what you're listening to." He snapped my headphones over his ears and picked up the CD player, squinting at the buttons.

I couldn't explain why, but as much as I'd been embarrassed

not to know this music when I was at the sleepover, I was equally embarrassed to have Teddy catch me listening to it. "Just some stuff that Izzy's friends showed me," I said. "I don't think it's really your—"

He pressed play and a muffled, uncensored version of "I Wanna Love You" by Akon resumed mid-song, loud enough that I could hear it even without wearing the headphones. His eyes widened and his mouth went taut, like he was making a very conscious effort not to laugh. My face was on fire.

After a long couple of seconds, he took off the headphones, mussing his dark curls. "I'll have to burn you a CD," was all he said, handing me the player back.

I cracked a small smile. "You'll send me music, and I'll send you books."

CHAPTER

8

I pop a cartridge of dark roast into the Keurig. The machine grumbles and black coffee trickles into a mug that says #1 TEACHER on it—Reagan thinks her birthday gifts are funny. They do make me smile. "So I've been meaning to ask you," I say over my shoulder as I tear open packets of sugar and dump them into the mug, "what are your thoughts on party planning?"

Over at the table, Belinda Jones looks up from her sudoku booklet with a thoughtful frown. She's a small and lithe woman, her box braids pulled into a loose bun at the nape of her neck. Her microwave meal has filled the faculty room with the tangy aroma of teriyaki beef and broccoli. "I threw a surprise party for my ex-girlfriend, like, five years ago."

I drag out the chair beside her, metal legs grating on the laminate floor, and take a seat. I use my sleeve to sweep some crumbs onto the floor before planting my elbows on the table in front of me. "How did that go?"

"Fine, I guess," she says, returning to her puzzle. She always fills in her sudoku with glitter gel pens—a bold move, if you ask me, but she never seems to get them wrong. "I kind of forgot that she scares easily. She punched her boss in the throat."

I raise my eyebrows. "You invited her boss to her surprise party?"

She holds up her hands, gel pen laced between her fingers. "Hey, I said it went 'fine,' not great. Mistakes were made." She fills in a square. "We all had a good laugh about it over drinks, later."

"I could use some more people on the gala subcommittee," I say. "We're meeting once a week. Location to be determined."

She stabs a piece of broccoli with a plastic fork. "Who's we?"

"Professor Harrison and myself."

She gives a mildly interested *mmm* as she chews, twirling her fork in a circle. "He's the visiting lecturer or whatever."

"Visiting scholar," I say.

"What's he doing on a committee?"

"He's doing me a favor." She shoots me a questioning look, and I loose a breath. I figured I might have to explain this part. "We went to this sleepaway camp together, when we were teenagers. Up in the Blue Ridge Mountains."

By the way her eyebrows are climbing even higher on her forehead, I get the impression that her curiosity isn't quite sated, but she does me the mercy of dropping it, at least for now. "So, what do you need from me?"

"I need you to come to the subcommittee meetings."

"What time?"

"Fridays at four."

"Can't," she sighs, nudging a piece of broccoli around her bowl with a fork. "I meet with my Krav Maga instructor on Fridays."

I sip my coffee, trying to think up a way to convince her. It's not easy, recruiting colleagues to a subcommittee that doesn't actually benefit them. Sure, there's the altruism of raising scholarship money for students who need it, but even that proves poor motivation for faculty who are already overworked and underpaid.

Bel is my only hope. We're both young women in a relatively

male-dominated department, and there's a sense of camaraderie in that, even if our friendship has never quite extended beyond the workplace. "Nothing's really set in stone," I say. "We could meet at a different time." When she doesn't look convinced, I sigh. "And it would be kind of nice to have you there. As a . . . buffer, of sorts."

I can tell by her expression that she's intrigued, but she doesn't ask what I mean by that. She gets up and crosses the room to toss the broccoli beef container in the trash. "Do you want my honest answer, or my work answer?"

"Honest answer, always."

"Honestly"—she plunks down into her seat and drags the sudoku back in front of her—"I'm adjunct. I don't even know if I'll renew my contract next year. I'm not sure I can justify devoting the extra time."

I sigh. "Can't fault you for that." It's looking like it's going to be just me and Teddy this Friday, and I'm not sure how I feel about that. It's already Tuesday and he still hasn't texted me about the location, nor have I bumped into him around campus. Habitually, I check my phone. "Fiddlesticks," I say, pushing out of my chair. "I've got class in five minutes."

I dump the rest of my coffee down the sink and rinse the mug beneath the faucet, stowing it in one of the overhead cupboards. Bel watches me with an unreadable expression as I grab my jacket from the back of a chair and tug it over my ruffled blouse.

"Text me when you figure out a location for the subcommittee," she says. "I'll see if I can pop over. At least feel things out before I outright reject it."

"Appreciate you," I say, and then I'm out the door.

* * *

HIST-102 is my least favorite class to teach. Nothing against the subject matter—the first few weeks of the semester usually overlap somewhat with my specialization in Tudor history—but it fulfills a core requirement for most majors, so the tiered lecture hall is chock-full of unenthusiastic students who wouldn't be here if their advisors hadn't pushed it on them. But seeing as I don't yet have tenure, I don't get priority when it comes to selecting classes, hence my third semester in a row slogging through World History Since 1500.

I hand off the sign-in sheet to a student in the front row. Lecture halls have a way of feeling a little cold and detached—especially when compared to the intimate Socratic seminars I grew accustomed to in grad school—and Britteridge 130 is no exception. It's a large, curved room like a movie theater, the folding seats filled with disinterested faces lit by bluish laptop screens. A bulky ceiling-mounted projector hangs at the center of the room. Last semester, I had to ask one of my taller students to pull down the projector screen for me, but only after a demeaning thirty seconds of me standing on tiptoe like a kid straining to reach the candy jar on top of the fridge.

Today, I eschew the projector in favor of scrawling key points on the whiteboard, dry-erase marker squeaking. We're covering the early days of Spain's colonization of the Caribbean right now—subject matter that's probably more up Teddy's alley, but I do my best to make it engaging and interesting. I enjoy teaching, but general ed courses always manage to make me feel like I'm holding students against their will, so it's a bit of a relief when the clock tower above the administration building chimes three. Students are already zipping up laptop bags and slapping their notebooks closed.

"Before I let you go," I say, and some of them sink reluctantly back into their seats; others hover with backpacks slung over a shoulder. I use the butt of my dry-erase marker to tap the bottom left-hand corner of the whiteboard, where I've copied down a series of due dates. "Your first reading responses are due next Thursday. Chapters twenty-two and twenty-three, half a page each. These aren't going to be graded, but they'll give me a feel for where you're at."

Hands spring up like dandelions. Can't help wondering where this participation was during lecture. I point to a student in the third row whose name I haven't memorized yet, a willowy young woman wearing a long-sleeved volleyball jersey emblazoned with the U of I Raptors' mascot: a goshawk in flight.

She lowers her hand. "I assume we'll be writing in Chicago?"

"Yes, thank you for reminding me. I want you to treat these reading responses like you'd treat a paper. Cite the readings. Give me a couple footnotes. For many of you, I assume this is your first time writing a history paper at the college level, so I want to get a feel for where you're at. If you have any other questions, my email and office hours are on the syllabus."

Thus dismissed, the students form a bottleneck at the classroom door, stampeding toward freedom. A couple of them mumble *Thank you, Professor Fernsby* or *Have a good week*, but for the most part, they keep their heads down and avoid eye contact.

In the middle of packing up my things, I reach into the front flap of my messenger bag to check my phone. I always mute it during lecture, but it doesn't matter, because no one's texted me anyway. I unmute it and stow it back in my bag before grabbing the dry eraser to wipe down the whiteboard, reaching for the upper left-hand corner of the board, where a student left a note last week about a Manga Club meeting that's already passed.

"I've heard if you stretch extra hard, you might actually grow an inch or two."

I settle back on my heels and glance over my shoulder. Reagan is standing behind me, no makeup on and her hair in a messy topknot. I breathe a laugh, finishing up with the whiteboard and setting the eraser aside. "I thought you were in class."

"Canceled. Professor Masrood emailed this morning." She

leans forward, arm resting on the desk, and picks up an orphaned Bic pen, closing one eye as she lines up her shot. "I've got an hour until my next class so I figured I'd come bug you." She tosses the pen like a mini-javelin and it lands in the pencil holder with a ceramic clatter.

"I'm just about to head back to the Hall of Letters."

"I'll join you."

"Isn't it, like, super uncool to be seen walking around with an instructor?" I ask, ducking my head to loop the strap of my messenger bag around my neck. Another thing that's uncool, according to Reagan: messenger bags. *It's like a forward slash between your boobs,* she says.

"Hey, you're the one who's embarrassed to be seen with me, not the other way around," she reminds me. I shoot her an exasperated look. Not entirely true—it's more her driving that embarrasses me than anything. "Besides, it's a beautiful day."

She's not wrong. The weather when we step outside the Britteridge Center is bright and cool. The tips of the leaves on the maples in the quad, a verdant green during the summer, have turned gold to herald the changing of the seasons. We stay on the sidewalk, passing by students kicking around soccer balls or lounging on beach towels in the grass. I'm reminded of my own time in undergrad, carrying moving boxes up the steps outside La Plata at the start of my freshman year—and everything else that happened that night.

I shake the memory. "What do you want for dinner tonight?" I ask. "There's that Thai place I've been meaning to try. I was thinking we could order in, maybe watch something on—"

When I turn to gauge Reagan's reaction, I find that her attention has diverted to her phone. She's texting, manicured nails clacking against the screen. "Actually, I'm meeting up with a few classmates tonight. We're trying to get a study group going."

"Making friends already," I observe. "What are their names?"

Reagan tucks her phone in her back pocket, lips curved in an amused smile. "Are you going to ask to read my diary, too, Mother?"

"Sorry. I'm just curious. I haven't met any of your friends." I worry sometimes whether she's hanging around the right people. But the trouble with Reagan is that her friends have always seemed to change every few weeks, so there's no way to even keep track, let alone impart any unsolicited wisdom.

"Sure you have. Nat's in one of your classes."

"I don't know who Nat is," I admit. I haven't had enough time to memorize new names. "But I'll keep an eye out for her. Do you know which—"

Reagan's phone chimes, and I pause—no point talking if she's going to be too wrapped up in answering messages to actually hear me, but she makes no move to check it. "Aren't you going to answer that?"

"Yeah, because I'd totally leave notifications on," she says dryly. I give her a blank stare. "It's not *mine*," she clarifies, eyebrows raised.

"Oh. Must be me, then." I pat around my messenger bag until I find my phone and withdraw it.

Teddy: 116 Bridge St, Irving, MD 21532

Teddy: For the meeting on fri

I furrow my brow at the screen. Strange that he's sending me an address as opposed to a room number. Bridge Street is downtown, a good six or seven blocks from campus, but I haven't really familiarized myself with all the businesses there because I have no social life. I tap the address to pull up the map. *The Falconer*, 4.2 stars. Beneath that, in the business category, my worries are confirmed: it's listed as a bar and grill. I tap out a quick reply.

> Clara: This address is for a bar

> Clara: ??

"You're texting Professor Hottison?" Reagan asks over my shoulder.

I angle the screen away from her, swatting like she's a mosquito buzzing in my ear, but she manages to dodge my hand. "Didn't Mom ever teach you that it's rude to read other people's messages?"

"Mom doesn't know texting etiquette," she reminds me. "She still thinks 'lol' means 'lots of love.'" I concede the point with a dip of my head. It's an exaggeration, but only just. We pass Martin Hall, where construction is ongoing—at the moment, a two-man team is hauling a crumbling roll of carpet padding through the eastern door, making way for whatever shiny new flooring they plan to install. "What's going on with you two, anyway?"

"I'm supposed to meet him Friday for a subcommittee meeting."

"At a bar."

I raise my eyebrows. "Would you like to give another dramatic reading of my journal while you're at it?"

"Diary," she corrects me, her expression a tad too smug for my liking. A memory surfaces of a nine-year-old Reagan standing barefoot on the glass coffee table in her pajamas, reading a particularly angsty passage from my teenage diary while I was home from college for the holidays—apparently, she'd been rooting around my room while I was away. Mom didn't even try to stop her. She sat on the couch, glass of Shiraz in hand, roaring with laughter over the fact that teenaged me had tried to use *sanguine* in a sentence. And that Reagan had then tried to read it out loud, but she pronounced it like it rhymed with *linguine*.

"You know, if I were a lesser woman, I'd almost think you were overdue for a good old-fashioned sibling beatdown." Not that I ever gave her those when she was little. Our age gap was too drastic. But now we're both adults, so maybe it's overdue.

"I'm just saying"—she holds up her hands—"he's asking you for drinks. That's totally a date."

"Maybe things are different with dating apps these days, but in my world, drinks between colleagues don't have to mean anything." When she opens her mouth to argue, I rush to cut her off. "Please, just drop it."

Reagan sniffs. "Maybe if you showed some interest in someone else, I could bug you about them instead."

I don't have a retort, because she's right. Maybe, if my life was the slightest bit interesting, she'd find something else to pester me about. And really, it's my fault for bringing up Teddy with her in the first place. She probably wouldn't have even recognized him after all these years, had I not said something beforehand.

My phone chimes again.

Teddy: Yes

Teddy: Happy hour til five on Fridays

Not much of an explanation, but at the very least, drinks will help break the ice. A nice public setting to slice through the tension. I copy the address and send it to Bel, even if it's a long shot. The more, the merrier.

CHAPTER

9

PRESENT

It's Friday, and for the first time in as long as I can remember, I'm headed for a bar. It's a crisp evening, the first whiff of autumn on the air, but inside The Falconer Restaurant and Pub is warm and stuffy. It's a poor imitation of its counterparts overseas—it's not distinctly English, nor Irish, nor even Scottish or Welsh, but rather an amalgamation of them all, with Guinness on tap next to Newcastle and politically incongruent flags dangling from the wood-beamed ceiling. But it seems to be popular, a mix of students and townies mingling in front of the bar. I find Teddy at a high-top table toward the back, water stains stamped into the worn finish and a highball glass of gin and tonic already in front of him.

"Why do I get the feeling I'm going to have to play catch-up?" I ask, hooking my messenger bag beneath the table and hoisting myself onto the stool.

"I was giving a lecture until three thirty," he says. "Only got here ten minutes ago."

A server stops by our table to take our order. "I'll do the cold brew martini, please, except could I get that with gin in-stead of vodka?" Someone once told me that it's not techni-cally a martini without gin, and now I can't order it any other way. I bend beneath the table to extract a pen and notepad from my bag.

"What are you doing?"

"Taking the minutes," I say, flipping past my grocery list to a blank page, where I scrawl *Gala Subcommittee—September 13th.* "This subcommittee doesn't exactly have a secretary."

"Actually, I was hoping we could talk first." He sets his glass on the table. It's already half empty. "We haven't really had a chance to catch up."

Since the moment I walked in the door, I've busied myself with looking everywhere else—at the table, at the waitress, at my notepad—but now, I set down my pen and force myself to look at him. He's not wearing his glasses for once, his honey-brown eyes cast almost black by the dim Edison bulbs dangling from the ceiling. He looks tired. There are dark circles under his eyes and a few days' worth of stubble dusting his cheeks and jaw.

"Sure." I flip the notepad closed. I'm not sure what sort of catching up he has in mind, but I recall the question I'd meant to ask him last week, and I decide to start there. "How are your parents?"

"My mom is good, for the most part," he says, staring into his drink. There's a pause, and I almost think he might leave it at that. But then he adds, "My dad passed away, December before last."

I'm stunned into silence. I never met his father—from everything Teddy told me, he was a difficult man to get along with, and they'd had their share of ups and downs. But he's still wearing his dad's ring, so they must've made their peace, in the end. "Teddy, I'm so sorry." My voice is small, strained, almost lost in the chatter of the bar and the Van Morrison song drifting from the smart jukebox. "Your ring—" I'm thinking out loud, letting my mouth get a running start on my thoughts. I swallow, looking down at my notepad. "I should have known."

I should have guessed, at any rate, but I also should have been there. Maybe if I hadn't been so tactless all those years ago, I would've been. It would have been me, and not Mindy, who helped him through it all.

"You don't need to be sorry," he says quietly.

My words catch in my throat. I'm thankful when the server delivers my coffeetini, giving me an excuse to tear my gaze away. I mumble a thank-you and take a large gulp to loosen the fist-sized lump that's wedged itself in my esophagus, and then another for good measure.

He clears his throat. "They moved to Dormont to be closer to his sister after he had the first stroke. Almost nine years ago, now."

He locks eyes with me across the table, both of us remembering the same thing. And my heart, I'm certain my heart is breaking for him, for us—except I'm pretty sure that part of it chipped off a long time ago, lost somewhere in a dark cavity of my chest. "That's how you ended up in Pittsburgh," I whisper.

He nods, folding his arms on the table. He only just got off work, so he's still wearing one of his button-up shirts. But the top button is undone, and he's rolled up the sleeves a little, revealing lean forearms dusted in dark hair. "I finished my last year at Chicago and then I moved back down to be closer to them. Taught at a community college for about a year before I got offered a tenure track position at Carnegie. I didn't know how long my dad would be around, and I knew Mom would need someone there for her after he was gone."

I give him a weak smile. "I'm sure she's glad to have you close by."

There's an irony to all of it, so bitter that I could almost cry, but I don't. I keep it together, sipping my martini, because that's what adults do. But it feels like I've missed out on so much, and worse, it feels like so much of it was for nothing—insisting that we go live our own lives, chasing our dreams on opposite ends of the globe, refusing to repeat the mistakes our parents made . . . only to end up teaching at schools two hours away from each other, in the same states we grew up in.

"With Dad gone now, she's sort of put down roots, figured some things out," he's saying. "She says she's fine on her own, so I guess I'm trying to get a feel for other opportunities, but it's just . . ." He blows out a breath, running a hand through his curls. "It's different now. I don't know that I want the same things I wanted when I was in my twenties."

"Mindy?" I ask, before I have a chance to stop myself.

"We ended things," he says. "A couple months before my dad passed."

Almost two years ago, then. I have so many questions. Most of them are probably none of my business, but I don't get the chance to decide whether I want to ask them, because we're interrupted by the legs of a stool grinding against the plank floor.

"Sorry I'm late," Bel says, climbing up next to me. Her long pinafore dress is rumpled and she's slightly breathless. "I got totally mixed up and thought the meeting was on campus. James Stambaugh talked my ear off about the Schleswig-Holstein question for twenty minutes. Still confused, for the record." Her gaze follows a direct path from me to Teddy, like my unspoken questions are somehow palpable, an invisible thread dangling between us. "Am I interrupting something?"

"It's nothing," Teddy says in tandem with my very emphatic, "Not at all!"

We look at each other. Bel looks back and forth between the two of us, frowning.

I need another drink. "We were just catching up a bit before getting started," I say.

"Right." She doesn't sound convinced, but she must decide that it's not all that important, because she folds her arms on the table and says, "I rescheduled my Krav Maga lessons for this, so this better look good on my resume when I buy a one-way ticket back to Atlanta."

"It will," I promise.

"So," she says, leaning into the table, "what's my title?" Before I'm able to say anything, she points an accusatory finger at the notepad and pen. "And don't you dare try to pawn secretary off on me."

"Treasurer," I offer. She purses her lips, displeased.

"Or vice chair, maybe?" Teddy suggests.

"Excellent," she says, planting her bag on the table in front of her—a recycled tote that proclaims LIFE IS SHORT & SO AM I.

I glance at Teddy, holding his gaze for a split second before dragging the notepad toward me. I need to banish his breakup from my thoughts. At least for tonight. "So. First thing on the agenda is to pick a location for the gala. Any ideas?"

He rubs a hand along his jaw, pensive. "The Alumni House, maybe. It's university property. So long as we can work around wedding rentals and other events, it should be available at no expense."

"You've done your research," I say, impressed. I jot down the suggestion. "Okay. We can circle back to that. What about timing? I was thinking maybe sometime in late October."

"Isn't that a little soon?" Bel asks. "That's less than two months to plan, send out invites . . ."

"November is already swamped for me, and I need to have something to show the advisory committee by December," I say. Plus, the sooner I get this knocked out, the sooner I can focus on everything else—putting together the rest of my dossier, coordinating the guest speaker from Edinburgh, submitting to journals. When there are no further objections, I press on. "So we see about securing the Alumni House, and then what about asking the Alumni Association to mention something in those emails they send out?"

"That could work," Bel agrees. "We could also post an event on Facebook. I feel like most of our donors would be in the Facebook age group, wouldn't they?"

I make a note. We iron out a few additional details—finding someone willing to cater for a reasonable price presents a challenge, so we agree that we'll ask around and see whether we can unearth any connections before reconvening in two weeks. We also touch briefly on the dress code, and while Teddy nods along with my suggestion of business casual, Bel emphatically shoots me down. "No one has ever, in the history of galas, been like 'Wow, you know what I really want to wear tonight? That pair of khakis I bought off the clearance rack at Kohl's.'"

"Thank you, Anna Wintour," I mutter, scratching out the idea with my pen. "What do you suggest?"

Bel splays her hands and leans into the table like she's about to divulge a juicy secret. "A costume party."

Teddy and I exchange a dubious look.

"Think about it," she says. "It's the weekend before Halloween. All these donors on the invite list, half of them haven't been to a proper Halloween party since they were kids. Give people an excuse to wear a costume, and they'll show." When I don't look entirely convinced, she adds, emphatically, "I promise."

"All right," I say. "But we need to make sure we keep it secular, you know, avoid ostracizing anyone who doesn't celebrate."

"We could call it a fall festival," Teddy suggests.

I tap my lips with the end of my pen, thinking.

"I'll create a Facebook event," Bel says excitedly, already tapping away on her phone. I can't help wondering whether *she's* the one who's looking for an excuse to wear a costume. "Get a feel for how much interest we can generate."

Afterward, Teddy goes up to the bar to pay the tab while I collect my bag and stow the notepad. "Thank you for being here," I say to Bel. "Really. It means a lot."

In the middle of reapplying her ChapStick, she shoots me a smile. "Hey, that's what friends are for." She rubs her lips together, popping the cap back on. She casts a glance over at the bar, where Teddy appears to be caught in an awkward encounter with a drunk student while he waits for the bartender to cash us out. "You mentioned that you know each other from camp," Bel says slowly, "but is there something—" She cuts herself short but raises her eyebrows, expectant. Like I'm supposed to fill in the blank. There's a couple seconds' delay before I catch her meaning.

"No," I say. "Nothing like that."

She purses her full lips. "You want my honest opinion, or my work opinion?"

"You already know what I'm going to say."

"Maybe you've gotten used to telling yourself that it's nothing, and maybe you've started to believe it, and if that's the case then I assume you have your reasons." She stands on tiptoe to hoist her oversized tote off the high-top table. "But for what it's worth," she says pointedly, "I don't believe you."

CHAPTER

10

Less than two weeks after camp had ended, a bubble envelope from Pennsylvania arrived at my parents' house, wedged inside the mailbox alongside a credit card offer and an AT&T bill. I was so excited that I tore it open right there at the curb, extracting a clear plastic CD case with a folded piece of plain printer paper inserted in the cover. He'd written on it in thick blue Sharpie, *Teddy's Mix*, and doodled a pair of headphones.

I spent the whole afternoon lying in the hammock beneath the oak tree, my CD player on my lap as I cycled through every track, replaying them to try to understand the lyrics. It was filled with all sorts of music: Taking Back Sunday and Arctic Monkeys and MGMT. A lot of it was moody and weird and some of it was angry. It was way different than the stuff I'd grown accustomed to listening to, but I didn't hate it.

After I'd listened all the way through a couple times and the sun was already sinking somewhere out beyond the bay, I climbed out of the hammock and went inside to ask my dad for permission to use the computer. Mom was still on my case about using the phone too much, so the first thing I'd done after arriving home from camp was create a Myspace profile. I'd called Teddy that same week to tell him to do the same.

"My parents still have dial-up," he'd said, "so I might not be able to check it whenever they're using the phone and stuff, but I'll try."

There was really no reason for either of my parents to have a home office, but we had a spare bedroom and few guests, so the room overlooking the backyard had been converted into a computer room. There was still a twin bed in the corner, but it was buried beneath donation bags and piles of old clothes. My parents had bought the computer years ago, when I was still pretty little, because my mom had insisted that they needed to make sure I was technologically literate. Mostly, it had involved them forcing me to play educational games like *JumpStart Typing,* but I'd also stashed a few cereal box games that I used to play when they weren't looking.

It took a few minutes for the computer to boot up, but once it did, I went to check Teddy's profile—he hadn't customized it at all yet, his default picture still set to the generic *no photo* graphic. It didn't look like he was online, but I sent him a message anyway.

From: Clare Bear ♥
Date: October 14, 7:52 P.M.
Subject: THANK YOU!!
Body: Thank you for sending the CD!! I listened to the whole thing already. Some of the songs you put on there are kind of intense, but I did like one of the ones you put at the end, once I got past the shouting and all the stuff about stakes to the heart. I think it was track ten.

How are you liking the book? I figure it'll be easier to write out our thoughts on here instead of talking about it on the phone, because on the phone my brain gets all scrambled and I can't remember all the things I wanted to say.

From: Theodore
Date: October 14, 10:06 P.M.
Subject: Re: THANK YOU!!
Body: Clara,

The song you're referring to is "Vampires Will Never Hurt You" by My Chemical Romance. It's about not wanting to be part of the crowd. I thought you might like it. If you like that one, I could burn you a CD with some of their newer stuff.

I read the introduction to Hegel but I'm not sure I really get it—he's not really writing about history, more about the history of people studying history? It seems overly complicated to me. Why not just write about the history itself?
Sincerely,
Teddy

From: Clare Bear ♥
Date: October 15, 9:06 A.M.
Subject: Re: Re: THANK YOU!!
Body: Yes, please send more!! I would just download them myself but I got in trouble last year for using LimeWire after I accidentally downloaded a virus and then we had to hire this guy to come reinstall Windows and fix everything and my dad only just started letting me use the computer again, sooooo. xD

He does talk about actual history eventually, but I agree that Hegel is sorta confusing. Maybe we should start with something else. I'll look through my books tonight and mail something tomorrow!!
    <333
Clara

From: Teddy
Date: October 16, 12:33 P.M.
Subject: Re: Re: Re: THANK YOU!!
Body: Clara,
What does xD stand for?
Best,
Teddy

* * *

My selection of history books didn't cater to any one particular interest. Mostly, I read whatever I could find for a couple dollars at the local thrift store, often not geared toward high school reading—sepia covers of *Images of America*, pop history paperbacks curling up at the corners, textbooks with yellow USED stickers slapped over the spines. Sometimes I understood the stuff I read just fine, sometimes I didn't, but maybe something with more exciting subject matter would be a good starting place for Teddy. I unearthed one of the books I'd read during my short-lived pirate phase, *Under the Black Flag*, and stuffed it into an envelope.

While my first book recommendation might've fallen flat, Teddy's music certainly hadn't; I found myself listening to the same CD on repeat during my walks to the library, and then, when the weather turned, blasting it from the stereo in my bedroom. When the next bubble mailer arrived, it sent me further down the rabbit hole: burned copies of *Three Cheers for Sweet Revenge* and *The Black Parade,* the track listings inked in that familiar blue Sharpie.

"So is this your favorite band, or something?" I asked Teddy the next time we talked on the phone.

I could practically hear him lift his shoulders, shrugging it off. "It's one of them, I guess."

But it didn't really matter whether they were his favorite or not, because they were quickly becoming *my* favorite band. I wasn't even sure I was their target audience—I didn't always relate perfectly to the lyrics, but they sucked me in anyway. Instead of December evenings spent hunched over the coffee table working on thousand-piece puzzles, I spent hours watching YouTube videos and scrolling through forums. I rented *The Lost Boys* and *Interview with the Vampire* from my local Blockbuster because a lot of the songs referenced vampires. I asked my mom to get me an iPod for Christmas, which was met with some hesitation, and I also asked whether I could dye my hair, which was met with outright distress.

"I don't understand where this is coming from," she said in the middle of peeling potatoes over the sink for Christmas dinner. "It's already such a pretty color."

Pretty was relative, I thought. It was a dull sort of dishwater color, perhaps the most noncommittal of all hair colors: Was it blond or was it light brown? No one seemed to agree. "I was just thinking maybe I'm ready for a change," I said.

She thought about it for a few seconds, potato skins falling from the peeler in curlicues. "No, I don't think so," she said finally. "Once you dye it, it's impossible to get it back the way it was. You'll only end up regretting it."

I tried arguing with her, telling her that she couldn't possibly know whether I would regret something or not, but it was no use. I woke up Christmas morning to a refurbished iPod Nano—"Beggars can't be choosers," Dad explained—and a set of colorful clip-in extensions, much to my chagrin.

Teddy and I called each other on our neighboring birthdays, just like last year, but we didn't see each other again until March, when he got his license. He asked if I could convince my parents to drive me to meet up somewhere for a day, and so I hopped into Mom's Jeep and we met in the middle: Middletown,

Delaware, fittingly enough. It was a forgettable town with few things to do and fewer places to eat, but we got Hardee's and went to a park, where we sat on swings damp with last night's rainfall, and he told me he was going to enroll at his local community college over the summer.

"But you're only sixteen," I said.

He dragged his feet, carving deep ruts into the cedar chips. "Yeah, but it's not like I have anything stopping me."

I didn't have a counter for that, despite a strange sort of discomfort bubbling beneath the surface. What would happen when he made older, cooler friends in college? What if he got a girlfriend? Where would that leave me? "What do you think you'll major in?" I asked instead. I didn't wait for an answer before adding, uncertain, "*Do* you choose your major at community college?"

"I think you can. And I'm not sure yet. I guess I haven't really found my calling." He swung his swing sideways to nudge my foot with his, shooting me a wry smile. "But that's what college is supposed to be for, right? Figuring it out. Plus it'll get me out of the house. Away from my parents. Mostly my dad."

"Tell me about them," I said, without really thinking. He shot me an odd look. "It's just that you've mentioned them before. It sounds like you don't really get along."

"I get along with them just fine. It's more . . ." He seemed to hesitate, searching for the right words. "They don't really get along with each other. They got married pretty young, I think. My mom, she always wanted to open a restaurant, but he didn't want her to work. He said it was the way Harrisons had always done it, the man works, the woman stays at home and takes care of the kids. So she stayed at home. Didn't fight it." He scrunched up his face against the bright gray overcast. "I've always wondered if she decided to homeschool me just because she didn't have much else to do."

It was a familiar story—familiar enough, at any rate. My

mom had given up her career to raise me, though she did take night classes to finish her degree when I was a toddler. But my parents didn't resent each other. They were happy, I was pretty sure. "What sort of restaurant did she want to open?"

"Greek," he said. "But not, you know, one of those places with the blue shutters and a mural of the Hill of the Muses or anything. We'd always pass by this empty brick building downtown and she'd describe it to me, the way she pictured it. All fancy. White tablecloths and chandeliers and stuff."

"Too fancy for Allentown, Pennsylvania?" I guessed.

He held back a smile. "Maybe. Somebody finally rented it out, a couple years ago. It's an office space now."

We sat in contemplative silence for a minute, the swings creaking faintly.

"So, you go to college, build a career, and rent it out for her," I said, hoping to lighten the mood. "Help her realize her dream."

He chuckled under his breath, but he was staring at his feet. "More like I don't let anyone stand in the way of my goals. I can't imagine anything worse than just"—he shrugged, but even for a shrug, it lacked gusto—"repeating their mistakes."

I nodded. I thought maybe I understood. Going to college early was proactive. Smart. But there was also this nagging feeling that our friendship had been a mere convenience, superfluous once he got out in the world and started meeting all sorts of interesting people. People who slotted in to the life he envisioned for himself with ease, like they were meant to be there. I wasn't that person. We lived hours apart.

Over the past year, Teddy had become my closest friend, and above all else, I was terrified of losing that.

* * *

But I shouldn't have worried.

Summer came and went, and my world didn't come crashing

down around me. When he mentioned his classmates, it was mostly in reference to group projects they were forced to work on together, or an answer he disagreed with—apparently, they weren't all that interested in befriending a sixteen-year-old home-schooled kid. And when September rolled around, he signed up for all late-start classes so that he could still come to camp.

It was the third year in a row that they'd dragged us on a mandatory foraging hike along the Appalachian Trail—so, naturally, rather than spend another afternoon hunting down dandelions and wood sorrel and wild strawberries so small you could fit them in a thimble, we snuck off on a hike of our own, and Izzy and Darvish followed, both outright refusing to be left behind. We clambered over rocks and fallen branches up a steep incline, following the route that promised the best view. It was the third week of September, and some of the trees had started to turn, casting a warm golden glow over the trail.

"These fucking mosquitos," Darvish moaned, swatting at the air. "They're eating me alive."

"Language," Teddy muttered. "Have some manners."

Izzy was leagues ahead of the rest of us, hardly breaking a sweat in her cut-off shorts and a bucket hat with the drawstring tightened beneath her chin, but our voices carried out here in the woods. She turned around to walk backward and spread her arms wide. "What, just because we're girls, you can't cuss in front of us?"

"I'll cuss for you," Darvish called up at her, clutching a hand over his heart and reaching out to her like Romeo in Capulet's orchard. "I'll say whatever you want me to say."

"Sorry," Izzy called back, "not my type."

I bumped Teddy with my shoulder. "I've heard the sort of music you listen to. They're not exactly shy with the word choice."

"Just because I listen to a few songs doesn't mean I *say* them."

"How old are you again?" Izzy asked from her perch atop the jagged stump of a fallen tree, the decaying bark riddled with moss and lichen. She was already tall on level ground, but now, she towered over us.

"I'll be seventeen in December," he said.

She hopped down from the stump, landing back on the trail with a crunch. "Have you *ever* said the word 'fuck'?" she asked as we kept walking. We were nearly to the top of the hill.

Teddy hunched his shoulders. "Once or twice."

Izzy and I looked at each other, wide-eyed. "He totally hasn't," I stage-whispered.

"I've said plenty of . . . words," Teddy protested. "I just prefer to save them for when I need them. You know, when I'm actually mad about something."

"I was mad about the mosquitos," Darvish said, but it went largely ignored because we crested the hill. A few yards away, the tree line ended in an outcropping of rock, and beyond that, sloping mountains stretched into the distance. The treetops were a mosaic of greens and golds, darker wherever the shadows of clouds passed over them.

Darvish bounded right up to the edge of the rock, so thoughtlessly that Izzy and I both let out sounds of protest. He planted his hiking boots wide, cupped both hands around his mouth, and shouted so loud it echoed across the mountaintops. "FUCK!"

A pair of chickadees skittered out of a mulberry bush, alarmed by the sudden sound. I turned to Izzy, my mouth agape. Her eyebrows were so high, they'd disappeared somewhere inside her bucket cap. For a few seconds, we just looked at each other. Then we burst into a fit of giggles.

"Real mature," Teddy grumbled, plopping himself cross-legged on the stone.

In a flash, Izzy had joined Darvish at the cliff, throwing her arms wide enough that she almost smacked him in the face. "Son of a bitch!" she yelled at the sky.

"Come on." I nudged Teddy's shoe with mine, standing in front of him so that my body cast a long shadow. He squinted up at me, but he wasn't saying no. "There's no such thing as bad words," I pointed out. "Just bad intentions."

"I'm not sure that's true," he said, but by the muscle twitching in his cheek, I could tell he was holding back a smile. Wordlessly, I offered him a hand, and he accepted. With our fingers interlaced, I couldn't tell whether it was my pulse or his that raced as I dragged him to his feet and led him over to the edge. Izzy and Darvish had probably already scared off any wildlife within a ten-mile radius. I let go of Teddy's hand, held my hands to my mouth, and shouted at the top of my lungs. "Asshole!"

Teddy scrunched his face in the bright sun. "This is so childish."

"What?" I teased. "Are you too mature for the rest of us, now that you're a college student?" I poked him in the ribs and he flinched.

"No," he said, covering his ribs with a protective hand.

"Then say a bad word."

"What are you, five?" he asked, but he was laughing now.

"Say a bad word, Teddy!"

On his opposite side, Darvish had started a low-but-rising chant of "Say it, say it," and Izzy joined in. Teddy's gaze remained locked on me. The chanting got louder. I arched a brow and he shook his head, almost imperceptibly, but he was leaving me with no choice here. I joined the chant.

"All right, fine," he said, exasperated. He took a deep breath and held it, his jaw working as he seemed to mull over his word of choice. Then he released it all at once, in a half-hearted, "Crap!"

Darvish gawked at him. "Man. That was *weak.*"

Teddy mumbled something under his breath.

Izzy curled a hand around her ear. "I'm sorry, what was that?"

"I said 'That's bullshit,'" he said, a little louder this time.

"You have to shout it!" I said. His gaze flicked over me, at the excited way I was bouncing up and down on the balls of my feet, and he held back a smile. "Please," I added, because suddenly this felt like some sort of ritual, binding our friend group together, and if he didn't participate, I was worried that meant he already had one foot out the door.

He shook his head, holding my gaze for just a second longer before he turned to face the overlook.

And this time, he shouted as loud as he could.

* * *

We stayed at the overlook for most of the afternoon, shouting until our voices were ragged. We started the hike back down a couple hours before sunset, to give ourselves plenty of time to make it back to camp before it got dark. Darvish insisted that he and Teddy hike ahead, "just in case there are any bears or mountain lions or anything." I didn't have the heart to point out that there were no mountain lions this far east, and I was pretty sure neither of them was any match for a bear, but I hung back anyway. Izzy alternated between staring down at her dust-covered boots and throwing odd, covert glances at me, like she was trying to parse something out.

"What?" I asked after a while, feeling antsy beneath her gaze.

"You like him."

I turned to her like a deer in headlights, startled into inaction.

"Teddy, I mean," she clarified, nodding at the trail ahead, where Darvish had picked up a fallen branch and was brandishing it at his friend like a rapier. "I had a feeling last year, but

I wasn't sure, and then today, the way you guys kept looking at each other—"

I didn't say anything, but her declaration made my heartbeat stumble, clumsy and awkward in my chest. Because it was true, but I hadn't wanted to admit it even to myself, put words to this nervous jealousy that had taken over my life the past few months. I wasn't just scared of Teddy meeting other friends. I was scared of him meeting a girlfriend, because then everything would change. But I was equally terrified of speaking those feelings out loud, because then our friendship would change anyway.

Slowly, I nodded.

"I knew it," she hissed. "Oh my god, you have to tell him."

Panic rose in my chest. "No," I said, grabbing her sleeve. "Izzy, you can't say anything, promise me."

"Okay, okay," she said, holding up her hands in surrender. "I won't say anything." After a moment's hesitation, she added, "But you should."

I shook my head, swallowing around a fist-sized lump. "I can't."

It was safer this way. Better to preserve what we already had than risk ruining it by admitting to something I could never take back. Something that didn't quite fit into his careful life plan. It was only a crush. It would probably go away.

CHAPTER

11

Frostburg Antique Mall always smells like an ashtray, mingling with the faint ammoniac odor of the litter box tucked behind the creaky door of the single bathroom. But a handful of the vendors offer Saturday morning deals and it's right around the corner from a coffee shop, which means iced coffee and antiquing has become a semi-regular weekend pastime, when I'm not drowning in an ocean of ungraded homework.

Usually, it's a pastime I enjoy alone, but today a very blond and nosey shadow decided to tag along—supposedly because she was bored, but she's been interrogating me about last night. It was a few minutes past six when I got home from The Falconer, but I'm being scrutinized like I turned up after breakfast still wearing last night's makeup. "Like I said, it was a work thing. I had a few drinks with some colleagues. Nothing exciting."

"Bummer," Reagan sighs, snatching a vintage bucket hat off the rack and trying it on in the mirror. "I was kind of hoping you guys had an actual date." She poses, inspecting her reflection at different angles, and then flings the hat onto a nearby chair, startling one of the nameless shop cats so that it darts beneath a Victorian sideboard.

"I fail to see how my love life is any of your business, anyway."

Reagan shrugs as we peruse a hoard of costume jewelry, all of it marked *Buy One Get One Free*. "I mean, it's not. If you want to die alone, by all means. But getting railed every now and again might be good for you. It would help you, I dunno, loosen up."

I snort into my paper coffee cup. "We are not having this conversation."

We skip over a booth filled mostly with mid-century baking utensils—stained wooden rolling pins and metal cookie cutters so bent out of shape that it's hard to tell whether they're supposed to be bells or Christmas trees or snowmen—in favor of a vendor selling vintage clothes and shoes.

"Statistically, it's less likely with each passing year that you'll find someone, you know," Reagan is saying as she bends to inspect a pair of scuffed-up Dr. Martens. "And even if you *do* find someone in the next five years, getting married in your late thirties tends to lead to a higher divorce rate than, say, if you had gotten married in your late twenties."

Slightly depressing, from my vantage point. "Did you Google that?"

"Nope. I learned that in Psych 101, my last semester at Chesapeake."

"So what are you prescribing me, doctor? Arranged marriage, stat?" I select a sport coat from one of the racks and check the size.

"A good old-fashioned friend-with-benefits." She gives a meaningful waggle of her eyebrows.

"No way," I say. "He's not even my friend." Even after all these years, it still stings to admit that. Last night, talking for the first time in a long time, I was almost able to convince myself that maybe we could be friends again. But after a long and restless night of grading HIST-252 reading responses and a series of hazy, stress-induced dreams, things look different by the light of day.

"You're assuming he'd be interested," I add. I pull the sport coat over my T-shirt and examine my reflection in the floor-length mirror, imagining how it might look with my usual work clothes. One of the lapels is moth-eaten and it's got bad eighties shoulder pads that make me look like David Hasselhoff. Nope. Not going to work.

Leaning against an old vanity, Reagan arches a brow over the lid of her cup of coffee. "He's a red-blooded male."

"That's . . . no." I shrug off the coat and return it to the hanger, warmth crawling up my neck. I'm reminded of a different coat, of hangers clattering around in a musty closet. "Teddy's different."

"Oh, my sweet summer child."

I can't help but laugh. "I just mean he's practically a robot." I slide metal hangers out of the way in pursuit of something I might actually get away with wearing. "On his list of priorities, sex probably rates, I don't know, somewhere in between doing the dishes and brushing your teeth." Even as I'm saying it, I know full well that it's a lie. But it's a lie that I hope Reagan might buy, seeing as she only knows him as her professor. Not as a best friend. Not as something a little more.

"I think you underestimate the whole thoughtful, studious thing he has going," Reagan says. "He's probably a total freak in bed."

"Okay, that's enough." I wave a hand to stop her, as though I can wave the images right out of my head. Warmth seeps into my cheeks, though I'm not totally sure what I'm embarrassed about. Sure, it's inappropriate to be talking about my colleague this way, but it's not like I'm the one hypothesizing about Teddy's sex life. I stuff a pair of woolly pants back onto the clothing rack and grab my half-melted iced coffee off a nearby table. I'm not really in the mood for looking at a bunch of itchy old clothes.

* * *

My phone vibrates as I'm unlocking the front door. I fish it out of the pocket of my skinny jeans—a fashion blunder that Reagan keeps insisting on rectifying, because apparently flares and mom jeans are back in. Izzy's smiling face has taken over my phone screen.

I slide to answer and lift the phone to my ear.

"I'm *so* sorry it's taken me so long to call back." She's talking before I have the chance to say anything, rattling the words off quickly and a little breathless. Probably walking to her car, or at the gym climbing the StairMaster, or out running errands— Izzy's largest issue with the phone is that she can't sit still, so on the rare occasions that she does make a phone call, it's usually when she's in the middle of doing some sort of physical activity that doesn't require too much focus. "Things have been completely bananas the last few months. Work is chaos and I had to renew my residence permit last month. Total nightmare."

I smile even though she can't see me. She accepted a TESOL position teaching schoolchildren in Lisbon five years ago and never left, so I imagine *chaos* to mean Portuguese kids learning how to curse in English. "I know the feeling. Well, not the residence thing, but life has been . . ." I trail off. I'm not sure I want to announce my application for tenure until I've secured it—it feels premature, somehow. "Interesting."

"Good interesting, or bad interesting?" comes her eager voice.

I move into the kitchen, where I deposit the plastic Subway bag and reach into the overhead cupboard for a glass. Reagan steals her sandwich out of the bag and disappears down the hall, where the door to her bedroom closes with a snap. Apparently, we're not eating together. Works for me, since I'll probably be on the phone for a while, but Reagan has a special talent for making me feel less like an older sister and more like a parent to a hormonal teenager. "Just interesting."

Izzy sighs. "Tell me about it. You'll never believe who added me on Facebook."

I pour myself some water from the Brita and settle onto one of the barstools at the kitchen counter. Light streams in through the curtainless window above the sink, tinged gold by the changing leaves of the old maple. "Brandi?" I guess.

"Mohammad Darvish."

I pause in the middle of unwrapping my cold cut sandwich. There's a name I haven't heard in a while, but she managed to say it with as much ire as when we were teenagers. "He's aware that no one uses Facebook anymore, right?" I ask.

"You updated your profile picture like last week."

"I'm old and uncool, as Reagan likes to remind me. Isn't Darvish supposed to be some big tech guy or something?" Last I heard, he was working in Silicon Valley, but that was years ago, now.

"He's a programmer for some dating app because he obviously can't get a date the old-fashioned way," she rattles off. "But that's not important. We got to messaging. He mentioned something about Teddy accepting a temporary teaching position at a school in Maryland."

I slow my chewing. We've avoided talking about Teddy ever since the falling-out happened, because an argument with Izzy had followed not long after—nothing on the same scale, but when I'd called her to complain that he was ignoring my calls, she'd told me that I deserved to have them ignored after turning him away the way I did. *Cold-hearted,* I believe were her exact words. I resented her for it at the time, but it was the truth.

"Is that true?" she demands.

"Yes," I admit.

"Why didn't you tell me?"

I hesitate. I'm not sure why I didn't tell her—I told myself it was because I didn't want to bother her, but that's maybe not the whole truth.

Izzy and I were never meant to be best friends. She had a whole number of friends away from camp, and I had Teddy. Izzy's wonderful, and I love her with all my heart, but we don't have all that much in common. She thinks my history books are horribly boring and my taste in music is garbage. I think she's flighty and occasionally too honest for her own good. We can recognize those things about each other, but it doesn't mean we love each other any less. It just means we're not each other's person, and that's okay.

But over the years, it's like I've defaulted to her, and she's accepted it sort of like one accepts a stray cat. It starts with setting kibble on the porch to make sure the poor thing doesn't starve, and then suddenly there's cat hair all over your pillow and you're scooping out a litter box on your hands and knees.

"It didn't seem like the sort of thing I should bother you about," I say. "I don't know, Iz. It's just . . ." I trail off, munching on a potato chip. "It's complicated, you know?"

"Is it?" she challenges.

I'm not really sure what I'm supposed to say to that. In her mind, it's probably not all that complicated. I'm the lost cat on the *found* flyer and this is her opportunity to shove me back into Teddy's waiting arms, except it's not, because I can't just take back the things I said. I'm about to explain as much when Reagan enters the kitchen, combat boots clopping on the tile. My eyes narrow as they sweep over her outfit, taking in the cropped tee and pleather shorts. I hold the phone away from my face. "Where are you going?"

"What?" asks Izzy's faraway voice.

Reagan grabs one of her Diet Cokes out of the fridge, shrugging. "A party."

"What party?" I press.

"It's just this thing with Kappa Sig. Nothing too wild."

"Is that Reagan?" Izzy shouts into the phone, loud enough that we can both hear her. "Tell her I haven't forgotten about my flat iron."

I ignore the flat iron in favor of more pressing issues. "Will there be alcohol?"

"It's a frat party, what do you think?" Reagan pops the tab on her Coke and takes a sip as she backs toward the door. "Even I know you're not *that* out of touch."

"I pride myself on being out of touch, thank you. Hey," I rush to add as she turns to leave. She spins on the heel of her chunky boots to look at me, her face fixed into the very picture of patience. "Stay safe. Don't leave your drink with anyone."

"Yes, Mom."

"Child," I call after her before returning the phone to my ear. "Sorry. Reagan's taking off to some party."

"Six years," Izzy laments. "Six years without that flat iron, and I've never found another like it. They just don't make 'em like that over here."

"I'll tell her to mail it to you."

"No. International shipping prices are highway robbery. And I'd have to use one of those adapter thingies with it, and I'm not sure it's the right voltage anyway." The price you pay when you throw caution to the wind and run away to Europe, I guess. "Maybe I'll hit her up on Instagram. Ask her to Zelle me."

"She probably wouldn't see it," I point out. "I'm pretty sure she has like two thousand followers."

"Yeah, because she went to public school. That's normal for them."

"Speaking of Instagram"—I'm eager to steer clear of any more questions about Teddy—"I saw you deleted all the pictures with Margarida."

She heaves a loud sigh. "I dumped her ass after I caught her riding around on her moped with some little exchange student. She said she was just giving her a ride, but the girl was clinging to her back like a spider monkey."

"One girl's heartbreak is another girl's *Lizzie McGuire Movie.*"

"At least I've *had* my main character moment," Izzy shoots back. "When was the last time you went on an actual date?"

"Why has everyone picked today to bully me about my love life?" I ask, dodging the question because I genuinely have no idea when my last date was. "Reagan was on my case all morning about 'getting laid.'" I throw air quotes around the phrase like it's some kind of hip new slang—which is maybe proof that I do, in fact, need to get laid, but I shove the thought to the back of my mind. Archive it, catalogue it. I'll get back to it later.

"Maybe because you live like a freaking monk. Irving doesn't require its professors to take a vow of celibacy, last I checked."

"I don't live like a monk," I protest.

"Do you even own a vibrator?"

"Yes, actually." A little silver number I ordered off a late-night infomercial while wine-drunk on the couch after spring finals.

"When was the last time you used it?"

I haven't touched it since the unboxing. "That's personal."

Izzy laughs in my ear. "Right. So it's been a while."

"I just—I'm super busy," I sputter. "I mean, what would I even fantasize about?" I leave the underlying concern unspoken—not a question of what, but who.

"Read some smut, maybe. I have a whole reading list I can send you."

"Anything with vampires?" I ask through a mouthful of potato chips.

"No, but I do have a bunch of dark romance. Oooh, there's this one book where the guy chases the girl through the woods. I'll mail you my copy," she says proudly. "Actually, no. It's kind of a big book, now that I'm thinking about it. I'll gift you a copy on Amazon."

I pick at what's left of my sandwich, my hunger sated. Other things not so sated, if I'm being honest. "That's part of the problem. I don't have time to read four-hundred-page novels. If I'm reading, it's always research. Otherwise I'd never get any work done."

"Then maybe you should fantasize about Napoleon or something."

I snort. History never was Izzy's strong suit. "Thanks, but no thanks."

* * *

It's been a long week, so I take the evening off from grading reading responses. I permit myself exactly two episodes of *True Blood*—in my search for good vampire shows, I find myself returning to all the stuff I watched when I was younger—and then I peel myself from the couch and head to the shower. Afterward, I throw on my robe and shuffle into the bedroom, where I remove my coin necklace and place it in the little dish on my nightstand before flopping into bed. It's only then that I allow myself to access the day's archives, the thoughts I've stuffed into the deepest and darkest filing cabinets of my brain. It's something of a nightly routine: review every social faux pas, every awkward conversation, before I drift off to sleep.

In today's news: apparently, everyone's under the impression that I'm some sort of sex-starved hermit.

They're not wrong. It's been at least—actually, no, I don't want to think about how long it's been, because I'm pretty sure the last encounter was toward the end of grad school. It's not the lack of sex that bothers me so much as the lack of desire. I haven't *wanted* to have sex with anyone in particular, so I've been content to just go about my life without really dwelling on it. But now, lying here with my damp hair in my decidedly unsexy robe, I think maybe it would be nice to want someone. To actually care. To dwell on a living, breathing person, and not on people who have been dead for nearly five hundred years. Even Teddy has put more time and effort into adult romantic relationships than I have.

My mind drifts to his hand around the glass of gin and tonic last night. He's always had nice hands—large, masculine, dark hair encircling his wrist. It's been so long since I've even allowed myself to entertain the thought. Remembered the feeling, however fleeting, of those hands on my body. I can just picture that intensity of his, that laser focus, all of it directed at me.

Warmth builds in my lower abdomen at the same time as it tinges my face. I shouldn't be thinking about this. It feels off-limits, but at the same time it feels so *good* to let myself fantasize a bit, and really, what's the harm? I set my phone face down on the nightstand and ease open the drawer, where the small and silver contraption lies innocently among old hair ties and cough drops and dried-up pens.

A buzz rattles the dresser and I leap out of my skin.

Not the vibrator. My phone. Heart hammering in my throat, I slide the drawer shut and flip the phone over to see who's calling. Reagan. Any lingering heat fizzles out of me. Taking a few breaths to calm my frustration, I swipe to answer. "What's up?"

"Professor Fernsby?" asks a hesitant voice—one that I'm certain doesn't belong to my sister. "This is Natalia. From History 111?"

I haven't memorized all the new students this semester yet, so I can't put a face to the name. But whoever she is, she must be a friend of Reagan's. "Why do you have my sister's phone?"

"She's—" Natalia stops short. Bass thumps in the background, mingling with raucous voices. "I don't want to get her into any trouble."

I withhold my exasperation. Unusual circumstance aside, this is a student of mine, and I need to remain professional. "She's an adult. I'm not going to ground her."

After a moment's hesitation, Natalia continues. "We had to take her keys. She hasn't tried to drive or anything, but I'm not sure . . ."

"No, you made the right choice." I'm already hoisting myself back out of bed and searching for clothes to throw on. I worry enough about Reagan's driving when she's sober. I don't want to imagine what it would look like drunk. "Thanks for calling me. I'll come get her. Keep an eye on her until I get there."

CHAPTER

12

PRESENT

It's a quick drive across town. I slow on the narrow and shadowy roads that branch off from campus, the glow of the old streetlamps dimmed by overgrown trees. Greek Row comprises mostly converted residentials—technically not part of campus, and therefore not an area I'm super familiar with. I was picturing kegs and people passed out on the front lawn like something straight out of a teen movie, but the lacy old Victorians and structured bungalows are innocuous in the dark. No sign of the yellow Jeep parked along the cut-stone curb.

Reagan had mentioned the name of the fraternity—Sigma Nu? Omega Something? I ring my sister's phone, hoping Natalia will pick up, but there's no answer. I should have asked where they were earlier. Unsure of what else I should do, I drive a block over to the familiar faculty parking lot outside the Hall of Letters, where I throw my car into park and open my messages. I shoot a quick text to Reagan's number—What party did you say you were at again?—before I switch over to my browser and pull up the University of Irving website. There's got to be a listing of all the fraternities somewhere on here, and then once I have a name, I might be able to figure out where their house is located.

Except these names are all Greek to me—literally. Kappas

and Gammas and Omegas, but none of it is ringing a bell. I scroll through pictures and descriptions of each fraternity like that's somehow going to help me, but it doesn't. Maybe she said it was a sorority party. Weird how you don't hear that phrase half as often as you hear *frat party*. Giving up, I try ringing Reagan's cell again, but this time it goes straight to voice mail. That can't be a good sign.

Something knocks against the passenger side window, hard.

I yelp, clutching my hand to my chest, where my heart thuds violently beneath my sweatshirt. A silhouette waves at me from beyond the dark tint of my windows. My finger hovers over the controls. I probably shouldn't roll down the window—there's rarely any trouble on campus, and we have private security on patrol around the clock, but better safe than sorry.

"Clara," a muffled voice calls through the glass. "It's Teddy."

I exhale, the unease lifting off me, and roll down the window. "You scared me. I thought I was about to get robbed."

In the dim light, I can just make out the way his eyes flick over my battered Volvo, over the dings and sunbaked paint. He raises his eyebrows, an expression that screams *not sure you'd be their first target.*

"What are you doing here?" I ask.

"I prefer grading homework in the office," he says. "Why are you sitting in your car?"

"I'm trying to find my sister. She's at some frat party or something, and one of her friends called me, but I can't find the house and now they're not answering." For good measure, I check my phone again, but there are no texts or returned calls.

"Kappa Sigma," he provides without missing a beat.

I look up from my phone to gawk at him. "How'd you know that?"

"A couple of my students in 121 were talking about it in the middle of class."

I imagine him pulling the ultimate teacher cliché: *Would you like to share with the class?* Most professors can't even be bothered because we're dealing with legal adults, not children, and if they want to waste their time, then that's on them. But Teddy's always been by-the-book in a way that makes me suspect he *might* actually use that line.

I make a mental note to look him up on Rate My Professors later. Because I'm curious.

"Here." He reaches inside my car, patting around blindly for the lock. I swallow, all too aware of the inappropriate thoughts I was having about those hands not thirty minutes ago. I'm thankful it's dark, because heat has crept back into my face. I press the button to unlock the door and he settles into the seat beside me, his long legs folded in the cramped space. He's dressed more casually than I've seen him in years—jeans and a plain black T-shirt that's snug over his broad chest, his well-toned arms on full display. It is the weekend, after all. He pulls up the map on his phone. "Looks like it's over on Dartmouth," he says. "I'll give you directions."

I glance over my shoulder as I back out of the space. Driving is a convenient excuse to look anywhere other than his arms. Or hands.

I clear my throat, trying to redirect my thoughts. "You didn't have to come with me, you know," I say. "You could have just given me directions."

"It's no problem." He pauses just long enough for it to sound half-hearted—and maybe a touch bitter—when he adds, "What are friends for, right?"

With a pang of longing, I glance at him sideways. He's staring out the windshield, shadows shifting over his features as we pass beneath a streetlight. I don't know what he expects me to say to that—or if he expects me to say anything, for that matter.

I lick my lips, trying to conjure up a response, but there's none forthcoming.

"Right, turn right," he urges, jarring me from my thoughts, but I react a second too late. I've missed the turn. It's a good thing I have this job at the university, because I'd make a terrible Uber driver.

"Okay, right at the next stop sign," he amends. "We can loop back around."

We ride in silence until we pull up outside a drab-looking bungalow, a dark flag fluttering from the porch. The windows glow a warm yellow, but there's no one outside. It's not until I step out of my car and into the crisp autumn night that I hear faint, thudding bass. Teddy joins me on the lawn, folding his arms and hunching his shoulders against the chill.

Without exchanging a word, we head for the door. As we draw near, I realize it's not the Maryland state flag or even a school flag flapping from the gable, but instead one that proclaims that SATURDAYS ARE FOR THE BOYS. Under normal circumstances, I might have knocked, but considering my sister is drunk and not answering her phone, I barge right in. This is university property, after all.

The would-be doorman—aka some drunk kid in a Kappa Sigma sweatshirt—leaps from the sofa, one hand spread wide as we cut through the living room, the other clutching a can of lite beer. "Whoa, whoa, dicks are five dollars," he says to Teddy. Then he teeters, eyes narrowing as he sizes both of us up. "Wait. You're not cops, are you? I mean, no offense, but you're kinda old."

"We're faculty," Teddy says in a sharp, authoritative voice that I'm not at all familiar with. "Now, excuse us." He brushes past the doorman and the kid's face goes slack. Taking advantage of the lapse in vigilance, I follow Teddy farther into the house.

It's sparsely decorated, the walls adorned with black-and-white photos of Kappa Sigmas past. The rare bit of furniture looks like it was ordered from Amazon and assembled by a drunken toddler. We pass a folding table adorned with a half-racked game of beer pong, one of the red Solo cups knocked over and beer trickling onto the tile. There are speakers set up on the half wall, still pulsing with what I assume is supposed to be music, but there's no one left to listen to it. This party is well and truly over. So where the heck is my pain-in-the-ass sister?

The dining room leads into a warm, earth-toned kitchen, the sink piled high with dirty dishes and an impressive collection of liquor bottles lining the granite counter. There, leaning against the island, is Reagan. I loose a breath, the full weight of my relief settling over me. She's got a glass of tap water clutched in her hand and mascara tracks beneath her eyes, but she lights up the moment she recognizes me.

"Clare Bear, you're here!" She throws her arms open to pull me into a loose-limbed hug. Drunken affection. This is new. When she pulls away, she blinks back and forth between me and Teddy, trying to clear the haze. "And you've brought— wait." She looks back at me. "What's he doing here?"

"I ran into Professor Harrison on campus," I explain, hoping that a subtle reminder that he's her *professor,* in charge of her *grade,* will keep her from saying anything too untoward. "Where's your phone? I've been trying to call you."

She waves a dismissive hand, eyes fluttering shut. "Natalia has it."

I try to be gentle but firm, gripping her shoulders to steady her. "And where's Natalia?"

"Here, Professor Fernsby." From one of the adjoined rooms, Natalia materializes. I recognize her now that I have a face to go with the name: sleek black hair, soccer sweatshirt. She's from out of state, here on an athletic scholarship, if my memory serves. "Her phone died. I'm sorry."

She hands me the phone and I release one of Reagan's shoulders to accept it. Reagan rocks but steadies herself. "Thank you for this," I say. "Do you have the keys to the Jeep?"

Natalia produces the Irving-maroon lanyard. I suspect she had to wrestle it from Reagan's neck. "It's parked over by the administration building. I think she walked."

"My Jeep," Reagan says feebly, fumbling for the keys, but I pocket them and steer her by the shoulders toward the front door.

"I'll take you to pick it up tomorrow," I say. "Come on. Let's get you in the car."

Stragglers watch, bemused, as two of their professors march a student out of the party and into the back seat of my car. Okay, so maybe we *do* look like plainclothes cops, if cops drove dinged-up Volvos. Teddy jumps back in the passenger seat. By the time I make it around to the driver side, Reagan has already poked her head between the seats, eyeballing Teddy with the sort of brazen curiosity that's only fueled by alcohol.

"Professor Hottison, I don't know if you remember me—"

I balk at the ridiculous nickname, but my protest falls on drunk ears.

"—but I'm in one of your classes this semester. The American history one."

A smile tugs at Teddy's mouth, but he doesn't comment on the nickname. "Of course I remember you. You're Clara's little sister."

I shoot another uncertain glance at him before pulling away from the curb, but he's not paying attention.

"I *am*," Reagan says proudly, reaching into the front to grip my shoulder in what I can only assume is supposed to be a loving gesture. Yep, she's completely hammered. "And you guys have known each other"—she hiccups on the word, and for a split second, I fear she's going to blow chunks all over the center console, but then she gulps and continues—"known each other forever. Like, a really long time."

"Seventeen years," Teddy confirms with a sideways glance at me.

Reagan exhales and I catch a whiff of beer breath. "That's, like, almost as long as I've been alive."

Teddy swivels to look at her. "Are you twenty-one?" His concerned eyes dart to me. "Is she twenty-one?"

"Yes, she's twenty-one. Barely," I add with an admonishing look in the rearview as we roll down the dark street toward campus. I'm not sure Reagan notices—she's too busy staring at Teddy, a funny look in her eye. And that's when it hits me, seconds too late. It's not *actual* vomit I should be worrying about.

It's word vomit.

"Maybe this is weird to say," Reagan slurs, folding her arms and leaning forward on the center console so that her head and shoulders are fully in the front seat, "but my friends think you're, like, the hottest professor on campus. Has anyone ever told you that?"

I want to grab her by the shoulders and shake some sense into her, but then she might throw up for real. "That's inappropriate," I cut in. "And put on your seat belt."

"I'm wearing it." To emphasize the point, she hooks a thumb under the overextended shoulder belt and lets it snap back into place.

The look on Teddy's face is somewhere between amusement and embarrassment. His gaze snags on mine and my stomach does a backflip. "Ah, no," he says. "They haven't told me that."

Reagan's eyes are wide as saucers, though the haze remains. "Well, they should tell you. Clara, tell him."

"I'm not going to—" I stop short, huffing in indignation. There's no point even arguing with her. She's drunk.

She pouts at me. "I don't understand why you're being so weird about it."

Teddy's curious gaze flits from Reagan to me. "Weird about what, exactly?"

Well, that's a loaded question, one that I have no intention of answering, but I'm also not sure how to brush it off without seeming suspicious. In the interim, Reagan tries to lean forward, but I come to a stop sign and her seat belt locks. She flops back into her seat. "You need to sit down," I order. I'm not saying I stepped on the brakes harder than normal, but I'm also not *not* saying that.

"Fine," she says, belligerent. "Then I'll say it from back here." She takes a deep breath. "Professor Harrison, you should know—"

"That's enough, Reagan—"

"—that my sister is most definitely in love with you."

I sputter a laugh, as though that could ever diffuse the tension that settles over the car in the wake of that simple statement, all the memories I'd shoved to the very back of the archives, left to collect dust. I am not in love with a man I haven't spoken to in over a decade. I hardly know him. But I did love him once, in my own way. And maybe that doesn't ever go away completely.

I pull into the parking lot and park in a faculty space. Reagan can't possibly know everything she's dredged up, but she tries to resolve it with a lot of drunk babbling that I only half hear—*oh my god, I was just kidding, you should see the look on your face,* that sort of thing. The person I wish would say something is Teddy, but then again, what could I possibly expect him to say? *No, you're wrong, Clara's not in love with me and she never has been?* I throw the car into park and glance over at him, tentative. He's watching me, his brow lightly furrowed, like he's trying to work something out.

"Thank you for the help tonight," I say, my voice tight. I clear my throat. "And I'm sorry." I jerk my head at the back seat. "For my sister."

"Hey!"

He shakes his head. "You don't need to apologize."

Now that we're no longer moving, Reagan pops up between the seats again. She swipes a lock of tousled blond hair out of her face. "This isn't going to affect my grade, is it?"

Teddy tears his eyes from me to give her an appraising look, like he's actually considering docking a few points. After letting her sweat for a few seconds, he concludes, "What my students do on their own time is none of my business." He unbuckles his seat belt, but pauses with his hand on the door handle. "Just— don't bring it to class," he amends, quite seriously. I'm not sure if he's referring to the drinking or the whole *Professor Hottison* thing. Maybe all of the above.

Reagan nods once, gives him a sloppy little salute. "Yes, sir."

We exchange a quick good night and he leaves without any of the usual hesitation—we've finally established, it seems, that we're not on hugging terms. I watch his retreating back and wonder whether we ever could be again.

The hardest part about loving someone is, in my experience, stopping. Maybe because I've never had to grapple much with the opposite, with choosing to keep on loving them despite everything. There was never much choice involved, for me. Falling in love was like falling asleep on a road trip: you let yourself get comfortable and then suddenly you wake up and you're already there. Falling out of love, in contrast, was like a car crash: you slam on the brakes, but you don't just *stop*, because the momentum is still there. And years later, you might've recovered, but you still have the little aches and pains, and maybe you're a little scared every time you hop back behind the wheel, because look what happened before.

I back out of the parking space and turn down one of the dark campus drives, lost in thought.

"I'm not *wrong*," Reagan says, breaking the heavy silence. I toss a glance at her in the rearview. Her face is shadowy in the back seat, but I don't need to see her to know what she's referring to. I heave a sigh. I'm not sure I have the energy to keep denying it.

CHAPTER

13

"Stop looking at it," Izzy ordered. "You're making me antsy."

It was an especially dark and blustery November, the sidewalk cold where we sat with our backs against the stucco wall outside Baltimore Premier Cinemas. That year, I'd gotten my driver's license, finally convinced my parents to add me to the cell phone plan, and Izzy had dragged me to the midnight premiere of *The Twilight Saga: New Moon*. We'd camped out since two that afternoon, until only the lights in the parking lot and the orange glow of a *Fantastic Mr. Fox* poster illuminated this side of the building.

I closed the sliding keyboard on my phone with a sheepish smile. "Sorry."

"Seriously," Izzy said, but it was very hard to take her seriously when her arms were folded over a Team Edward shirt, Robert Pattinson's pale face peeking out from behind her colorful jelly bracelets. She'd flat-ironed her thick black waves until they were pin-straight just for the occasion, with a side part so dramatic that a chunk of hair kept falling over her right eye. "Didn't Einstein say in his theory of relativity that the more time you spend waiting around for something, the longer it takes to actually happen?"

"I'm pretty sure the theory of relativity has nothing to do with waiting on a text message," I pointed out, unzipping my backpack to tuck my phone away. Out of sight, out of mind. "I won't check it again until we're in the theater, and then I'll mute it. Promise," I tacked on, because she didn't look convinced.

Teddy was nearing the end of his second semester at Northampton Community College, and between that and working to graduate high school a year early, the past few months had kept him incredibly busy. Texting had made things easier—instead of needing to boot up the computer to log into Myspace, we'd send messages throughout the week, but his responses grew less and less frequent. We'd had to put The Long-Distance History Club on hold because he said he couldn't keep up. A paperback waited patiently on my dresser, pages marked with colorful sticky flags. He swore he'd make time over winter break, and he'd already asked whether I could fit a few of my favorite books in my suitcase for him to borrow this summer, but that was a long way off.

Whatever feelings I'd started to develop for Teddy, I'd shoved them down for the sake of preserving our friendship. Sort of like packing my suitcase for camp every year: slightly overfull of unvoiced thoughts and words and emotions, but if I rolled some of them into a tight little ball and threw my weight against them, I was able to make it all fit long enough to zip it closed. But I still found myself checking my phone a little too often, my heart skipping a beat whenever I got a text message notification.

They didn't let us into the theater until half an hour before showtime. While Izzy extracted contraband bags of Sour Patch Kids and Flaming Hot Cheetos from places I didn't even know they could fit, I unzipped my backpack and checked my phone. No notifications. Which meant he still hadn't answered the message I sent over fourteen hours ago, but I opened my texts anyway.

"You're obsessed," Izzy hissed, shoving a box of Mike and Ikes at me.

"Am not," I muttered, even as I reread our messages from this morning.

> Teddy: Good morning. What are you doing today?

> Clara: Meeting Izzy in Baltimore! We're going to the mall and then we're going to see the new Twilight movie

> Clara: I know it's kind of silly but Izzy's read all the books

> Clara: Speaking of reading I was wondering what have you been reading for school? Anything interesting? I was thinking we could restart Long-Distance History Club(1/2)

> Clara: if I read some of the same books that your teachers are assigning you. That way you don't have to do a bunch of extra work. What do you think?(2/2)

The lights dimmed around me as I stared at the bright screen. Why hadn't he replied? Perhaps my last couple texts simply hadn't gone through. That sometimes happened with the longer texts—only one half of the message would find its way to the other end, the other half lost in cyberspace. I typed out a follow-up text asking whether he'd received the messages, but hesitated before hitting send. Would it look desperate if I texted him again?

I deleted the drafted message and silenced my phone before shoving it in my backpack. If he didn't answer by tomorrow, maybe I'd text him again then. Or maybe I wouldn't—at least, that's what I told myself. It wasn't like he was my boyfriend, and the last thing I wanted to be was *obsessed*. We were friends. Nothing more.

* * *

We filed out of the dark theater, moviegoers chattering excitedly around us. I fished my phone out of my backpack. I had several missed calls from Mom, but more importantly, Teddy had finally texted back.

> Teddy: Sorry for the delay, have a paper due tomorrow

> Teddy: That sounds good. I've got a bunch of assigned reading. Just a minute

> Teddy: How was the movie?

He followed this with a grainy photograph of a course syllabus, packed with unfamiliar articles on early American history. The texts were hours old already, so there was a very good chance he'd already gone to bed, but I typed out a quick reply.

> Clara: No worries! Movie was pretty good.

Clara: I haven't read any of those.
I'll have to see if I can find them

"I can't decide who's hotter: Robert Pattinson or Kristen Stewart." Beside me, Izzy was chattering happily about the movie as we made our way across the chilly parking lot. "I mean, did you see that moment when Edward was about to expose himself to all those people? Goose bumps just thinking about it. *Goose bumps.* Look at my arm." She shoved the arm in question out in front of me, nearly clotheslining me because my eyes were glued to the phone screen.

"I'm not sure 'expose himself' is the right choice of words," I said, pushing her arm down.

"Whatever, you know what I mean." She scrunched her nose. "And can you please stop obsessing over your phone? Staring at it isn't going to make him text you back any sooner."

"I know," I said with a sigh, tucking my phone in my pocket so that I could feel if it vibrated. We climbed into my car, a 1999 Volvo S40 that I'd bought with money earned babysitting for the next-door neighbors, the peeling blue paint tinged greenish by the warm glow of the streetlight. I'd left the volume turned up on the stereo and it blasted a Taking Back Sunday song as soon as the engine turned over. I turned the dial to low and drove to the nearest McDonald's because it was the only fast-food place still open. The air inside the car was thick with tension and cheap pine-tree air freshener. Izzy had her hands in her lap, twisting and stretching a pale pink jelly bracelet she'd pulled from her wrist.

"You need to just talk to him," she said after we placed our orders and I pulled up to the first window. "Like, tell him you want him to text you more often or something. That way you're not just sitting around"—she made a vague gesture at me, jelly bracelet still in hand—"obsessing."

I opened my door to dump out the remnants of an iced coffee. "I'm *trying* to talk to him." I tossed the cup over my shoulder and into the back seat, where it would join the rest of my hoard because I hadn't cleaned my car out since the day I bought it off some guy on Craigslist. "But I can't just ask him to text me more. It's not like that."

"Okay, then you need to do something about it," she argued instead. "It's like Bella with Jacob, right?"

I was a little distracted as I accepted my change from the cashier. "I'm not following." I dumped the coins in one of the drink holders.

"They're friends, right? Practically best friends. But then they're more than friends, or Bella thinks maybe they *could* be more than friends, and she has to decide whether she wants to be more than friends or not. You know?"

"Okay," I said slowly. My phone buzzed in my pocket and I resisted the temptation to check it.

"And sometimes when you're not totally sure how you feel, you have to just"—another indecipherable wave of her jelly band—"*do* something. Try your feelings on for size. See whether it all makes sense."

I wasn't sure when or how Izzy had become an expert in feelings—I suspected it had something to do with the tutelage of one Stephanie Meyer—but I gave her a blank look, shaking my head. My feelings were supposed to stay packed away and zipped up tight, and I was terrified that if I unboxed them, tried them on and found that they didn't quite fit, I'd never be able to go back to not knowing.

"That's it," she said. "I'm loaning you the books. You're all into vampires anyway, about time you actually read them." I opened my mouth to protest—I wasn't sure I counted the vampires in *Twilight* among actual vampires—but Izzy cut me off, pointing a finger in my face. "And don't you dare tell me you're not going to read them. You have your whole book club thing with Teddy. You can make time for my book club, too."

My phone vibrated again and this time I couldn't resist the urge to check it. My heart sank into my stomach where it sat, a dead weight.

> Parental Unit: Why aren't you answering your phone?!

> Parental Unit: you need to come home and watch Reagan. NOW.

> Parental Unit: it's your father. There's been an accident

"See?" Izzy said, self-satisfied. "I told you. As soon as you stop staring at your phone, he texts back."

"It's not Teddy," I breathed, turning the screen to show her. Her face was illuminated whitish-blue in the dark car and her eyes widened as she scanned the messages. "It's my mom."

* * *

A fall. That was how Mom explained it as she hurried out the door, keys jangling. He fell while he was on a job. The eventual discharge paperwork was more descriptive: Dad had fallen from a boom lift while away on a weekend job near Richmond, suffering a pelvic fracture in two separate places. Mom made the three-hour drive down to Chippenham Hospital that night. His recovery would be a long and arduous one, filled with surgeries and lots of uncertainty, but one thing *was* certain: he wouldn't be going back to work any time soon. There was a chance he'd be able to get worker's comp, if he could prove that the fall was the fault of his employer and not an error in judgment, but there were no guarantees. Mom sat me down in the living room the week of Thanksgiving and explained, as delicately as she could, that she was going to have to look for a job.

"You can't get a job," I said, like it was simple, a matter of fact. She'd always been at home. I knew that she had taken night classes when I was younger and earned a bachelor's in childhood development—she was still paying back the loans—but that was because she thought it would help with the homeschooling. It wasn't like she ever planned to *work*.

"Yes, I can," she told me. "You have a year left of school—"

"A year and a half," I corrected.

"—which you're more than capable of finishing on your own. I'm not sure I've taught you anything since you discovered Wikipedia."

I stared, only half-seeing, at the unfinished puzzle scattered around the coffee table—a picturesque cottage fractured into a thousand pieces. She wasn't wrong. As I'd gotten older, I'd spent fewer days hunched over the kitchen table with Mom hovering over my shoulder and more days cross-legged on my bed, surrounded by textbooks with my music blaring. "What about Reagan?" I asked, changing tactics. "I can't sit around babysitting her all day. I still have schoolwork to finish, and I'm supposed to start thinking about what colleges I want to apply to in the fall."

Mom shrugged. "She's old enough. We'll just have to enroll her in public school."

* * *

She applied to every opening she could find, but with fifteen plus years out of the workforce, she only earned a call back for a sales associate position at the Bath & Body Works in Salisbury. It was surreal, how quickly it all changed. My parents had fallen in love young, the perfect, cookie-cutter life practically falling into their laps, and in a second, it was all ripped out from under them.

They argued more. Shouting matches over bills and debts and the future. I'd always thought of them as a cohesive unit, a model of what love was supposed to look like, but I started to see them more as two separate people—a begrudging alliance, tolerating the other's presence, but there wasn't any joy in it. I had trouble remembering if there ever was. Maybe if they had taken things slow, I thought, planned their lives a little better . . . maybe it all would've been easier on them.

Maybe, if you were careful, you wouldn't have to struggle to hold it all together, even as your life was coming apart at the seams.

For my part, I focused on finishing out my junior year. I binged all the *Twilight* books in less than a week. I also found PDFs of the same papers Teddy was assigned, texting him my thoughts as I went and asking what his professor and classmates had had to say. We talked on the phone a couple times over winter break, on Christmas and his birthday, like always, and he broke tradition by calling me shortly before midnight on New Year's Eve to wish me a happy new year and promise that things would balance out once he was finished with his senior year of homeschooling and could focus on college full time.

Long-Distance History Club once again fell by the wayside during the spring, which was fine, because both of us were busy. But as the months wore on, I started to feel lonely being at home for the first time in my life. I spent a lot of time blasting music in my room, flipping through books I'd already read, nothing quite holding my interest. Mom worked long hours, Reagan was enrolled in first grade, and Dad mostly stayed in bed watching daytime television, except on the days he had physical therapy.

I missed camp. I missed my friends. I managed to tough it

out until spring break, at which point I knew I needed to get out of the house, at least for the day, as a matter of self-preservation.

Clara: What are you doing this weekend? I could use a distraction right about now.

Teddy: My schedule's wide open.

Clara: Meet in Middletown on Sat for lunch?

It shouldn't have felt like anything out of the ordinary—we'd hung out before, texted often enough that I counted him among my closest friends, if not the closest. But with my phone lying on the quilted comforter next to my calculus textbook, the hours wearing on, I started to get nervous. Maybe I overstepped, made it sound too much like a date. He'd made it clear he was busy, at least until summer. When he finally texted back, it was curt, to the point.

Teddy: I have another idea.

CHAPTER

14

PRESENT

Reagan's blond hair is fanned across her pillow. I resist the urge to chuck the bag of McDonald's at her head, instead opting for setting it on her nightstand. Am I not merciful? Actually, I'm not, because I proceed to throw open the curtains, admitting the blinding gray of an overcast morning into her bedroom. She groans in protest, tugging the quilt up over her head.

"I don't think so." I yank it back down, and she doesn't have the strength to fight me. She scrunches up her face, throwing an arm over her eyes instead. I jostle the fast-food bag to get her attention. "I brought you McDonald's."

She lifts a lifeless arm just enough for one bloodshot eye to squint at the nightstand. "I'm on a diet."

"I don't want to hear it." I take the bag and shove it at her. "You probably drank, what, a thousand calories' worth of alcohol last night? And McDonald's is the perfect hangover cure."

"Why can't you let me sleep?"

I drag her desk chair and position it beside the bed like I'm about to give her Last Rites. She probably thinks the McDonald's is a peace offering, but I like to think of it as buttering her up before the impending interrogation. "Be glad we're having this conversation now and not earlier."

Grumbling, she props herself up against the headboard and begins rifling through the bag with half-lidded eyes. After shoving a few fries into her mouth, she gropes in her sheets—probably searching for her phone, which is currently on the kitchen counter, where she left it last night after I forced her to down a couple glasses of water. Giving up the search, she blinks at me, bleary-eyed. "What time is it?"

"Eleven thirty."

"What time did I get home? How did I—" She stops in the middle of unwrapping her Big Mac to stare at me in horror. Last night's eyeliner is smeared across one of her cheeks. "You picked me up last night."

"Her memory returns," I announce to the barren room. Aside from the odd teapot or moth-eaten armchair from the local antique mall, I haven't bothered decorating much of the house, but Reagan's room is the most neglected. Just a twin-sized bed, a thrifted rolltop desk, and a nightstand, the lot of which she's accented with fairy lights and haphazardly strewn laundry. She's lucky there are curtains—they came with the rental.

"Where's my Jeep?"

"Safe and sound where you left it. I'll take you to pick it up later today." I eye her, wary. "If you're not still drunk."

"I'm not still drunk," she protests through a mouthful of hamburger.

I'm not convinced, but we'll see how things are looking after the McDonald's. In the meantime, I have bigger Filet-O-Fish to fry. "So, you don't remember anything else, I take it?"

Reagan must note the edge in my voice, because she lowers her Big Mac, chewing slowly. Biding her time. When she swallows, she asks tentatively, "Was Professor Harrison with you?"

Okay, so she does remember. I'm not sure if that makes it better. "*Now* you call him by his actual name."

Her eyes widen. "Oh my god. I didn't. Did I?" When I neither confirm nor deny, the panic sets in. Her Big Mac lies forgotten on her lap, and she scoots closer to the edge of the bed. Closer to me. "What else did I say?"

I take a deep breath. I can do this. Relay the events. Just the cold, hard facts. No emotions involved. It's all in the past, right? Reagan might have unintentionally dragged a few memories out of storage and shaken the dust loose, but it's not like any of those things matter now, well over a decade later. So I'm not going to take my frustration out on her. I'm going to handle this like an adult.

* * *

"Get off me," Reagan wheezes from where her cheek is smooshed against the bed.

The quilt and sheets are tangled, collateral damage from the struggle that ensued after she told me that I should *thank* her for giving me an easy opening with Teddy last night. What with her hangover, it took less than a minute for me to gain the upper hand, and I promptly secured my victory by sitting on her back, flattening her against the bed. "Apologize first."

"You're going to make me throw up!"

"You won't throw up if you just say sorry."

She sighs, her body deflating beneath me. "Fine. I'm sorry I told Professor Hottison about your stupid crush."

"*Former* stupid crush," I correct her. "And I've told you to *stop calling him that.*"

She groans. "Whatever. Now let me up."

I relent, and she gasps like I've been dunking her head underwater. Which, now that I'm thinking about it, sounds like a great punishment for the next time I have to babysit her like this.

"I'll be back in a couple hours," I say, "and then we'll see about going to grab your Jeep."

Rubbing her chest, she manages a glare. "Where are you going?"

I don't feel like getting into details, so I just say, "I'm meeting up with someone."

If anything, my elusiveness only stokes her curiosity. "What, like a date?"

"Sure." Actually, I'm meeting with potential caterers for the gala, but she doesn't need to know that. If she thinks I'm going on a date, maybe she—and Izzy, for that matter—will get off my case for a little while.

"It's with Teddy, isn't it?"

"Do you want to get squashed again?"

"You only won because this hangover is a bitch."

I bow my way out of the room. "I'll leave you to your recovery, then."

"Say hi to Professor Hottison for me," she calls, just as I shut the door behind me.

We'll see who wins round two, once she's good and sober.

❊ ❊ ❊

I don't have much to offer local caterers in exchange for donating their food, time, and hospitality to the gala, save my gratitude—which, let's be real, doesn't amount to much in the world of business. My first stop is Lucretia's, a family-owned Italian restaurant in one of the old brickwork buildings. I'm greeted by a teen-aged hostess, who—after I explain why I'm here—goes to fetch the owner, poking her head into the kitchen and shouting for *Nonna*. A white-haired woman with a beauty mark on her chin emerges from the back, wiping her hands on an apron and already shaking her head.

After a polite but firm rejection, I cross Lucretia's off the list in my notepad. And then I scratch the local seafood place out, too, when I walk a couple doors down and discover the C sanitary inspection grade taped in the window. The Falconer's food menu is limited and I doubt they're staffed for catering, so I skip the bars in favor of popping into Subway. The assistant manager is pleasant—a college-aged kid with his blond man bun wrapped in a hairnet. He nods along with everything I'm saying and expresses enthusiasm in the idea before reluctantly explaining that I would have to reach out to the franchise owner . . . who's on vacation in Cabo San Lucas for the next three weeks and won't be taking any business calls until he gets back to the States. I jot down a name and phone number on the back of receipt paper, but I leave feeling less than hopeful.

The last stop on my list is Bucky's Burgers and Dogs. The owner comes out from around the counter and introduces himself as Mack, shaking my hand like he's trying to strangle a python and ushering me outside. He insists that he likes to do business "in the great outdoors"—better known as the Bucky's parking lot, overlooking an overfilled dumpster, the O'Reilly Auto Parts across the road, and a Dodge Ram parked in the handicapped space with a vanity plate that reads TAILG8R. Mack is a little older than me, his sparse hairline half-hidden beneath a red Phillies cap, and he chain-smokes Camel Crushes while I pitch the gala to him at one of the steel mesh tables.

"All right, I'll do it," he says, snuffing out a cigarette in the ashtray and cracking the filter on a fresh one before pinching it between his lips. "I've been looking for an excuse to roll out the new food truck. Got a couple conditions, though." The cigarette bobs as he talks and he pauses to light it, taking a few puffs and emitting a cloud of pungent, minty smoke before continuing. "I want a banner put up at the event. A big one."

I waft the smoke away with a hand. "Done." That's almost

too easy, considering we already had plans to print banners listing all the major donors and participants. "Anything else?"

"A scholarship," he says. "Named after Bucky."

I ignore the more interesting question—if this guy is Mack,
then who, precisely, is Bucky?—in favor of a practical approach
to his demand. "A scholarship is dependent on funding," I
explain. "An endowment, usually, or maybe a yearly cash donation."

He arches a wiry brow. "You're putting on this whole thing
to raise money, aren't you?"

"Yes, but—"

We're interrupted by a teenaged employee poking his head
out the door, disheveled red hair sprouting up from his visor.
"There's a customer on the phone about a to-go order," he says,
looking on the verge of tears. "She found an onion ring in her
fries and says she's allergic to onions and now she's threatening
to sue."

Mack sighs, stabs his half-finished cigarette in the ashtray,
and rises to his feet. "Wait here. This'll just be a minute."

I do as I'm told, waiting with my hands folded on the table
until Mack's hoarse shouting carries through the front door.
Not knowing what else to do with myself, I grab my phone out
of my messenger bag and flick through my unread texts. I have
a habit of neglecting them for days on end—mostly because I
don't really get texts from anyone I actually care about. Izzy pre-
fers her phone calls, Mom has never quite learned to text, and
while Reagan sometimes messages me to meet up for lunch, we
have plenty of opportunity to talk in person. But I do get plenty
of texts asking me who I'm voting for, or letting me know that
it's 40 percent off on custom framing this week at Michaels.

Except today, there's another contact gracing my inbox. At
the sight of his name, my stomach swoops like I've hit a dip in
the road while driving—an uncomfortable, lurching sensation.

Teddy: Home safe?

When I got home last night, I collapsed face-first into my pillow, so I must've been asleep when the text came in: it's time-stamped 1:36 A.M.

Clara: Yes

Clara: Thank you again for the help last night.

Clara: Sorry about Reagan.

Teddy: No problem

Teddy: I actually thought she was sort of funny

Not the word I'd use, but better that he thinks the situation is funny than being awkward about it, I guess.

Clara: She's a handful when she's drunk.

Clara: I really am sorry

I waggle my thumbs as I debate whether I want to add anything else. I feel compelled to let us both off the hook. To make sure he knows that regardless of whatever was said last night, he doesn't have to worry about rehashing the past. But before I figure out what exactly I'm going to say, my previous message switches to read. Ellipses pop up, then disappear. I stare at the screen.

"Sorry about that," Mack says, pushing out the door and sitting back down at the table. "So, back to this scholarship business."

"I'll have to discuss it with my colleagues," I say, setting my phone face down. "I can't make any promises, but we might be able to divert a small amount of funds into an award, as a thank-you for your generosity. It would have to be on a limited basis, of course. Maybe one scholarship given out in your—Bucky's—name, for the next five years, or something like that. Without an endowment earning interest, it won't be possible to set it up indefinitely."

"Hey, that's good enough for me." With a grin so broad that a gold-capped molar glints in the sun, he thrusts a hand across the table. We shake on it, his grip so strong I wonder whether the circulation is being cut from my fingers. "Consider yourselves catered."

* * *

I spend the remainder of my lazy Sunday driving Reagan to pick up her Jeep and composing an email for Julien Zabini's former colleague—Dr. Lorna P. Foster, an Honorary Fellow at the School of History, Classics & Archaeology at University of Edinburgh, and author of several books, including *Meeting in the Middle Ages: The Intersection of Archeology and Manuscripts in Understanding Early Medieval Britain*. Going off her headshot on the university website—unsmiling, her white hair slicked into a military-grade bun and an enamel pin of a white rose fastened to her tweed lapel—I have a strong suspicion that she's one of those no-nonsense types, which frankly makes sending an unsolicited email a little scary.

I can only hope Julien reached out to her first, but considering he didn't mention it, I'm probably on my own here.

From: Clara Fernsby (clara_fernsby@irving.edu)
To: Lorna P. Foster (lorna.foster@ed.ac.uk)

Date: September 15, 7:42 P.M.
Subject: Invitation to guest lecture
Hello, Dr. Foster,
My name is Clara Fernsby. I'm a colleague of Julien Zabini's at University of Irving in Maryland. He passed your email along to me to see whether you might be interested in coming to campus to give a guest lecture while you're visiting D.C. in November. I realize it's a bit of a drive, but I'd be more than happy to arrange transportation if you're at all interested.
Thank you for your time.
Warm regards,
Clara Fernsby

I send off the email before letting myself fret over it any further and set about making some dinner. Reagan's suffering enough that there's no chance of her disappearing on me again, so I stick my head in her bedroom. "Mac and cheese, or fettuccine Alfredo?"

She's buried beneath a fuzzy Halloween blanket covered in pumpkins and witches' hats, but she peeks out from behind her phone. She's been flicking through TikTok videos for long enough that it's probably starting to melt her brain—whichever part's still left after last night. "They're the same thing. They're both pasta with cheese."

"No, they're not. One is macaroni and cheese and the other is fettuccine Alfredo." To be fair, I'm not sure I could explain what the actual difference is. "So, no preference, then?"

"Mac and cheese," she grumbles before tugging the blanket up over her head.

I'm in the kitchen waiting for the water to boil when my phone buzzes against the counter. I flip it over, half-expecting it to be Teddy finally answering my last message, but instead it's an email.

From: Lorna P. Foster (lorna.foster@ed.ac.uk)
To: Clara Fernsby (clara_fernsby@irving.edu)

Date: September 15, 7:48 P.M.
Subject: Re: Invitation to guest lecture
Julien mentioned you'd be reaching out. Let's get something on the books—I have a conference I'll be attending on the 7th, 8th, and 9th, but I should be free on the 6th or the 11th. I imagine the 10th won't work very well, seeing as it's a Sunday.
Cheers,
Lorna

It's almost 8 P.M. here, which means it's well after midnight in Scotland. But a surprising number of academic types seem to operate on odd hours, working until two in the morning and answering texts in the middle of Red Bull–fueled research sessions. Growing up homeschooled, I was never really aware that the world thought there was such a thing as a good or bad sleep schedule, because sleep was just sleep when you didn't have anyone to answer to. It made for a bit of rude awakening my first year of college, when my classes didn't wait for me to wake up.

I send Lorna a quick and enthusiastic reply—*The 11th would be great!*—as well as a few questions to iron out details before I open the box of dried elbow pasta and dump it into the boiling water. I should be in a good mood—today's been a pretty productive day—but it feels like my head's everywhere *except* today. In the past, in the future, in a strange sort of in-between, thinking about what the past might have been and what the future will never be. And for some reason, I'm thinking about Federal Hill Park.

Maybe it's the long-distance emails. Maybe it's last night and the unanswered texts and that nagging compulsion to let us both off the hook, because if I'm being honest with myself, I probably need that more than Teddy needs it. He seems to have no trouble ignoring things—I mean, he still hasn't answered my text—yet here I am, thinking about everything.

I pick up a wooden spoon and stir the pasta, even though it probably doesn't need stirring. I'm not going to think about it.

I'm not.

CHAPTER

15

"What do you think so far?"

I thumbed the corner of the page, trying to decide how I wanted to phrase my thoughts. We were lounging on the hill overlooking the Inner Harbor, boats meandering past the Baltimore skyline on the other side of the water. It was a cool and gray spring day—not ideal for a picnic, but we had stopped by a local café to grab a couple sandwiches to go. Now, post-lunch, we sprawled on a rough, key-patterned blanket on the grassy knoll behind the park benches, swapping books.

Teddy nudged my foot with his, trying to get my attention. He was lying on his back, my own battered and annotated copy of *The Wars of the Roses* fanned across his chest.

"It's good, but it feels . . ." I hesitated, not wanting to hurt his feelings. He'd recommended the book, after all. "I don't know. Reductive? I just feel like history is more complicated than the author's making it out to be."

He marked his page in Gillingham with a finger before propping up on an elbow to look at me, squinting one eye against the blinding gray overcast. "It's more enjoyable if you remember that it's sort of interdisciplinary," he said. "It's not written for historians so much as for the average reader. Someone who wouldn't normally pick up a history book."

"No, I get that," I said. "It's just that—well, it's really *broad*. I don't necessarily disagree with him, but . . ."

". . . but it's maybe not your favorite approach to history?"

I gave him a weak smile. "Maybe not."

He leaned back against the blanket, folding an arm behind his head. "I've thought a lot about what you said that one time. About how you like history because people have always been people."

"Did I say that?" I flipped onto my stomach so that I could read more comfortably.

He nodded. "I think I like it because they're all dead."

"Wow. That's dark."

He chuckled under his breath, casting a sidelong glance at me. "I just mean . . . you can spend your whole life trying to figure people out and they'll still surprise you. You never know for sure what they're going to do next. But everybody in here"—he tapped the cover of *The Wars of the Roses* with his index finger—"their whole lives are behind them. And we've got it all in front of us, charters and log books and love letters, and it's all down to what we make of it. How we choose to interpret it."

"Makes sense," I said. "But even dead people can surprise you."

He hummed thoughtfully. For a moment, we fell silent. A light breeze swept over the hillside, whispering through the budding trees and rustling the pages of my book so that I had to hold them down with a finger.

"I've been thinking that might be what I want to study."

"Dead people?"

"History," he said, with a slight tilt of his head, like he was conceding that it was more or less the same thing. "I've done a year of general ed, I'm overdue to pick a major. And it's the only thing that really interests me." He paused again, contemplating. I tried not to feel too flattered that my passion for history had rubbed off on him, but it was almost impossible. "And if I focus on research, I might not have to deal with all that many people," he said finally.

"Living people, that is."

"Right."

"I don't know why you worry so much," I said with a sigh. "You get along with me just fine."

"I've told you." He shifted onto his side again, closing his book and setting it on the blanket between us. He rested his hand there, firmly on the book but mere inches from my waist. "You're different."

"I know you've said that." I licked my lips and his gaze dropped to my mouth. "I guess I've just never really known what you mean by it."

"Sort of like—" He hesitated, then groaned and rolled onto his back. "Never mind. It's going to sound ridiculous."

"No. Tell me."

He sighed. "Do you think it's possible that you're meant to meet someone?"

"What, like fate?" I asked.

He was quiet for a long moment, head angled toward me, eyes searching my face. My heart was pounding, though I wasn't sure why. "I don't know," he said softly. "Maybe."

With most things, I was a skeptic. I didn't believe it until I'd googled it, read everything I could find on a given subject. But maybe I wasn't so skeptical about fate. After all, maybe it was fate that we met in the cafeteria that rainy day, fate that we drew the same number during the three-legged race. Fate that our birthdays were a day apart, as though Teddy was born and the universe realized the next day that it had almost forgotten his twin flame.

I didn't mean to leave him hanging. But him staring at me like that was making me feel all sorts of things I shouldn't have been feeling, so I forced myself to look down at the book, still splayed open in front of me. "Blueprints and Borrowed Letters," the chapter title read—and beneath that, the page was freckled with water. I looked up at the sky, flinching when a drop landed on my cheek. "Looks like it's starting to rain."

Teddy glanced skyward. "Huh."

And then, before either of us had a chance to react, the sky opened up, like it had only been waiting for acknowledgment.

I squealed as we gathered everything haphazardly in our arms, books and crumpled-up sandwich wrappers. Teddy canopied the blanket over our heads and I ducked in close, the scent of him mingling with the earthy smell of rain. We made a beeline for the Volvo. At the driver side door, I fumbled with the keys. Teddy waited until I was inside the car to hurry around to the passenger side and then collapsed into his seat.

We looked at each other, breathless and laughing. I remembered two things at once: first, a similar sprint to shelter, one I took with Izzy three years ago, the day Teddy and I first met; second, that he had asked me a question just moments ago, and in our bid to outrun the rain, I hadn't answered.

"Yes," I panted.

His grin faltered. His eyes darted to my lips and back up again. "What?"

"Yes, I believe in fate."

He held my gaze for a beat, his damp hair curling at the ends and glasses flecked with water. The rain beat against the roof of the car, streaked down the windows, shielding us from the outside world. Then he leaned across the center console, took my chin in his hand, and pulled me toward him, lips meeting mine in the middle.

It was only awkward for a second, finding our bearings,

but his mouth was warm and inviting, and so I melted into the kiss. His tongue parted my lips, sending a wave of heat crashing through me. I'd never been kissed before; I'd tried to imagine it countless times, but this was so much more *real*.

And that terrified me. I broke the kiss, drawing back a little. His eyes searched my face, thumb still tracing my jaw.

"Sorry," I whispered. "It's just—"

"No, I'm sorry." He sighed and leaned back in his seat, hand sliding from my face. "I shouldn't have done that."

"No, it's—" I shook my head, reaching for his hand and interlacing my fingers with his. "I'm glad you did it." There were a million thoughts buzzing around my head, emotions that I didn't know how to name. But we were only seventeen. I remembered what Teddy had said last year about not letting anyone stand in the way of his goals. I pictured my future the way Teddy talked about the past—primary sources spread across a desktop, tattered books and text messages and half-finished applications to Ivy Leagues. I couldn't afford to feel this way, because it could only mean one of two things: either we'd suffer through years of long distance, or one of us would have to compromise. Kissing dream schools goodbye for the sake of living closer to one another, one of us working a dead-end job while the other earned a degree they might never use. Like my parents. Like his parents. The thought of it was suffocating.

That didn't mean I wanted to let go of whatever this was. But Teddy was my best friend. And I needed a friend right now, more than I needed a boyfriend. I took a deep breath. "Teddy, I—"

"I'm leaving for Greece," he blurted. I snapped my mouth shut, stunned into silence. "As soon as the semester's over. To visit my aunt and uncle for the first week, but then my lab partner invited me to go backpacking around Europe with some friends."

I should've been relieved. And I was, in a way—relieved that he wasn't asking anything of me, wasn't making any grandiose promises that neither of us would be able to keep in the long run. But equally, I was sad. A sort of premature loneliness washed over me, knowing that I wouldn't see him for a while. I wouldn't be able to text him that I needed a distraction and have him show up at my door the next day, a folded blanket tucked under his arm and his backpack crammed with used books.

The rain outside had lessened, but water still streaked down the windshield so that Federal Hill Park looked like an Impressionist painting.

"Just for the summer," Teddy clarified. "I'll be back in August for school."

"I guess that means we should maybe put a pin in the whole conversation," I said quietly. "If I'm not going to see you for a few months."

After a moment's deliberation, he nodded once, decisive. "Okay. We'll wait."

CHAPTER

16

September breezes by so fast that before I know it, we're already in the first week of October, and the gala is looming ever closer. I'm trying not to stress, because for the most part, it's coming together. Various local businesses agreed to donate gift certificates for the raffle. Limitless Party Supply donated two boxes' worth of autumn decorations—last year's overstock that would've been sold this year for 75 percent off anyway, because apparently mushrooms and orange twinkle lights have fallen out of fashion sometime in the last twelve months, but for my purposes, they're perfect: cute, secular, and inoffensive. And on Monday, I'm picking up the vinyl banners from the office supply store the next town over. But I'm starting to feel a little overworked, strained—a button sewn on with a single thread, threatening to pop at the slightest movement. I keep reminding myself that it won't be like this forever, that this is only one semester, but between my classes, the gala, and rewriting my dossier, I haven't had a lot of time to myself. I haven't touched my article about Elizabeth of York in weeks, let alone polished it up enough to submit to journals.

I burst into Franklin 106 like a storm banging through the shutters, causing everyone's heads to snap up. "Sorry, sorry," I say, breathless. I'm fifteen minutes late to our Thursday meeting. I let my messenger bag drop from my shoulder and it hits the floor with a *thump* as I plant myself in the seat between Bel and Teddy. "One of my students had a few questions about the midterm and I lost track of time."

Teddy's brows pinch together and I give him a tiny shake of my head.

"Fine. Great," Gary says, his tone a mixture of boredom and annoyance that doesn't sound anywhere near *fine*, never mind *great*. "Let's get this thing over with, shall we?"

We cruise through everything on the agenda at breakneck speed, partly because everyone's over this and just wants to get on with their day, but also because there isn't a ton to address. Beside me, Bel fidgets with an acorn-shaped earring, twisting it between her thumb and forefinger. Asking her to participate on the scholarship committee wasn't part of our deal, but subcommittee members are technically required to be part of the overseeing committee, so she's shown up like clockwork every Thursday—looking bored out of her mind, sure, but present, and words can't express how much I owe her for all this. As soon as I declare the meeting adjourned, everyone pops up like dandelions, collecting their things. I've met students less eager to escape a classroom.

"Before we go," I say, earning a murderous look from Bel and a very audible sigh from Gary, "this is off the record, not official committee business or anything, but I just wanted to ask to see whether you guys have any local performers to recommend for entertainment. For the gala," I clarify, because Trina is looking at me like I'm from Mars.

"I haven't listened to music since '83," Gary says, deadpan. I can't tell if that's his idea of humor or if he's serious. Neither would really surprise me.

"I could ask my band," Dean Goodman offers, running a

hand through his thinning blond hair so that it stands on end like he's Beetlejuice. Trina narrows her eyes at him, like he's betrayed some secret pact to barricade my progress every step of the way. Considering how standoffish they've all been, maybe he has. But he just shrugs. "I might not buy into this whole gala business, but a gig is a gig."

"What sort of music do you guys play?" I ask.

"We're a cover band. Mostly indie rock or alternative. Think Arcade Fire, Death Cab for Cutie, that sort of thing."

Not exactly in my wheelhouse, but not that far off, either. "Are the songs clean?" I ask. "I mean, are the lyrics sort of family friendly?"

Goodman squints. "We could *make* them family friendly."

"Then great," I say. "That works for me."

He digs around in his laptop bag and unearths a business card that identifies the band as Eleventy-One Elephants, complete with an Instagram handle and a SoundCloud. Afterward, Goodman and Trina and Gary all leave in a whirlwind of notebooks slapping shut and book bags swinging from slumped shoulders. Bel and Teddy are left behind, both seeming to purposefully linger, and I'm not sure whose purpose I'm dreading more.

"So I won't be able to make it to the subcommittee meeting tomorrow," Bel says. I already suspect she's abandoning me for Krav Maga. "My aunt is flying in from Atlanta and needs a ride from the airport."

Okay, so maybe not Krav Maga, though I can't rule out an elaborate cover story. "No worries. I'll email you the minutes."

Bel mumbles a *thank you*. She'll likely never read the minutes even if I do email them—and to be fair, I don't blame her, because she's only really in this for me. And maybe for her resume. She scurries out of Franklin 106 and I follow not far behind, slinging my messenger bag around my neck as I go.

"Hey, wait up."

I turn. Teddy jogs to catch up with me in the bright, fluorescent hall of the Franklin Complex. I wasn't *trying* to skip out before he had a chance to talk to me, but if I'm being honest, I've thought about him more than I'm comfortable with these past few weeks. I feel like I need to put a little distance between us.

"So for tomorrow," he says, "I was thinking maybe we meet at The Falconer again."

"Why?" I ask. We'd met on campus the past couple of meetings after I emailed administration and managed to secure one of the conference rooms on the third floor of the Hall of Letters.

"To be entirely honest, because you look like you could use a drink."

I snort. He's not wrong, but I don't want to admit that he's *right,* either. I push through the glass double doors, emerging into the brisk evening. The beech trees have turned yellow and the maples have faded to a dull ochre; their leaves sweep up in the wind. "How do you figure?"

He gives me a sidelong look, because there's nothing he could say that I don't already know. *I've known you since you had braces, so I can sort of tell when you're stressed out and overworked.*

I press my lips together. "Right."

He flips around and walks backward so that he can look at me, his coffee-brown curls tousled by the breeze. "So, The Falconer, then?" he asks. When I just keep walking, he ducks down in a way that forces me to look at him, all puppy dog eyes. That's a new one. I guess he's learned a few tricks over the years. "Please say yes. If I'm being honest, I could use a drink, too."

I sigh, resigned. "The Falconer it is." I'm certain this is a bad idea, but I'm helpless to put a stop to it.

* * *

By the time I arrive at The Falconer on Friday, seven minutes behind schedule, it's packed with people. A Dropkick Murphys song rattles the dark wood paneling, so loud that it's hard to hear myself think. I find Teddy at one of the booths, a pair of drinks already on the table. He's almost drained his gin and tonic, the wedge of lime bled dry. The other drink—a chocolatey one in a skinny martini glass—sits untouched on the opposite side of the table.

I slide into the booth across from him. "What's this?" I ask, indicating the martini. I have to raise my voice to be heard over all the chatter.

"A cold brew martini with gin." Upon noticing my raised eyebrows, he explains, "That was still your drink of choice, last I checked. Which was"—he pretends to consult an invisible watch—"a couple weeks ago, I'm pretty sure."

"Thanks." I pinch the stem between my fingers and raise it in a quick toast before taking a sip.

And then I cough.

He winces. "I might've asked them to make it a double shot," he admits. "Thought you might need it."

I shoot him an exasperated look before taking another, more experimental sip. It's a bit strong, sure, but this time I'm expecting it, and he's also not wrong. I probably do need it.

"You look nice," he says. "The . . ." He waves his hand around his own face. "Makeup, I mean. And the hair."

"High praise," I mumble, though I can't help feeling mollified that he noticed. I asked Reagan if I could borrow some of her makeup, because I figured if I'm once again going to find myself in a bar on a Friday evening, I might as well look the part.

Teddy looks like he might say something else, but he's distracted by a guy with a neat, square beard standing on a stool in front of the bar so that he towers over the throng. He flips on a cheap karaoke microphone and it squeals from the proximity to the speakers. Some people cover their ears. Teddy doesn't react, save a slight lilt of his dark brows.

"All right," our host says after stepping down from the stool and dragging it between bargoers to put sufficient space between himself and the nearest speaker. He pops up again like a meerkat. "Welcome to The Falconer Quiz Night. Before we begin, let's lay down a couple ground rules."

"I'm sorry," I say, turning to Teddy, "did he just say 'quiz night'?"

"First Friday of every month," Teddy confirms, raising the remainder of his gin and tonic to his lips and downing it. He lowers the glass, frowning at my expression. "Don't look so scared. It's team based."

"I'm not worried about beating you," I say sharply. He *did* beat me at trivia on that rainy day in the cafeteria the summer we first met, but he hasn't beaten me since, and he knows it. "I guess I'm just—we're supposed to be having a meeting here. Maybe we should go somewhere else. My car or—"

Wait, scratch that. My car, alone with Teddy, is an obviously bad idea.

"Clara. Look at me." His deep voice is so authoritative that I listen almost instinctively, turning and blinking at him across the table. "Everything for the gala is on schedule," he says firmly. "Better than on schedule. You've gone above and beyond to make this thing work. I think you can afford to take the night off."

"I really shouldn't."

"Please." His brown eyes soften, pleading, maple syrup running over pancakes. "For old times' sake, if nothing else."

I blow out a breath. *For old times' sake.* Practically the magic words, though I'm not sure he knows it. Everything about him is always so nostalgic and sticky-sweet, and that's exactly why rekindling our friendship is a bad idea.

One of the pub employees passes out handheld whiteboards with markers. They're blank, wiped clean of most of the evidence of last month's quiz night. "It's been a while since I've played trivia. And I still suck at sports questions."

The employee fills in a series of team names on a chalkboard behind the bar, like QUIZ ON MY FACE and THE CUNNING LINGUISTS, because this isn't sleepaway camp anymore. When the host adds I AM SMARTACUS to the board, I suck a surprised breath and my head whips back to Teddy.

"I'll handle the sports questions," he says, eroding my resolve. "But I'm pretty sure you'll nail the rest."

The quiz kicks off with science questions. The host reads from a sheet of paper and everyone scribbles their answers on the whiteboard, holding them up when the timer goes off. The blackboard behind the bar tracks the scores, with bartenders pausing in the middle of pouring beer from the tap or shaking cocktail shakers to add chalky tally lines next to each of the team names. We make it through a question about Nikola Tesla without argument, but then the host asks, "Which planet in our solar system has the most moons?"

I lean into the table so that Teddy can hear me beneath all the noise. "Saturn," I say, thinking back to that night sixteen summers ago, cross-legged in the damp grass and staring up at the sky with a chart splayed on my lap. "I think."

"Not Jupiter?" he asks uncertainly. "Ganymede, Io, Europa, what's the other one, Calypso?"

"Callisto," I correct him. "And anyway, just because you can name more of Jupiter's moons doesn't mean it has more. Look at the size of Saturn's rings."

After a hushed debate, we agree to write Saturn, and I scrawl it across our board just as the timer goes off. Around the room, teams are holding up their respective answers. Most of them say Saturn, though a couple say Jupiter.

"The correct answer is Saturn," the host confirms, and I lower the board back to the table.

"Told you," I say, wiping the board clean.

We work our way through the questions. Despite my initial reluctance, I've always been a little bit competitive about trivia, and that familiar rush pushes past any lingering reservations. I want to get the answers right, bickering with Teddy over Jane Austen characters and the invention of penicillin. He nails a question about *Game of Thrones,* which I've never actually watched, and in our excitement, we exchange a high five across the table. Another team—Dazed and Confused—has taken the lead, but we're not that far behind, and between the two of us, I'm pretty sure we can catch up. After struggling through a couple questions and breezing through others, we finally reach the history section.

"What year did Martin Luther nail his Ninety-five Theses to the door of the castle church in Wittenberg?"

"That would be, what, sometime in the sixteenth century? You ought to know this," Teddy says.

"I mean, I specialize more in early Tudor history than continental stuff," I say, which is mostly true. But I also wrote a paper about the formation of the Church of England for undergrad, and I'm sure I mentioned Martin Luther somewhere in there. It's been so long, my honors thesis is little more than a vague and foggy memory, buried somewhere on the hard drive of my old MacBook. What about more recently? I had an article published in *Renaissance Quarterly* a couple years ago, analyzing the tone of a letter written by Anne of Cleves in response to Henry VIII's request for annulment. Anne was born in Germany around the time the reformation started, and her family had some involvement in it. What involvement? I should know this. But that doesn't mean I do. Not when I'm put on the spot with Teddy deferring to me. "Anne of Cleves was born in 1515. And I think . . . I think maybe it was a couple years after that. 1517."

"How certain are you?" he asks.

"Not a hundred percent," I admit. "Call it an educated guess. Unless you know the answer?"

He doesn't, and he writes the year down in sloppy, square numbers. His handwriting has grown careless over the years, like he doesn't have time to ensure it's neat and legible anymore. We wait for the timer to go off.

"The correct answer is 1517," the host announces, and we grin at each other across the table, victorious. Teddy orders a couple of shots of whisky when a server passes by our table, and despite the fact that I haven't done a shot since undergrad, I accept it, clinking glasses with him before stamping it on the table and tossing it back. A comfortable, toasty feeling settles over me. I'm starting to feel like it's okay to be here, enjoying this. It's Friday, and aside from grading a few discussion posts on Sunday night, I don't have anything looming over me.

We sail through the rest of the history questions with relative ease, but so do a number of other teams. It's neck and neck right now, anyone's game. And then the host announces the theme for the next round of questions.

Sports trivia.

When I was growing up, on the rare occasions my dad was actually at home before his injury, he would sometimes force me to sit on the couch and watch the Orioles game with him. Baseball was America's Pastime, he said, and to not enjoy it would be very un-American. His intentions were good, but it backfired during my teen years, when sitting on the couch with my dad was the last way I wanted to spend my weekend. The end result was that I pledged to never watch another game, baseball or otherwise. And I've done a pretty good job of sticking by that. I've never been to one of Irving's football matches. I refuse to watch the World Cup or Wimbledon. The only sport I get any real enjoyment out of watching is those mock jousts they put on at the

Renaissance Faire, and that's not really a sport—it's more like choreographed entertainment.

Which has all been fine and good, until now. Now, my competitive streak is cursing me for not paying attention. Teddy said he'll handle the sports questions, but I'm not sure he's much of a sports person, either—or at least he didn't used to be, but maybe that's changed. Maybe Mindy dragged him to hockey games and bought him monogrammed jerseys and shared hot dogs with him at PNC Park.

I shouldn't be thinking about her. It's not her fault we drifted apart, and I know that she's well out of his life now, but it's always felt a little like salt in an open wound. I'll never forget that afternoon in the sandwich shop, three whole years after we'd fallen out of touch. He couldn't even look at me.

The host reads off a question about basketball, something about hoops and points that sails right over my head, but Teddy writes down an answer—which turns out to be wrong. Next comes a question about which city hosted the 1936 Summer Olympics.

"Oh, I know this one," I say.

"I'm pretty sure a lot of people know this one," he reminds me with a gentle smile, and the tallies confirm it. As of right now, we're tied with The Cunning Linguists. There's a chance we might actually win this.

"How many times have the Philadelphia Eagles appeared in the Super Bowl?"

Teddy leans back in his chair, folding his arms—which I can't help but study, the sleeves of his dress shirt rolled to the elbow, toned forearm muscle and a dusting of dark hair visible—and stares thoughtfully at the ceiling. "Two," he says, when he comes back down to earth. "I'm thinking two."

"How certain are you?" I ask, echoing his earlier question.

He teeters his head back and forth. "Fairly certain. My dad was always an Eagles fan."

Not particularly reassuring, but I don't have a leg to stand on, so we go with two.

The answer is four.

"All right, last question of the night, for double points," the host announces. I turn away from Teddy and straighten in my seat, prepared to give the question my full and undivided attention. If we can just answer this question, we might overtake The Cunning Linguists. "How many horses are on each team in a polo match?"

And with that, my heart plummets. I have no idea. At least baseball and football are the sort of games blue-collar families go to, the sort my dad tuned into every Sunday, but polo is a world away. I glance at Teddy, but he shakes his head faintly. He doesn't know either. Why does it feel like neither of us ever seem to have the answers? We've done fine at this quiz night, sure, because we've always been book smart, good at the *facts,* the research, the technical stuff.

But it's never been enough.

"You have thirty seconds," the host calls out.

"We have to write something down," Teddy says. "Maybe . . . I don't know . . . ten?"

I shake my head. "Ten sounds like too many." Don't ask me why it sounds like too many, considering I've never seen a polo match in my life, but it just does. Like there aren't enough stuck-up rich folks to maintain those numbers.

"Eight seems reasonable," he suggests instead, holding my gaze.

Nothing about what I'm feeling right now is reasonable. I press my lips together, wishing he would just take the plunge. Commit to a probably wrong answer. But neither of us wants to be the one to do it.

"Ten seconds."

He exhales. "Should we go with eight and call it a day?"

"It's too many," I say again.

"Five," the host begins counting down.

"Well, what do you suggest?" Teddy demands.

"Four," the host says.

"Four, just put four," I say in a panic.

"Three."

Teddy's dark brows are sky high above the frame of his glasses. "You're sure?"

"Two."

I just shrug. I don't have time to say anything.

"One."

He writes a hasty four on the board.

"Time's up. Let's see those answers."

I swivel on my stool to see what the other teams have written down. One of the kids at the table behind us holds their whiteboard aloft, and written on it is a magnificent, sloppy four. It's sheer luck that we got it right, but I know that we got it right, because now the host is announcing "The correct answer is four" and one of the bartenders is using his free hand to tally on the chalkboard. And we've won. We beat a bunch of drunk college kids at a quiz night. We high-five across the table, laughing a little at our own ridiculousness, because we *better* have beaten them, if we think we're qualified to teach.

We order some waters and talk a little about work while waiting for the buzz from the drinks to wear off, and then we call it a night at seven thirty, because apparently we're getting old.

"I guess maybe you were right," I concede as Teddy walks me to my car. Wind rustles the trees and dead leaves clatter in the gutters, and I hug myself, wishing I'd brought a coat. "I did sort of need this."

He peers at me curiously. "Is that a 'thank you' I'm hearing?"

I give him a tight-lipped smile. "Maybe something like that."
We stop when we reach my dinged-up Volvo. "Well, this is me,"
I say, and then I immediately feel dumb, because of course he
remembers my car. I've only had it forever. "Oh! Let me get you
for the drinks."

I unlock the driver side door and bend across the seat to dig
in the change-filled cupholder, looking for the ten-dollar bill I
stuffed in there a couple weeks ago after picking up the McDonald's for Reagan. "No, really, it's fine—" Teddy tries to protest,
but he cuts himself short as he leans over my shoulder, close
enough that I can feel the heat radiating from him, a little too
inviting in the evening air. "You still keep change in that thing?"

"And bills, sometimes. Aha!"

I straighten up with the crumpled ten in hand, victorious—
and bump into Teddy in the process. He steadies me with a
hand on my upper arm, lingering a couple seconds longer than
necessary before letting it drop to his side. "I can see why you
worry about getting robbed. You're aware that leaving money
lying in plain sight is probably a bad idea?"

I pat the side of the Volvo. "So is this thing being allowed
on the road, but the Maryland Motor Vehicle Administration
hasn't put a stop to me, yet." I smooth the crumpled bill against
the window, leaving behind scattered, smudged fingerprints before holding the money out to Teddy.

He stares at it, shaking his head. "I'm not going to accept
this."

"Donate it to the scholarship fund," I tease, pressing it to his
chest. The muscle is firm and warm beneath the fabric of his shirt,
and against my better judgment, I don't pull my hand away.

"That endowment would earn . . ." He casts a glance skyward, like he's doing the math in his head. "A penny a year, by
my calculations." His gaze drops back to me, irises swallowed
up by black in the dim glow of the yellow streetlamps. He takes

a step toward me, so that it's just my hand separating us. My heart thumps in my fingers—or maybe that's his heart. It's impossible to say.

"I think your math might be a little off," I say, my voice barely more than a whisper. "It would definitely earn less than a penny."

He chuckles under his breath, reaching up to touch something—to touch *me*. "Numbers were never really my strong suit." My breath catches in my throat as his fingers find the Tudor coin pendant I've always worn, his thumb brushing over the burnished nickel. I wonder whether he reads into me wearing it, thinks it's anything other than force of habit, something for me to fidget with when I'm lost in thought. His eyes flick back up to my lips.

I swallow. My mind has gone blissfully blank. But he doesn't bend to kiss me. Seeming to emerge from some sort of trance, he shakes his head faintly and takes a step back. I try not to feel too disappointed.

"I should get going," I say. "I told Reagan I'd pick up dinner."

He only nods, his face an expressionless mask.

I bid him good night, climb into my car, and fix my eyes on the road. I'm on a sort of autopilot for the drive home, headlights and ruby-red brake lights passing across my windshield in the night. I'd like to believe that this, too, will pass. But it occurs to me that I am very much in danger of the thing I've been most afraid of: loving a man who knows better than to open his heart to me again.

CHAPTER

17

That summer was hot and boring. Earlier that same year, we'd had back-to-back blizzards that blanketed Maryland in more snow than I'd ever seen in my life, but the summer that followed was largely forgettable. I never thought of myself as struggling to find things to do—I'd spent a good chunk of my life at home, after all, and had gotten pretty good at entertaining myself—but for those three months, I felt a little lost. Come September, I'd have to start thinking about college, mapping out my future, but in the meantime, I existed to make my parents' lives easier. There was an uneasy sort of truce in the house—my parents had stopped arguing every night, but now it felt like they hardly spoke to each other. I drove Dad to his physical therapy appointments and watched Reagan while Mom was at work. I couldn't find the motivation to pick up a book and I barely saw my friends.

I kept in touch with Teddy over Facebook; his replies were sporadic, dependent on whether he had internet access in whatever hostel he was staying in. So naturally, when I booted up the computer on a random Wednesday morning in July and realized he was online, I decided to post a status update to mess with him.

Well-behaved women seldom make history—Eleanor Roosevelt

Within minutes, he'd liked the status, and then an instant message popped up on my screen.

> Teddy: How do you suppose Laurel Thatcher Ulrich feels when you attribute that quote to Eleanor Roosevelt

> Teddy: ?

> Clara: Who is Laurel Thatcher Ulrich? I thought it was a quote by Anne Boleyn

> Teddy: Haha

> Teddy: You can't fool me

> Teddy: I know a Mary Todd Lincoln quote when I see one

> Clara: I've missed this

> Teddy: I've missed you

> Teddy: Free for a video call?

Ten minutes later, I'd set up my webcam, hurriedly swept my fingers through my hair to make sure I didn't look like I'd just crawled out of bed, and clicked to accept. Teddy materialized on the screen, a little pixelated at first, but then it cleared. Warm light spilled through the hostel window and his handsome face split into a broad grin. "Hey," he said.

"Hi," I said back, smiling so hard my cheeks hurt. "How's Europe?"

"Great. We're in Bruges right now, but tomorrow we'll catch a train back to Brussels, and then it's over to London." He said this very fast, with breathless wonder, as though it was still surreal, even for him. "Clara, there's so much history over here. You'd love it."

My heart squeezed in my chest, an ache and a relief all at once, like massaging a sore muscle. I wanted to be there with him, to decide for myself. But I didn't voice that; we hadn't discussed what transpired that day at the park, just as promised. It could wait. "Bruges," I repeated. "They're famous for, what? Painting?"

"Lacemaking," he corrected me, "but I think most people visit for the architecture."

"How's the weather?" I cringed even as I was asking it. It was a throwaway question, impersonal, the sort of thing my mom asked strangers while paying the cable bill over the phone. But I wanted to live a little vicariously, to imagine something other than being cooped up in the house.

"Pretty mild," he said. "It was hotter down in Marseille, though."

They'd spent at least two weeks backpacking through Provence-Alpes-Côte d'Azur, couch surfing and staying in cheap hostels. The Mediterranean had treated him well, it seemed. His olive skin was tanned to a deep bronze and the shadow of stubble traced his jaw. He looked good. *Really* good.

"I hope you're taking lots of pictures," I said.

"I am, but I won't be able to upload them until—" He was interrupted by knocking and pivoted at the waist to look over his shoulder. Hinges groaned and a male voice drawled somewhere off screen, but I couldn't quite make out what it was saying.

"Right," Teddy said to him. "Yeah, I know. Be there in five." He turned back to me, raising his eyebrows in that way that said, wordlessly, *This guy is annoying the hell out of me.* "Sorry. Not a lot of privacy, traveling like this."

A triple bunk with a metal frame was pushed up against the wall behind him, the bleached white sheets tangled on the bottom bed. I wondered what he needed privacy for. Insecurity bubbled to the surface, because maybe he wanted to bring girls back to his room, but I shoved that thought back down.

It wasn't any of my business what he was doing, because we'd put that conversation on hold, at least *for now*—however long that was. And while it was hard to get a read on things without seeing him in person, I could tell that our friendship hadn't gone back to normal, exactly. The kiss had changed things, a shifting of tectonic plates that had settled but left a permanent fault line.

"Hey, so I've been meaning to tell you," he continued, "but I wanted to wait until I could actually do it, you know"—he indicated the camera—"face-to-face, sort of, or at least as close to face-to-face as we can get. My application for transfer got accepted. I'm going to Cornell in the spring."

I blinked at him, processing the new information, because my mind was still on him flirting with French girls. "But that's all the way up in New York."

"I was expecting something more along the lines of 'Congratulations, Teddy, that's great.'"

"I'm sorry, it's just—" I tried and failed to put what I was feeling into words. This was exactly why we couldn't be anything more. I didn't want to resent Teddy for getting in to his dream school, for succeeding in all the things he wanted to do. But it felt as though the plates were shifting again, the fault widening.

I put on a tight-lipped smile. "Congratulations. I'm happy for you. I really am."

"Thank you," he said, a little wary.

I could sense that he was still a little bothered by my initial reaction, so I elected to change the subject. "So, London."

He swept a hand through his hair, mussing the loose curls. He hadn't had a haircut in months, probably, but it suited him. "For a few days. Then it's over to Cardiff."

"I'm so jealous," I breathed. I'd always wanted to travel, but the farthest I'd ever been was my grandmother's house in Knoxville. And my parents certainly weren't in a position to pay for any summers spent abroad, so I likely wouldn't get to go anywhere until I could pay for it myself.

"I'll bring you a souvenir," he said, like it was my consolation prize, but I looked forward to it anyway.

* * *

We didn't see each other for an entire year.

Because he'd finished with the homeschooling program a year ahead of schedule, Teddy didn't attend camp that September. A part of me mourned, because it hadn't crossed my mind that last year would be *his* last year, and now it was my last year and it didn't feel the same without him.

I hadn't told anyone about the kiss in the spring, but I ended up confessing to Izzy the first week of camp. It was an usually warm day for September, and we'd decided to lie out by the lake. "It's like Allie and Noah in *The Notebook*," she said, a lithe brown arm slung over her eyes to shield them from the sun. "Sometimes people drift apart because the timing's not right, but if they're meant to be together, they find their way back to each other in the end."

I picked at a loose terry cloth fiber in the towel I was lying on. "Okay, but they were actually in a relationship. Teddy and I are just—" I broke off, because I wasn't sure *friends* summed it up anymore.

That night, drowsy after a day of sunbathing and swimming, she insisted on putting *The Notebook* on her laptop before bed—for "educational purposes." I'd seen it before—several times and often under duress, because it was one of my mom's favorites—but when Izzy passed out about ten minutes in, drooling on her pillow, I had little else to occupy my thoughts. I lay awake on my side, propped up on an elbow with only the cold light of the laptop screen for company.

When the movie reached the first fumbling sex scene, my heart sped up. I was going to be eighteen by the end of the school year and I hadn't had sex yet. I didn't know if eighteen was late for that sort of thing, and I felt all the more naïve for not knowing. I shut the laptop and rolled onto my back, staring at the ceiling in the dark. Teddy was the only boy I'd ever kissed. I never thought of myself as particularly sheltered—I'd had unrestricted access to the internet in recent years, with plenty of time to look up sex terms like *Eiffel Tower* on Urban Dictionary, only to X out of the window, mortified—but I also had very limited practical experience.

"Izzy," I whispered. She didn't respond, so I shook her shoulder. "*Izzy.*"

"Mmm?"

"Are you a virgin?"

She lifted her head a couple inches, disheveled hair spilling around her like a lion's mane. "Virginity is a social construct."

"No, but I mean—have you done anything? With anyone?"

"Yes."

"With who?"

"Skylar. You met her, at the sleepover that one time."

I considered this for a moment. "What sort of stuff did you guys do?"

Izzy made a noncommittal noise into her pillow. "Touching," she said, her voice muffled. "And I sent her some pictures."

"Pictures?" I hissed, surprised. "What kind of pictures?"

"Just me in a bikini. And underwear, one time." She lifted up to fluff her pillow and turned her head to the other side. "Can we go back to sleep now?"

"Sorry. Good night." I crawled out of Izzy's bed and back to my own bunk, but I didn't fall asleep. I lay awake for hours, thinking about pictures. And I wondered if any girls had sent pictures to Teddy.

* * *

As soon as camp ended in October, I drove to a couple local universities to meet with admissions counselors, some of whom did more discouraging than actual counseling.

"But my test scores came back really good, and my GPA is almost perfect," I'd argued during a Skype call with an advisor at University of Pennsylvania, when she told me she just couldn't see how to frame my application in a way that felt competitive. "The only reason it's not a 4.0 is because I got a B in Latin, and that was an elective. I got an A in French I *and* II. I got As in everything."

She gave me a paper-thin smile. "To be frank with you, dear, I'm not sure that counts for much of anything when your mother's the one who graded you."

"But my mom's *not* the one who graded me," I said, my face hot. "I have an independent study teacher who checks all my work. The program is accredited. It's a *public* charter school, the same as any other public school, we just do the work at home."

The counselor heaved a sigh. "Well, I can't stop you from applying," she conceded. "All I'm saying is, I wouldn't get your hopes up. These homeschooling programs, they don't look great on college applications."

I applied anyway, to all the schools on my list. Penn rejected me with a polite but impersonal letter, as did several others, but

I was accepted to both Duke and Johns Hopkins—without the sort of financial aid packages that I'd hoped for. The only school that seemed to take pity on me was University of Maryland, just a stone's throw away on the outskirts of Washington D.C.

"Maybe it's a blessing in disguise, Clare Bear," Dad told me one day. I was moping at the dinner table, pushing my mashed potatoes around my plate with a fork so that the gravy spilled down the sides in rivulets. "Now you'll be closer to your family."

I suspected he felt guilty, like it was his fault for getting injured, his fault that my parents had burned through my would-be college fund when our family needed it most. I didn't resent them for it. If it weren't for our difficult financial circumstance, I probably wouldn't have gotten the aid to attend UMD at all. But it seemed lackluster compared to my friends' plans—Izzy taking a gap year to live with her cousins in Brazil, or Darvish's parents covering his full tuition to UC Berkeley.

By the time the holidays rolled around, my schedule was just too jumbled to coordinate anything with Teddy. I'd picked up a job at a local sandwich shop to help sock away money for college. Mom suggested that I invite him for Thanksgiving, but his parents wanted him to spend Thanksgiving with them, so we came to a sort of stalemate. We tried to revive Long-Distance History Club, but it was more a series of history memes and fragmented texts than any meaningful conversation.

An envelope arrived in the mail addressed to me the week before Christmas. Enclosed was a brief note from Teddy, along with the souvenir he'd promised: a reproduction Tudor six-pence on a simple leather cord. It wasn't lavish or particularly high quality—more like the sort of thing I imagined they sold in the gift shop at Hampton Court Palace—but I took to wearing it anyway.

My mom dragged us down to Knoxville for Christmas to visit my grandma, and to my surprise, Dad came as well, though neither of them talked all that much on the car ride down. Teddy and I sent our respective *Happy Birthday* texts a few days later. Our eighteenth birthdays, a turning point in our lives. We were adults now. Perhaps him more than me, in some ways—while he was away at college, I was still plunking through my last few high school requirements.

But it was also a turning point for our friendship. The longer we put this conversation off, I realized, the greater the likelihood that it would be irrevocably complicated. Maybe he'd get tangled up with some girl at school, or I'd start dating some guy in my dorm next year, when I started college. But it wasn't until the day after my birthday, New Year's Eve, that I found the courage to actually bring it up.

My family had gathered around the yellowed oak table in my grandma's dining room with plastic flutes of Martinelli's, watching Times Square on the boxy old television set. My phone buzzed in my lap and I checked it beneath the table.

> Teddy: Happy New Year's Eve. Any resolutions this year?

> Clara: Not exactly

> Clara: Do you have time for a quick phone call?

Within seconds, my phone started ringing. Incoming call: Teddy Harrison. I got up from the table.

"Where are you going?" Dad asked, indicating the television. "You're going to miss the ball drop."

"I'll just be a second," I said before slipping out of the room. I wandered over to the living room, well out of earshot from my parents. The tree was still up, decked in multicolored lights and ugly, sentimental ornaments. I held the phone to my ear. "Hello?"

"Hey," Teddy said, his voice low—like he, too, had stolen away to some dark corner to talk to me. "So what's up?"

It was only a few minutes to midnight, so there was no time for beating around the bush. "Do you remember last spring, that thing that happened in the car?"

"Well, yeah."

"We said we wouldn't talk about it. Or that we'd talk about it later, I mean." I was speaking fast, frantic, trying to get it all out before anyone came looking for me. "I'm tired of not talking about it."

"Okay," he said slowly. "What do you want to say?"

"I wanted to let you know that it's been really confusing. I'm not blaming you, it just—" I broke off, twiddling a pink light on the tree, the bulb warm to the touch. "I've thought about it. A lot. And I think it's pretty obvious that it wouldn't work. At least not right now."

Teddy chuckled awkwardly. "It's not like I asked you to marry me."

"I know, it's just—" I lowered my voice, not quite a whisper, but quiet enough that I knew there was no chance of it carrying into the next room. "That's the thing. We both want to focus on our futures. Right? We don't want to end up like our parents did."

"Right," he agreed.

"But we kissed and we're still friends." I paused, waiting for him to understand what I was saying, the big *eureka* moment, but the line was quiet. "So, I've been thinking, you know, maybe—" I took a deep breath. "Maybe we can. Kiss. And do other stuff."

"What, you mean just as friends?" he asked.

"Yes." Another pause, but still he didn't say anything. "You're being quiet. What are you thinking?"

He sighed, a rush of air into the phone. "I'm thinking that I care about you. A lot. I don't want you to get hurt."

"Then don't hurt me," I said. "As long as you keep being my friend, I promise, I won't get hurt."

I wished I could see his face, get a better read on him, but even over the phone, I sensed his hesitation. In the other room, my family started counting down to midnight.

Ten.

Nine.

Eight.

My dad's voice cut through the chant: "Where's Clara?"

Six.

Mom stepped into the living room, a flute of champagne in one hand, my Martinelli's in the other. "There you are."

"Give me five minutes to convince you," I whispered into the phone.

Three.

My mom pressed the plastic flute into my hand and ushered me back into the dining room.

Two.

One.

"All right," Teddy agreed.

I hung up just after the clock struck midnight, without ever wishing Teddy a happy new year. Grandma pulled the string on a popper, showering the table in confetti. My parents shared a quick, chaste kiss, like they were actors on a stage, trying to convince the rest of us that they were happy. Reagan blew on a paper horn, a relentless *honk, honk, honk* that drowned out whatever rendition of "Auld Lang Syne" was playing over the television. I toasted my plastic flute, downed it in two gulps, and excused myself to the bathroom, taking my phone with me.

I locked the door, peeled off my sweater, and checked my reflection in the bathroom mirror. I was wearing a coral-pink bra trimmed with lace, not a push-up or anything fancy like the stuff Izzy wore, but it didn't look bad. I tousled my hair with my fingers and stepped back from the mirror for the full effect. I felt like it looked weird to leave my jeans on, so I shimmied out of them, revealing black boy shorts. It didn't match. Was it supposed to match? But I only had a couple minutes left, so I didn't have time to change. I opened the camera on my phone and snapped a quick picture. It actually looked pretty good. Pulse hammering, I pressed send.

Afterward, I dressed and went to tell my family good night, but all I could think about was Teddy. The minutes ticked by, but he wasn't answering. I'd never sent anyone a picture like that before, and I felt suddenly more than a little self-conscious. Was he just going to ignore it? Maybe it wasn't a good picture after all.

It wasn't until I was lying in bed that he finally texted back. I reached for my phone on the nightstand, the screen blinding white in the dark.

> Teddy: I've figured out your New Year's resolution

I stared at the message, my brow knit. Maybe he didn't receive the picture. Or maybe he was trying to change the subject. I started to text back, but then he sent a follow-up message:

> Teddy: Wear that for me. In person.

CHAPTER

18

PRESENT

A heavy rain on the day before the gala forces a last-minute change of plans. I checked the forecast for weeks beforehand, with consistent results: we were due to have a big storm roll through on Thursday, the night of Halloween, but the Saturday before was predicted to be partly cloudy and mild. So it made a lot of sense to set up tables and chairs on the sprawling lawn in front of the Alumni House. Especially taking into consideration the unexpected but enthusiastic response rate on our event page on Facebook. The house itself simply isn't large enough to host this many people, but with the weather forecast uncertain for tomorrow, it's looking like the house won't have much of a choice.

"Mack, listen to me," I say, phone pressed between my shoulder and my ear as I try to disentangle myself from the fall foliage garland I'm pulling down from the pediment. We decorated the outside just two days ago. If the weather app could've been a bit quicker on the uptake, it would have saved me a whole heap of trouble, but . . .

"Would you please stop inter—" The stepstool teeters beneath me and I break off mid-word to steady myself. "For two seconds, please, *please* just hear me out without cutting me off,"

I beg, because the last five minutes have been a constant stream of complaints and vague threats like *keep your scholarships*. I'm on the verge of hanging up. "I *know* rolling out the food truck was part of your reason for agreeing to this gig"—make them feel heard, that's the first step—"but people aren't going to want to stand in line for a food truck in the rain." I step down from the stool, gathering the garland in my arms and carrying it inside.

Teddy is in the great room with Bel, who has the orange twinkle lights spooled around her arms. She enlisted him to drape the lights around the hooks in the crown molding. Mack's ranting in my ear about how this isn't what he agreed to.

"I understand that," I say. I deposit the garland on the coffee table and switch my phone to the other ear. Teddy arches a brow and I return the expression, blowing out a breath. "Well, if that's the case, then I'll just have to—" I'm interrupted by a fresh string of curse words. "I'm not sure that sort of language is necessary." Teddy abandons the twinkle lights and moves toward me. "If you could just—"

The phone is snatched from my grasp before I have a chance to react. Teddy holds it up to his ear. "Hello, Mack?" he says. There's that authoritative voice again. "I'm on the scholarship committee with Clara. What seems to be the problem?"

Everything goes quiet while he listens with his brow knit. I look over at Bel. She shrugs and pulls a face like *at least you're not having to deal with it.*

"Uh-huh." I can't make out exactly what Mack is saying, but whatever it is, it doesn't sound polite. A muscle twitches in Teddy's jaw. "Fine by us. We'll just have to remove your logo from the banners."

The phone's not on speaker, but there's no mistaking Mack telling him exactly where we can shove those banners. Teddy draws the phone away from his ear, frowning at the screen.

And then he presses the screen to end the call.

I toss a hand in the air, dropping it with such force that it slaps my thigh. "Great. So we're down a caterer." I spin on the spot like I'm going to walk off, but then immediately spin back again. I don't know what to do with all this pent-up frustration. I plant my hands on my hips and fix him with a glare. "I was trying to talk him down."

"Very professionally, I might add." Teddy hands me my phone, all easy posture, his other hand tucked into the pocket of his sweatpants. We all dressed comfortably today, but whereas my threadbare Phi Alpha Theta hoodie and black leggings make me look like I'm desperately clinging to my college years, he manages to look good in sweats and a T-shirt.

"What do you want me to do, cuss the guy out?" I ask.

"He seemed to have no problem cussing you out."

"Which I was willing to overlook because he was doing us a *favor*. It's not like we were paying him."

Teddy scoffs. "Guys like that don't work for free. He was doing it for the exposure." He flings a hand at our surroundings, stacks of colorful flyers and scattered autumn decorations, like a tornado ripped through a crafting store. "The scholarship and the banners."

"The banners!" I slap a hand to my forehead, rounding again to where the vinyl banners lie in a haphazard pile, waiting to be hung. I lift one by the corner like it's contaminated, a used napkin or a dirty dishrag. The oversized Bucky's logo is printed among our other sponsors. "We don't have time to get them reprinted."

"I'll paint over them," Bel volunteers. Teddy and I both turn to look at her. "What? I have white paint. It'll be like using Wite-Out, only bigger."

"What about the food?" I ask.

"Let me make a quick call," Teddy says before excusing

himself and cutting across the hall. His deep voice carries from the other room, too muffled by the old horsehair plaster to hear what he's saying.

I look over at Bel. "Do you think ordering pizza would be tacky?"

She shrugs. "No tackier than burgers and dogs."

"Touché." I search for local pizza places on my phone, to get a feel for my options. Without the full scholarship committee backing this decision, I'll have to pay out of pocket.

A moment later, Teddy steps back into the great room, pocketing his phone. "All right," he says on a sigh. "So I found us a caterer." I open my mouth to ask who, and where, and *how,* but he cuts me off, holding up a finger. "On one condition."

I'm pretty sure I'd accept any condition, right about now. But there's a mischievous twinkle in his eye that makes me wary. "What's that?"

The corner of his mouth quirks, like he's holding back a smile. "I have to bring you to meet her."

* * *

An hour and a half later, I'm parking outside a restaurant in a town just south of Pittsburgh. The lot is empty, but the building is lit from within, *Taverna Eliopoulos* glowing in neon blue cursive above the entrance. Teddy's Datsun creeps into the space next to mine. He shuts off his headlights before stepping out into the brisk evening. We agreed to drive separate so that he can check up on his apartment in Pittsburgh and drive back down with the food tomorrow morning.

"So when you said 'put down roots,'" I say, coming around to meet him at the curb, "you meant that she finally did it. She got her restaurant."

Teddy stares up at the white brick building with black-framed windows, the boxes trimmed with greenery that probably flowers in the spring. The lights in the dining room are dimmed, but a warm glow emanates from what I assume is the kitchen. "She sold the auto body shop after my dad passed," he explains. "Didn't seem like I was very likely to take over, given—"

"Given your impressive post-doctoral career," I say, tossing him a sad smile.

He laughs under his breath. "I don't know about all that."

"Is she here? There aren't any cars."

"She parks around back. Come on."

He opens the door, unlocked despite it being after hours, and steps aside to usher me in. Faint music carries from somewhere deeper in the building, and he ushers me toward it, past square tables set with wineglasses. The dining room is stylish and modern, with sleek light fixtures hanging from a coffered ceiling. Either the heater's cranked or someone's baking. It's warm enough that I shed my hoodie, folding it over an arm. I'm not exactly dressed to impress tonight, but I don't have any time to worry about whether or not I look presentable, because we're rounding the corner into the kitchen.

The kitchen is all gleaming stainless steel. Amidst the assortment of half-chopped vegetables lying on the prep table, a portable speaker blasts "Tainted Love" by Soft Cell. A woman in perhaps her mid-fifties hovers over a metal stock pot, a black apron thrown over her double-breasted chef's jacket. There's a familiar furrow to her brow as she lifts the lid, steam billowing around her. Her thick brown hair is knotted away from her face and streaked with wiry grays.

In a blink, I know that Dimitra Harrison is not the meek housewife I've always imagined.

"Ah!" Noticing us, she pops the lid back on the pot and wipes her hands on the apron. "There you are. I didn't hear you come in."

"Can't hear anything when you're blasting the music like that," Teddy says irritably, gesturing at the portable speaker. "And what have I told you about leaving the door unlocked after hours? It could've been anyone walking in here. You wouldn't have heard a thing."

She makes a *pfft* sound and pats around her apron. "I only unlocked it because you said you were coming." She pulls her phone out of the front pocket and pauses the music, but the kitchen doesn't quiet—it's filled instead with the bubbling of pots, the ticking of an egg timer. She pockets the phone and fixes me with a broad smile. "Hell-o!"

"Mom, this is Clara," Teddy says. "You remember, she's the one—"

She interrupts with an impatient wave of her hand. No rings, her unvarnished nails cut short. "I know who Clara is."

I extend a hand, businesslike. "It's lovely to finally meet you." I'm not sure how to address her. If she were a stranger, I'd have no problem calling her Dimitra, but somehow, even at thirty, calling my former best friend's mom by her first name feels too familiar. But Mrs. Harrison feels too formal.

She clasps my hand in both of hers, not shaking it, merely holding it. There's a warmth to her expression that's a little disarming. She leans in, conspiratorial. "You know"—she casts a glance at Teddy as though checking to see whether he can hear us, even though she's stage whispering—"I had almost given up on meeting you. So many years of Clara this, Clara that, but he never once asked to bring you home."

I laugh. "Was he supposed to?"

Teddy drags a hand down his face, but by the time he pulls it away, he's barely containing a smile. "Do we have to do this right now?"

"Oh, that's right. You're on a schedule." She rolls her eyes at the drop ceiling. I get the impression that she's the sort of woman who operates on her own time. For a commercial kitchen, this whole place is immaculate. And here she is, working alone after hours. "Aprons are hanging over by the walk-in. Let's put you both to work."

I wasn't expecting to help prep the food, but who am I to complain? This is an unexpected window into Teddy's life. I grab one of the black aprons off the wall next to the walk-in freezer and tie it around my waist, double-knotting for good measure before joining Dimitra over at the prep table. She suggests moussaka and pastitsio for the entrees, both casserole-type dishes that would be easy to store in serving trays and reheat, and instructs me on how to slice and rinse the eggplants before soaking them in a colander.

Teddy's already prepping ingredients for a vegetarian pastitsio like it's second nature, and I suppose maybe it is. He wasn't always forthcoming about his parents. His relationship with his dad was strained at times, I knew, and I always got the impression that his mom was overbearing. But maybe that was a side effect of her circumstance—having so little control over her own life that she felt the need to exert control over the one person she could.

"I was so sorry to hear about your husband's passing," I say in the middle of peeling potatoes for the moussaka. I'm not sure what else to say—*I wish Teddy would've reached out to me. I wish we never had our falling-out, and then maybe I could have been there for him.*

She sucks her teeth, a sort of sympathetic *tsk,* and touches my elbow as she moves around me to grab the colander of sliced eggplant. But she doesn't say anything, none of the usual platitudes about how she misses him but knows he's in a better place. I imagine it's complicated. They weren't exactly happy, the way Teddy relayed it. But they still shared a life together.

We work in silence for a while, and when we get tired of

that, to a soundtrack of eighties synthpop, which Dimitra blasts so loud, the little speaker rattles the stainless steel. "Helps me concentrate," she shouts over Depeche Mode. I meet Teddy's eye from across the prep table, both of us chuckling. His eyes crinkle at the corners and even after he looks back down at his work, the smile lingers. And I'm suddenly, acutely aware of just how much I've missed him.

How many moments like this, how many late nights and shared laughs have we missed out on? I don't have to do the math to know that it's too many. But somewhere between him showing up here at the start of term and now, I've started to think of him as a friend again.

Dimitra's speaker has run out of battery by the time we finish up for the night. I'm not sure how many hours of work we put in, but Teddy promises he'll come back first thing in the morning to finish up any prep work.

Dimitra serves a small cup of espresso to help me stay awake on the drive home. "Best of luck with your gala."

"It was really lovely to meet you," I say again, but it's less of a formality this time. I didn't expect to stay up past midnight tonight, but it's been a delight.

She winks. "I hope I'll be seeing more of you."

With that, she slips out the back. Teddy excuses himself to the dining room to lock up for the night. "We'll leave through the back, too," he explains, walking backward out of the kitchen. "Front door always sticks when you try to lock it from the outside."

I nod and watch him go, my hip leaning into a prep table that's covered in flour, bits of onion skin, and dirty knives, which Teddy insists he'll clean in the morning. I'm wired enough that I'm not even sure I need the espresso, but I sip it anyway. It's thick and bitter and a touch tart, nothing like the coffee I brew at home. But I like it.

Teddy returns a moment later. His glasses are hooked on the neck of his black T-shirt, which is dusted in white. "You are covered in flour," I inform him, brushing off his shoulder with a hand, but it's a fruitless effort.

He reaches into a measuring cup and pinches out some flour, swiping it across my cheek. I scrunch up my face. "So are you."

I laugh, setting down my espresso, and swipe my cheek.

"Ready to head out?" he asks.

"Yes," I lie.

His gaze sweeps over me and he quirks a brow. I look down. I'm still wearing my apron. With a snort, I push off the table and reach behind my back. I fumble trying to undo the double knot. Funny how the simplest tasks are complicated by the smallest shift in perspective. Like reaching for the shifter when you're seated on the right side of the car, or trying to tie someone else's shoe.

"Here, let me."

Teddy steps up behind me, his fingers brushing against mine. I clasp my hands in front of me and stare down at the breast pocket while he works, my cheeks heating. *Taverna Eliopoulos* is embroidered there in sleek black thread, camouflaged on the dark fabric. "Who is Eliopoulos?" I ask, just to break the silence.

"That's her maiden name." His fingers work the knot loose and I duck out from under the apron, turning to face him. We're standing quite close, but he makes no move to back away. I can feel the warmth radiating from him, see the flour dusting his hair, tinting the brown white.

I fold the apron and set it on the table, my hand resting there. "So you must've been raised really Greek."

"Define 'really Greek.'"

"I don't know." Really, I have no idea what I meant by that. It just came out, something to fill the silence. "Like the family in *My Big Fat Greek Wedding.*"

He laughs under his breath. "Ah, no." I peer at him, questioning, and after a few seconds he deigns to elaborate. "My mom was kind of isolated from her family, to be honest. I didn't meet her sister until I took the trip to Europe that one summer."

His hand rests on the table next to my apron, fingers splayed wide. His dad's ring is on his finger, flour and dough packed into the hairline engraving. I wonder why he wears it, what was said before his dad passed. Maybe it's because he shares his dad's name; sometimes things are as simple as that.

I don't want to leave. I don't want to drive home, suffering through an hour of silence, or cranking up the radio in an attempt to drown out my thoughts.

"This was nice," I say. "Unexpected, but nice." I drag my gaze back to his, willing myself to just say it, to get it out in the open, because denying it hasn't done me any favors. And he did invite me here, tonight. That has to count for something. "I've missed you. I think—" I hesitate when he doesn't immediately say it back, but he doesn't cut me off, either. His Adam's apple jumps in his throat. "I think more than I realized, if that makes sense. It was easier to pretend I didn't miss you when I barely even remembered what it was like having you around."

After a heavy pause, he speaks, his voice gravelly. "You keep calling me Teddy. No one's called me that in years."

It's not quite the response I was looking for. I stare at my hand, curling my fingers in the fabric of the apron. "You know what they say about old habits." I try to force my voice to sound light, airy, but it comes out a bit shaky. I'm nervous. I've just put myself out there a little and it feels like he's trying to change the subject. I shouldn't have said anything.

His hand moves and his fingers brush against mine. "I like it," he says. "I've missed hearing it."

Our fingers intertwine. I tear my gaze from our hands and meet his eye, my blood pumping. Without his glasses, he seems more exposed, in a way, nothing between me and his emotions, which are on full display. Right now, his pupils are wide, brown swallowed up by black. He shifts, angling his body closer to mine. I give him a tiny nod, permission, and he bends to kiss me.

It's slow and longing at first, remembering each other, trying to find our footing. There's something so surreal about this—kissing him again. It's not like it never crossed my mind, but I'd filed it away as an impossibility. But this is happening. His hand finds my lower back and drags me against him so that our bodies are flush. His tongue moves against mine and a whimper escapes me.

Desire crashes through me like water broken from a dam, a hard rush of something I've held back for years. I reach for him on instinct, my hands raking over his chest, broad and firm beneath his T-shirt. The hand around my back tightens, crushing my hips against his. It's almost too much, the flood of emotions and lingering questions and just pure *need*. Maybe we should stop and think this through, but instead, we're stumbling, and then the cold steel of the prep table presses into my backside. Teddy hoists me up onto it and I spread my legs, dragging him between them. He's hard, straining against his sweatpants where his hips settle into the apex of my leggings.

Any semblance of coherent thought is ripped up and scattered to the wind. I should scramble after the pieces, try to make sense of them, but Teddy's hands are skating up my sides, over my ribs, brushing against the thin cotton bra beneath my shirt. He groans into my mouth as I move my hips against him, wanting him closer. I reach for the hem of my shirt to tug it over my head, needing to feel his hands on me—

And then the back door bangs open.

It's as though we've been doused in a bucket of cold water. We spring apart—or rather, he springs back, almost crashing into the gas range stove. I slide off the prep table, tugging my shirt back down, my pulse still pounding through me.

"Made it three blocks before I realized I left my purse," Dimitra calls from somewhere, her voice echoing off the tile. Her movements are partially obscured by the heating lamps hovering low over the prep tables. "Don't mind me."

I'm not sure she saw anything, but I'm flooded with embarrassment anyway. It's like I'm experiencing déjà vu, transported to a night thirteen years ago, when we were similarly interrupted. Compelled to busy myself, I snatch the apron off the table and go to hang it by the freezer. My stupid leggings are caked in flour now, like I'm bread dough someone rolled around to give a good dusting. Dimitra bids us good night again before stealing away through the back door.

"I should probably get going," I announce, without looking at Teddy.

He clears his throat. "I'll walk you out."

I wait outside while he double-checks that everything's put away in the fridge and shuts off the lights. It's a cold, clear night and the moon is a small sliver like a fingernail. I hug my sweatshirt close, lost in thought. Teddy steps outside and gives the handle a good tug to make sure it's locked.

"I'll text you when I'm heading down tomorrow," he says as we walk around to the front of the building, where we parked our cars.

I manage a tight nod. "Sounds good."

He lingers, frowning off into the middle distance. The traffic lights at the intersection change from yellow to red, but there are no cars. "Something's bothering you," he says finally.

I'm not sure I want to talk. But there's this feeling, words bubbling up in my throat. Less word vomit and more confessional, because if tonight is a night for getting things out in the open, then I want to do it right. I want him to know the truth.

"I loved you."

The words spill out, the circumstances so different from all the times I'd imagined telling him. I never said those words to him, not even as friends, but they were always there, just beneath the surface. In the little things: phone calls at Christmas and counting the days until summer. Long drives to meet up in the middle of nowhere and history books with annotations in the margins, neat square handwriting beneath my own slanted scribbles. Drinking Pepsi because it reminded me of him, of that first summer, skipping stones by the lake with crutches tucked beneath my arms.

But the whole is lesser than the sum of its parts. There's nothing to show for it, all this wasted love with nowhere to put it.

He just looks at me, his eyes sad.

"Why didn't you follow me?" I ask. "Stop me? That day in the sandwich shop. You let me walk away."

He bows his head, staring at the ground. "I was seeing someone. You know that."

"We could've been friends," I say with a weak shrug.

"You didn't want me to follow you. Not as a friend."

I hate how well he knows me, that he could read me like that even when we'd gone years without talking. But there's more to it than that, more that I wanted out of him, then and now. "I know that I hurt you," I continue, trying to keep my voice steady, "and I'm sorry for that. I'll be sorry for the rest of my life." I pause. I want to give him time to absorb the words, to feel the full impact of what I'm telling him. Because I can't let myself fall for him again until I get it out in the open. Lay all the cards on the table, so that we both can make an informed decision.

I take a deep breath. "But I need you to understand that you hurt me, too."

He reaches for me. "Clara—"

"No, don't 'Clara' me right now." I step out of his reach. "You were supposed to be my best friend. And you abandoned me, like I was trash, like I didn't mean anything—"

"You abandoned *me*!" he cries, throwing his arms wide. He turns like he's about to walk off, then rounds back, chopping his palm to emphasize each point. "My dad had just had a stroke. All of my goals, everything I worked for, I had to put it on hold. I needed you. And you weren't there for me."

An incredulous laugh escapes me. "Oh, I was there for you. I answered all your calls, all your texts, I probably blew a thousand dollars on my cell phone bill alone—"

He tries to talk over me, but I don't even hear what he's saying, because now I'm on a roll.

"—but none of that matters, apparently. It only counts if I was there for you on your terms." My laugh morphs into a sort of dry sob, my voice quivering. "I would've still been there, Teddy. Through everything. I wanted to be. You're the one who shut me out."

A muscle feathers in his jaw, but he doesn't argue, doesn't even try to contradict me. He rips his gaze from mine, staring off again like he can't bear to look me in the eye.

I swipe a stray hair from my cheek. I already regret bringing this up. I don't know what I expected. "Right." I sniffle. "It's late. We can talk about this tomorrow."

I walk around my car and shove the key in the door, my eyes burning.

"I'm not sure you should be driving right—"

"I've been making my own decisions for nine years without your supervision!" I cry before ducking into the car. "No need to start worrying about me now." I shut the door with a snap, my punctuation mark on this whole conversation.

He just stands there as I back out of the parking spot, flip the car around, and pull out onto the street. Tears blur my vision, the streetlights spreading into starbursts. I wipe my eyes on the back of my hand. It takes every ounce of my willpower not to look back.

CHAPTER

19

It started with texting.

I still didn't see Teddy right away after our New Year's exchange; he left the second week of January to move into his dorm at Cornell. I probably wouldn't get to see him until spring break at the earliest, and I texted him to complain about it—a conversation that was quickly derailed by his innocent-not-so-innocent inquiries as to *why* I wanted to see him, and what I planned to do with him when I did.

Long-Distance History Club quickly fell by the wayside. Mostly because he was swamped with schoolwork, because there was a whole new breadth of subject matter to explore together, and—for a brief, fleeting window—because I found something that eclipsed my interest in history. I wanted to know everything. How to kiss, where to touch. I wanted to learn what he thought about in the shower, whether he ever used his hand and pretended it was me, and when he told me that he did, I realized how badly I wanted it to be *my* hands on him. My mouth. Me.

A part of me must have known that this was a bad idea, that we were blurring the lines between friendship and a relationship, but I never brought it up. And neither did he, after the phone call on New Year's. Maybe this was how it was always meant to be between us, or maybe we were just so caught up in the discovery of it all, we didn't let ourselves consider the consequences. It felt good, talking to him like this. And that was all it was. Talking. It soon progressed to phone calls, hushed conversations while lying in the dark. But we didn't send any more pictures because we agreed that we'd rather see each other in person.

But spring break didn't go as planned. Teddy drove down to Pennsylvania to stay with his parents, but a couple days into his stay, he got into a pretty heated argument with his dad— the elder Theodore Harrison didn't understand why his son was buying into college and all that *stuffed-shirt nonsense* when he could be learning the auto body trade, the family business that would eventually land in his lap. Teddy called me that evening to let me know that his dad had kicked him out, ignoring his mom's tearful protest.

"It looks like I'll just have to head back to school early," he said. "I'm sorry, Clara. I know we had plans."

But I wasn't willing to accept defeat so easily. I tried and failed to arrange for him to come stay at my house for the remainder of the week.

My mom was still dressed in the long-sleeved black shirt and jeans she wore beneath her Bath & Body Works apron. Warm Vanilla Sugar wafted off of her as she set her purse on the arm of the couch and toed off her Skechers. "You're not bringing a boyfriend into this house, not without us meeting him first."

"He's not my boyfriend," I argued, following her into the kitchen. "And anyway, you can meet him first and then decide. We could invite him over for lunch tomorrow."

"And then what?" she asked. "He sleeps on the couch, sneaks into your room every night when he thinks we're not looking?" She shook her head and opened the fridge.

"It's not like that." Never mind that I'd already considered the possibility.

"No. No," she said again, like the first "no" wasn't enough. "I'm not having you fool around under my roof. You're a teen-ager."

"I'm eighteen," I shot back.

"When you have your own place, you can invite over who-ever you want." She cracked open a can of Coke with a sharp hiss. "But until then, eighteen or otherwise, you'll just have to follow the house rules."

* * *

A couple weeks later, I caught wind that My Chemical Romance would be playing in D.C. in May. I was determined to secure tickets and have Teddy go to the concert with me. It seemed overdue, seeing our favorite band together, but yet again, life got in the way.

"But that's right before finals week," he said. "I want to be there, really, I do, but—"

"It's no pressure," I insisted. As much as it felt like he should be the person to accompany me, it was a nearly six-hour drive from Ithaca to D.C. I was a little disappointed that I wouldn't get to see him, but I understood. This was why we couldn't have a real relationship. We didn't have the time for it—not right now, anyway. So I dragged Izzy to the concert instead.

Calling the end of high school a graduation would be gen-erous—I didn't actually walk, and I only had a picture because my mom ordered the cap and gown off eBay, but I did receive a diploma in the mail, so I was a high school graduate regardless. Meanwhile, Teddy tentatively repaired his relationship with his father by agreeing to help out in the body shop over the sum-mer. I drove up to visit him a couple times, and we kissed and touched each other in the back seat of the car, but we didn't have anywhere else to go, and we didn't push it further than that. At least not until the week before I was due to start college.

I arrived on campus early to move into my dorm. I was assigned to La Plata, in a two-person room on the second story; they'd sent me contact information for my roommate in mid-July, but I was more focused on my job at the sandwich shop and getting ready for the semester than I was in making friends, so I hadn't bothered reaching out. Teddy was back home in Allentown until his fall quarter started in a few weeks, so he drove down to UMD to help me move in, despite my insistence that I could handle it myself.

I stood in front of the trunk of my Volvo, hands planted on my hips. Everything I needed for the school year had been loaded into the trunk: clothes and a stack of three-ring binders and a couple Kirkland boxes filled with books. "Like I said, it's really not that much stuff." I pointed at one of the boxes of books. "If you want to get that, I can—"

Teddy stacked two of the boxes on top of each other before hoisting them up, and I watched his arms, mesmerized. His biceps strained against the sleeves of his gray T-shirt and a vein trailed up his forearm. He'd always been on the lean side, tending toward athletic, but during the spring, he'd started to make use of the gym on his campus.

He followed my gaze, glancing down. "I could use the workout," he said, a little sheepish, and I couldn't tell whether he was just being modest or if he genuinely thought there was room for improvement.

I turned back to the trunk. My clothes I'd just tossed in on their hangers, so I hooked as many of them as I could on my hands and we marched up to the second floor. The room was vacant when we arrived. I bumped on the lights and tossed the clothes onto the bed. Teddy deposited the book boxes over by the dresser. "Your new roommate?" he said, only half a question as he nodded in the direction of the Joy Division poster that was taped above an empty bed. Whoever she was, she'd clipped

Instax pictures on a clothesline and assembled a collection of tiny, potted succulents on the windowsill. A stress ball shaped like a hamburger sat in the middle of the nightstand, its surface wrinkled with use.

"They said in an email that they paired us up based on personality, but . . ." I shook my head faintly, not really trusting UMD's vague understanding of whatever they thought my personality was. I had to resist the temptation to squint at the Instax pictures to get a better idea of who I was dealing with here. Spying on my roommate straight out the gate was probably a bad idea.

We headed back downstairs to grab more stuff out of the trunk. It was evening, the sky all cotton candy clouds and the weather surprisingly dry and cool for late August. Teddy hoisted another heavy box of books into his arms. "So you never did tell me how your last year at camp went."

"Oh," I said, a little surprised. We'd talked about a thousand things between then and now, but talking about the day-to-day had been moved to the back burner. I collected a stray bottle of nail polish remover and a can of dry shampoo that had rolled around loose in the trunk. "It was fun, I guess. I enjoyed catching up with Izzy."

He gave me a curious look, like he knew I was dodging the question, and I was. There was something expectant, seeing him today, a sort of tightly coiled tension that I was eager to dispel, and talking about camp wasn't the way to dispel it.

We finished hauling everything upstairs and then we walked to get iced coffee and sandwiches from a nearby café. By the time we made it back to the dorm, it was dark out, but my roommate hadn't made an appearance. I invited Teddy to stay and hang out for a bit, in part because I knew he had a long drive back, but also because this was our first time alone, in a room that conveniently had a bed. My heart pounded in my ears as we settled onto my new bed, watching *The Twilight Saga: New Moon* on my laptop, a movie choice that Teddy had accepted with a mixture of bemusement and reluctant interest.

"Jesus, why do they have to make it so complicated," he mumbled, dragging a hand down his face when Alice said she had the vision of Bella jumping off the cliff. When I didn't say anything, he glanced over at me. "You're being awfully quiet."

I lifted my shoulders. "I'm watching the movie."

"Hm." He turned back to the computer, but I could see by the glossy look in his eyes that he wasn't really registering the plot anymore. His glasses reflected the shifting light of the screen. After a few seconds, he said, "Just normally you have more commentary. You analyze things."

"I've seen it before. Anyway, I guess I'm just sort of . . ." I peered at him sideways. He was leaned back against my pillows and his T-shirt had ridden up his stomach a few inches, so that a trail of dark hair beneath his belly button was visible, leading down into his boxers. ". . . distracted."

Now he didn't bother pretending to be engaged in the movie. He turned to look at me, giving me his undivided attention. "By what?"

My heart clambered up into my throat, lodged itself there. "You."

He didn't say anything, but he held my gaze. We were both reclined, and somewhere in the midst of our fragmented conversation, we'd angled our bodies toward each other. The air crackled with anticipation. I scooted closer to him, shutting the laptop and nudging it down the bed with a knee. His gaze dropped to my lips.

"Kiss me?" I whispered, grazing my hands over the firm, muscular planes of his chest. His heart hammered beneath my fingertips, a steady rhythm that reassured me I wasn't the only one who was nervous.

He pressed his forehead to mine, his eyes fluttering closed. "I want to."

"Then—?"

I didn't get a chance to finish the question, because his mouth sank into mine. I let out a surprised *mm* before returning the kiss. We'd kissed only a handful of times, the last time well over a month ago, but the mere memory of those encounters had enough staying power that there was nothing tentative or exploratory this time around. His tongue moved against my own and he swallowed the tiny moan that escaped me. My hands skated down his flat stomach until my fingertips brushed against warm skin and hair. I traced the waistband of his boxers with shaky hands, teasing. Testing.

With a growl of approval, he flipped me onto my back and his hips settled between my legs. Near the foot of the bed, something clattered to the floor—something that, in my haze, I knew was *probably* my laptop, but any concerns were smothered by Teddy's weight pressing into me. Heat bloomed between my legs, spreading like wildfire. He rocked his hips against mine and I arched off the bed in reply, wanting to feel more of him. He broke the kiss and pressed his mouth to my neck, running his tongue over my skin. His hands burrowed up the sides of my sweatshirt, fingers digging into my ribs, but they stopped there, like he wouldn't let himself take this any further.

"Touch me," I said, but it came out sounding more like a sob. He lifted his head to look at me, his hair tousled and any traces of brown in his eyes swallowed by black. Holding my gaze, his hands skimmed the sensitive skin of my ribs, nudging my sweatshirt higher until it was pushed up over my lace bralette. We dropped our gaze together, staring at my hard nipples beneath the sheer lace fabric. "Please," I whispered.

He swallowed hard, hooking a thumb in the lace and tugging it askew, freeing a breast. "They're so pretty," he rasped before flicking a tongue over me. I sucked a breath through my teeth, my hips rolling involuntarily. Seeming pleased by this reaction, he took my nipple into his mouth. It was warm and wet and the sensation was almost too much to bear—I clapped a hand over my mouth to keep from making too much noise.

Teddy moved back up and pulled my hand out of the way to cover my mouth with his, his other hand massaging my breast. His erection pressed into me, hindered by my spandex leggings and the denim of his jeans. I reached for his zipper, fumbling ineffectually with the button. I'd never taken someone else's pants off before. My hands were shaking. I wondered if I even remembered how to undress *myself.* I broke the kiss. "I want you," I muttered, and I pressed kisses into his jaw, up to his ear, where I sucked on his earlobe. "I know you're worried about hurting me, and maybe it'll complicate things, but I need—I want it to be you."

At this, he jerked back like I'd bitten him, just far enough for his eyes to search my face. "What are you talking about?"

"I'm—" I hesitated, embarrassment rising, because what did *he* think we were talking about? I might have been inexperienced, but I knew enough to understand where this was obviously going. There was only one place it *could* go. "I thought we were talking about sex. And I don't want to start college without ever—"

"So what, I'm just the free trial?" He pushed himself off me, kneeling between my thighs. "Take me for a test drive before trying other cars?"

"We agreed that we're not ready to date," I said, but even as I was saying it, I was aware that we hadn't agreed to that. Not in so many words. We'd touched on the idea of fooling around while staying friends, but we hadn't laid down any ground rules, hadn't set clear boundaries for what, exactly, we were doing.

"I can't stand the thought of you doing this sort of thing

with other guys while I'm not here," Teddy said. "It's not—" He broke off, shaking his head. "This doesn't feel right."

"I'm not going to," I insisted.

"So we're exclusive, then?" he asked. "What, exclusive friends with benefits? Because that kind of sounds like a relationship to me."

I didn't have an answer for that. We sat like that for a moment, him kneeling, me on my back, propped up on my elbows. It seemed we were at a sort of impasse. Nothing about our situation had changed; we both had a whole future ahead of us, we weren't in the position to be making promises. But maybe, if it came down to it—

The door banged open.

I shoved Teddy backward with a foot. It was pure instinct—the somebody slamming into the room had set my heart racing, activating my fight or flight, and having nearly two hundred pounds of muscle on top of me hindered my ability to fight *or* fly.

A girl strolled in. She had a large denim jacket thrown over a floral-print dress and a Patagonia beanie tugged low over short, yellow hair, all of it eclectic in a way that somehow managed to look intentional. "So," she said with flourish, "which one of you is the roommate? No offense"—she inclined her head toward me, apparently to indicate that I was the one who shouldn't take offense—"but I'm sort of hoping it's the Clark Kent look-alike."

I stared at her, this total stranger, and shook my head faintly, because *what?* Teddy looked back and forth between the pair of us, rubbing his chest where I'd kicked him. "Actually, I was just leaving."

"What?" I asked, taken aback.

"Don't leave on my account," the girl said, staring as he scooted to the edge of the bed and tugged his tennis shoes back on. "I'm cool with just watching. You know. Whatever you guys are into."

Teddy shot her a quick, vexed look before pushing to his feet. "I need to get going. Long drive."

I grabbed him by the T-shirt sleeve to stop him from walking away from me. "Hey, wait," I said, trying to instill meaning in my words while also keeping my voice low, because my new roommate was hanging onto our every word. I wouldn't have been surprised if she'd unveiled a bag of popcorn from under her skirt and started munching on it. "We weren't done talking."

"I'm sorry. I can't—" He shook his head with a tired look. "I'll call you later?"

A lump the size of a baseball had formed in my throat, so all I could do was nod. I let go of his sleeve, and he left.

"Whoops," my new roommate said, flopping down on the bed directly across from mine. "I didn't mean to intrude."

I wanted to flip her off, but then we'd *really* be getting off on the wrong foot, so instead I grumbled, "Don't worry about it." I stood to collect my laptop from the floor. It had landed face down, the whole thing lying flush against the vinyl flooring. Just looking at it, it was clear that it was broken, but I picked it up anyway. The screen flapped uselessly; the hinges connecting it to the keyboard had snapped, and the whole thing had gone dark. I tapped the space bar a few times, but it was no use. It wouldn't turn on.

"What's your major?" my roommate asked, oblivious.

"History." I tossed the broken laptop on my bed and just stood there, not sure what to do with myself. "Yours?"

"Undeclared, but I'm thinking maybe I'll major in psychology." She lay with her boots still on her feet, crossing one ankle over the other, and grabbed the hamburger stress ball off her nightstand, tossing it up into the air and catching it. "Or business, maybe. I like anything that deals with people."

I didn't say anything. My mind was stuck on Teddy. I turned to my bed so that my new roommate wouldn't see as I swiped the tears from my eyes with the back of my hand.

"That guy that just left," she said slowly. "He's your boyfriend?"

I sniffed once, hard. "No." I busied myself with hanging my clothes up in the closet, needing a task to keep me from dwelling too heavily on whatever had just happened.

"Why not?" she pressed. I released a sound that was somewhere between a sigh and a laugh, because of *course* I couldn't have a roommate that allowed me to wallow in peace—that would be too much to ask for. She must've picked up on some of my irritation, at least, because she added, "Sorry if I'm being nosey. I'm just saying. I'd climb that like a tree."

"Yeah, well . . ." I scratched an itch at the base of my skull, where my braid was thickest. My hair was a rat's nest after rolling around on the bed with Teddy. I searched for an excuse to change the topic. "I don't think I caught your name?"

"Oh, dude, my bad." She sprang off the bed, tossing the rubber hamburger aside, and made short work of the room, thrusting a hand at me. "Miranda Schooner," she said, chipper. "But my friends call me Mindy."

* * *

I tried calling that night to talk things through, but he didn't answer. I told myself that he was just busy driving, that we'd talk about it later and everything would be fine. My phone buzzed the next morning when I was in the middle of freshman orientation, seated in the top row of a massive lecture hall. But it was a text, not a call, and my heart sank as soon as I opened it.

Teddy: I think maybe it's best if we go back to just being friends.

CHAPTER

20

PRESENT

Rain lashes my windshield as I search for a parking space, my wipers on full speed and fighting a losing battle. I squint through the downpour, but I'm not having any luck. I brake to let a family of four dressed as the *Incredibles* pass, Elastigirl gathering her children under a black umbrella.

I'd planned to arrive a couple hours early to finish prep, but Teddy insisted he had it handled and I'm not overeager to face him after the way we left off last night, so I took my time getting ready before heading to campus. But now the parking lot closest to the Alumni House is full, so it looks like I'll have to park on the street. The world outside is dark and oil-slicked as I turn down one of the dark side streets, where the streetlights are shadowed by barren branches and a handful of cars dot the cut-stone curb.

I park and grab my compact umbrella off the passenger seat, craning my neck to check my reflection in the rearview mirror. My makeup looks good, courtesy of Reagan—a dramatic, vampy look with winged eyeliner and a bold lip. It's the sort of makeup I wanted to wear in high school, only I didn't think to look up YouTube tutorials, so I never quite got it right. I bare my teeth. Fangs: check. No lipstick on them either, which feels like an achievement. Enough stalling. I open the door.

When I step out of my car and into the gale, the storm nearly rips my umbrella from my hand. It feels like autumn's been holding back; it's hardly rained since August, so now it's coming down all at once. My heeled boots clomp on the wet, uneven sidewalk as I find my footing, the concrete ravaged from beneath by gnarled, overgrown roots.

I send Bel a quick text as I power walk toward campus. Lot B was full. Walking that way now. How is everything?

She sends back a thumbs-up.

With my free hand, I fasten a couple of the snaps on my raincoat, which I've thrown over a knee-length black dress—the vampire costumes at the local Spirit Halloween weren't exactly what I'd call work appropriate, so I had to get creative. I pass by a woman standing beside a minivan, her date holding an umbrella for her as she runs a lint roller over a flapper costume. Everyone's still wearing their costumes, weather aside; I take that as a good sign.

The Alumni House is perched at the crest of a small hill in the oldest section of campus. A road winds between beech trees, but there are no streetlights to guide guests—only the yellow glow of the building itself, reflecting off the wet asphalt. It's a brick federalist home with twin chimneys, built in 1812, but it's long since been updated—I cringe at the history lost—into an event space.

As soon as I'm sheltered from the rain by the porch, I shake out my umbrella and fold it before stepping into the traffic jam happening in the entryway. By nature, the gala is a town and gown event, so I'm surrounded by a handful of faces I recognize and plenty of faces I don't. After a few hellos, I drop my umbrella at the umbrella stand and cut through the great room, where orange fairy lights twinkle near the ceiling. A dour oil

portrait of the former university president hangs above the fireplace, the lacquer crackled with heat and age. Just above it, Bel's
strung up the banner: CULTIVATING COMMUNITY it reads, with
the logos of our various sponsors on either side. The Bucky's
logo is blotted out, leaving a large, empty space. I feel a little
guilty that we didn't have time to replace it with Taverna Eliopoulos instead.

The air is thick with chattering voices. I shrug out of my coat
and make my way into the kitchen. A foldout table is lined with
foil chafing dishes of moussaka, vegetarian pastitsio, and grape
leaves. People are standing in line with paper plates in hand.
Behind the serving table, Teddy's alone and looking a little har-
ried. He's not wearing his glasses tonight, dressed in a sort of
drapey tunic covered with an apron. A crown of laurel leaves
perches in his hair. This is bound to be a little awkward, but it's
now or never.

I jump behind the table. "A little on the nose, don't you
think?" I joke under my breath as I knot the apron, hoping to
break the ice. I grab a serving spoon and take over the dolma
tray.

"Don't remind me," he mutters. "The website called it a 'Roman senator costume.' I didn't know we'd be serving Greek food
when I ordered it last week."

I withhold a laugh. "*Et tu, Brute?*"

"Don't make me stab you with the spatula."

I snort and he casts a tentative smile my way. As ridiculous
as the costume is, it doesn't look bad on him. His biceps are on
full display, his skin bronzy against the alabaster fabric, and the
rain has mussed his curls, making them a little unruly.

Bel pokes her head into the kitchen. She's dressed as Velma
from *Scooby Doo*, her hair in a short twist out. "The band just
got here. They're asking where you'd like them to set up."

"Jinkies," I say. "Tell them to set up in the great room."

She peers at me over the top of her fake glasses, disapproving. "I know that's what you *said*, but Goodman is complaining about the acoustics . . ."

I sigh, glancing over at Teddy. "I should go handle that."

"I think I can manage without you for a couple minutes," he teases.

I find the members of Eleventy-One Elephants standing around in the foyer. Their black instrument cases are flecked with rain and they've dressed up as—what else?—elephants. Goodman's wearing a loose gray onesie, a rubber trunk affixed to his nose with a string, but he has the audacity to look me up and down and ask, "Who are you supposed be, vampire Martha Stewart?"

I fold my arms over the apron. "I'm helping in the kitchen. What seems to be the problem here?"

He waves a hand at the great room. "There's too much clutter. Going to mess with the sound quality."

We cleared a space for the band while we were decorating yesterday, but there's still plenty of furniture for people to sit, the coffee table already littered with paper cups and plates. "You'll just have to make do."

It takes some back-and-forth, but once I've made it clear to the members of Eleventy-One Elephants that the great room is the only room large enough to host their six-person band, they relent. The rest of the night goes off without a hitch. I split my time between the kitchens and the rest of the party, shaking hands and thanking people for coming. Music drifts through the halls, mingling with conversation, but things quiet down when the president of the Alumni Association stands on an ottoman to make a brief announcement about the raffle. Afterward, Eleventy-One Elephants plays an alternative cover of "Thriller," but with the exception of a possibly drunk group of older alumni dancing out of step, it's not much of a crowd-pleaser.

We've nearly run out of food by the time Teddy unties his apron and joins the festivities. He wanders over to where I'm standing in the parlor, sipping water from one of the paper cups. "So," he says. "All this for tenure."

"For the scholarship fund," I correct him. "The possibility of tenure is an added bonus."

"Is it worth it?"

"What do you mean?"

He waves around the room, paper cup in hand. "This school. The job."

"It's tenure," I say, like that should be the end of it. "It's everything I've wanted. Everything I've worked for."

"That's like saying you've always wanted to get married. You don't just marry the first person who comes along." He fixes me with a serious look. "So, why Irving? There must be a reason."

If we're going with his simile, then Irving *is* the first person to come along. I'd applied to a number of schools, but this was the only one to offer me a position on the tenure track when I was still fresh out of grad school. It had seemed like a good enough reason, at the time. "They'll help with Reagan's tuition, once I'm tenured."

"What about your parents?" he asks. "They can't help at all?"

I wobble my head back and forth, noncommittal. "They're doing better now, financially." Better in general. "Dad's still dealing with the whole worker's comp nightmare, but Mom moved up to assistant manager a couple years ago. But they can't afford this. And I hate the thought of Reagan drowning in loans."

Teddy considers this for a beat. "I'm not sure that's your responsibility."

I stare at him. "She's my sister."

"Yeah, well." He shrugs. "She's an adult. If this is the school she chose, I'm sure she knew what she was signing on for."

He's not entirely wrong. I tried to encourage Reagan to

apply to other schools, but she was set on Irving. Something about the old buildings, the intimate campus, appealed to her. Maybe because she's a bit of a romantic at heart, no matter how much she tries to bury it beneath layers of snark. She *is* a literature major, after all. "Anyway, I don't know why you're questioning me," I say, deflecting. "You're on the tenure track at Carnegie, you seem to be happy enough."

He shakes his head.

I frown. "No, what? No, you're not happy?"

"I'm not tenure track. I'm adjunct."

"What?" It comes out louder than intended, apparently, because several people in our immediate vicinity turn to stare. I lower my voice. "Why?"

"Well, my plans got sort of derailed after my dad had the first stroke," he says, matter-of-fact. "It took me a couple years after that to finish my thesis. But I guess you could say I just haven't found the right school yet." He tosses me a cheeky grin. "Not ready to tie the knot."

I shake my head and roll my eyes, but I can't help smiling. We're interrupted by Trina Madhani, who drags him away to meet one of her former advisees. I end up chatting with Wendy McAllister from the Communications Department about the renovations on Martin Hall, but I find that I keep glancing over at Teddy in the next room. After a little while, I excuse myself and cut through the crowd to take momentary refuge in the kitchen.

It's empty except for Bel, eating what remains of the pastitsio directly out of the aluminum serving tray. My stomach grumbles just looking at it—I've been rushing around so much that I forgot to eat.

"Feels like it's going well," she says.

I pluck the last dolma out of the tray with my fingers and

bite off the end, leaning my back against the counter as I chew. "Better than I'd hoped."

"So," she says slowly, "are you ever going to tell me what the story is with you two?"

She levels me with a significant look. I can't pretend that I don't know what she's asking about. "We just—" I try to find the right way to sum everything up, to explain where it went wrong. "I was really focused on school." She waits for me to elaborate, and for some reason, I do. "My mom, she was working this dead-end job at the time, and everything about it just looked so bleak. Not having anything for yourself. Counting on someone else to make it all better. I didn't want to end up like that, so I sort of just put everything else on the back burner."

As soon as I've finished talking, I feel like I've overshared. But Bel just nods, like she understands. "Right person, wrong time?"

"More or less."

"But now it's . . ." She waits a beat for me to fill in the blank, but I don't. "The right time, maybe?"

I pop the rest of the dolma into my mouth and push off the counter. "I'm still trying to figure that part out."

The remainder of the night is spent shaking even more hands, thanking donors, announcing the winners of the raffle. Guests begin filtering out by eight thirty. At eight forty-three, the band stops playing and Goodman steps outside with the bassist to smoke a joint beneath the portico, the rain coming down in sheets. Bel complains that she pulled a muscle hanging up the banner, so instead of asking her to stay to help clean up, I tell her to head home and draw herself a hot bath. I think she suspects that I'm doing this on purpose, but she doesn't call me out for it.

By nine, it's just me and Teddy. He heads upstairs to change back into his normal clothes and find his glasses. When he comes back down, he plays some music on his phone, a throwback playlist that fades into the background while we clean—"Famous Last Words" and "Demolition Lovers," songs he used to send me on burned CDs. We exchange few words and fewer glances as we work. We'll have to talk before the night is over, but for now, we crisscross through the rooms, boxing up decorations and bagging up trash, paper cups and plates that were left on the mantel and upright piano. I'm standing on a stepstool to reach the banner above the fireplace when he finds his way over to me.

"Looks like this is the last of it," he says, staring up at the words CULTIVATING COMMUNITY.

I tug a pushpin out of the horsehair plaster and the top left corner of the banner flutters over my hand. "Can you grab the other end?" I ask.

He reaches to help and then I climb down from the stepstool. We meet in the middle, lining up the corners of the banner, which he folds and sets aside. I cross over to the coffee table and pop my fake fangs from my teeth one at a time, stowing them in a plastic bag in my purse.

When I turn back around, Teddy's offering me a hand, palm up.

I stare at him, wary. "What are you doing?"

"I'm asking you to dance."

A surprised laugh sputters out of me. I've never been asked to dance in my life—there's no prom when you're homeschooled, and the last wedding I attended was when I was the flower girl for my aunt Gillian when I was eight. "You want to slow dance to 'Ohio Is for Lovers'?"

A smile tugs at the corner of his mouth. "You do look the part." I roll my eyes and turn away, but then he adds, "You look beautiful."

I hesitate.

"I'll put on whatever song you like," he says. "It doesn't matter to me as long as I get to dance with you."

"I can't dance," I say.

"I'm not sure there's much to it."

"You're not sure," I echo, arching a brow.

"Pretty sure I'm supposed to lead anyway, so you're not the one who should be worried."

I should probably decline, insist that we talk things out first. But there's something so tempting about just giving into impulse for once, so instead I'm letting him lead me to the middle of the faded Turkish rug. We don't even bother changing the music. His hand settles on my hip, drawing me toward him, and we sway out of time. Like we're dancing to a song that only we can hear, something soft and slow.

I stifle a giggle.

"What?" he asks.

"This is ridiculous," I say, nodding in the direction of the music playing from his phone.

"I don't care," he says.

I focus on our shoes, sobering. I'm all too aware of how close we're standing.

"I'm sorry for last night," he says after a moment. "For how I reacted."

I shake my head. "I'm sorry for bringing it up the way I did."

"You don't need to apologize. Everything you said was true." The hand on my waist drags me in close, so that our bodies are almost flush. He mutters into my hair. "I should've paid more attention to how you were feeling, back then. I had tunnel vision. All I could think about was how unfair everything was, and when I called that night—I thought that if you were here, if I talked you into coming home, then at least I still had you." He takes a deep breath, chest rising and falling against mine. "It was selfish thinking. I'm sorry for taking it out on you."

I rest my cheek against his shoulder, absorbing everything he's telling me. His heartbeat is strong and steady. Him holding me like this, being this close to him, it does something to me. A weakening of my resolve, or maybe a strengthening of it—that all depends on what I actually want, and I'm not sure I've figured that out yet. "Can I ask you something?" I say finally.

"Anything."

"Why are you here? You could've applied to work as a visiting scholar at any number of universities. But you chose this one."

"I might've mentioned something earlier," he says, breath warm against my ear, "about how I haven't found the right school yet."

"And what do you think of Irving?"

"It's the faculty that really makes a school." He's quiet for a minute. "I think, if you're set on staying here, then maybe I should extend my visitation."

I draw back so that I can look at him. "Teddy—"

"You have to know, it was never about the school, for me." We've stopped swaying now, standing stock-still with our bodies pressed together. His eyes search my face. "The past couple years put things into perspective. The whole idea of building a better life, making sure it all goes according to plan, it's all wasted if you miss out on the things that made that future worth building in the first place."

"We knew each other a long time ago," I whisper.

With a hand, he angles my face up, thumb brushing against my bottom lip and sending a shudder through me. "Then I guess we have a lot of lost time to make up for."

He bends to kiss me.

CHAPTER

21

PRESENT

My mouth opens against his, eager to pick up where we left off. He responds in kind, his tongue dipping into my mouth, sending a fresh wave of desire through me. I loop a hand around the back of his neck to steady myself, my fingers finding that spot where his hair curls up at the nape of his neck. For a moment, we're simply mirroring the other night: savoring the kiss itself, our breathing heavy. His hands slide over my backside, down to my thighs, tracing the soft fabric of my dress. Then he scoops me up around his waist, swallowing the surprised noise that escapes me, and suddenly we're moving.

He walks me backward until we bump into the sideboard in the parlor, where he swipes a stack of donation forms out of the way before setting me down. "Lock the door," I gasp against his lips. I don't want to stop kissing him, but the last thing I want is a repeat of last night—even worse if one of our colleagues were to walk in.

He obliges, but he's back in a flash, his mouth devouring mine. He puts his hands on me, cupping one of my breasts through the thin fabric of my costume, and I reach behind me to unzip the back, tugging the dress down around my waist. Inviting him to touch me. I'm not wearing a bra—thanks to the fabric of the dress, I didn't need one—and my nipples pinch at the sudden rush of cool air. His teeth sink softly into my lower lip before he draws back to drink me in.

For a few seconds, he just stares at them, his own chest heaving. "That night in your dorm," he says, "these"—he cups both of my breasts, tests the weight of them in his hands before one thumb flicks over a nipple, and I close my eyes at the fleeting touch, my head spinning—"were the sexiest thing I'd ever seen. I've thought about that night so many times"—his eyes flick to my face—"wishing I'd handled it differently. I've wanted you so badly, Clara, ever since the day I met you."

I swallow. "I've wanted you, too."

He presses an open-mouthed kiss to my collarbone before sinking lower, his nose dragging over smooth, sensitive skin. His tongue flicks over a nipple and then he takes it into his mouth. My head lolls back, a sound halfway between a sigh and a moan escaping me. "I've always imagined your—" I break off, distracted as he trails kisses across my breastbone before lavishing the other nipple with the same attention. "—hands."

He draws back just far enough to look at me, half-laughing despite the heat of his expression. "What?"

"You have nice hands," I say, warmth stinging my cheeks even as it settles between my thighs. "I used to . . . touch myself. And pretend it was you."

He leans in to press a kiss between my breasts. "You fantasized about me?" he asks against my skin, his warm breath sending a shiver through me. I nod. "Where did you picture me touching you?" He stops kissing me and holds out a hand, and for a moment, I'm not sure what he wants me to do with it. But then he says, "Show me."

I take his hand and guide it back to my breast. "Here," I whisper, my eyes never leaving his face, though he's momentarily distracted. He pinches the nipple, just hard enough that

I suck a breath through my teeth, and he plants a kiss on the other.

"Where else?"

I move his hand down to my hip bone, making him grab me. "Here, sometimes."

He mirrors the touch on the other hip, taking advantage of the excuse to yank me toward him. His arousal presses into the apex of my thighs through the rough denim of his jeans. My dress has given up, at this point: the slinky fabric is gathered around my middle, leaving my underwear fully exposed. His gaze locks with mine, challenging me.

Pulse pounding, I drag his hand across my stomach and slip it beneath the waistband of my underwear. He sucks in a breath when his fingers brush against me and he feels just how turned on I am. "This," I say, "is where I've always wanted you."

He presses his forehead into my shoulder. Need throbs between my legs, so hard it almost hurts, but he doesn't offer me any sort of relief yet. "It's not fair what you do to me," he mutters against my skin.

I want to protest, because he's the one who's doing something pretty unfair to *me*, currently, but all that comes out is a faint, "What am I doing?"

"Make me so hard, I can't fucking think."

"Show me," I breathe, echoing his earlier words.

He draws back from my shoulder, leaving a quick kiss in his wake. "Don't you want me to touch you first?" he asks, thumb moving back and forth over me, lightly teasing.

I shake my head weakly. "I can't . . . I mean, not without a vibrator."

I expect him to argue with me, to give the whole *with me, it's going to be different* spiel that every other man has given me, but after a few seconds, he nods slowly. "Do you have one?"

"In my purse."

A husky laugh escapes him. "You brought a vibrator to a costume party," he says, like he doesn't believe me.

"Gala," I correct him. "And let's just say I was optimistic about us talking through things. Though I didn't expect we'd do anything here. I thought maybe we'd go back to—"

Without warning, he scoops me up by my thighs. I squeak in surprise and sling my arms over his shoulders for some semblance of balance, but I'm not sure it's needed—he's able to support my weight, no problem. He trails kisses over my neck as he carries me over to the chaise. His hips settle between my legs, still separated by my underwear and his jeans, and then he's kissing me again. My fingers scrabble at the back of his T-shirt and he seems to catch the hint, grabbing it at the neck and tugging it over his head in one swift motion. It's technically not the first time I've seen him shirtless; I saw him swimming now and again at camp, but now he has a man's body. The hard planes and ridges of his muscles have more meat on them, covered in dark hair. He bends to kiss me again and his chest brushes against my hardened nipples, the sensation sending a zing of pleasure coursing through me.

He breaks the kiss and leans over to the coffee table, reaching into my purse.

I place a hand on his arm. "Actually"—he looks at me, confused—"can it just be us, for right now?" I want him to take a little longer to learn my body, for me to learn all the sensations of being with him, first.

"Okay," he says, with a feather-light kiss to my naked shoulder. "Just us, for now."

I reach for his jeans and fumble with the button, and he's more than happy to help matters along, straightening up to step out of his jeans. Next come his boxers, and then the hard length of him springs free. For some reason, it's this moment of all moments that's so surreal, my brain might break. I lift my hips off the chaise and he helps me out of my underwear, and then I tug the bunched-up dress over my head so that we're both completely vulnerable for one another. I'm surprised when he reaches to the floor to fish his wallet out of his jeans, grabbing a condom. Something resembling uncertainty must cross my face, because he catches my eye and explains, "I don't normally keep them on hand, but after last night—"

"Optimistic," I paraphrase, dragging him toward me for a kiss. "Got it."

He breathes a laugh, but it's swallowed up as our mouths meet again, open and hungry. He rolls on the condom and notches himself inside me and we both suck in a breath. He draws his head back just far enough to look back and forth between my eyes. "Are you sure?" he asks. "Because we don't need to rush into this."

I answer by kissing him and rocking my hips against his, nudging him deeper, and he releases a groan. "God, you feel amazing." He thrusts home, slow and purposeful, and the sensation is almost too much. I clench around him.

"No, don't—" He closes his eyes and exhales, his body tensing over me. "I need to focus." Slowly, torturously, he draws back and sinks into me again, resting his forehead against mine, his face screwed up as he tries to concentrate.

My body moves against my will, hips rolling beneath him. "Don't hold back."

"I'll come too fast."

"Don't care. Please," I whine. "Want you to mean it."

"I do mean it," he says through gritted teeth. "But I've wanted you for too fucking long. There's no way I'm going to last."

Despite his words, though, the undeniable need for release seems to command his body for him. He moves in and out of me again, and then again. Before I know what's happening, my legs are hooked around his back and his thrusts quicken. If there was any lingering concern as to whether we both wanted this, our bodies are more than happy to hash it out for us. After a moment, he pushes himself up onto his knees so that he can watch my face, and the shift in angle is almost too much. My fingers scrabble for purchase.

He's almost breathless, his brow knit in careful concentration, but he manages to ask, "You sure you don't want me to—?"

I shake my head, because no, I'm not sure, before realizing that could be interpreted either way. "Silver," I sputter. "In the pocket."

He reaches for my purse, clumsily, and manages to grab the small silver vibrator out of the front pocket. I expect him to stop and ask questions, but he only inspects it for a brief moment before twisting the end to turn it on—I am immensely relieved to discover that I must have put batteries in it at some point, and that they still work—and lowers it to me, his hips all the while maintaining a steady pace. Tension threads through my body until my legs constrict around him, slowing his hips. I bite my lip, trying to muffle the strangled cry that escapes me, but he catches my mouth in a rough kiss instead.

"Don't hold back," he says, nipping my bottom lip. "I want to watch you come undone."

It's the same authoritative voice I've heard him use before, only its effect right now is entirely different. Pleasure racks me until I'm seeing stars, seeing nothing, but I feel his pace speed up again and then falter. A groan rips from his throat. The vibrator is abandoned somewhere off to the side. Shuddering to a stop, he collapses on top of me, chest heaving against mine.

We lie like that for a long moment in a sort of reverent silence. Finally, still winded, I say, "That was—" But I'm at a loss for words, so I don't bother finishing.

"Overdue." Teddy kisses me one more time before heading to the kitchen to throw away the condom. Still dazed, I search for my clothes and try to re-dress myself on teetering, wobbly legs, but the zipper on my dress is caught and I can't seem to get it working again. Teddy comes up behind me and takes over, zipping me up. He brushes my hair to one side and plants a feather-light kiss on the back of my neck. I turn to face him.

There are still questions buzzing around my head—*what does this mean, and where do we go from here?*—but I elect to ignore them, at least for now. Instead, I ask, "Do you want to come back to my place for the night?"

CHAPTER

22

People have a way of convincing themselves that they're the exception, not the rule.

Maybe it's ego. Maybe it's a self-preservation thing—we have to believe that we're not doomed to repeat everyone else's mistake, or else we'd be paralyzed into inaction, too scared to take the leap. Or maybe it's a strange form of solipsism, where you convince yourself that everyone else is running on autopilot, and you're different because your decisions are deliberate, informed; you know what you're doing. You can share firsts, learn to bare your soul to someone without it having to be at the expense of your friendship. All those other people, the people who fell in love, who made things messy, who woke up one day and realized they could never go back to the way things were—those people were nothing like the two of you.

Except in all the ways you were exactly the same: in the way he looked at you every time he saw you, like you were the first rain after a long drought—palms turned up, catching droplets, because to have some small part of you was better than having none of you at all. In the way your pulse raced beneath your skin whenever he touched you. And in the drifting apart, that moment when you realized you were no longer on the same page. That you wanted two different things.

I think maybe it's best if we go back to just being friends.

What he was asking wasn't possible.

As much as I didn't want a relationship, we couldn't go back to the way things were. Our conversations became awkward, stilted. With little happening in my life to distract me, I dove headfirst into that first semester of college, volunteering in the food cupboard on campus and joining the Sigma Tau Delta book club to keep myself occupied between classes. Teddy seemed all too willing to fade into the background—or maybe we were both just busy, but I resented it all a little more for every week we went without a phone call, every time a text message came through with a one-word answer or a thumbs-up. When neither of us called the other on Christmas that year, a part of me mourned the loss of our friendship. But I told myself that I understood: life went on.

Determined to get out of my funk, I applied to a semester abroad program, and the following year I packed my bags for Queen Mary University in London, where I fell in love with the city and its history. Maryland had a long history of its own, but everything in England felt so much older, like walking every gum-riddled sidewalk and zebra crossing was walking in the footsteps of ghosts. It was easy to romanticize it all, being so far from home. The heavy gong of the bells at Westminster Abbey; the colossal plaster cast of Trajan's Column in the Victoria and Albert Museum; touring the cold sepulcher of the royal tombs in the Lady Chapel, footsteps echoing off the high ceiling as I stared into the gilded faces of long-dead royals, lying in repose. Back home, history had felt like something contained, bound in books full of names and dates. But here, it bloomed outward like a spiderweb of veins running beneath the city—living, pulsating.

Despite my efforts to distract myself, I wanted to call Teddy, to share this sense of wonder with him, because I knew that he would understand it. I'd downloaded WhatsApp so that I could keep in touch with my parents and Izzy without racking up my phone bill, but messages from Teddy were few and far between—wishing me a happy Easter, or sending a picture of a textbook beneath a yellow lamp in the library, accompanied by a short message lamenting a deadline—and I'd left half of them on read. After a while, the messages stopped altogether.

Plans for Izzy to come visit me over spring break fell through when she failed to renew her passport on time, so I spent a week sightseeing by myself, on quiet bus rides with my earbuds in, the English countryside zipping past my window. It was raining when I visited Stonehenge, the grass slick beneath my tennis shoes and the snaps on my raincoat buttoned up to my chin, but I traipsed all the way from the drop-off point despite the weather—my mom had a coffee table book of famous landmarks with Stonehenge on the cover, and she always swore she'd visit one day, so I was determined to get a picture for her.

The stones were dark with water and freckled in lichen, and I was forced to stand a good fifteen yards away behind a cordon, hugging myself in the rain. Meanwhile, a crow landed on one of the lintel stones, preening feathers as wet and black as oil. I dug my phone out of the pocket of my raincoat, hoping to be quick about this. Raindrops speckled the screen as I pulled up the camera and snapped a few quick selfies.

"Do you want me to take one for you?" a man's voice called across the grass.

I looked over. He was standing a ways away, wearing a large and structured raincoat, and behind the stiff collar, a square jawline peeked over a turtleneck. I recognized him from the tour bus.

"Sure," I called back. "That would be great."

He drew near and I handed him my phone, noting as I did so that he wasn't bad-looking. His dark blond hair was damp with rain and he was average height, lean beneath the layers of warm clothes. He took a couple of pictures and handed it back so that I could check whether I liked them. I looked like a snap pea with just my face poking out of the raincoat, but my mom was the only person who was going to see these, so I thanked him and pocketed it.

"It's smaller," he said, his forehead wrinkled as he nodded toward the stones, "than I thought it would be."

"I don't know. Still pretty impressive that somebody was able to move them like that."

He turned to stare at me. "You're American."

I nodded. "I'm doing a semester abroad. You?"

"Canadian. Originally from Toronto, but I moved to London for work." I cast him a curious look, and he tacked on, "I'm a business analyst."

"I'm going to be honest. I have no clue what a business analyst does."

He chuckled. "You're asking the wrong person. I'm not really sure myself." We lapsed into silence, hands shoved in the pockets of our coats, both looking at Stonehenge more than we were looking at each other. But he didn't walk away. "What do you study?" he asked after a moment.

"History."

"My worst subject." I glanced at him and he gave me a self-deprecating smile. "All the names and dates, everybody's dead." With a pang of longing, I thought of Teddy. I hadn't heard from him in months. I was so lost in thought that I didn't say anything, and so after a moment, the stranger thrust out a hand. "Emmett, by the way."

My fingers were wet and numb with cold, but his hand was warm. "Clara."

"Clara," he said slowly, like he was savoring it, "I don't suppose I could convince you to grab a coffee with me." He inclined his head in the direction of a bus ambling up the road, exhaust billowing behind it. "After the tour, of course."

I gave him a tight-lipped smile. "I might be persuaded."

* * *

Emmett and I casually dated for the remainder of my semester in England. We had few things in common, and we had an expiration date right from the beginning in the form of my plane ticket back to Baltimore, but we found camaraderie as two people living outside their home country. And he was interesting in a novel sort of way, explaining things like forecast and variance analysis, stuff I'd never really studied. He tolerated my interest in history, meeting me in abbeys and museums but mostly looking bored, his face lit by his phone. "Work," he'd say when I shot him an irritated look. We had sex the week before I left, because even though it wasn't perfect, I liked Emmett enough. I never told him it was the first time, and if he noticed, he didn't comment on it. A week later, we broke up amicably. And while I would return to England several times over the years, for research or school, I never had any interest in looking for him. Our relationship had run its course.

I returned to UMD in the fall with a renewed sense of purpose. I resolved to write my capstone on Tudor-era England but had trouble pinning down an exact subject; my advisor, a dour woman with a white-blond pixie cut who taught intersectional courses in the Religious Studies Department, suggested that I focus on the formation of the Church of England, and—because I could use the guidance—I agreed. At the same time, I started looking into applications for graduate programs overseas. I'd learned during my year abroad that there were programs in the U.K. that would allow me to finish my master's within a year, back in the States in time for my birthday. It was the next logical step in my plan.

Since I'd returned home, things between me and Teddy had sort of leveled out. We were on speaking terms, at least, something that toed the line between friends and simply friendly acquaintances, texting intermittently about school and work and the weather. He was already knee-deep in a Ph.D. program, so he didn't have a lot of free time, but we met up for coffee once or twice. I told him that I'd received an offer for a full ride to University of Manchester. He seemed happy for me, but in a polite, surface-level sort of way. We didn't talk about us, or the future.

We were, as it turned out, the rule.

CHAPTER

23

PRESENT

I wake to the sound of the refrigerator opening and closing.

It takes a moment to register where I am. The living room is sideways because I'm lying on the couch. There's something warm and solid behind me—something that's *breathing*—and I turn my head to squint one eye at Teddy. He's in a surprisingly deep sleep. His muscular arm is slung over my waist, a dead, heavy weight, and while he's not snoring, his breathing is slow and heavy. I shift, trying to find a way to slip out from beneath his arm without disturbing him.

Bare footsteps slap against the tile floor and Reagan materializes in the doorway between the living room and the kitchen. She leans a shoulder into the doorframe as she pops the tab on a Diet Coke and takes a long, slow glug. "Morning."

"You're supposed to be at Nat's," I hiss, pressing myself flat against the floral fabric and wriggling out from under Teddy's arm. We arrived to an empty house last night, so we turned on scary movies, polished off a bottle of wine, and ended up having sex again on the couch, more tender and less hurried. There's still a lot we need to talk about. The *where do we go from here* conversation is going to need to happen. But the rest of the night was surprisingly relaxed. Comfortable, even. So much so that—with my head against his chest while we watched *From Dusk Till Dawn*—the steady beat of his heart lulled me to sleep.

"And boy, am I glad that I'm not."

I manage to twist free, slinking to the floor. "Keep your voice—"

But it's already too late. Teddy blinks awake, rubbing a hand over his face. "Good morning," he mumbles. His eyes are bleary, his hair rumpled, and a strange, warm feeling blooms in my chest. I watch as he goes through the same series of thoughts I went through only seconds before: recalling where he is, what I'm doing there, why there's someone else in the room. Except at this last step, he squints hard across the living room. I hand him his glasses from the coffee table. He nudges them onto his face and blinks at Reagan before his sleepy gaze falls back to me. "What time is it?"

"Seven thirty," Reagan cheerfully provides. "Late night, Professor Harrison?"

Teddy scratches his head. "Um." He looks at me. "I don't remember what time we fell asleep."

I shrug, memories of last night flooding back, causing my stomach to swoop. "Late-ish."

"Right," Reagan says with a sage nod. "You were probably too busy to look at the clock."

"Get *out*," I say, grabbing a balled-up napkin from eating nachos last night from the coffee table and chucking it at her head. I miss by about a foot, the napkin sailing over her shoulder into the kitchen. "Go to your room or something."

"So, does this mean I'm going to get special treatment?" she asks Teddy, ignoring me entirely. "As your future sister-in-law and all that. Because I'd really like an A, but I suppose I could settle for—"

"Out," I order, pointing down the hall, and she finally obliges, vanishing from the room with an evil cackle. "Sorry about that," I say once we're alone again. I push myself off the couch and head to the kitchen, the tile cold beneath my bare feet. "She doesn't know when to mind her business," I call over my shoulder. I put on a pot of coffee and open the refrigerator in search of something to eat. "Are you hungry?" I ask. "Closest thing I have to breakfast is an expired carton of eggs, but we could go out and grab something to eat, if you want."

He enters the kitchen, his hand finding my waist. "Actually, I need to get going." He pulls me toward him and catches my mouth in a kiss. "But I'd like to take you out for dinner tonight. I think a proper date is about fifteen years overdue."

He collects his things and I walk him out to the car. We share a long kiss leaned up against the driver side door of the Datsun and then he leaves with a promise that he'll text me later before picking me up for dinner. I head back inside, butterflies fluttering around my stomach. Reagan is waiting in the kitchen with her arms folded on the counter, a smug smile on her face. "About time."

I hide my smile by turning my back to her, pouring myself a mug of coffee. I grab a couple sugar cubes from the lemon-shaped sugar dish and drop them in. "I don't know what you're talking about."

* * *

Despite the spring in my step all morning, I am determined not to rush into anything with Teddy. We're both adults, and both practical to a fault; we know that whatever this is, it comes with a little baggage. One of our biggest roadblocks has always been communicating—sure, we've mostly said whatever we felt, but there's also been this persistent pattern of waxing and waning, pulling back whenever it was convenient, but there's no backing out this time. Our lives are inextricably intertwined.

Dinner feels less like a date and more like a negotiation.

Sitting across from each other at an orange-lit booth beside a faux-brick wall in Lucretia's, we talk at length about what this is, where we see it going, the numerous reasons it might or might not work.

We work together.

We're very similar.

Perhaps too *similar?*

But we've known each other long enough to work around that; or at least we should be able to, in theory.

We've both wanted this forever.

We have a lot of history.

It's not clear if this last point belongs in the pros or cons column. I'm well aware that our track record is far from perfect—but then again, we were practically kids when most of it happened. I was twenty-one when I stood outside the Manchester Cathedral, my thumb numb with cold as I pressed the screen to END CALL, effectively shutting down whatever might have been. Our track record ends there. It's been a whole decade since.

"So we take things slow," Teddy says. "See whether we can get it right, this time around."

* * *

Julien asks me to swing by his office after my HIST-111 lecture on Monday afternoon. I knock at the frosted glass door and it swings wide.

"Ah. Good. I was wondering whether you got my email. Come on in, have a seat." He's already moving over to the bar cart, unscrewing the cap on a bottle of single-cask Macallan. "Care for a glass?"

I settle onto the chair, crossing my legs beneath my breezy skirt. "Please," I say, because why not? As much as it might offend the very American sensibilities of our colleagues, it's not technically against campus policy. And you know what else isn't against policy? Getting romantically involved with visiting faculty. I triple-checked the rules because I'm a little worried that that's why Julien called me in here today—that he's somehow found us out. But I'm prepared to stand my ground. My only concern is whether it will reflect poorly on me when it comes time to go before the advisory committee in December, but so long as Julien is on my side, hopefully word won't spread.

He pours me a finger, placing it on the desk before walking around to his chair. "I wanted to commend you on the success of Saturday's gala." He settles into the creaky, worn leather, swirling the amber liquid around his own glass before downing it in a single go. "I'm sorry I couldn't be there."

I exhale, some of my tension unraveling. "Thank you. But I can't take full credit. I couldn't have done it without the help of the other committee members. And the generosity of all our sponsors."

He smiles, setting the empty glass on the desk with a dull *clink* and leaning back in his chair. "Always a good idea to acknowledge the efforts of those around you. Though a word to the wise: when you describe your contributions to the school in your dossier, be sure to take some credit."

"Of course."

"Speaking of which," he continues, "I've been meaning to ask how that's going. Your dossier."

"Fine," I say. "Great. I arranged with Lorna for a guest lecture next Friday."

"I'm glad to hear it." He squints at me. "A solid application for tenure also requires the recommendation of your colleagues, as I'm sure you're aware. People who have worked with you on the day-to-day, who have a good sense of your teaching style, whether your methodologies align with the ethos of our institution."

I take a sip from the crystal highball glass. The scotch is earthy and smoky and burns in my throat. I cough, covering my mouth with the sleeve of my sweater. "Belinda Jones might be willing to write something," I choke out, my voice hoarse.

"Fantastic. Though I think it would be prudent to get recommendations from tenured faculty, as well. People who have been in your shoes and can speak to whether they feel you deserve to move forward with the process."

I clear my throat. "I can ask the other members of the scholarship committee. Beyond that, I'll have to think on it."

Satisfied with my progress, he dismisses me from his office. I pause in the middle of collecting my messenger bag to toss back the rest of the scotch—waste not—and then I'm out the door.

* * *

Whether Julien didn't know about me and Teddy or simply didn't care, I didn't ask. But it doesn't take long for the rest of the faculty to start suspecting that something is up. I'm not even sure what we're doing to give them that impression—aside from our Thursday meetings, we're rarely together on campus, and whenever we are we keep a professional distance. But regardless of our efforts, by the following week, there are two disparate rumors circling: the first being that Teddy and I have been together for years and that's why he applied for the visiting scholar position in the first place, and the second being that he had to file a Title IX report over the weekend because I've been harassing him to go on a date with me.

I don't have much time to worry about correcting either rumor, though, because today is the day that Dr. Lorna Foster is coming to campus for her guest lecture. I meet the Uber outside the Britteridge Center, right on schedule. Dr. Foster steps out of a black suburban wearing a houndstooth blazer and white slacks that swish when she walks. "You must be Clara," she says, her Doric accent making my name sound more lyrical than normal, at least to my ears. Her white hair is pin-straight and blunt around her shoulders and she's wearing a stern-looking pair of cat-eye glasses, but her smile is warm. "Glad to meet you."

We shake hands and then I lead the way. "It's just inside." I glance over my shoulder. "Do you need anything before getting started? Some water, somebody to set up the projector?"

"A dram and a willing audience."

"You'll have to see your friend Julien about the first one," I say with a wry smile, "but the second is taken care of."

"I read your paper," she says as we walk. "On the first marriage of Lady Margaret Beaufort. Riveting stuff." Were she not an archeologist herself, I might've thought she was being sarcastic. Only someone who has a genuine passion for history would ever call a paper on a six-hundred-year-old annulment *riveting* and actually mean it. "I don't know whether you've any interest in Margaret Tudor, but if you do, University of Edinburgh would be just the place."

I smile. "I'll keep it in mind. Though I'm actually in the middle of trying to get tenure here, so I'm not sure I'll be traveling any time soon."

"Well, feel free to reach out, if you're ever considering it. I'd be happy to vouch for the quality of your work. We've quite a robust program for visiting researchers."

"Thank you," I say, a little taken aback.

The turnout for the guest lecture is good for what it is. Various members of the history and anthropology faculty were persuaded to offer their students extra credit for attending, so the folding auditorium seats are dotted with note-takers, with stragglers filtering in and ducking down the aisles. After a few minutes of chitchat, Dr. Foster pulls up a PowerPoint. She kicks off her lecture with an anecdote about an excavation on a

Pictish hillfort at Knockfarrel. I climb the stairs to a dark row toward the back of the hall, where Teddy waits in one of the aisle seats.

He leans over to whisper in my ear. "How'd it go?"

"Fine, I think." I jiggle my leg, a little nervous, though there's nothing left to be nervous *about*. Julien set up all the dominoes for this; I was just responsible for giving them a little nudge.

His hand settles on my thigh, stilling it. "Hey, you did great. You got her here in one piece, right?"

I incline my head, because yes, I did, but then again, that's not much of an achievement. A few rows down, a professor from the English Department swivels to stare at us. We're not being especially loud, but I don't think she turned because she heard us, anyway. She leans and whispers something to the person seated beside her. You really would think that a bunch of academics would have more interesting things to talk about than who's sleeping with whom, but alas. At least Teddy sitting next to me should put the harassment rumors to rest.

"What happened to people minding their own business?" I whisper, glancing up at the ceiling. The recessed lighting is dimmed, only a cluster of lights pointed at Dr. Foster in front of the projector screen. Julien watches her from the shadowy wings, his hands clasped in front of him.

"We could give them something to talk about," Teddy growls, his breath warm against my ear.

I nudge him with an elbow, holding back a smile, torn between professionalism and the very *un*professional thoughts his suggestion inspires in me. Dr. Foster uses a clicker to change slides, and a picture of a large, jagged boulder with a serpentine inscription slides on-screen. *Brandsbutt Stone*, the header on the slide reads, inspiring a slew of stifled giggles from students.

"So, I know we said we're going to take things slow," Teddy continues in a low voice, angled toward me even as we're both pretending to pay attention to the lecture, "but I was thinking maybe we could spend Thanksgiving together. If you're interested."

I draw back a little to look at him. In all the years we've known each other, I have countless memories of all the holidays we spent apart—mailed birthday gifts and phone calls from different time zones—but we've never actually spent a holiday together. Maybe this could be good for us. A sort of reset button. I hadn't really reflected on it, but now that he's brought it up, the thought of spending another holiday apart is anticlimactic. Like we'd be doing things the same way we always did.

"Reagan and I are planning to drive to our parents' place in Cambridge," I say, tentative.

"I wouldn't mind that." His dark eyes search my face. "Assuming you want me there. And assuming your parents don't completely hate me."

I laugh under my breath. "They don't hate you." Though he might be in the hot seat for the first hour or so, but I'm not about to tell him that.

CHAPTER

24

It had been a mild May, but the day of commencement was warm, and despite the ceremony being held inside the massive indoor arena, I was sweating beneath my black gown as we all waited for the speeches to wrap up. I was surrounded by strangers, passing acquaintances in caps and gowns. It was bittersweet, in a way. I was closing this chapter, but it also felt as though I'd barely cracked it open, maybe scanned the first few lines.

As soon as the ceremony was over, I shouldered my way through the crowd, searching for my parents. They weren't all that hard to spot—Mom and Reagan had taken paint markers and glitter glue to a poster board that said *WE ♥ YOU CLARA*, which Mom held above her head like she was picking me up from the airport gate all over again.

"I guess the apple falls pretty far from the tree," Dad said as soon as I was close enough to hear him over the chatter. Leaning on his cane, he drew me into a hug, his whiskers scratchy against my cheek. "Congratulations, Clare Bear."

Mom was already teary-eyed. She forgot all about the poster board and hugged me tight, whispering, "I hope you know I'm not trying to take credit when I say that I'm so proud of you."

"I think you deserve a little bit of credit," I said. "You did sort of teach me for most of my life." She released me and I smoothed my red stole and straightened my honors medal, maybe calling attention to it a little, but today was supposed to be a day for celebrating achievements, after all.

She gave me a grateful smile and squeezed my arm. "You taught yourself."

Reagan hung back, toeing the ground with a sneaker and looking bored. "Thank you for the poster. And the awesome cap," I said. She was in a crafting phase, and Mom had suggested I ask her to decorate my graduation cap for me. Considering I didn't really have the time to decorate it myself, nor did I have any ideas, I was more than willing to give my eleven-year-old sister free rein. She'd lined the edges with red and gold stick-on gems and used scrapbooking letters to spell out *AND I DIDN'T EVEN NEED A TUDOR!* I didn't know when she'd gotten so witty, but then again, we hadn't seen a lot of each other the past few years.

"You're welcome," she mumbled with a surly expression that suggested she'd rather be anywhere else.

"How about we get some food?" I asked.

"Hold on," Mom said. "Aren't there some friends hanging around that you want to take pictures with?"

With a twinge of embarrassment, I glanced over my shoulder, pretended like I was searching for someone in the crowd. In truth, I hadn't made many friends in college. "Not sure where they've gotten to. They're probably busy with their families." I shrugged and turned back to face my parents. "But it's fine. I have their phone numbers, we'll keep in touch."

"Will you?" a familiar voice said in my ear.

I spun around, my stole whirling. Teddy was standing there. His hair was cropped short and he looked a bit tired, but he was smiling. "Oh my god!" I squealed, so surprised that I threw my arms around his neck, the past momentarily forgotten.

He crushed me against him, so tight I thought my ribs might crack. "Hi, stranger." His voice hummed in his chest, our bodies flush. "It's good to see you."

It had been months since the last time we met up for coffee. We'd never quite gone back to normal—the chemical makeup of our friendship had been irrevocably altered—but he was still the closest thing to a best friend that I had. And he had shown up here. For me. There were a million things I wanted to tell him, but for some reason the first thing out of my mouth was, "You cut your hair."

"Figured I was due for a change."

After what felt like an eternity, we drew back, and it was like the world suddenly remembered to keep spinning. People milled around us in a sea of black and red. Reagan watched us with a kind of reluctant curiosity and Dad had tucked the poster board under an arm, like he was ready to leave. "Teddy wanted to surprise you," Mom explained. "Found our number in the white pages, believe it or not."

Teddy laughed under his breath, his gaze fixed on my face. "She means the website. I haven't seen an actual phone book since I was sixteen."

I grinned. "My family mostly just used them as doorstops."

We briefly discussed where we all wanted to eat dinner, which sparked a joke from my dad about how we could use the yellow pages right about now. After a couple suggestions, we settled on a restaurant and navigated the crowd toward the nearest exit. I led the way, sidestepping families and stopping for a crowd of classmates so that we didn't get in the way of their picture, but I was a little lost in thought—wondering what Teddy was doing here, whether he had some ulterior motive in showing up like this unannounced. Distracted, I shouldered my way past a group blocking the aisle, accidentally knocking a bouquet of daisies out of someone's arms.

"Shit, I'm sorry," I said, stooping to collect the flowers. The bouquet was thankfully still in one piece, protected by the cellophane wrapping.

"It's no problem, really, you don't have to—"

Her voice was familiar and I glanced up. Mindy, my old roommate. "Clara," she said, recognizing me. Then, seeming like she didn't know what else to say, she gestured at my graduation garb. "Congratulations."

I handed her the flowers back. "You, too." Teddy caught up with me, followed by the others. My mom was giving me a polite but expectant look, her eyebrows raised. "Oh, this is, um—" I stumbled over my words, feeling a little awkward.

"Mindy Schooner," she said, taking over and reaching to shake my parents' hands in turn, but she was looking over at Teddy. He had his hands stuffed into the front pockets of his jeans, looking as awkward as I felt. I wondered whether he remembered his last run-in with her—in the midst of the argument that pushed us apart.

"We were roommates, freshman year," I explained to my parents. It felt like I should say more, but we didn't know each other all that well. After spending my sophomore year abroad, I'd been reassigned to a different dorm, though I'd seen her around campus now and again.

"How about a picture of the two of you?" Mom asked, pulling out her phone.

We looked at each other.

"Oh, um—"

"Sure, why not—"

We scooted in close. Mindy put an arm around my shoulder, but it was feather-light, staged for the camera, like a celebrity posing at a meet-and-greet with a fan. I put on a tight-lipped smile and my mom said something to the effect of *big smiles, come on now, say cheese*. There was a flash and then we put some distance between ourselves before my mom had even lowered the camera.

Mindy looked at Teddy. "I recognize you," she said. "Your hair. It's shorter."

He ran a hand over the hair in question, looking sheepish. "I wanted to change it up."

"It looks better this way," she said decisively. "Cleaner."

There was an awkward pause, and then I said, "We're just on our way to dinner, but I'll see you around, maybe?"

She nodded. "I'll find you on Facebook."

Both of us were probably just saying these things to sound polite; there was little chance of us running into each other, and I wasn't even sure she knew my last name to look me up. I figured that was the last time I'd be seeing Mindy Schooner, and that was all the thought I gave the matter.

* * *

After dinner, we drove back to the house, where Teddy had parked his Datsun, but he wasn't ready to leave. We sat out on the curb catching up, because the walls in the house were paper-thin and my parents were notorious eavesdroppers. As it was, my mom had already poked her head out the front door twice under the guise of telling us she'd put together a vegetable tray and then again to offer us a glass of wine to celebrate. Our street was a dark suburban one with long lawns and few cars, and I had stretched my bare feet out into the road and crossed my ankles, my arches sore from standing for commencement in heels. I lay back on the sidewalk and stared up at the night sky. The concrete was cool and rough against my exposed shoulders.

"You remember when they made us do that astronomy thing at camp?" I asked. "We filled in that whole sheet and Ms. Fischer still marked it as incomplete because—"

"—because we missed Neptune," Teddy finished, folding an

arm behind his head and lying down next to me. "Ms. Fischer. I wonder where she is these days."

I turned my head to look at him, studying him in profile while he stared up at the stars. The shorter hair made him look older and flattered his bone structure, the hard corner where his jaw met his ear. But I missed the curls, and the desire to run my fingers through them. After allowing me a few seconds to ogle him in peace, he angled his head toward me, eyebrows raised in question.

"I don't like your hair," I said.

"Gee, thanks."

"It doesn't look bad, I just always like when it's a little longer, when you get the curlicues right here—" With a finger, I traced behind his ear, trailing down to the nape of his neck.

It was an innocent, feather-light touch, but his eyes fluttered closed for a moment, until I withdrew my hand. "I've been thinking a lot, lately," he said.

"When are you not?" I joked.

He breathed a soft laugh. "About us, I mean."

I propped myself up on an elbow, somewhat uncomfortable on the unyielding concrete. The word *us* had my heart running a marathon. I didn't know where he was going with this, but the possibility of him dredging all that up again sent me into a panic. I was leaving for Manchester in three months. "Us?"

"How little we've talked, these past few years," he said. "I've missed talking to you. I miss *you*."

"I've missed you, too," I admitted, and he didn't ask me for more than that.

CHAPTER

25

Irving to Cambridge is nearly a four-hour drive, and worse on Thanksgiving. We agreed to carpool, which I thought very little of at the time, but now—crammed into my Volvo with the heater blasting and Reagan in the back seat, her usual road trip playlist cycling through The Lumineers and Vance Joy—it all feels very domestic. Were it anyone else, it would probably be too soon for all this, but it's Teddy, so it's almost too easy. Familiar.

As soon as Reagan moves past her determination to embarrass me by rattling off stories about how I was always hogging the computer to Skype with Teddy whenever she wanted to play Club Penguin, we settle into a comfortable rhythm, alternating between talking and listening to music. When we pass over Bay Bridge, Teddy sinks in his seat and mumbles, "God, I forgot how long this thing is." I laugh and Reagan teases him. It's almost too perfect: a clear, windswept November day, the blue expanse of Chesapeake Bay stretched out on either side of us.

When we pull into my parents' driveway a little under an hour later, Teddy's the first to get out, groaning and stretching his legs.

"There they are!" Mom calls from the porch. Her Farrah Fawcett hair is fluffed away from her face, the grays half-hidden with box dye, and she's wearing a puffer vest and riding boots like she took a cue from an old Pinterest board. "How was traffic?"

I hold out a hand and tilt it back and forth, *so-so,* as Reagan bounds up the empty driveway and flings herself at our mother. The white work truck is gone, an oil stain the only evidence of its usual parking place. I remove my sunglasses and tuck them into the neck of my sweater as I draw near the porch. "Where's Dad?" I ask.

"Sent him to the store," she says, waving us inside. "Ran out of Old Bay."

Teddy shoots me a quizzical look as we cross over the threshold, and I know exactly what it's about, because what does Old Bay Seasoning have to do with Thanksgiving? But there's little need to explain when we're greeted by the salty tang of seafood on the air, a stainless steel vat bubbling on the stove. The Thanksgiving crab boil: a Fernsby family tradition. A long folding table is erected in the living room, surrounded by mismatched chairs and draped in a checkered tablecloth.

"So, Teddy, I'm curious," Mom says, stirring the large pot with a wooden spoon. "Where have you been all these years?"

I sigh through my nose and toss a vexed look at her back, though she doesn't notice. Wasting no time, apparently, but I should've known better than to think my mother would beat around the bush.

"Ah—" Teddy glances at me uncertainly, like he expects some guidance, but I have none to offer. He's on his own, here. "Pittsburgh, mostly."

"Mmm." She doesn't turn away from the stove, but I can tell, just from this small, noncommittal noise, that she's not satisfied with his answer. He could give her a breakdown of every place he'd set foot in the past decade, down to the latitude and longitude, and it wouldn't quite be the explanation she was looking for.

The front door creaks open, followed by the rustle of grocery bags. "I see a car out front," Dad calls. He alternates between his boots clomping and the click of his cane as he crosses over to the kitchen, depositing the bags on the counter. He pulls me into one of his sideways hugs and plants a scratchy kiss on my temple. "Clare Bear," he says. He leans over to plant a kiss on Mom's cheek, and she practically glows. All those months of arguing, years of struggling to get by, they're a distant memory.

Dad's ironclad stare has shifted to my date. He thrusts out a calloused hand. "Teddy. It's been a while." He manages to make it sound like a warning, but Teddy takes it in stride.

"Where's The President?" Dad asks.

"She ran to her room as soon as we got here," I say. "Or my room, maybe." She'd mentioned something about wanting to go through my old clothes, which my parents never had the heart to donate. Apparently the low-rise jeans I swore I'd never wear again are back in style.

"The sewing room, you mean," Mom corrects me—never mind that I'm supposed to be sleeping in it. We packed our bags to stay overnight rather than make the four-hour drive back to Irving after dinner. There was still an extra bed, last I checked.

* * *

Thanksgiving dinner consists of Maryland blue crab and corn on the cob, boiled with a generous helping of Old Bay Seasoning and served with melted butter. It's just the five of us; my grandmother refuses to leave her house in Knoxville these days. Things are a little stiff, at first, but my parents ease up on Teddy once we all start eating, and by the end of the evening they've dropped their line of questioning entirely, just happy to have somebody here for the holiday. Mom serves her red velvet cup-cakes for dessert.

My parents know better than to bother trying to insist that Teddy sleep on the couch, but it's *more* awkward telling them good night, knowing that they know damn well we're going to be sleeping in my old room together. A part of me wishes they would've just pretended to be old-fashioned about things and saved us all the weirdness. I shut the bedroom door and lock it behind us. There's a plastic organizer full of sewing supplies and a brand-new Singer sitting on the dresser, still in the box, but otherwise, it's like a room frozen in time. The walls are papered in album covers I printed off Photobucket and the bookcase in the corner overflows with used books, colorful sticky flags still peeking out of tattered pages.

"They seemed to warm up to me again," Teddy says, "after a while."

"Yeah." I flop onto the bed. It's full-sized, a generous bed for a teenager but not quite large enough to comfortably accom-modate two adults, but we'll have to make do.

"What did you tell them? About everything that happened, I mean."

"Nothing really," I say. "Just a . . . rough outline, I guess." It's an evasive answer, but I don't feel like getting into what all my parents were privy to—Dad especially. I called him and broke down six years ago, when I realized that this wasn't just another road bump in our friendship, when it seemed I'd lost Teddy for good.

Teddy sits on the edge of the bed and bends over to kiss me. His hand skates up my arm. I'm still wearing my sweater and jeans; I need to change into pajamas. "I have a lot to make up for," he says against my lips.

"We have all the time in the world."

He draws back a little, his gaze softening as it flits around my face—not searching for answers, but just looking, like he means to memorize me. As though either of us could ever forget what the other looks like. His eyes snag on my necklace and he takes it into his hand, polishing the nickel with a swipe of his thumb. "I can't believe you still wear this thing."

"I never stopped."

His gaze rises to meet mine. In those three words, I've told him everything, bared my soul. We're not talking about my necklace anymore. And in three more words, he confirms what I already know: "Neither did I."

My breathing hitches. "We're supposed to be taking things slow."

"It's been seventeen years." His eyes drop back to my lips. "It doesn't get much slower than us."

With that, he kisses me, slow and oh so tender. He shifts over me, his body a pleasant weight. I pop the button on my jeans and shimmy them down my body until they're around my ankles, kicking free. He reaches for me, his fingertips tracing the lace trim of my underwear before he inches up to the hem of my sweater and lifts it over my head, tousling my hair. I'm left in my bra and underwear. He kisses me again, his tongue flicking over mine, and I arch my body against him.

"This doesn't seem very fair," I point out, breathless. "You still have all your clothes on."

He answers by kissing lower, skimming my jawline and trailing down between my breasts before he nudges my knees wider and positions his head between my legs. I lean back on my hands, watching as he tugs the fabric of my underwear to the side. When he puts his mouth on me, I have to bite.my lip to keep from making noise. His fingers press into my thighs to keep me from squirming.

Pressure builds and ebbs inside of me, but I know I can't come like this, so after a moment I drag him back up to my mouth, kissing him hard. He fumbles with his belt, and then with the button on his pants before freezing with a hand on the zipper. "Fuck," he mutters, pressing his forehead against mine. "I forgot to bring a condom."

I nudge his hand aside, reaching into his boxers and wrapping my fingers around him. "Birth control," is all I say.

His eyes, normally so serious and pensive, are swallowed in a sort of haze, but he's lucid enough to ask, "Are you sure?" even as his hips seem to move almost against his will, thrusting into my hand.

We've talked about this in passing; I know there's no one else. I nod. We might have promised each other to take things slow, but right now, I'm pretty sure I'm sick of slow. I drag his hips toward me, our mouths tangled up in each other, and then he's pushing inside me, both gasping at the new sensation.

After that, there's no taking it slow. He rocks into me again, swallowing the sound that escapes me, and then again, his pace quickening. Clumsy fingers find my bra straps and tug them over my shoulders, pushing my bra down around my waist so that he can cup my bare breasts. His hands skate over my body, like he wants to touch me everywhere, all at once. They settle on my thighs, his fingers sinking into soft flesh, angling my hips toward his.

The sensation is too much; I can't think. There's nothing but him inside of me, and then he's touching me. I left my vibrator at home, but my thoughts are so wrapped up in him that I forget to remember that I can't come without it. I'm completely vulnerable with him right now, and he's patient enough to bring me to the edge. My arms are around his back, hands scrabbling for purchase in his shirt. And before I know what's happening, I come undone. I muffle the strangled cry that escapes me with his shoulder, and his thrusts grow more erratic, like he was waiting for me to come first, regardless of whether I'd insisted I couldn't.

He catches my mouth in a rough kiss and we collapse into each other, our energy spent.

Afterward, we lie naked in bed together. He plants a soft kiss on my shoulder. "I love you," he says, barely more than a whisper.

"I love you, too." The words hang between us for a moment, so much more real now that we've spoken them out loud. A part of me has always known, even in the intervening years when I tried to convince myself that he was a man I had *loved*, past tense. And when he showed up this semester, I tried to tell myself that we were strangers. That I couldn't let myself fall back in love with him. But there was no falling, this time around—there was only remembering how to love him, a sort of muscle memory. "Where do we go from here?" I ask softly.

He pops up on an elbow, tracing the contours of my body with a hand. "I'll stay through the holidays, head back to Pittsburgh to put in my resignation at Carnegie, tie up any loose ends. And then I suppose I'll see about finding a position here in Maryland." There's a pause, and then he adds, "If you're set on the tenure thing, that is."

I adjust my head on the pillow, frowning at him. "You keep making those little comments."

"I'll support you, whatever the decision," he says quickly. "I just can't help wondering what a Tudor historian is doing in Maryland."

"You specialize in the colonies," I point out. "History of the Mid-Atlantic. It's not like there would be a ton of jobs for you in Edinburgh."

"I specialize in colonial *maritime* history," he corrects me. "Key word there. Which generally involved a lot of back-and-forth across the Atlantic, so I think I'd be just fine." Another pause, during which he seems to fully absorb what I just said. "Why Edinburgh?"

I shift, suddenly a little self-conscious. "Just something Lorna Foster mentioned before the guest lecture. I sort of got the impression she was offering to vouch for me, if I ever wanted to apply to be a visiting researcher."

He looks at me like he's worried I'm coming down with a fever. "Why wouldn't you take her up on that?"

"Because I might be getting tenure here," I say, defensively. "And then it'll be years before I can take sabbatical, and anyway, I don't know."

"Strong finish to a strong argument."

I shoot him an exasperated look. "And what would you do if I packed my bags and jumped on a plane to Scotland tomorrow?"

"Follow you," he says, not missing a beat.

"Without finding a job first?"

"I've got enough in the bank that I'd be fine for a year or two. I could take my time. Focus on research. Write. And if you decide you want to stay longer, I'd just have to look for a job."

It all sounds so simple, when he says it like that. Idyllic, even. I've spent so much of my life chasing after security, both emotional and financial. But somewhere along the way, it feels like I lost sight of the finish line. "I don't know," I say again. "It's a lot to think about."

"Then take your time," he says. "Think on it."

CHAPTER

26

The remainder of November is hectic, spent meeting one-on-one with students to discuss their final papers and piecing together my dossier between classes. It's dense work, breaking down every contribution I've made to Irving these past however many years, and to academia at large. Pages discuss at length my research, publications, the courses I've taught, my services to the school. A curriculum vitae detailing my work experience, the years of adjunct professorship while I worked on my Ph.D. at University of Notre Dame, the Fulbright award that took me back to England for six months to conduct research for my dissertation. It's all very stale and methodical, but also deeply personal, in a way: my life's achievements, stuffed into a manila envelope too flimsy to bear the weight.

I submit it for consideration on the first Monday in December, the last week of instruction before finals week. Letters of recommendation are submitted separately by the recommenders, so I have no idea what they say—not even Teddy's, which Julien suggested I add after our work together on the gala. Teddy offers to let me peek at it, but it feels like cheating, so I decline. "Okay," he says in a mock-concerned tone, leaning over his desk with his hand on the mouse, threatening to click send.

"Just wait until you find out that I've told them all about that time you misattributed a Winston Churchill quote."

"I've never quoted Winston Churchill." I widen my eyes, feigning worry. "Or maybe I didn't know I was quoting him."

He shuts down the computer and straightens up, taking me by the hand and dragging me toward him in the privacy of our shared office. "'It is a good thing for an uneducated man'—or woman—'to read books of quotations,'" he recites, hooking his arms around my waist.

I arch a brow up at him. "Is that a suggestion?"

"No. That's Churchill."

He tugs my body flush against his, but we're interrupted by my phone vibrating between us. I draw back just far enough to dig it out of my pocket to check who's calling.

Izzy.

That's weird. Save for a handful of texts, we haven't spoken for the past month, so this is a little out of the blue. My knee-jerk reaction is to assume something's wrong. "Sorry," I say, slipping out of Teddy's grasp, "one sec." I swipe to answer, stepping out into the hall.

"What are you doing December fourteenth to nineteenth?" Izzy asks by way of greeting.

"I don't exactly have my schedule in front of me," I say slowly. "That's right after finals week, so probably not much." The board should have made their decision by next Friday, so that will be out of my hair by then.

"I'm planning a visit," she explains. A keyboard clacks in the background. "My parents have been begging me to come home for the holidays the last couple years and I figure I might as well squeeze in a trip to see you while I'm at it."

"Oh," I say, my eyebrows raised. I don't mean for it to sound disinterested or ungrateful, but it's fairly short notice with everything else happening. Still, we haven't seen each other in a few years. And no matter how long we go without talking, how long we spend apart, the moment we're together again, it's like nothing's changed. Not unlike my friendship with Teddy, actually. We all adapted to spending time alone during our formative years, managing friendships through periodic visits and long-winded catch-ups. Everyone always says that home-schooling doesn't prepare you for the real world, but maybe it does, at least in this regard: it prepares you for how disparate your lives are going to be.

"Unless that doesn't work for you," she says uncertainly. "We could always plan something separate. Maybe in the summer."

"No, that should be fine. Sorry, zoned out there for a minute."

Behind me, the door to the office cracks open, and I step out of the way. Teddy locks up and pockets his keys. We're supposed to be headed for lunch. "Everything okay?" he asks in a low voice, meant only for me. I nod.

Izzy pounces at the faintest hint of a male voice in the background. "Who's that?"

"That was Teddy. We're just heading to lunch."

"Teddy, huh?" she echoes, a little too curious. "So, care to share what's going on there?"

"It's a long story," I say mildly. "Let's just say we have a lot of catching up to do."

* * *

The scholarship committee meets for a final time the Thursday before finals week to review applications for the spring. It's al-ways a little begrudging, this last meeting of the semester—more so than our usual meetings, that is. And then we don't talk. We sit around the table in silence, scanning essays, sorting them into piles: *No* and *Yes* and *Needs further review*. We steal things out of each other's piles. Voice when we're particularly impressed by an applicant. Gary yawns wide, an empty can of Red Bull sitting atop a stack of rejections. Trina absently presses the butt of her pen against the table, a rhythmic *click, click* like a metronome.

"This one's not bad," I say, passing an essay for The Samuel Chase Scholarship across the table. "Gary, if you want to take a look—"

We review the submissions anonymously to prevent any biases creeping in, sticky notes slapped over the students' names and ID numbers, but depending on the application requirements, we sometimes still get a rough sketch of the person behind the paper. In this case, it's a pre-law student who mentioned a minor in political science in his introductory paragraph, so Gary will double-check to see whether it holds up to scrutiny.

I've never been overly fond of this whole process—passing judgment on students, deciding which are worthy of financial help and which are not, but someone has to do it. This year it feels ickier than normal, though. Or maybe I'm just more attuned to it because I can empathize: my dossier is up for review any day now. There's another committee somewhere on this campus who are going to be judging *my* merits, *my* contributions to the school.

I pick up the paper that Goodman just set in the *Yes* pile, scanning over the contents. Scholarship recipients are generally decided by consensus, though the opinions of committee members who work in the relevant department tend to hold a bit more weight. This one's a critical essay submitted for The Lizette Woodworth Reese Award. A critical analysis of some work or another by Sylvia Plath. I'm inclined to trust Goodman's opinion, seeing as poetry isn't my expertise. I add a star to the sticky note and toss it back into the pile.

* * *

Julien emails me the Sunday before finals week to let me know that I have a meeting scheduled with the tenure advisory committee that Wednesday. I'll admit it's a little unorthodox for them to meet with you face-to-face, he notes in the body of the email, but all this means is that they likely have some questions they want to ask you, and that they haven't ruled you out yet. Try to think of it like a job interview. Best foot forward and all that.

There's no two ways around it: it's downright intimidating, being interviewed by a panel of your would-be peers. The advisory committee comprises twelve tenured professors, tasked with providing guidance to the president on the granting of tenure. I spot a handful of familiar faces when I step into the classroom, but most of them I only know in passing. Andrew Greene in a cranberry sweater. Henry Nguyen, a lanky biology professor with ink-black hair and a permanent glower. Wendy McAllister from the Communications Department, who gives me a smile and a half nod. She can't be all that much older than I am, her auburn curls cascading over an infinity scarf.

At least there's no bench at this tribunal. We're gathered in a classroom in the Franklin Complex, the committee members seated around a U-shaped table arrangement and a trigonometry problem still scribbled on the whiteboard. Teddy walked me to the room, but they asked him to wait outside. I take a seat at one of the ends, but there's no escaping the twelve faces pointed at me.

"Good afternoon, Clara." Andrew shuffles the papers in front of him. Looks like he's going to be leading this interrogation. "Let's not waste any time getting to the heart of the matter. I'm sure we're all ready to get on with our holiday break."

A couple committee members chuckle under their breath. I give a curt nod. Ready to get this over with.

"You come with an enthusiastic recommendation from Julien Zabini, Michael Jeong"—he lifts the corner on the paper in front of him, double-checking something underneath—"as well

as a number of your colleagues on the scholarship committee."
The page flaps back down. "Your dossier is more or less satis-
factory. The problem, unfortunately, lies not in what you have
to recommend you, but in your relatively young career. I can't
help feeling this application is a little rushed."

Henry Nguyen nods his agreement, more to himself than
to anyone else in the room, because his eyes remained fixed on
the page in front of him. They all have papers in front of them.
Notes.

"Julien suggested that I apply for tenure early," I explain.

Andrew scratches his brow with the eraser of his pencil as
he flicks through the papers. "It's not *un*heard of. But you have
to understand that it's made tricky by your lack of prior experience, save this brief position while you were in grad school—
assistant professor?" He glances up for confirmation and I nod.
"I also wanted to ask you about your high school education. It's
listed here as a charter school. Does that mean it was private?"

"More like independent study," I say.

One of the older professors clears phlegm from his throat.
"I think we can all agree that a homeschooled education is often—" He looks to his colleagues for input, though no one is
forthcoming. "Well, it's often a little subpar. There's no curriculum, and the parents are incapable of imparting information
to their children that they don't fully understand themselves."

"My homeschooling program was accredited," I explain, a
little irked. I can't quite believe I'm still arguing this, after all
these years, with everything else I've accomplished. "My mom
had a degree in early childhood education. Not to mention I
graduated from University of Maryland summa cum laude, I
hold a doctorate from Notre Dame, my research has been published in the *Tudor Quarterly Review*—"

"It's no matter," Andrew interrupts with a wave of his hand.

"More just a curiosity. There was also a question about one of your recommenders—Theodore Harrison?"

"What about him?"

"He's visiting, isn't he?"

"Yes, but we worked together on the gala subcommittee, which I highlighted in my—"

"But you knew each other prior," Andrew interrupts.

"Yes," I say, hesitant. I'm not sure where this is going.

"For how long?"

I glance at the other committee members like someone might rescue me from this odd line of questioning. As soon as Wendy McAllister meets my gaze, her blue eyes flick downward, and she pretends to scribble something on the paper in front of her. "Does it matter?"

Andrew holds up a hand, placating. "Curiosity."

An unfortunate side effect of the rumors floating around campus. "Seventeen years."

"There are . . . concerns," a steely-haired woman from the Engineering Department offers up, "about impartiality in your department, or a lack thereof. I understand the pair of you are sharing an office."

"Julien Zabini makes those decisions," I say, looking around at all of them. "You're not implying that Julien is biased."

"We're not implying anything," Andrew says. "We're simply trying to sort out the facts."

This, I realize, must be the reason they called me here. Not to talk about my lack of previous work experience or the fact that I was homeschooled, once upon a time. All that was pretense.

"Look at it from an outside perspective," Henry Nguyen pipes up. "You're a favorite of Julien's. An adjunct professor from Carnegie Mellon applies for a visiting scholar position that would typically be granted to someone a little more"—he waffles his head back and forth—"established. And you have—excuse the pun—but you *have* history. You have to admit, the sharing an office together, working on the same committee, it all looks a little odd."

"Not to mention your sister being enrolled in one of his classes," someone says.

"The committee is open to any faculty members who are willing to dedicate their time," I say. "And my sister signed up for classes like everyone else. I doubt she even checked beforehand to see who the instructor was." I'm not bothering to hide it now—I'm annoyed. This is a waste of my time. And frankly a little insulting to everyone involved. "I don't really understand what you're implying. Do you really think I asked Julien to give him a job? Assign us to the same office?"

The room falls silent. Okay, so maybe that's exactly what they're implying. I huff.

"Our goal here is to clear the air," Andrew says. "It might look one way from the outside, but I'd hope that your inside perspective might clear a few things up."

"I had no idea that Professor Harrison had applied for the visiting position, and if I had, I wouldn't have vouched for him." It sounds harsh, but it's also the truth—had Julien somehow found out we knew each other and asked my opinion on the matter, I would've been more likely at the time to try to *dissuade* him. "Julien never mentioned him by name until after I found out we were going to be sharing an office."

I do everything in my power to keep my temper in check for the remainder of the meeting, but by the time they shoo me out of the room to leave them to their deliberations, some of my anger must show on my face, because Teddy takes one look at me and furrows his brow. "How'd it go?"

"Not great." While we make our way down the hall, I do my best to summarize everything in undertone.

"It's just faculty gossip," Teddy says as soon as I've finished. We make our way through the quad, the dormant grass dusted with frost like confectioner's sugar. A bitter cold clings to the air and silver clouds overhead threaten more snow. "They're bored. Nothing's going to come of it. And the tenure advisory board doesn't even have the authority to reprimand Julien, certainly not at any school I've worked for."

I *am* worried about Julien. He's one of the few allies I've had at this school, and I fully intend to tell him about this meeting. But I am also, selfishly, worried about more than that. "What about you?" I ask.

Teddy stops walking, a confused laugh escaping him. "What about me?"

I hesitate a few paces ahead, my arms folded to fend off the cold. "There's no way you're going to get approved for another semester. Not if word gets out—"

"So I find a position somewhere else," he says, tossing up his hands. His intensity catches me off guard. "I'll teach at a community college if I have to."

I wait for him to add *or we run away to Edinburgh,* to really drive the point home, but he seems to know better. "Don't you realize what we're doing?" My voice cracks, but I'm determined to make him see reason. "We're doing what we always swore we wouldn't do. We're letting this dictate our decisions; you're talking about quitting your job for me, moving away from Pittsburgh and your mom's restaurant, giving up all these things that you wouldn't give up if it wasn't for—" I break off. Frustrated tears are welling in my eyes, stinging in the cold. "I'm terrified of you waking up one day and resenting me because you gave up too much."

"I'm talking about doing those things because I want to," he says. "Not because you're asking. You *haven't* asked."

"You're right," I say, stressing the words. "I haven't." It sounds a little more heartless than I intended, but I need to say it. I need him to know that I'm not asking any of this of him. I want him to stay. So badly that my chest hurts, a fist squeezing around my heart. But I can't voice that, because as soon as I do, I've tipped the scales. He'll be making a decision for *us*, not for *him*. And I can't stand the thought of it—an imagined argument, five or ten years from now, that culminates in *I wish I never quit that job for you.*

I wish we didn't get so caught up in the moment.

I wish we never met.

The muscles in his face draw tight, masklike, though not with any discernible emotion. "What, so now you don't want me here?"

"I didn't say that."

He blinks before ripping his gaze from mine. "You know, you mentioned once that you enjoy history because humans haven't changed all that much. You said that like it's a good thing." He pauses, like he's waiting for me to recollect, but it's not like I'd be inclined to forget. I've built a whole career out of my love for history. "I agree that people haven't changed," he continues. "People *don't* change, really. But I think that's one of the worst things about us. Here we are, with entire histories at our fingertips, answers to all your questions only a Google search away, but the reality is that people never learn a goddamn thing."

I don't know what to say to that, but I can't quite bear to look at him, so I stare across the quad, arms folded. The campus is largely abandoned this late into finals week, save the intermittent straggler, darting from one building to the next to escape the cold.

I feel Teddy's eyes on me, looking for some reaction. "We fucked this up once before and I'm pretty sure we both regretted it," he says slowly. "I have no interest in repeating my mistakes."

"Neither do I," I whisper.

He nods to himself, staring somewhere just beyond my shoulder. "Right. Okay." He exhales through his nose. "Take your time to think it over." Despite his best efforts to maintain composure, the soft sadness in his voice is utterly devastating. "You turned me away once. I'm not going to rush you to do it again."

And with that, he walks away.

CHAPTER

27

I moved to Manchester for my M.A. program, my old roommate found me on Facebook, and Teddy and I were close again. It started slow, a steady trickle of information, texts to check whether my plane landed safely and cell phone pictures of beautiful old buildings. Teddy had completed all his required coursework for his Ph.D., which meant he had moved from student to candidate, and while he was still exceptionally busy, he seemed a little less distracted—though I suspected his workload hadn't lessened all that much, if at all. He still had a dissertation to write and he was working as an assistant to one of the professors, feeding Scantrons into a scanner to flesh out his resume.

For my part, I spent large swaths of my time playing around on WhatsApp, keeping in touch with my parents and exchanging fleeting updates with Izzy. She'd kept busy in recent years, jumping straight out of her bachelor's into a volunteer program in Honduras, where she was being eaten alive by sand flies and posing for pictures with white-faced capuchin monkeys on Roatán. But I texted Teddy most often—not because I was expecting more than friendship, but because he was one of the few people in my life who'd been in my shoes. My family didn't quite understand why I had to be so far away, why I needed to be in *this* master's program as opposed to one closer to home; dispersed throughout the family group chat were prodding comments like *It's a shame you won't be home for Thanksgiving* and *It must be lonely, living in a strange country all by yourself.*

But it wasn't lonely, not really. For one, England wasn't all that strange—they spoke our language and I'd lived in London for an entire school year, so any semblance of culture shock was washed away with the first rain. My classes kept me busy, and my thesis busier. Several of the grads in my program arranged to meet for what they called History Happy Hour at a local pub, which I joined intermittently, but mostly I was focused on my work.

In October, Teddy called me. I thought it was strange because he almost always messaged me first to see if I had Wi-Fi—I wasn't eager to rack up my phone bill. I was in one of the study areas in Rylands Library, just off the main hall, my textbooks spread across a single-person desk beneath a latticed window. "Hey. I'm in the library," I whispered into the phone. But it was quiet. I pulled it away from my ear to make sure I'd answered the call. After a few seconds, I heard something—breathing, I thought—and my stomach sank. Something was wrong. "What is it? Is everything okay?"

"It's my dad," he said. "He had a stroke."

"Oh my god, Teddy. I'm so sorry." Immediately, I sprang into action, packing up my things so that I wouldn't have to whisper.

"I don't know what to do," he was saying. "They need me. He can't manage the business like this, he's not the same now, Clara, it's—" He broke off, breathing hard. "I don't think he can go back to work."

I slung the book bag over my shoulder and made my way out onto Deansgate. It was busy at that hour, the pavement shaded by brick-and-mortar buildings. "Don't panic," I said in what I hoped was a soothing voice. "The same sort of thing happened to my parents, and they ended up—"

"It's not the same thing," Teddy argued. "Your dad was able to get worker's comp. You were still living at home, you helped take care of him. It's completely different."

I tried not to feel too irked by his immediate dismissal of my experience. I needed to be patient and empathetic. "You could sell off the business," I suggested. "The auto body shop. It's not like you're going to run it."

"He'd never forgive me."

"If he can't work—"

"You don't get it," Teddy interrupted. "Clara, I'm worried I'm going to have to drop out."

* * *

I couldn't fathom it. There was no way that Teddy—who'd been eager to start college early, remained laser-focused on his goals through his late teens and into his early twenties—would just walk away from everything he'd worked so hard to achieve. He resolved to finish out the semester before flying home for the holidays, but everything beyond that was up in the air. We talked on the phone almost every week, but he was often distracted, a little scattered, and I was content to just be a listening ear.

For my part, I decided not to fly home for the holidays after my parents told me they planned to take Reagan to visit Grandma for a few days. Nothing against my grandmother, but the thought of flying home only to drive eleven hours to Knoxville—or even flying directly into McGhee Tyson, and then spending a week sleeping on a forty-year-old mattress that smelled like mothballs—sounded miserable, so I politely declined.

Instead, I spent the week leading up to Christmas wandering Manchester, growing increasingly aimless. I didn't regret staying put for the holidays, not exactly, but the weather was bleak and I was bored waiting for school to start up again, to give me purpose. For years now, I'd compartmentalized my life into a series of end goals: get into a good university; earn my bachelor's; get into *another* good university; earn my master's and my Ph.D. or DPhil so that I could get a tenure-track job and have all the emotional and financial security I'd dreamed of. I tried not to think about what goals I'd set after that, or how I'd function without a five-year plan.

On Christmas Eve, I wandered the Christmas market on Brazennose Street, where the spicy smell of gingerbread clung to the nippy air. I bought a cheap bottle of white wine at Lidl, fully intending to spend the evening drinking it alone, but then one of my classmates invited me to a dinner at her flat. A pity invite, I assumed, but with nothing better to do, I went. I sat with strangers around a long table with a red tablecloth and too much food. There was something a little surreal about it, like it was all staged—a movie set mimicking what a holiday dinner should have been, the guests paid actors, talking about meaningless things that sounded interesting on paper but that I couldn't convince myself to care about.

Afterward, I walked back to the student housing by myself, feeling uncharacteristically listless. But I knew this feeling would pass; I only felt like this because it was my first Christmas alone. Even the streets were empty and cold. My breath fogged the air and the pavement was absent its usual foot traffic, no black hackney carriages pulling up to the curb.

All I had to keep me company was my phone, and it jingled in the pocket of my puffer jacket, alerting me to an incoming call: Teddy Harrison. I didn't have Wi-Fi out on the street, which meant no WhatsApp, so a phone call would probably cost me an arm and a leg. But it was Christmas Eve, so why not? I slid to answer.

"Sorry," Teddy said as soon as I answered. "What time is it there?"

I pulled my phone away from my ear to check the clock. "A little after ten. I'm just walking back from dinner."

"By yourself?"

I didn't miss the concerned tone. "It's pretty safe," I said. Actually, in retrospect, I'm not sure that it was safe, but I didn't really think much of it at the time. Walking home alone, at night, in the cold had seemed like the perfect solution to shock me out of this strange and melancholy ache—not quite homesickness, but a hollowness, like a jigsaw puzzle with a piece missing.

"Anyway," I said, "how's everything across the pond?" I couldn't imagine he was calling just to wish me a good Christmas Eve, not when a Christmas Day phone call had always been our tradition. Every time we'd talked lately, it had been because he needed a sounding board. And I was happy to be that right about now. Something to give me purpose.

"Fine," he said. Then, taking a deep breath, he added: "I'm going to take a year off. Figure some things out."

I nodded to myself, processing this. "What about the shop?"

"Dad had a couple guys working in there with him," he said. "My mom figures we can rent the space out to them. There's some legal stuff to figure out, and I'm not sure how exactly we're going to budget, but—" He broke off. "Clara, this isn't why I called."

I'd reached the cathedral, and any other night, I might've marched on past. But tonight, I stopped to look at the Gothic clock tower, its knuckled spires all the more menacing in the dark. They'd erected a Christmas tree on the lawn, the wind-tattered boughs strung with lights that glowed a soft, buttery white. "Why'd you call, then?"

"I miss you."

"I miss you, too," I said, a little wary.

"I mean it when I say that, you know. I think about you every minute of every day." His deep voice was hoarse, raw with some unnamed emotion. Maybe he'd been drinking, too. "I thought about flying out there to surprise you, to talk about everything in person, before I realized that was completely idiotic," he said with a gruff laugh. "I don't even know your address."

My eyebrows pinched together. "What are you talking about?"

"I'm talking about us."

Us. One word, and the whole conversation shifted, like the world's axis was nudged slightly off-kilter.

"God, I'm butchering this," he said with a humorless laugh. "It's just that all this, Dad having the stroke, trying to juggle everything with my research, it's a lot. And I've been thinking. You're the one thing in the world that makes me happy right now, you've been there for me through all of it. I guess I don't really understand why we're still wasting time."

I shook my head even though he couldn't see me, feeling small in front of the colossal Christmas tree and looming cathedral. In some ways, I'd wanted there to be an *us* for a long time. But at the same time, transitioning from friends to something more felt like taking a leap across an ever-widening chasm, hoping we'd find our footing on the other side.

"We're not wasting time," I said. "We're working toward things. Focusing on—"

"But what's the point, if we could turn around and lose everything tomorrow?"

I tossed up a hand. "What's the point in anything?"

"Sorry, I don't think I'm—" he said, sighing, a rush of wind in my ear. "I'm not saying we both drop out. I'm saying that I don't want to waste another day not being with you."

His voice sounded tinny through the phone, small and faraway. There was something unsatisfactory about it, to not have him standing in front of me, looking me in the eye as he said all these things. Things I might've liked to hear, under different circumstances—*later,* I wanted to beg him. *Tell me these things later.* Because right now, all they did was hurt. "I have to finish school," I whispered.

"Then finish it," he said. "I'm not asking you to drop out. You've got six months left in Manchester, and then you can come back here, find—"

"I'm not talking about my master's," I interrupted. "I've applied to a doctoral program at Notre Dame. In Indiana," I added, with emphasis, when he didn't immediately say something.

"Then we try long distance," he said, undeterred.

"That never works."

"It could work with us."

"It's a distraction," I blurted, throwing my free arm wide. "You're only saying all of this now because you don't have anything better to do." It shut him up; the line went deathly quiet. "Shit." I pressed my fingers into my forehead, hanging my head. "That didn't come out right. All I meant is that you might feel differently once you're back in school."

"You're not listening," he said. "You matter more to me than school. More than some stupid plan, tenure by thirty, whatever else I thought I was going to—I mean, what the hell, I'm only studying history because *you* showed me how to fall in love with it." My heart stuttered at the mention of love, even when he wasn't directly confessing it. "You're always there, Clara. In everything I do. You've always been it, for me. Tell me you don't feel the same."

What scared me most was the temptation to say yes. Frustrated tears had welled in my eyes, smudging all the lights on the Christmas tree, because I already knew what I had to say, and it was going to kill me to say it. *Later* wasn't an answer. *Later* would only create a false sense of hope, warp our friendship into some sort of sadistic waiting game—though maybe it had always been that, in a way.

"No."

"No, what?" he asked, annoyed.

I took a shaky breath. "No, I don't feel the same."

His voice cracked a little as he said, "You're lying."

I shut my eyes tight. It killed me, hearing him like that. But I had to stand my ground. "I'm telling you no."

He fell silent, breathing hard. I just stood there, wiped my nose on the back of my sleeve, waiting for him to say something. The minutes seemed to stretch on, until finally, he managed a quiet, "Merry Christmas, Clara," and the line went dead.

CHAPTER

28

PRESENT

I spend Friday washing bedsheets, Swiffering the hardwood floors, and scrubbing the grout on the countertops, as though Izzy's going to march in here tomorrow and immediately swipe the nearest surface to inspect it for dust. I'm pretty sure I could live in a hovel, for all the difference it would make to her, but it helps keep my mind off things. Thick snowflakes whirl beyond the kitchen window as I toss empty bottles of salad dressing and overripe fruits from the fridge. The weather hasn't relented since this afternoon; there's five inches on the ground and counting, unusual for December in Maryland, but there are no signs of it stopping.

As terrible as I feel admitting it, I wish I hadn't promised to pick Izzy up from the airport tomorrow morning. It's all just been ... a lot, the past couple of days. I didn't hear from Teddy all day yesterday—not that I blame him. We left things where we've pretty much always left them: inconclusive. Except I know that if I let him walk out of my life again, this time he won't come back.

Maybe I'm letting my stubbornness get the best of me. It's not like he's asking me to move closer to Pittsburgh, rewrite my entire life. On the contrary, he's offering to follow wherever I go. Some would call that romantic. Izzy certainly would. Maybe a love like that is wasted on me. I never sat around dreaming about meeting my soulmate, falling in love. Maybe that's because I met the only person for me when I was fourteen. Love never had to be added to my list of never-ending goals because it was just . . . already there. A constant in my life, something I took for granted, and I didn't quite appreciate it until it was long gone.

When my phone chimes in my pocket, I straighten up in the middle of wiping out the bottom shelf of the refrigerator to check it. But it's not Teddy. It's an email from Julien, and the subject line makes my stomach bottom out.

From: Julien Zabini (julien_zabini@irving.edu)
To: Clara Fernsby (clara_fernsby@irving.edu)

Date: December 13, 6:12 P.M.
Subject: Tenure Decision Letter
Clara,
Attached is the decision letter from the tenure advisory board. I know it's not quite what we hoped for, but it's not all bad. Let's discuss.
J

I take a long and measured breath. Okay. Sounds like they rejected me. I can't say I didn't have time to prepare myself for this, but I'm feeling a little nauseated anyway. I open the letter, because why not? Better to get it all over with at once. It's a PDF file, the letter emblazoned with the university crest:

Professor Clara Fernsby, History Department
University of Irving
1200 E Richmond Ave
Irving, MD 21532
Dear Clara,
I am writing as a follow-up to our meeting on Wednesday.
I'd like to thank you once again for taking the time to meet
with us and your patience in answering our questions.

I scoff at this, because I don't think I was all that patient. I
was pretty short with them, actually. But I keep on reading.

I regret to share that opinion was divided in regard to
your application for tenure, with the majority feeling
that your application was premature. While we are
immensely grateful for your contributions to our university,
particularly your growing collection of published works and
your extradepartmental activities, we ultimately felt that
your overall relevant experience was lacking. This opinion
was conveyed to the president, who elected not to move
forward with your case for tenure.

We would, however, like to invite you to apply for an
associate professor opening for the upcoming academic
year. I'd also invite you to reapply for tenure again once
you've reached the seven-year mark; while your career
shows promise, the committee is in agreement that we'd like
to see a couple of years' more experience under your belt
before considering your application again.

Warm regards,
Andrew Greene, Ph.D.
Chair
Tenure Advisory Committee

I kneel in front of the refrigerator, scanning the letter again. It's not unheard of for assistant professors to be offered a slightly better position in lieu of tenure, but I'm not even sure they're offering—just inviting me to apply. I wait to feel something. Indignation, maybe. But I'm numb.

It was always a long shot, securing tenure so early in my career. I don't resent them for denying me. I don't resent Julien for encouraging me to apply. I don't feel anything. It's as though suddenly, out of the blue, the thing I've put first for my entire life—my career, my professional reputation, my future—it doesn't matter to me either way.

Reagan skirts around me as she enters the kitchen, tossing me an odd look. She grabs a mug from one of the overhead cupboards and fills it beneath the tap. "What's the matter with you?"

I glance over at her. "They rejected my application for tenure." It comes out sounding so calm, measured. I stuff my phone back in my pocket and drag myself to my feet, collecting the sponge and spray bottle of disinfectant that I was using to clean out the fridge. I set them on the counter.

Reagan tracks my movement. "I'm sorry," she says after a minute. It's uncharacteristically gentle, coming from her. But then she adds, "They're a bunch of fucking fossils."

I sputter a laugh, but she's not even smiling.

"Seriously," she says. "They don't know what they're missing out on. You're pretty much the smartest person I've ever met."

My gaze snaps to hers. She just shakes her head at me, her jaw set, like she really believes what she's saying. It makes me feel a little less numb, maybe. I'm tempted to hug her, but I'm not sure how that would go over.

"They also invited me to apply for an associate professor position," I say. "It's not tenure, but it's still a step up."

She rolls her eyes—now *that's* a Reagan face I'm much more familiar with. I press my lips together.

"You're not going to apply," she says, disbelieving.

I don't say anything.

"Nope," she says. "No way. You give them the middle finger. There's literally no other option."

It's a little melodramatic, all things considered—the advisory board hasn't directly insulted me. Or maybe they have, but *c'est la vie*, because when you're a young woman in academia, there's bound to be some old guy lurking around the next office over, looking for an excuse to call you incompetent. *Inexperienced*. Whatever.

I lift my shoulders and let them drop. "I don't know."

"What does Teddy think?"

"We haven't really talked about it."

She sets her mug on the counter. "Well, why not?"

"Because it's my decision," I say, though even to my own ears, it sounds like a half-hearted excuse. "And whatever he does is his."

"Are you kidding me right now?" She tosses up her hands. "It's like you're determined to waste your whole life sitting in the fig tree."

I blink at her. "The what?"

"It's from Plath." When I just give her a blank look, she prompts, "*The Bell Jar*? It's a metaphor. Your life is split off in all these different branches. Work. Family. *Love*." She places extra emphasis on this last word, like she feels the need to make sure I understand she's talking about my relationship and not my job. I glower. "You convince yourself that you have to choose just one, only one fig, but you can't decide which branch to pluck from, and you take so long to make up your mind that you never reach for any of them, and they all start to go bad, and at the end of the day you're left with nothing because you were too scared to choose."

She's rambling now. Not unlike the way *I* sometimes ramble, like when I've bottled something up for so long it just comes spilling out, and once it starts, there's nothing I can do to stop it.

Yup. It's word vomit.

"Except for you"—she flings a hand at me, her voice pitching up—"you're convinced you've already picked your fig and you're just going let all the other ones rot. Perfectly good figs!" She finishes her rant with an emphatic swing of her arm.

"I'm trying to think about what's best for everyone," I snap. "Including you."

She scrunches her whole face in a frown, incredulous. "What does this have to do with me?"

"Your tuition. The student loans. If I'd accepted an offer of tenure, the school would've covered half the cost. But a promotion, that's almost as good. I'll just have to help you out of my own pocket."

She shakes her head. "I don't want it."

"What are you talking about?"

"I don't need you to make this decision because of me," she says. I don't think she realizes, and I'm not about to be the one to point it out, but she sounds like me. "This has nothing to do with me."

"So you're going to make a poor financial decision because of your stubborn—"

"Stop mothering me!" she explodes. "I'm not a child and you're not Mom." For a moment, I'm stunned into silence, and she takes advantage of it. "Ever since Dad's injury, it's like you decided that it's your life's purpose to do better than they did, like you can fix it—"

I find my voice, but she continues talking right over me, both of us half shouting. "I wouldn't have to mother you if you didn't act like—"

"—already applied for a scholarship, so I don't need your stupid money—"

"—or showed even a modicum of responsibility."

We finish at the same moment, only half hearing what the other said because we both wanted to say our piece. It takes me a few seconds to process the bits I did hear, but when I do, I look at her with fresh eyes. "Sylvia Plath," I say, disbelieving.

"What about her?" Reagan snaps.

"You wrote the essay for the, which one"—I snap my fingers—"the Lizette Woodworth Reese Award."

She makes a sound that's probably meant to be a sarcastic laugh, but it comes out a little strangled. "That's a mouthful."

I'm not laughing. "Did you write it?"

She seems to hesitate, jiggling her leg. "I wasn't supposed to tell you," she mumbles finally. "Since you're on the panel or whatever. They told me I'd be disqualified if you knew."

I nod to myself, bracing my hands on the kitchen counter, coming to a fast realization. I'll have to step down from the scholarship committee. No official decisions have been announced yet. If I step down now, I remove myself from the equation. Goodman would temporarily succeed me as chair. At least until they could find someone else for the job. And in the meantime, they'd probably still grant the scholarship to Reagan, without my input.

I cast her a sideways glance, guilt creeping over me. "I'm sorry for shouting," I mumble.

She stares at the floor. "I'm sorry, too."

I know better than to press my luck by asking her for a hug right now, but I make a mental note to hug her more often.

* * *

I slap cables on my tires before driving into the city early Saturday morning to grab Izzy from the airport. Perhaps *too* early

Saturday morning—traffic's cut in half on the weekends, and I arrive with a whole hour to spare, so I pull over to the curb and search on my phone for the nearest coffee shop with a decent rating. *Hot Off the French Press.* I set it as my destination and drive a couple blocks over, parking on the street and feeding some change from my cupholder into the meter. It hasn't snowed yet in Baltimore, but it's drizzling. The café is part of an old strip, gold peel-and-stick letters affixed to the window beneath a scalloped black-and-white awning.

Wait a second. I glance up and down the narrow one-way street, déjà vu washing over me. I've been here before. I remember the old-fashioned awnings, the comic book store next door, the Chinese restaurant just past it. And if I kept walking, just another door down . . .

Still, I'm not about to waste time driving around to find a different coffee shop, so I pop inside. It's cramped inside, but the coffee smells amazing, rich and earthy. An espresso machine hisses and trickles, steam rising from somewhere behind the counter. I order two black coffees to go, stop by the self-serve station to stuff a couple creamers and stir sticks in my pocket, and then I'm back out the door. I wait at the curb for a semi-truck to amble down the narrow road and then I walk around to the driver side, setting the coffees on the roof of my car so that I can unlock the door. I've really got to look into buying a new car—one with a working key fob, for example.

"Clara?"

There's that déjà vu again.

I peek over the top of my car. A woman stands on the sidewalk, car keys in one hand and a plastic bag in the other. She's got the hood of her raincoat thrown over her head. "Sorry. I knew I recognized that car." When I only gape at her, she points at herself with the keys. "Mindy Schooner."

Time stands still on the quiet side street. There's something surreal about seeing her here, now, just a few doors down from the sandwich shop. "I didn't think you still lived in Baltimore." It comes out sounding more accusatory than intended.

"I live just over that way. Wyman Park. Been in the same apartment for years."

I realize that I'm standing in the middle of the street and I move a little closer to the curb.

"I was craving a turkey melt"—she lifts the bag—"and nobody does it like Augie's, so . . ."

We stand there for a moment, the silence so thick you could almost reach out and swipe it away, like snow collecting on a windshield. "It's nice to see you," I say. "You look great."

By this I mean: *you look healthy, happy.* But it comes out sounding, at least to my ears, like *you look different.* Mellowed, somehow, and I wonder whether that's because of the years spent around Teddy or just getting older. It occurs to me for the first time that they might've been good for each other, in a way—not as life partners, but as life lessons, the sort of people who help you learn and grow, even if they don't stick around for good.

"Well, happy holidays," she says awkwardly, and she marches to her car a few meters away, unlocking it with a beep. A little shaken up, I start to climb into my car before realizing that I left the coffees sitting on the roof. I retrieve them, but not without glancing back at Mindy. She's bent across the front seat, her yellow coattails sticking out of the driver side door.

"Hey," I say, fully aware that I should probably just shut up, but I can't help it.

She straightens up.

"I'm sorry if I wasn't exactly friendly toward you in college. I've thought about it a lot since then and I think I might've been a jerk."

She laughs under her breath. "A lot of us were jerks in college, in our own way. I mean, I sort of just . . . barged my way in. I always had a bad habit of doing that."

"It's not a bad thing," I say, my voice small. "You kept things lively."

She snorts. "A lot of good it did me. You certainly didn't try to keep in touch with me afterward. No one did." I have no idea how to respond to that, but she saves me from having to say anything by adding, "And that's not me saying I want to be friends now, for the record."

"Well, I'm sorry"—I give a small shake of my head—"if you were looking for friends and I wasn't there. I sort of kept to myself, around that time. Head in the books and all that."

She gives me a close-lipped smile that doesn't quite reach her eyes. "That's probably something the two of you had in common."

There's no need to ask who she's talking about, but when I give her a quizzical look, she adds, "I realize that might sound sarcastic, but it's really not. You guys make sense together. I just"—she lifts her shoulders and lets them drop again—"didn't see it."

CHAPTER

29

I spent the remainder of my time in Manchester in a sort of trance: eyes strained from reading and writing, skimming and editing; my neck and shoulders aching from hours spent hunched over the computer; my feelings bottled up, talking to few acquaintances and fewer friends. In the midst of all of it, like a true masochist, I stuck to my plan. That March, I accepted an offer of enrollment from the History Department at University of Notre Dame, and by the end of the spring semester, I was packing my bags to move to another unfamiliar city.

For the first six months after that phone call on Christmas Eve, I tried to reach out to Teddy. I'd call, he'd send me to voice mail. I sent long-winded texts apologizing for what I'd said, emphasizing how much our friendship mattered to me. I sent short, nonsensical texts wishing him a Happy Presidents' Day or complaining about my professors. All went unanswered. When I tried to call him on my birthday and it went directly to voice mail, I assumed he'd blocked me and accepted my fate.

For the next couple years, I stalked his Facebook periodically, where he'd conveniently *forgotten* to block me (and I wasn't about to call attention to that by trying to message him). But my curiosity was never really satisfied. He was pretty inactive, save the rare occasions when he shared an article, usually without comment. So I clung to the little details, like when he changed his current city from Allentown to Dormont, or the day our mutual friends jumped from seven to eight. Miranda Schooner, of all people. It struck me as odd, and I dwelled on it for a few days, but they had met in passing a couple times, and I was just as soon distracted by my research.

* * *

I was a couple years into the program and finished with the required coursework when I decided to apply for a part-time job teaching freshman-level courses for an online college. It had seemed like the easiest option, at the time, but the application called for three letters of recommendation, preferably from different institutions. My thesis advisor was happy to comply. A quick email to one of my professors in Manchester garnered a reply that just said letter, as requested, with a glowing review attached. But my capstone advisor at UMD had to go and make things difficult.

I'd feel more comfortable recommending you if we had a chance to talk first, she said. That way you could update me on what you've been up to in the interim, your research, etc.

Professor Blanchett had retired a few years ago and plainly had too much time on her hands. I tried to suggest a video call, but she wouldn't hear of it, so I reluctantly agreed to meet up for lunch as soon as I was back in Maryland for summer break; thankfully, the deadline for the application wasn't until the end of July. We arranged to meet at a sandwich shop near Hampden.

On an afternoon in mid-June, I parked outside a Harris Teeter and marched three blocks with a messenger bag full of notes and papers slung over my shoulder, ready to make my case.

I never did get that recommendation. I suppose fleeing the restaurant mid-lunch because your former best friend turned up with his girlfriend makes you look *flighty* and *unprofessional*—at least according to Professor Blanchett's strongly worded follow-up email. I ended up sitting in my Volvo in the parking lot of the supermarket with my seat belt buckled, sobs racking my body. It was like everything I'd bottled up for the past three years was pouring out all at once. I'd lost my best friend, but I guess I didn't really feel the full weight of that loss until that day.

My hands were on the steering wheel at ten and two, but my vision was so blurry that there was no way I could drive. I needed to calm down. I needed to do something. I reached over to the passenger seat and grabbed my phone out of the messenger bag, blinking tears out of my eyes as I scrolled down my recent messages. I found my mom and pressed call. It rang twice and went to voice mail, so I called the house instead.

Dad answered on the first ring.

"Hey," I said, trying to keep my voice steady. "Mom's not answering her phone. Is she at home?"

"She's at work right now," he said. Then, after a beat: "Is everything okay?"

"Yeah, it's fine, it's just—" I took a shuddering breath and exhaled, calming down a little now that I was hearing a familiar voice. Now that someone was hearing *me* have a total breakdown. "Could I just . . . vent to you for a minute?" I didn't expect him to say much of anything back, to impart any sage wisdom or anything. This was my dad we were talking about.

"Of course," he said, sounding concerned.

So I did. I told him everything—well, almost everything—that had happened between me and Teddy: how we'd bonded over burned CDs and used history books, how we realized on an afternoon at Federal Hill Park that we might like each other as more than friends. How it all came crashing down over a phone call on Christmas Eve, and how I realized today that he'd never forgive me. That we'd never forgive each other. It actually felt good to talk to my dad for once, even though I was pretty sure he wouldn't know what to say by the time I was finished.

"That's a shame," he said slowly, after I'd recounted the incident in the sandwich shop. "He seemed like an all right kid. And you both like history, so that's—" I choked on a fresh sob, and he must've realized that even this lukewarm praise for Teddy wasn't helping, because he cleared his throat and switched tactics. "But you know what they say. 'It's better to have loved and lost than to never have loved at all,' and all that."

I shut my eyes, trying to stem the flow of the tears. "Please, Dad, I'm not in the mood for more idioms."

He chuckled uncertainly. "Don't know why you're saying 'more,' but I'm pretty sure that's not an idiom, Clare Bear. It's Shakespeare."

I was almost certain *that* wasn't right either. But I didn't have Teddy here to laugh with, to point out that my dad had attributed the quote to the wrong person, that that was actually what George Washington had said after he chopped down the cherry tree. I'd probably never get to share any of those inside jokes again.

It had been three years since our falling-out, but the wound felt fresh, opened anew. Somehow, this time, it was almost worse—because this time I got a glimpse of him moving on. The cruel irony was that it had taken me seeing him with someone else to realize how badly I wanted him for myself. Turning him away had resulted in the one thing that forced me to recognize the irrefutable truth, something that had become such a fundamental part of me that I didn't even notice it: I was in love with my best friend.

And I'd broken his heart anyway.

I couldn't possibly put all of that into words, not coherent ones, and my dad was waiting quietly on the other end of the phone. So I just said, "This really sucks."

"Clara, listen to me," Dad said. "I know it hurts right now, but you have to keep things in perspective. Everybody goes through rough patches. If you want to be together, then you'll find a way to be together, sooner or later. Simple as that."

"But it's not that simple. Everything gets so complicated—I mean, look at you and Mom."

"What about us?"

"I don't know." I sniffled. "You guys argue. Sometimes you don't seem happy."

"That's not true," he said, sounding a little offended. "Sure, we argue, but I couldn't ask for a better partner than your mother."

"But don't you ever wonder if you were really meant to be together?" I asked. "If it was . . . fate, or something, or if the person you're really meant to be with is still out there somewhere, and it would've all been so easy with them, but instead you're with the wrong person, you took the hard road—"

"Clara," he interrupted, more serious than I'd ever heard him, "love *is* the hard road. The person you're meant to be with is whoever you choose to be with. And you'll have to fight for it and make sacrifices for it every step of the way. You just have to choose someone who's worth all that trouble, and then you have to keep on choosing them, every day."

CHAPTER

30

PRESENT

I meet Izzy inside the airport. She's tan despite it being winter, her thick black hair gleaming beneath the harsh overhead lighting. I didn't know it was possible for hair to look that perfect after a seven-hour flight. She nearly runs over some lady's foot with her rolling suitcase as she dashes across the airport and yanks me into a hug.

"It's been too damn long," she says, her chin balanced on the top of my head. She's always been statuesque, but it's easy to forget just how tall she is. "It's so good to see you."

"You really have no idea," I mutter. My cheek is sort of pressed into her cleavage. I think *she* forgets how tall she is, when it comes down to it. "This week has been—" I blow out a breath. "Let's just say it's been a lot."

She pulls back, alarmed, holding me at arm's length like she needs to inspect me for bumps or scratches. "Are you okay?"

"No?" I say, not entirely sure myself.

"Is it the holidays?" she asks. "I'm sorry to ask you to pick me up in the middle of everything, I know this is a stressful time of—"

"It's not the holidays," I say.

After that, there's no avoiding it. Everything that's happened comes pouring out, word vomit right in the middle of the airport. People are giving us weird looks. Izzy ushers me out to the parking garage, where we sit in my Volvo while I explain the confrontation with the advisory committee, the rejection letter, the argument with Reagan, and Teddy. A lot about Teddy.

When I finish, I flip down the sun visor and swipe at my damp cheeks, trying to preserve the concealer I applied this morning to create the illusion that I'd actually gotten sleep. Izzy watches me, sympathetic.

"Do I sound like a total mess?" I wonder aloud. I'm not used to being the messy friend. I'm the neat, methodical one. The only person who's ever had me beat in that regard is Teddy.

"Honestly," she says flatly, "you sound like you could use a drink."

* * *

After dropping Izzy at the house so that she can shower and settle in, I swing by campus to talk to Julien. It's the Saturday after end of term, but when I emailed him asking whether he had a minute to talk, he suggested we meet on campus. Snow blankets the quad, pristine but for a few sets of footprints like baste stitching on an unfinished quilt.

I climb the stairs in the Hall of Letters to the third floor. The rooms are mostly dark, abandoned for the holidays, but I slow when I notice that one of the doors is propped open, warm light spilling out into the hall. It's not Julien's office, but I nudge it wider, announcing myself with a verbal, "Knock, knock."

"Holy balls!" Bel springs off the floor, clutching her chest. "You scared the crap out of me. What are you even doing here?"

Her desk is barren, battered cardboard boxes on the floor are stuffed with books and boxes of staples and sticky notes, and a roll of clear packing tape rests on the chair. "I could ask you the same question," I say, looking around at the mess. "What's all this?"

She settles back on the floor. "I'm packing. I've been offered a position on the tenure track at Georgia State."

"Congratulations," I say. Bel's been talking about wanting a job back in Atlanta since I first met her three years ago. "Seriously, that's amazing. I'm really happy for you."

"Thank you." She tapes up one of the boxes, but she glances over with mischief glinting in her eye. "Not sure my committee participation helped."

I seat myself on the edge of her desk. "Think they would've preferred the Krav Maga?"

"I'm not talking about my application." She smirks. "I wasn't a very good buffer."

"Oh, I don't know." I feign a sigh. "You might've buffered a thing or two."

She laughs. "Not gonna lie, there's not a lot I'll miss around here, but I will miss working with you."

"I'm going to miss you, too." I hesitate. I've lost count of the number of would-be friendships I let go, classmates and campmates that fell by the wayside in the hustle and bustle of my complicated life. "When do you leave?"

"Planning for Monday, though I technically have my apartment through New Year's. Want to spend the holidays with family, you know."

"You should come out for drinks tonight," I suggest. "I've got a friend visiting from Portugal. We're planning to stop by The Falconer later. I feel like you guys would really hit it off."

Bel raises her eyebrows at me, like she's not sure whether I mean hit it off or *hit it off*, but before either of us has a chance to say anything more, we're interrupted by a sharp knock on the open door.

"Thought I heard voices." Julien hovers in the doorway, arching a brow at the pair of us—Bel kneeling among the scattered boxes, me perched on the desk—before his gaze settles on me. "Sorry to interrupt, but did you still want to discuss—?"

He doesn't quite finish the question because I didn't tell him what I wanted to talk about. Mostly because I'm still not sure. Heart hammering in my throat, I hop down from the desk. He retreats into the hall and Bel mouths something at me behind his back, miming a texting motion with her thumbs. I give her a thumbs-up before following Julien down the hall, a silent march to Hall of Letters 301 that feels a lot like marching to my own execution. Once inside, he shuts the door with a snap and pours two fingers of scotch, setting the etched crystal glass on the mahogany desk in front of me.

"Let me be the first to offer congratulations," he says as he pours a second glass, and then holds it out in a toast.

I stare at him, nonplussed.

"I'm looking at our newest associate professor."

"The advisory board invited me to apply," I point out. "They didn't offer me a job."

"Yes, well"—he settles in his chair, leather creaking, his glass still held aloft—"formality. But it's already been discussed. You're a shoo-in at this point. The obvious woman for the job." He frowns. "The *only* woman for the job, when you really get down to it."

I stare into the glass of scotch. I'm not sure how to feel about that. I'm still angry, I suppose, at the way the advisory board handled things. But it's not a white-hot anger. It's more . . . tepid. Like I've left it sitting for too long. And I can't really be bothered to bring it to a boil. "Teddy—Theodore Harrison, I mean," I say. "He applied to extend his stay as a visiting professor." Julien doesn't say anything. He just waits for me to continue, so I do. "I know you don't get the final say, but you choose whether or not to push that application through. Or it can stop with you."

He dips his head, acknowledging this fact.

"I guess what I'm asking," I continue, "is whether you're going to push it through?"

He regards me curiously. "Are you asking me to push it through?"

I don't answer. No. Maybe.

"Clara." He sighs, sitting up in his chair, and sets his untouched glass on the desk in front of him. "You can't choose whether or not you want this job based on who's still going to work here in six months. I like you very much. You're professional. Goal-oriented. And a charismatic lecturer. Students like you because you're passionate about what you do, and that translates. Irving would be lucky to keep you around a little longer. You," he emphasizes, "not a package deal."

I nod. I understand all of that. But I'm also not quite satisfied by his explanation. All those things he's complimenting me on, it's nice to hear them—but they're not really *me*, specifically. They're a part of me in the same sense that they're a part of so many other professional, goal-oriented, passionate historians. I've strived to be all those things, but that doesn't change the fact that they're my most replaceable qualities. There are thousands of hungry grad students who'd be happy to be those things for Irving.

I guess it just would've been nice to hear how they value me as a Tudor historian in a department that has none. How my publications have contributed to the overall prestige of our institution. How I'm . . . I don't know. All the other things I am. But I suppose they haven't really been privy to all that. Whatever "that" is. I've buried it all beneath layers of *professionalism*.

I look up from my glass. "Did you know it's been like eight years since I've said the word 'fuck'?"

A smile tugs at the corner of Julien's mouth. "I did not."

"I thought it was unprofessional," I explain. "Never mind the fact that Gary Reid drops seventeen F-bombs in a single lecture."

"It's not against any university policy," Julien says diplomatically.

"I was also worried that it would be unprofessional if I told you that I didn't want to share an office with Teddy." I'm rambling now. "Which was fine, by the way, in the long run—I mean, he wasn't even in there half the time, and we obviously worked things out, so it didn't really matter—" I take a deep breath. "That's not the point. The point is," I say, "I'm going to take some time off."

He doesn't say anything. He just raises his eyebrows, the ghost of a smile on his lips.

"But assistant professors don't get sabbatical," I press on. "And associate professors—I'm guessing they don't either, not if they don't have tenure. Sabbatical is for tenured professors. Someone that the school has invested in, whom they trust to come back."

He dips his chin. "You'd be correct."

"So in that case, by 'time off'"—I hold my breath for a split second, wondering if I'm really about to do this, and *oh my god*, I'm about to do this—"I guess what I'm really saying is that I quit."

I'm met with silence. Julien sucks his teeth and picks up his glass, but he doesn't take a drink. I stare at him. He stares back.

"And I guess what *I'm* saying is"—he nods at his whisky—"I'll drink to that."

I blink at him. "You're not mad?"

"On the contrary," he says. "I'm happy to write you a glowing letter of recommendation, should you ever need one. Irving would've been lucky to have you, but off the record, I'm not sure I'd accept a consolation prize after the way you were treated, either."

I realize Julien's still waiting for me to join him in a toast, so

I clink my glass against his and then toss it back. The scotch is peaty and strong.

"The advisory board," I ask, leaning forward to set my glass on the desk, "they spoke to you?"

"They did."

"Did they—" I try to find the right way to phrase it. "Did they threaten to take any sort of action against you? Because I tried to make it clear that there was no bias involved, but—"

"You forget that I'm already tenured," he interrupts with an apologetic smile. "There's not much they can do to threaten where I'm at. Though I will say—again, off the record—that Andrew Greene has had it out for me ever since I was elected chair."

"Why?"

"He thought it should go to a more . . . *distinguished* member of the faculty."

In other words, Andrew Greene thought the chair position should've gone to him. I can't help smirking at that. At the risk of sounding completely corny, I say, "I'm not sure it gets much more distinguished than you."

As soon as I leave Julien's office, I dig my phone out of my messenger bag and scroll through my contacts while I'm making my way down to the parking lot. We'd exchanged numbers after the guest lecture, but I haven't spoken to her since. I'm so amped up, I don't even pause to consider the cost of making an international call. The least I could've done was open WhatsApp, maybe shot her a message first. Actually, it's like nine thirty at night in Scotland, and on a Saturday. Maybe I shouldn't—

"I was hoping I'd hear from you," she answers.

"Lorna," I say, "I am *so* sorry for calling after hours, I wasn't thinking about the—"

"Ah, no bother," she says. "I'm something of a night owl,

anyway. Any particular reason for your call, or are you just looking to have a blether?"

"You mentioned something in passing before giving the guest lecture," I say as I unlock my car, "about a program there in Edinburgh?"

"Yes, I was hoping you might be calling about—" A dog yaps in the background, and she holds the phone away to have a brief but heated argument with it—most of which I don't quite catch. "You know," she says, returning the phone to her ear, "let me send out a few emails tomorrow. Or, wait, what day is it?"

"Saturday," I say.

"Monday. I'll send them out Monday."

By the time we hang up a few minutes later, I'm feeling quite good about things. Well, *most* things. I still haven't spoken to Teddy. I guess maybe I've been putting it off, because a part of me is scared it'll be like last time all over again—calls sent to voice mail, text messages that go unanswered. But the longer I wait, the less chance I can mend whatever damage has already been done. So I suck it up. I press call.

It's ringing.

* * *

Izzy is probably going to wonder what's taking me so long . . . except who am I kidding? I already know it takes her two-point-five hours just to blow-dry her amazing hair. Not to mention, she's going to have to duke it out with Reagan over that flat iron.

It's still ringing.

For all I know, he's back in Pittsburgh right now. Maybe he packed his bags Wednesday and never looked back. I didn't even stop by our shared office to see whether he'd boxed up his things. He must've, if his application for next semester wasn't approved. Though maybe he doesn't know that yet.

There's a click, and for a moment, I wonder if he's sent me to voice mail. But then a familiar, deep voice says, "I was starting to worry."

I breathe a sigh of relief at the warmth in his tone—no hurt, no exasperation. "Hi."

"I thought maybe you weren't going to call," he says. "In which case I would've had to show up on your doorstep to beg you to reconsider."

"Of course I was going to call," I say in a small voice. But I don't really want to have another serious conversation over a phone call. "Can you meet me at The Falconer in maybe"—I hold the phone away from my ear to double-check the time—"twenty minutes?"

CHAPTER

31

It's after sundown and snowing again by the time I find parking behind Lucretia's, but I came prepared. I straighten my beanie before checking my reflection in the rearview. I look ridiculous, but oh well. Shocking revelations are way easier to swallow when they come from an almost-thirty-two-year-old woman in mittens and a pom-pom beanie, right?

Right.

Snow crunches beneath my boots as I make my way along Bridge Street, brick buildings cast sepia by the dim glow of the old streetlamps. Most of the businesses have shuttered for the night, but cars dot the curb. Music and voices drift from inside The Falconer. A gaggle of students push out into the cold, laughing and stumbling. They start up the street, back toward campus, the few that chose to stay in their dorms over the holidays. The group parts for a man in a peacoat and a plaid scarf, walking in the middle of the sidewalk.

Teddy.

We come to a stop maybe ten, fifteen feet from each other. His hands are stuffed into the pockets of his coat. It accentuates his broad shoulders. His nose is a little rosy with cold, which I find surprisingly endearing.

"I quit my job," I announce, lifting my arms and letting them fall to my sides. His lips part in surprise, but I hold up a mittened hand. "Don't say anything yet. I have my thoughts all organized and you're going to jumble them, and then it'll just be—"

"Word vomit?" he provides.

"Something like that." I take a deep breath, the air stinging my lungs. "I've been doing a lot of thinking. And I've come to some conclusions."

Teddy nods. *Go on.*

"A few hours ago," I say, "I was sitting in Julien's office, and something he said made me realize that I'm not really happy with just one fig. I want to be more than just Clara Fernsby, Associate Professor of History."

His eyebrows pinch and he sucks in a breath like he's going to say something—probably to ask *Associate since when?* and *What's this about a fig?*—but I just keep talking.

"I want to feel like I'm my own person, not constrained by this—this compulsion to force my life into these neat little boxes. I miss being the girl who stood on a rock with her friends, just . . . shouting random words, because I wasn't worried about what anyone else thought. I want to be a sister to Reagan, not a second mother. I want to finally dye my hair black and get a weird tattoo that students will ask me about and then I'll tell them the story about how I was drunk off my ass in Edinburgh and I thought it would be funny."

The words all tumble out in one go, so that I'm winded by the time I've finished, my breath rising in a fog. There's a glint of something in his eye, but I can't tell if it's love or admiration or if he simply thinks I've lost my marbles. Maybe this whole speech worked better in my head.

"But more than any of those things," I conclude, "I want to be all the things that I am to you."

"And what are you to me?" he asks without missing a beat.

I wasn't expecting him to ask that. "I don't know," I admit, feeling ridiculous.

He moves closer to me. The shoulders of his coat are freckled with snow and his hair is starting to do that frizzy, curly, disheveled thing that gets me every time. "The love of my life," he says, brushing a lock of hair from my cheek, but his hand doesn't leave my face. "We could start with that."

He bends to kiss me, his other hand rising to angle my mouth toward his. His hands are surprisingly warm, but just as I'm starting to lose myself in the kiss, he draws back.

"Someone with great taste in music"—he lifts a brow—"for a homeschooled history nerd."

I narrow my eyes. "Are you talking about you, or me?"

"The girl who was kind to me, even when I didn't have any friends." He kisses me, once. "And the most stubborn woman I've ever met."

I laugh against his lips, my eyes closed.

He draws back again, dark brown eyes flitting around my face. "And my best friend."

"We didn't talk for nine years," I say softly. I'm not sure I've earned it.

"Doesn't matter." He puts on a mock-serious tone. "The cool thing about best friends is that you get to decide who you think deserves the title."

I breathe a laugh. "Well, in that case, I choose you."

We kiss again, holding each other tight, wrapped in our own warm little bubble. I never want to lose this again. After a minute, we agree that we should probably head inside. Teddy stomps his shoes on the mat beneath the eaves, but freezes with his hand on the door, turning to look at me with his brow knit. "You said 'ass.'"

I give a tiny shake of my head, bemused. "What?"

"'Drunk off my ass,' that's what you said." He points at me, triumphant. "You cussed."

"I also said 'fuck.' In Julien's office."

"To Julien?"

"Not *to* him exactly, but—"

"Well, well, well." The snow crunches behind us and we turn in unison. Izzy plants her fists on her hips and shakes her head, her lips curved in a smug smile. Her hair is sleek and flat-ironed and she's wearing one of those waist-cinching thermal jackets. She looks more like she's going skiing in the Alps than bar-hopping in small-town Maryland. "I thought this day would never come."

"Feeling nice and vindicated?" I ask. "Because we'd like to get out of the cold." Teddy shoots me a questioning look. "Izzy knew that I had a thing for you since we were like—"

"Sixteen!" she exclaims.

Reagan materializes behind her, her hair in twin braids and her lanyard slung around her neck. In contrast to Izzy's form-fitting thermal wear, everything Reagan's wearing looks like she bought it three sizes too big on purpose.

"What are you doing here?" I ask.

"Someone had to drive me," Izzy points out.

Teddy looks at me, then tosses a thumb at Reagan. "Are we *sure* she's old enough to drink?" he teases.

Reagan rolls her eyes with a groan, throwing an arm around each of our necks and dragging us inside.

* * *

There's something magical about a crowded pub on a winter's night, the air warm and thick with friendly chatter. A Christmas tree stands beside the fogged window, strung in colorful lights and popcorn garlands; silver tinsel dangles from the exposed beams; and the whole place smells like peppermint schnapps, thanks to the holiday-themed cocktails scribbled on the menu. The four of us grab a booth and I order a round of eggnog for the table.

Izzy pulls a face when a mug is placed in front of her. "I forgot people actually drink this stuff."

The server delivered a fifth mug to the table, as requested, but there's no one here to claim it. It looks like Bel decided not to join us after all. I'm a little disappointed—maybe because it was my first time trying to establish a friendship outside of work in I don't know how many years—but I'm not going to let that put a damper on my mood.

I lift my mug in a toast. "To old friends."

"Hey," Reagan says.

"And their annoying kid sisters," Izzy amends. We clink glasses. Izzy plugs her nose before taking a sip, but stifles a gag anyway, beating her chest with a fist and coughing. "Oh my god, that's worse than I remembered."

Teddy clears his throat. "You know, I think there's actually a rule that says faculty aren't allowed to drink with their students."

Reagan shoots him a sardonic smile across the table. "Good thing I'm not your student anymore."

"What grade did you end up giving her?" I ask.

"B."

Izzy and I gasp in unison.

"I didn't know that!" Reagan cries.

He mimics her former smile, and somehow it's a lot more convincing on him. "That's because I haven't put it in the system yet."

The door to The Falconer swings open again. Snow chases Bel Jones inside. She scans the busy room, unwinding her long scarf before pushing through the crowd. "I hope you appreciate the lengths I've gone to for this friendship," she tells me, standing over our table. "First I join a subcommittee, now I drive to a pub in the middle of a snowstorm. That's love, right there."

"And I hope you know that I appreciate you more than I know how to articulate," I say.

She doesn't take a seat, but her eyes dart around the table, curious.

"Oh, right." I gesture at the other side of the table. "My sister Reagan you might've met, but actually I don't think so . . . and this is Izzy, an old friend from camp. This"—I lean across the table to nudge the last glass of eggnog toward her—"is Bel. My favorite coworker."

Teddy shoots me a mock-reproachful look and I shake my head. Technically, he's not my coworker. Though also, technically, Bel isn't either, anymore.

With Bel standing and Izzy sitting down, they're almost the same height, and they opt to shake hands on this equal standing—or seating.

"Together we almost form one whole name," Bel observes. "Izzy. Bel."

Izzy scoots over to make room on her side of the booth, wedging Reagan against the paneling. "My name *is* actually Isabel. But no one calls me that except for my grandma."

"What if we're both Isabels?" Bel asks.

Izzy arches a brow. "Are we?"

"That's for me to know and you to find out," she says coyly, picking the mug of eggnog off the table. It almost makes it to her mouth before she pauses, staring down at it with her nose wrinkled. "What is this?"

"Eggnog," I say, in tandem with Izzy saying, "Disgusting, is what it is."

Bel frowns at it, then shrugs. "I'll drink it if you will." She holds the glass in the middle of the table.

Teddy's eyebrows shoot up. "Are we toasting again?"

Bel looks around at all of us, her arm still outstretched. "You guys toasted already?"

"I wasn't sure if you were coming," I say, raising my own mug. "What should we toast to this time?"

"What was it last time?"

"'To old friends.'"

"Hmm." Bel glances around the crowded pub, looking for inspiration. "To . . . new beginnings?"

Seems fitting enough. "Sure. To new beginnings."

Still wedged against the wall, Reagan wriggles an arm free and grabs her mug, shooting a scathing look at Izzy—who's paying her absolutely no mind. Izzy sighs, raising her drink to meet ours. "Bottoms up, I guess."

I down the rest of my eggnog and stamp the empty glass on the table.

"Speaking of old friends," Teddy says, with a pointed look at Izzy, "Darvish sends his love."

"Rejected," Izzy says, though she can't hold back a grin. "Return to sender. Wrong address."

"Sorry, who's Darvish?" Bel asks, looking around at all of this.

While Izzy launches into a long-winded explanation, Teddy excuses himself from the table. "Sorry, I just remembered," he says in an undertone to me as he slides out of the booth, "I need to grab something out of my car."

I glance around at the crowd, trying to figure out where our server went so that I can order another round for the table—though maybe not eggnog, this time. That wasn't the hit I was hoping it would be. "Didn't expect it to be so busy tonight," I mutter.

"It's the middle of December in a small college town," Bel points out. "There's not much else for people to do."

Reagan lifts out of her seat and swings an arm, doing a much more effective job of capturing our server's attention than I was able to. She orders a round of cranberry kamikaze shots for the table, despite groans and protests from literally everyone else that we're too old to be doing shots. "Shut up," she says. "Your early thirties are not old."

Izzy casts a sideways glance at Bel. "How old are *you*, anyway?"

Bel purses her lips. "I'm immortal."

She's twenty-eight, actually, but I'm not about to spoil this for her. "Like Bella in *Breaking Dawn*," Izzy whispers reverently, more to herself than anyone else at the table. She's about two seconds away from offering to be her Edward, I'm sure of it.

The front door swings wide and Teddy shoulders his way back to the table a moment later, an arm tucked behind his back. "I thought maybe you were going to tell me that they gave you tenure," he explains, a little apologetic. "I meant it as a sort of congratulations, and kind of a joke, but . . ." He settles back into the booth and sets a package on the table. It's wrapped in a simple brown paper sack like a bagged lunch, the top folded over and neatly creased. He slides it over to me and scratches an eyebrow, sheepish. "Didn't exactly have a lot of time with the gift wrap."

I unfurl the top, shooting him a curious look, because I have no idea what this could be. I reach down into the bag and extract a book. It's a battered paperback, the spine creased with heavy use and the pages so badly dog-eared that it doesn't quite close correctly. *Lectures on the Philosophy of History*. I smooth the bent cover with a thumb, my vision clouded by tears.

"It's the first book you ever loaned me," Teddy explains, needlessly. "I never did mail it back."

I sputter a wet laugh, swiping beneath my eyes. "I tried to make you read Hegel when we were fifteen. What was wrong with me?"

He holds back a smile. "I believe your exact words when you handed it to me were 'required reading.'"

"No wonder you went ahead and started college early. I was already putting you through historiography boot camp." I flip through it, the margins graffitied with Teddy's notes and mine, passages traced in green and yellow highlighter, page corners folded over. I let it flap closed, except the cover remains curled back, the title page peeking out from behind it. There's something written there in soft gray pencil. I fold the cover back, scanning the script. It's Teddy's handwriting, but more recent than the notes in the margins—messier, less careful, like he spent less time thinking about how he wanted to write it and more letting the words just tumble out onto the page:

Clara,
Figured it was about time I returned this to you. Not sure what seventeen years' worth of late fees might look like, but I'm prepared to face the consequences.

I know our own history is imperfect, but I'm glad it eventually led me back to you. Abraham Lincoln once said, "We learn from history that we do not learn from history." Or maybe that was Georg Hegel. Either way, I disagree. It might've taken me a while, but I learned just fine, and what I learned most is that I will do whatever it takes not to lose you, this time around. I'm all in.
I love you,
Teddy

I trace a thumb over the words. I've spent so long dwelling on the past, wishing I could erase all the negative and do it over, but perhaps if our lives had gone any differently, we wouldn't have ended up where we are today. And I'm happy with where we are. There's no bad guy in our story, no one person who wronged any more than the other. There's just . . . life. Some-times it's messy and complicated, and sometimes there are forks in the road, anticipated and not.

"Thank you," I whisper, because words don't feel adequate, which almost seems a silly sentiment when he's giving me back a book I once owned, but it's not. That he's held on to it, and thought to give it back to me tonight, means the world. If our story were a book we picked up for Long-Distance History Club—not so long-distance, these days—then this feels like closing a chapter. Looking toward the future instead of just the past, because while the past has its value, it's not the end-all. I smooth the bent cover again before turning to look at him. "I'm all in, too."

He swallows, nods, bends to kiss me. The chatter of the bar ceases to exist, and I could almost pretend it's just the two of us, lost in each other—*almost,* but we're interrupted by the server delivering a round of cranberry shots to the table, the tiny red drinks garnished with lime, and then all the people I love are lifting their glasses in another toast.

"What are we toasting to this time?" Bel asks.

"I think we're running out of toasts," Izzy grumbles.

"How about . . . to looking ahead," I say with a glance at Teddy, because this is far from the beginning of our story.

But it's also far from the end.

ACKNOWLEDGMENTS

Everyone always says to write what you know, and I really took that to heart with this book, except for the part where I'm not a history professor and had, at the outset, only a vague idea of how tenure works. But I drafted and edited this story while wading through an ocean of grad school work, so close enough, right? Right?!

In all seriousness, this book wouldn't have come together without a lot of help. First and foremost, I owe a huge thank-you to my stellar editor, Eileen Rothschild, for all her insight and patience (I have a habit of taking one line of feedback and turning it into six new chapters and she somehow hasn't complained). I'm also grateful to the rest of the team at St. Martin's Press for all their hard work: Lisa Bonvissuto, Kejana Ayala, Alyssa Gammello, Marissa Sangiacomo, Ginny Perrin, Jennifer Rohrbach, and all the other wonderful, knowledgeable folks working behind the scenes. And thank you so much to Olga Grlic and Camila Gray for the most amazing cover. The colors! The cozy autumn vibes! It's everything I'd hoped for.

I feel so incredibly lucky to have the guidance of my agent, Amy Stapp, through every step of the publishing process. No matter what sort of story I throw at her, she sees the vision and works with me to make it the best it can be. Thank you to my foreign agent, Taryn Fagerness, for helping my books find a home in other countries (still amazed that anyone likes my words enough to translate them into other languages). Of course, I have to thank my critique partners and writing friends who took the time to read early iterations of this story: A. R. Frederiksen, Sarah Chapman, Michael A. Rubalcava, Desirée M. Niccoli, and Sylvia L. Leong. You're all amazing.

I always want to take the time to thank my husband, George, who happily lets me turn every car ride into a book brainstorming session. When I said I couldn't envision myself writing friends-to-lovers, he presented the idea for a romance about two professors while we were in the drive-thru waiting on chili cheeseburgers. And thank you to my best friend, Greta, who has cheered for me every step of the way. She used her killer bartending skills to create Clara's signature martini!

Last, but never least, thank you to all the amazing bloggers, Bookstagrammers, BookTokers, Goodreads reviewers, and everyone else who has helped get the word out about my books. I'd like to extend a special thank-you to Sude, for being an excellent character PR manager, and my fellow Kristyn, for helping me connect with readers and influencers. These stories wouldn't make it very far without all of you.

ABOUT THE AUTHOR

George H. Miller IV

Kristyn J. Miller is the author of *Seven Rules for Breaking Hearts* and other novels. A lifelong history nerd with a background in museum work, she finally earned her M.A. in history and museum studies at the University of New Hampshire in 2023. In between writing novels, she spends her free time wandering peat bogs, sampling craft beers, and restoring her old colonial house in rural Maine with her husband.